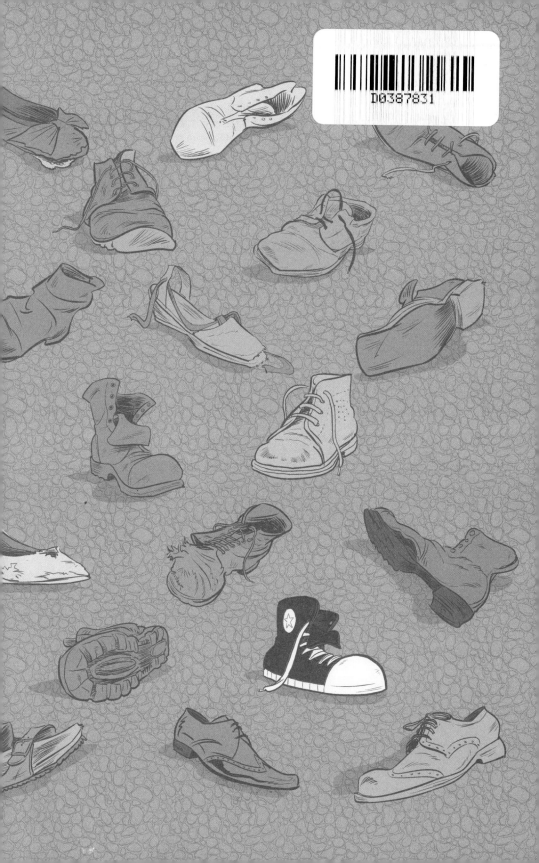

Eddie Pittman

Red's Planet

AMULET BOOKS
NEW YORK

Library of Congress Control Number: 2015946889

ISBN 978-1-4197-1907-3 (hardback) — ISBN 978-1-4197-1908-0 (paperback)

Copyright © 2016 Eddie Pittman

Book design by Eddie Pittman and Chad W. Beckerman

Published in 2016 by Amulet Books, an imprint of ABRAMS.

Printed and bound in China

10 9 8 7 6 5 4 3 2 1

Amulet Books are available at special discounts when purchased in quantity for premiums and promotions as well as fundraising or educational use. Special editions can also be created to specification. For details, contact specialsales@abramsbooks.com or the address below.

ABRAMS
THE ART OF BOOKS SINCE 1949

115 West 18th Street
New York, NY 10011
www.abramsbooks.com

To Mom and Dad—the storyteller
and the artist, and my first inspirations

Thanks to:

Norm Fuetti, Joshua Pruett, Tom Richmond, Dan Povenmire, Swampy Marsh, Jeff Smith, Kim Roberson, Mike Maihack, Travis Hanson, Tom Dell'Aringa, Steve Ogden, and Broose Johnson for their support, encouragement, and help along the journey.

Travis Hanson, Jose Flores, Sean Balsano, Janelle Bell-Martin, and Ginny Pittman for color and production assistance.

The readers, commenters, and fans of the *Red's Planet* webcomic for keeping me going.

Chad W. Beckerman, Pam Notarantonio, and the whole team at Abrams.

Judy Hansen, my super-ninja agent.

Charlie Kochman, my amazing editor, for taking a chance on this little book.

And to my beautiful wife, Beth, and my amazing kids, Ginny and Teagan—my first and most important audience.

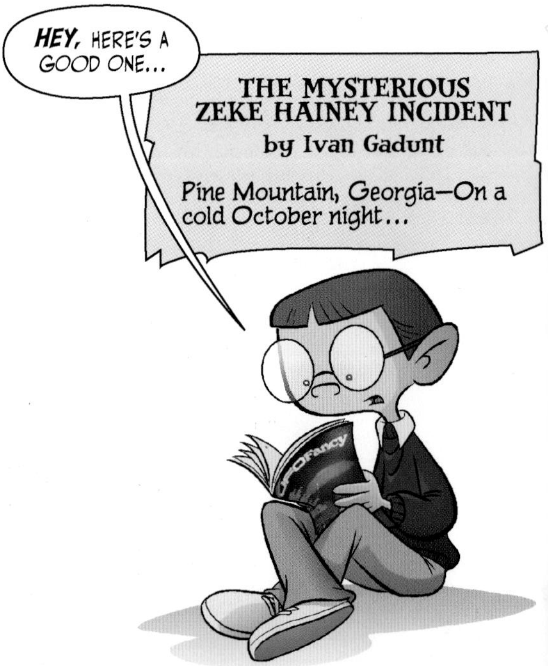
HEY, HERE'S A GOOD ONE...
THE MYSTERIOUS ZEKE HAINEY INCIDENT
by Ivan Gadunt
Pine Mountain, Georgia—On a cold October night...
UFO Fancy

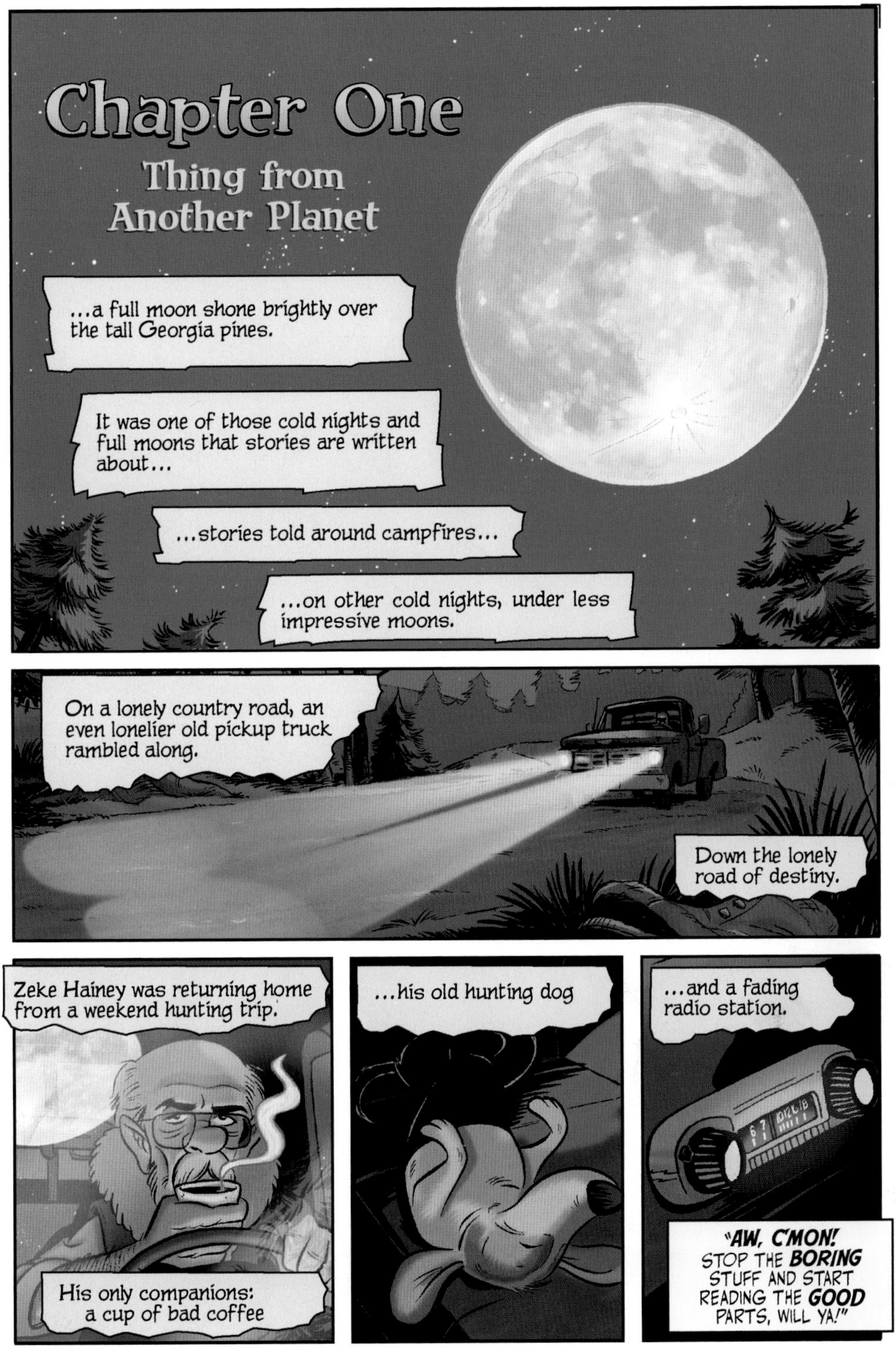
Chapter One
Thing from Another Planet
...a full moon shone brightly over the tall Georgia pines.
It was one of those cold nights and full moons that stories are written about...
...stories told around campfires...
...on other cold nights, under less impressive moons.
On a lonely country road, an even lonelier old pickup truck rambled along.
Down the lonely road of destiny.
Zeke Hainey was returning home from a weekend hunting trip.
His only companions: a cup of bad coffee
...his old hunting dog
...and a fading radio station.
"AW, C'MON! STOP THE BORING STUFF AND START READING THE GOOD PARTS, WILL YA!"

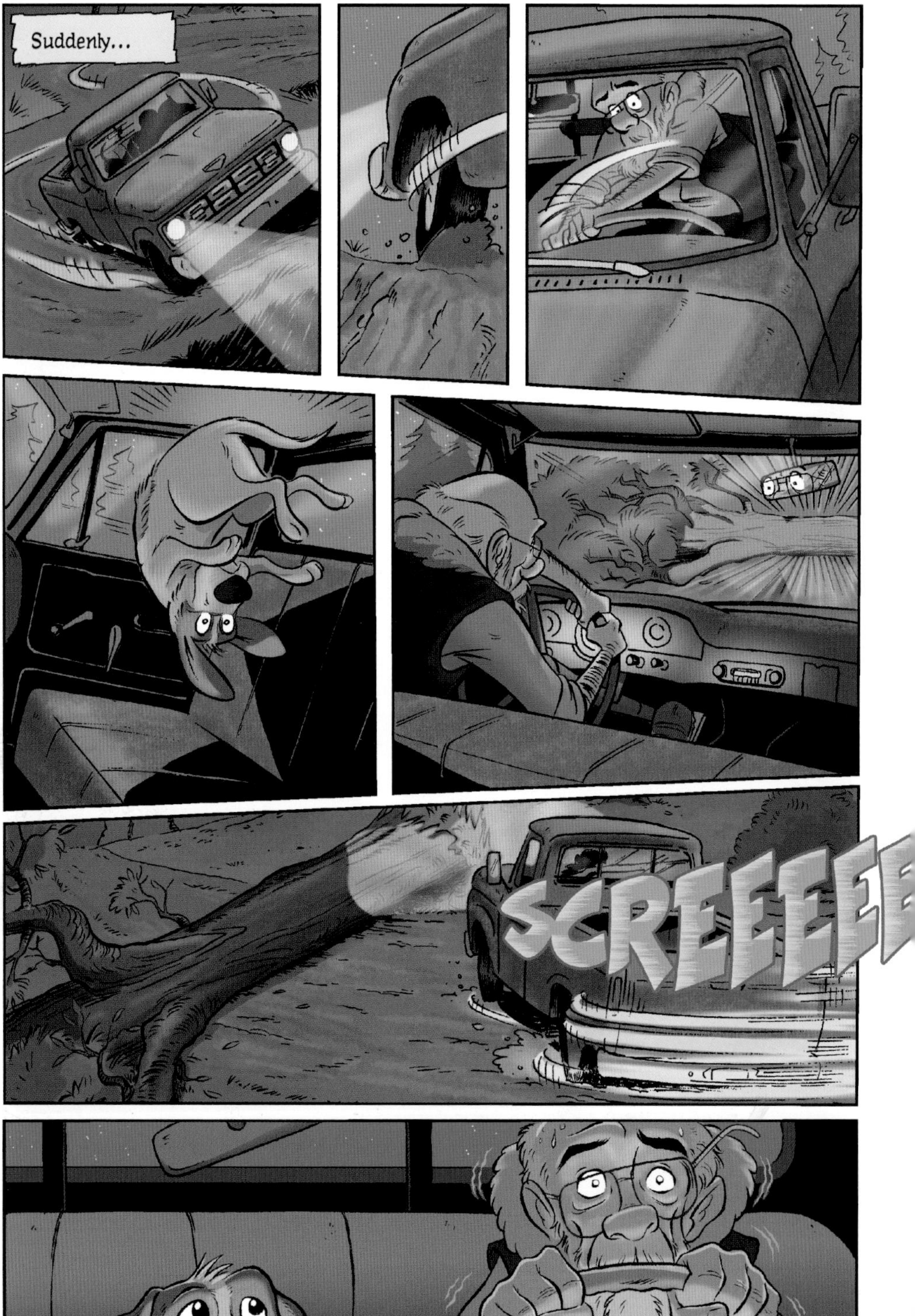
Suddenly...
SCREEEEE

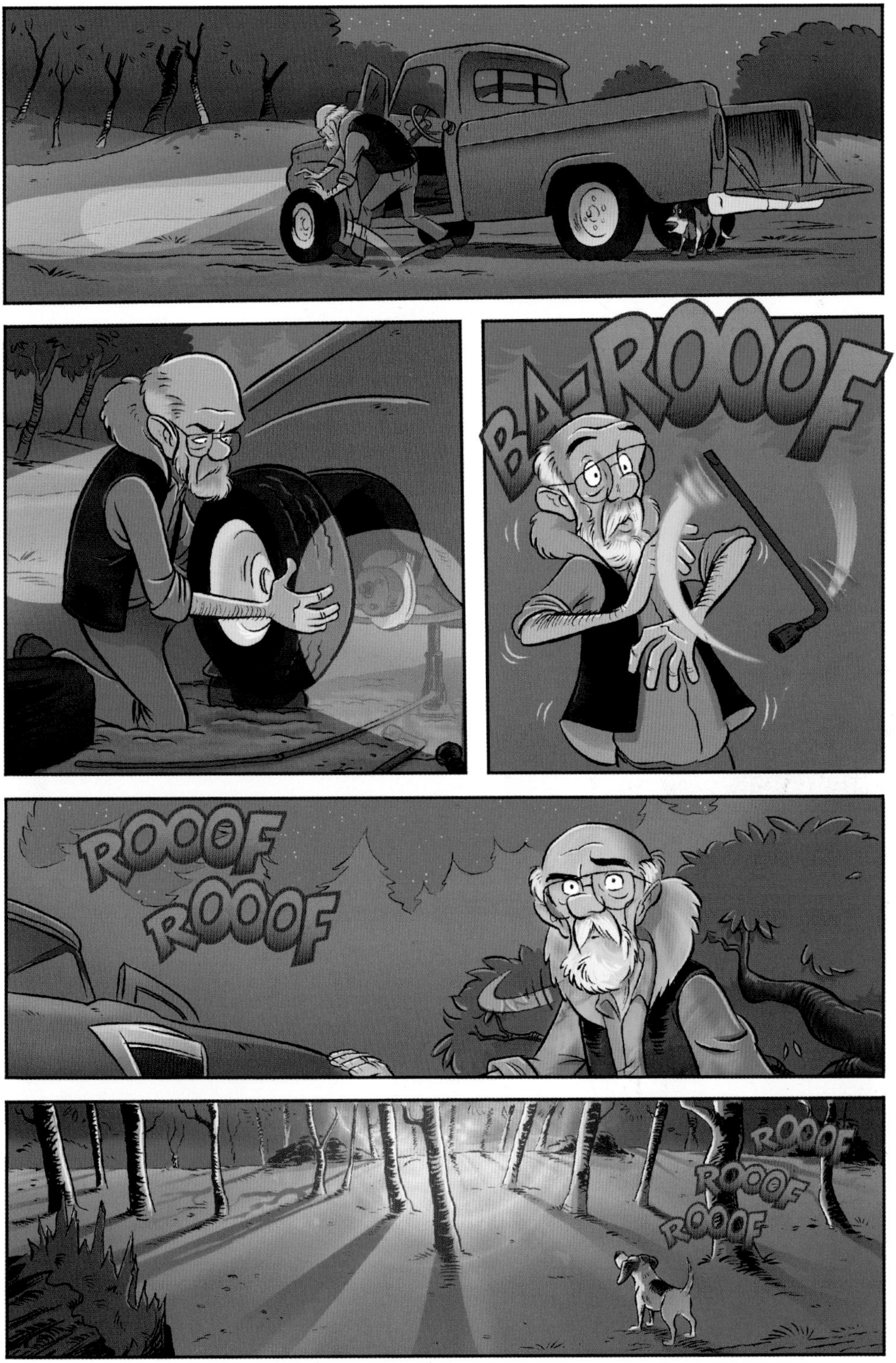
BA-ROOOF
ROOOF
ROOOF
ROOOF
ROOOF
ROOOF

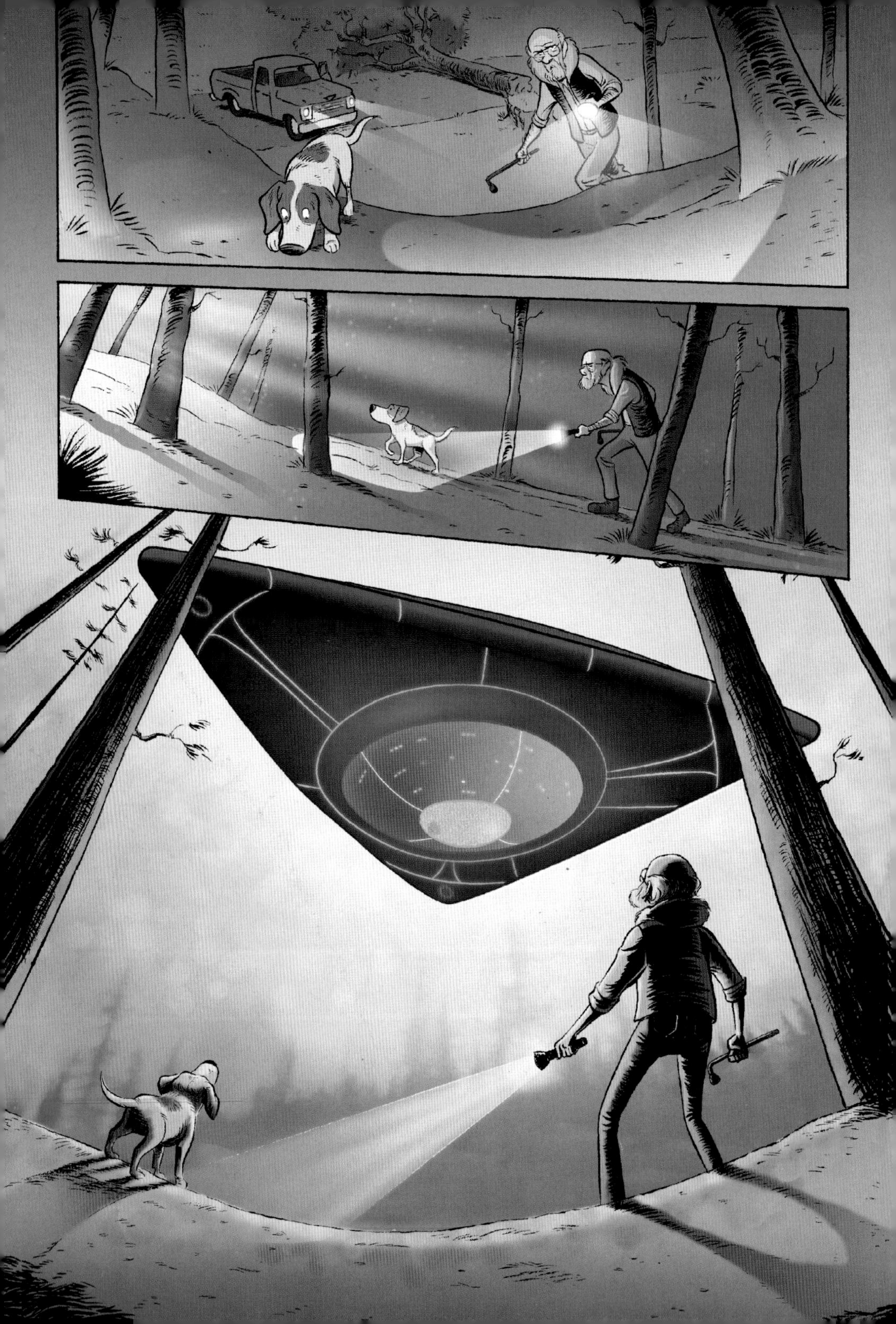

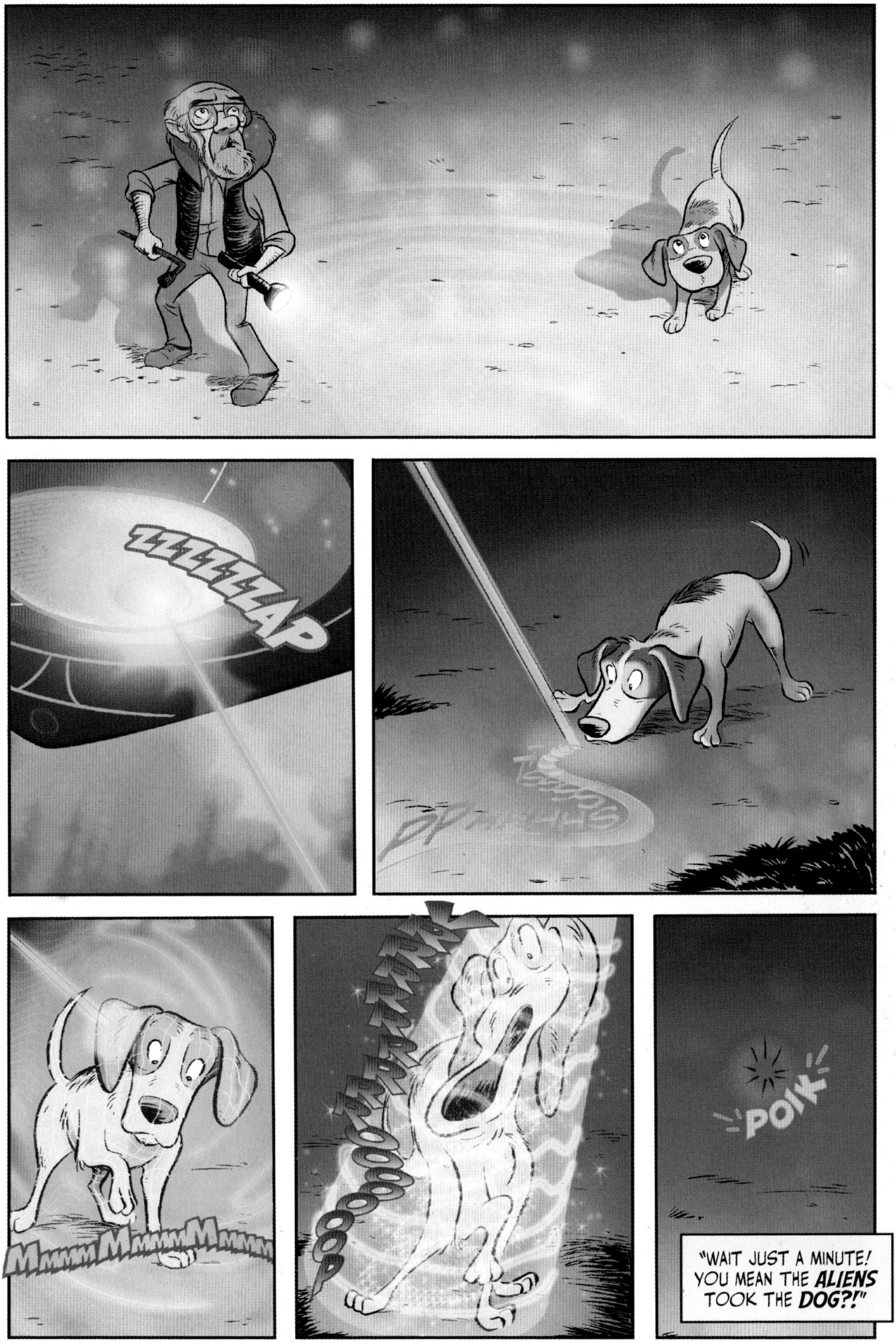
ZZZZZZAP
MmmmMmmmmMmmmm
POIK
"WAIT JUST A MINUTE! YOU MEAN THE ***ALIENS*** TOOK THE ***DOG?!***"

WHAT WOULD *ALIENS* WANT WITH AN *OLD* DOG, FOR CRYING OUT LOUD?!

WELL, IT *SAYS* HERE THEY TOOK THE OLD MAN, TOO!

SURE THEY DID! AND THAT'S *ANOTHER* THING...

THE MAN JUST GOT BACK FROM A *HUNTING TRIP*, RIGHT? AND *ALL* HE TAKES INTO THE WOODS TO CHECK OUT A *STRANGE* LIGHT IS...

A *TIRE IRON?*

ANYONE *ELSE* SEE A *PROBLEM* HERE?

NOT TO MENTION, IF *THEY* WERE *ALL* ALONE...

THEN *WHO* WAS AROUND TO TELL THE *STORY?*

WELL?

WHAT *IS* THAT MAGAZINE ANYWAY?

HEY!

GIMME!

UFO *FANCY?!*

UFOFancy
October 1974
Vol. 4 No. 8

ACTION RESEARCH REPORT
Jimmy Carter's Alien Rabbit Encounter

THE DEVIL'S
...LE
...y Alien
...Y?

...LUSIVE
PHOTOS
SUGGEST UFOS
ARE GRAINY

NAMU-NAMU:
...OS PROBE

TALK ABOUT YOUR *ANCIENT* ALIENS! HOW *OLD* IS THIS *THING?!*

IT'S LIKE FROM WAY BACK IN THE *1900S!*

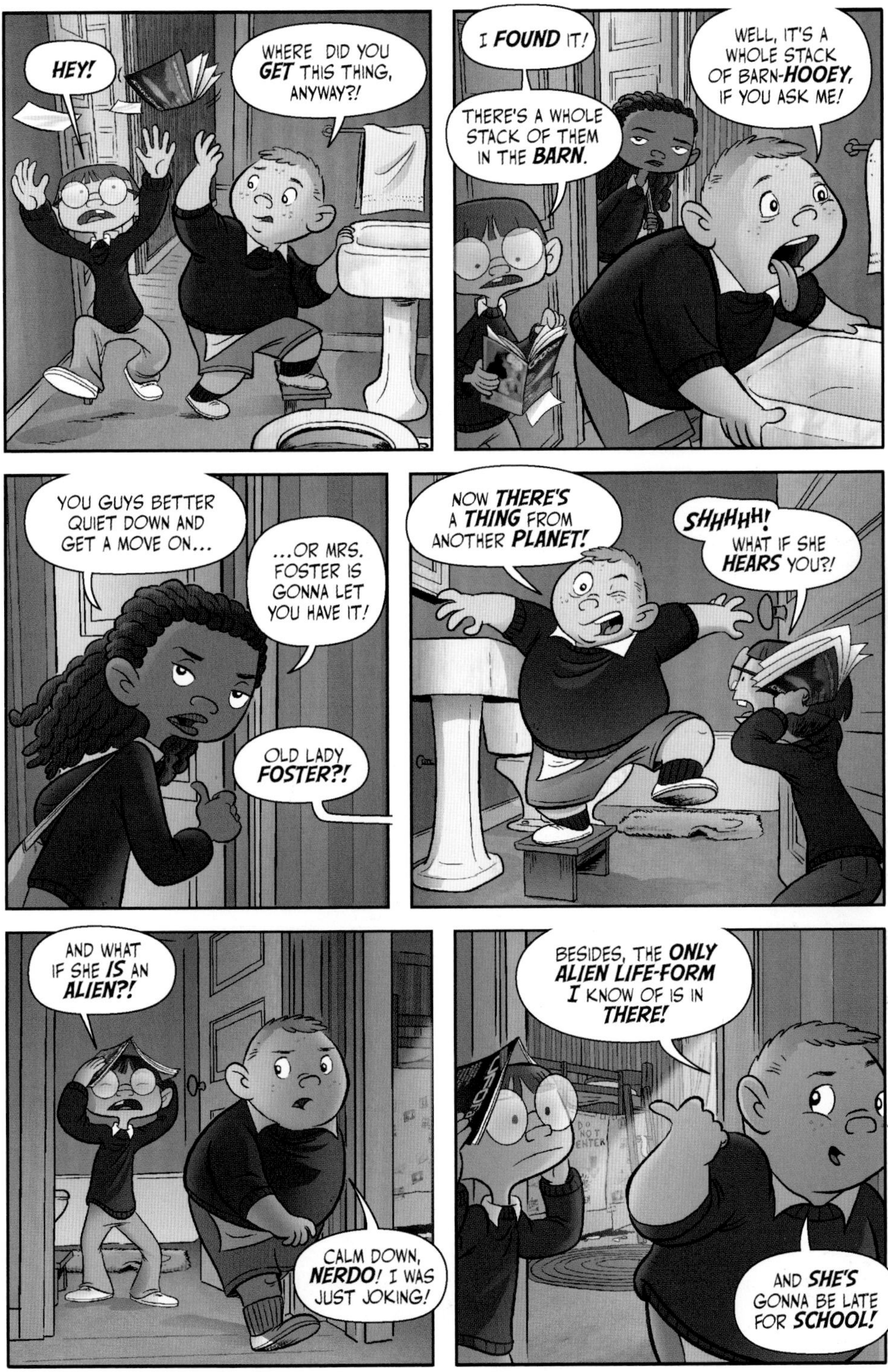
HEY!
WHERE DID YOU GET THIS THING, ANYWAY?!
I FOUND IT!
THERE'S A WHOLE STACK OF THEM IN THE BARN.
WELL, IT'S A WHOLE STACK OF BARN-HOOEY, IF YOU ASK ME!
YOU GUYS BETTER QUIET DOWN AND GET A MOVE ON...
...OR MRS. FOSTER IS GONNA LET YOU HAVE IT!
OLD LADY FOSTER?!
NOW THERE'S A THING FROM ANOTHER PLANET!
SHHHHH! WHAT IF SHE HEARS YOU?!
AND WHAT IF SHE IS AN ALIEN?!
CALM DOWN, NERDO! I WAS JUST JOKING!
BESIDES, THE ONLY ALIEN LIFE-FORM I KNOW OF IS IN THERE!
AND SHE'S GONNA BE LATE FOR SCHOOL!

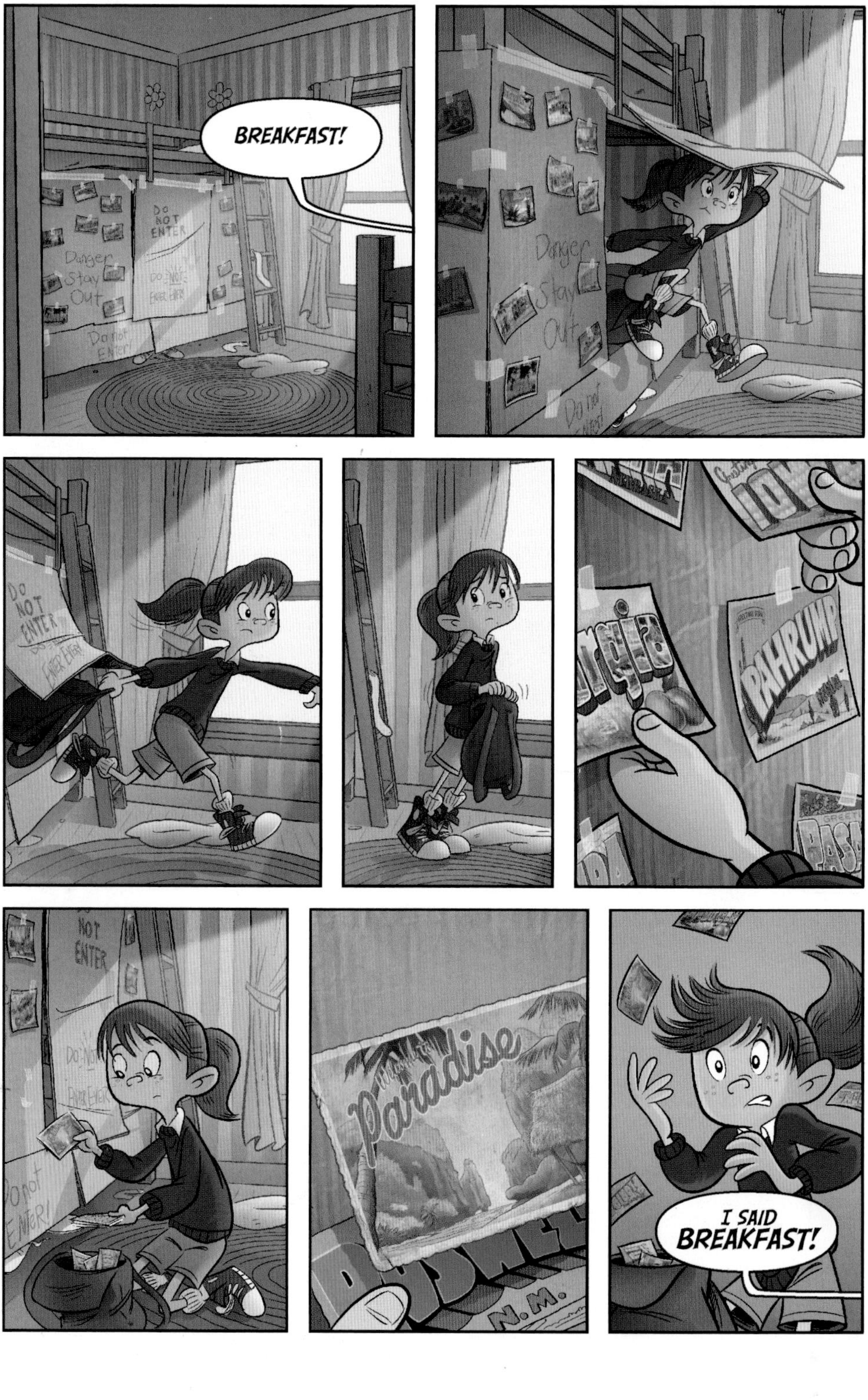
BREAKFAST!
DO NOT ENTER
Danger Stay Out
DO NOT ENTER EVER
Do not Enter
Danger Stay Out
Do not Enter
DO NOT ENTER
ENTER EVER
PAHRUMP
NOT ENTER
DO NOT ENTER EVER
Do not ENTER!
Paradise
N.M.
I SAID BREAKFAST!

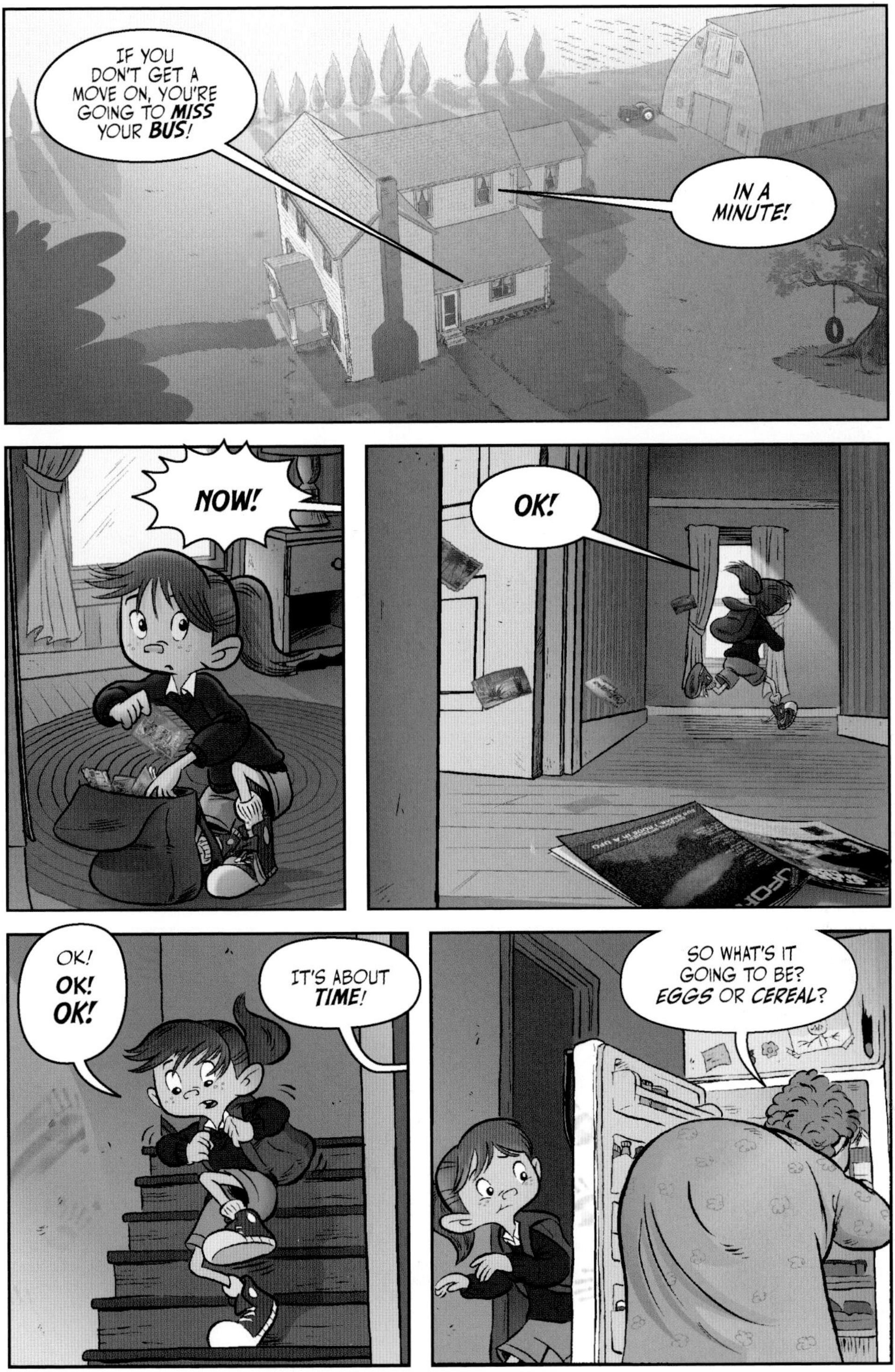
IF YOU DON'T GET A MOVE ON, YOU'RE GOING TO **MISS** YOUR **BUS**!
IN A MINUTE!
NOW!
OK!
OK! **OK! OK!**
IT'S ABOUT **TIME**!
SO WHAT'S IT GOING TO BE? *EGGS* OR *CEREAL*?

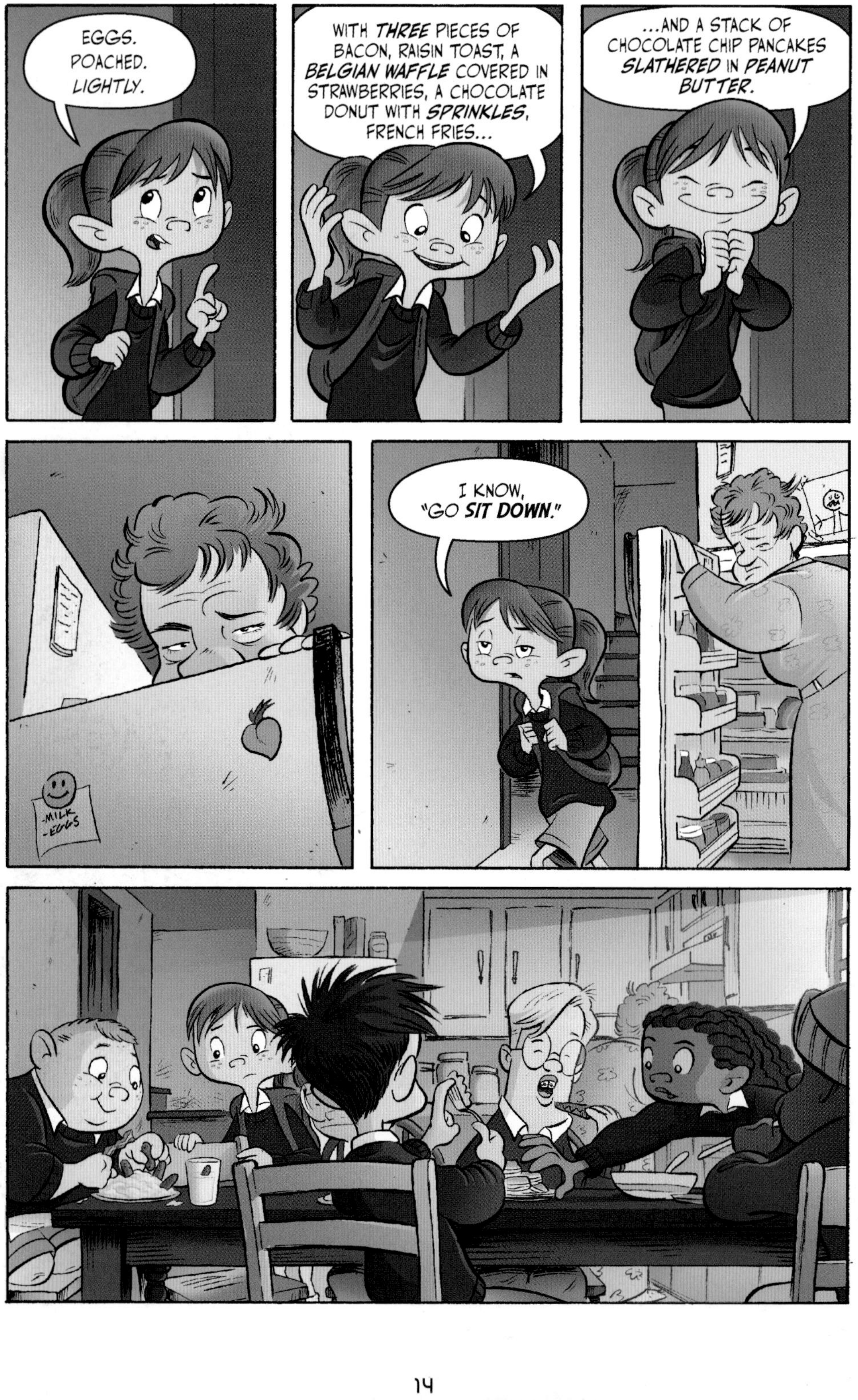
EGGS. POACHED. LIGHTLY.
WITH THREE PIECES OF BACON, RAISIN TOAST, A BELGIAN WAFFLE COVERED IN STRAWBERRIES, A CHOCOLATE DONUT WITH SPRINKLES, FRENCH FRIES...
...AND A STACK OF CHOCOLATE CHIP PANCAKES SLATHERED IN PEANUT BUTTER.
-MILK
-EGGS
I KNOW, "GO SIT DOWN."

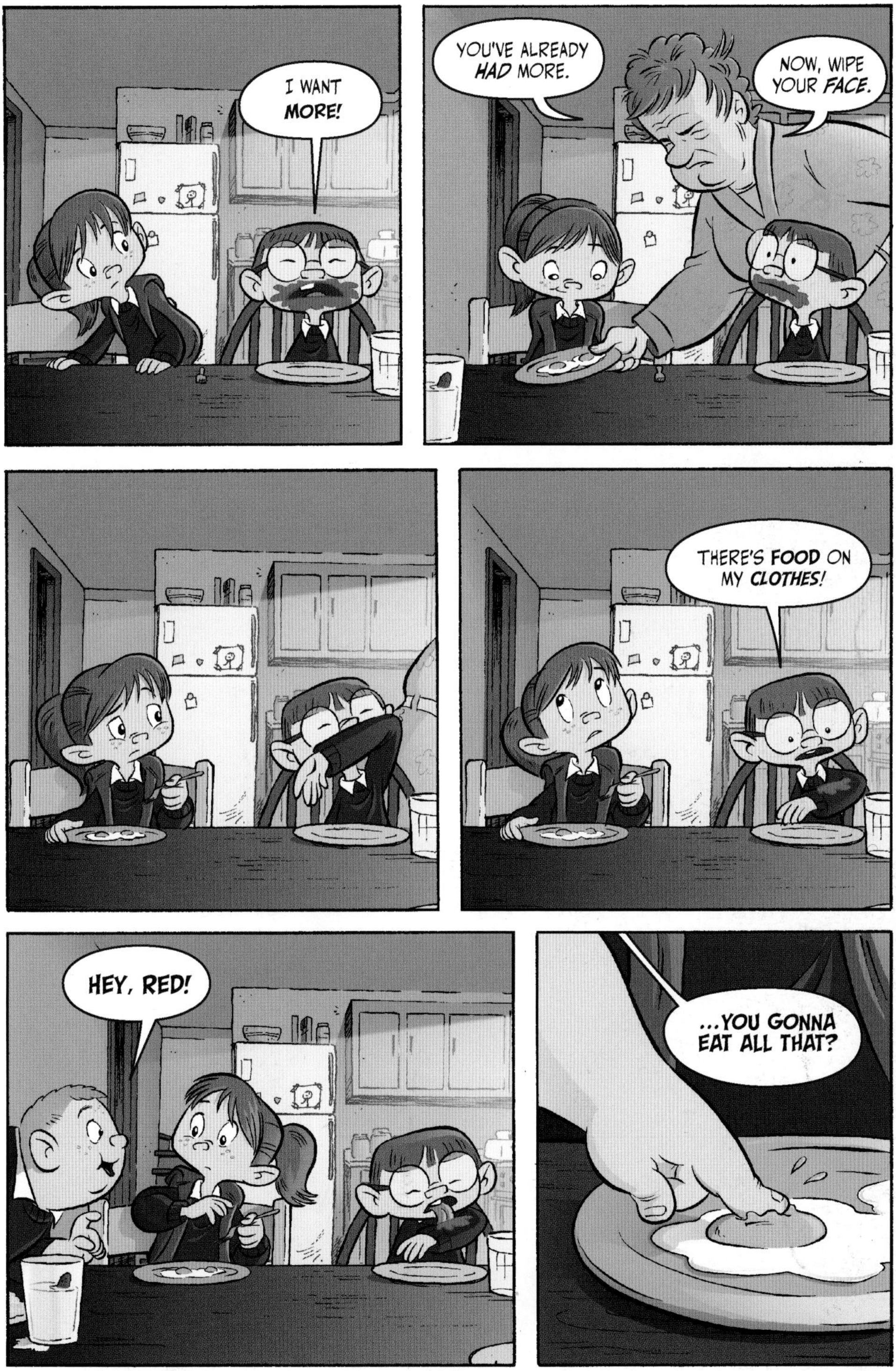
I WANT MORE!
YOU'VE ALREADY HAD MORE.
NOW, WIPE YOUR FACE.
THERE'S FOOD ON MY CLOTHES!
HEY, RED!
...YOU GONNA EAT ALL THAT?

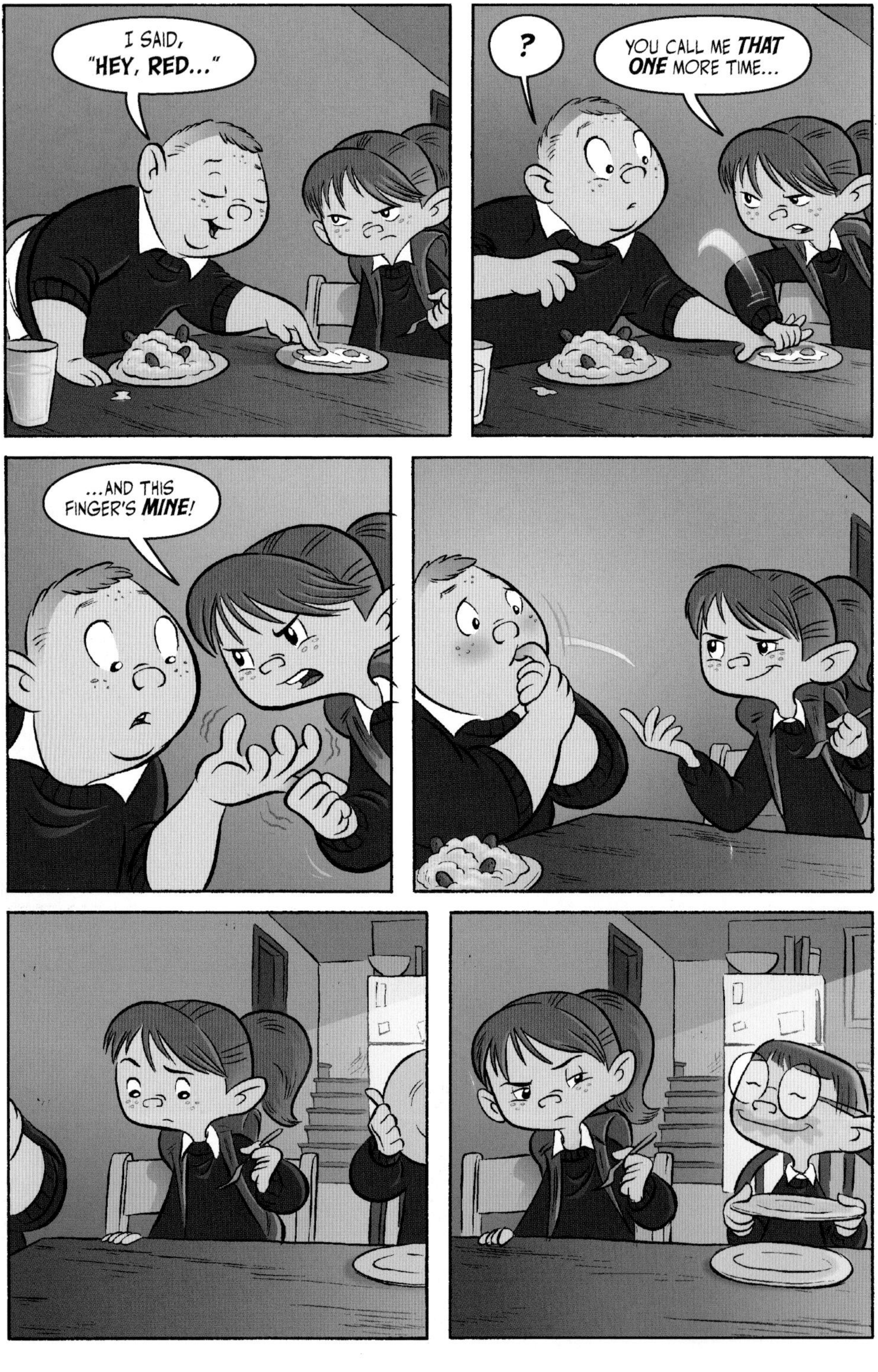
I SAID, "**HEY, RED...**"
?
YOU CALL ME ***THAT ONE*** MORE TIME...
...AND THIS FINGER'S ***MINE!***

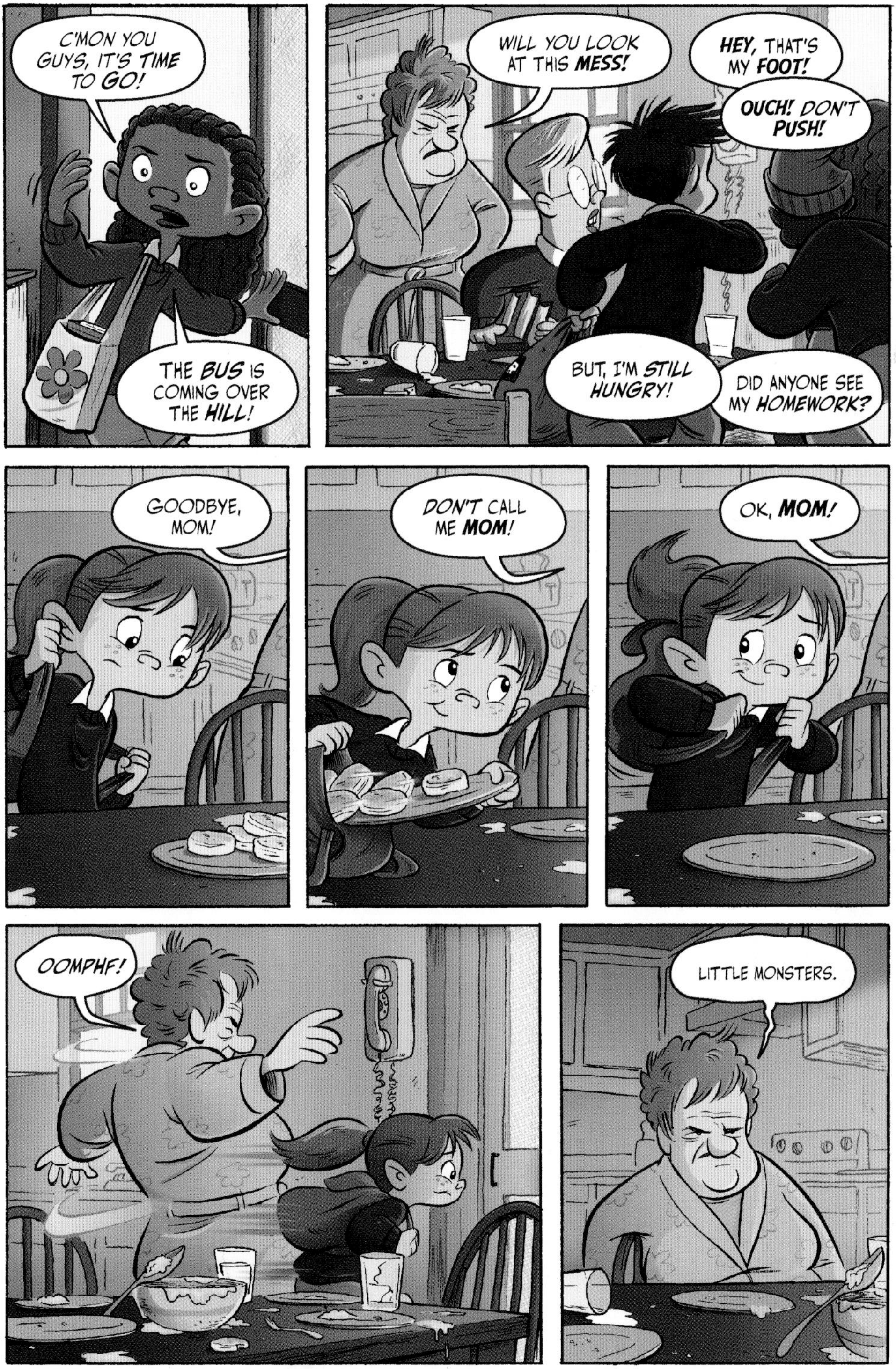
C'MON YOU GUYS, IT'S TIME TO GO!
THE BUS IS COMING OVER THE HILL!
WILL YOU LOOK AT THIS MESS!
HEY, THAT'S MY FOOT!
OUCH! DON'T PUSH!
BUT, I'M STILL HUNGRY!
DID ANYONE SEE MY HOMEWORK?
GOODBYE, MOM!
DON'T CALL ME MOM!
OK, MOM!
OOMPHF!
LITTLE MONSTERS.

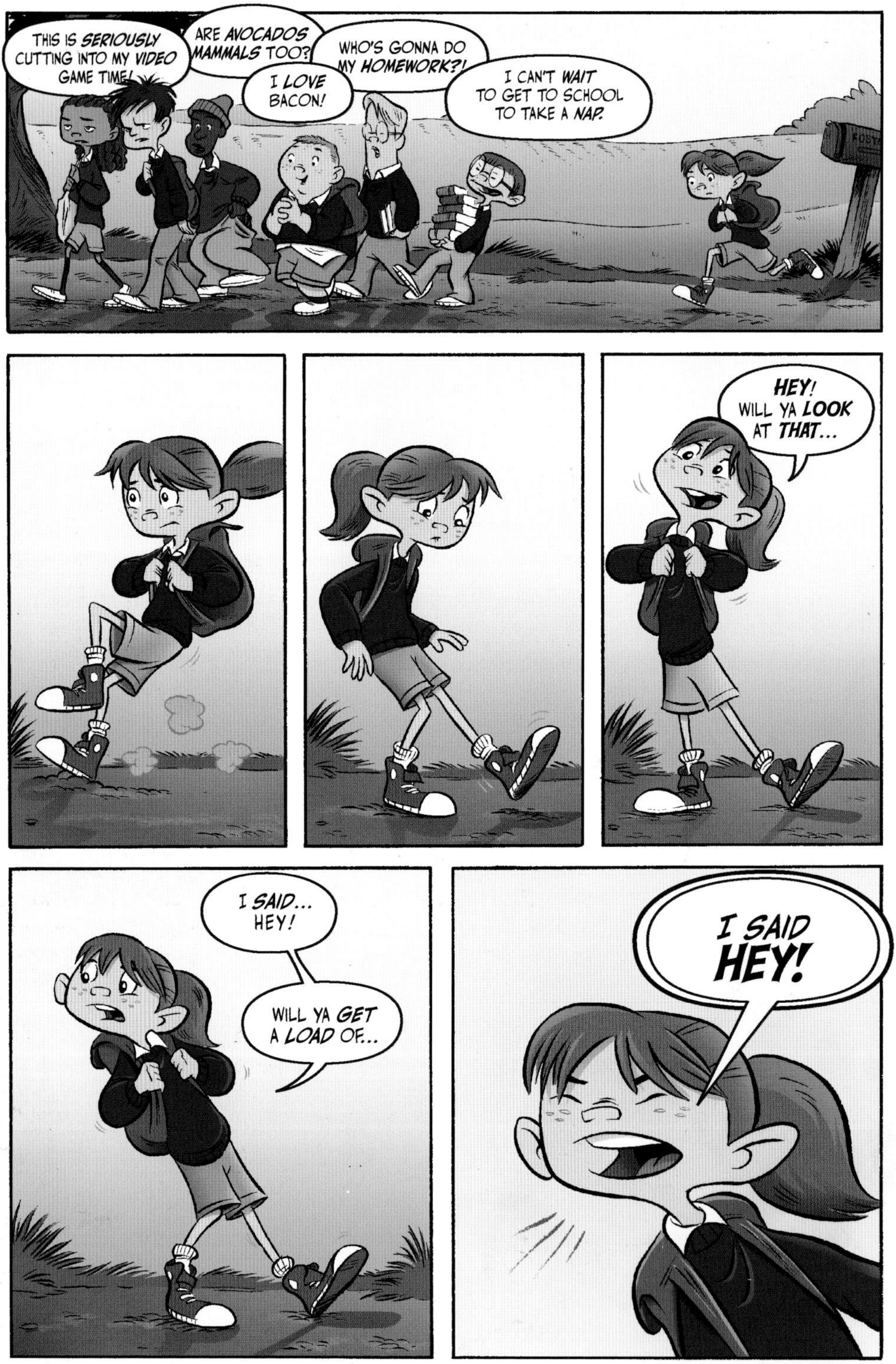
THIS IS SERIOUSLY CUTTING INTO MY VIDEO GAME TIME!
ARE AVOCADOS MAMMALS TOO?
I LOVE BACON!
WHO'S GONNA DO MY HOMEWORK?!
I CAN'T WAIT TO GET TO SCHOOL TO TAKE A NAP.
HEY! WILL YA LOOK AT THAT...
I SAID... HEY!
WILL YA GET A LOAD OF...
I SAID HEY!

UH...HEY...

...WILL YA *LOOK* AT WHAT I *DID*...

I WENT AND PUT ON THE *WRONG SHOES!*

AND I CANNOT WEAR *THESE* SHOES BECAUSE THEY ARE *NOT* SCHOOL *REGULATION* AS STATED IN THE COUNTY SCHOOL *DRESS CODE* SECTION 13, PARAGRAPH 4, AND I *QUOTE*...

...ALL STUDENTS *MUST* WEAR *APPROVED* WHITE, RUBBER-SOLED SHOES WITH FULL TOES AND HEELS AND THE AFOREMENTIONED SHOES *MUST* REMAIN TIED AT ALL TIMES UNDER THE PENALTY OF *DETENTION!*

ILLEGAL FOOTWEAR INCLUDES, BUT IS NOT LIMITED TO:

FLIP-FLOPS, SLINGBACKS, WINKLEPICKERS, SANDALS, SLIPPERS, SKATE SHOES, BEACH SHOES, MULES, PUMPS, CLOGS, MOCCASINS, CLEATS, SNOWSHOES, HORSESHOES, TAP SHOES, HEAVY, HIKING, CONSTRUCTION, COWBOY, COMBAT, *OR* GO-GO BOOTS *AND* **HIGH-TOP SNEAKERS!**

WHAT WILL I *DO* **NOW?**

WAIT A *MINUTE!* ARE *YOU* THINKING WHAT *I'M* THINKING?!

I'LL JUST *RUN* BACK HOME, CHANGE THESE SILLY SHOES, THEN CATCH UP WITH YOU KIDS *LATER!*

WHAT DO *YOU* KNOW ABOUT THE *TOOTH FAIRY*

MAN, I'D LOVE TO HAVE A *BACON TACO!*

STO... PUSHING...

I WON'T BE *LONG*, JUST GO *ON* WITHOUT...

19

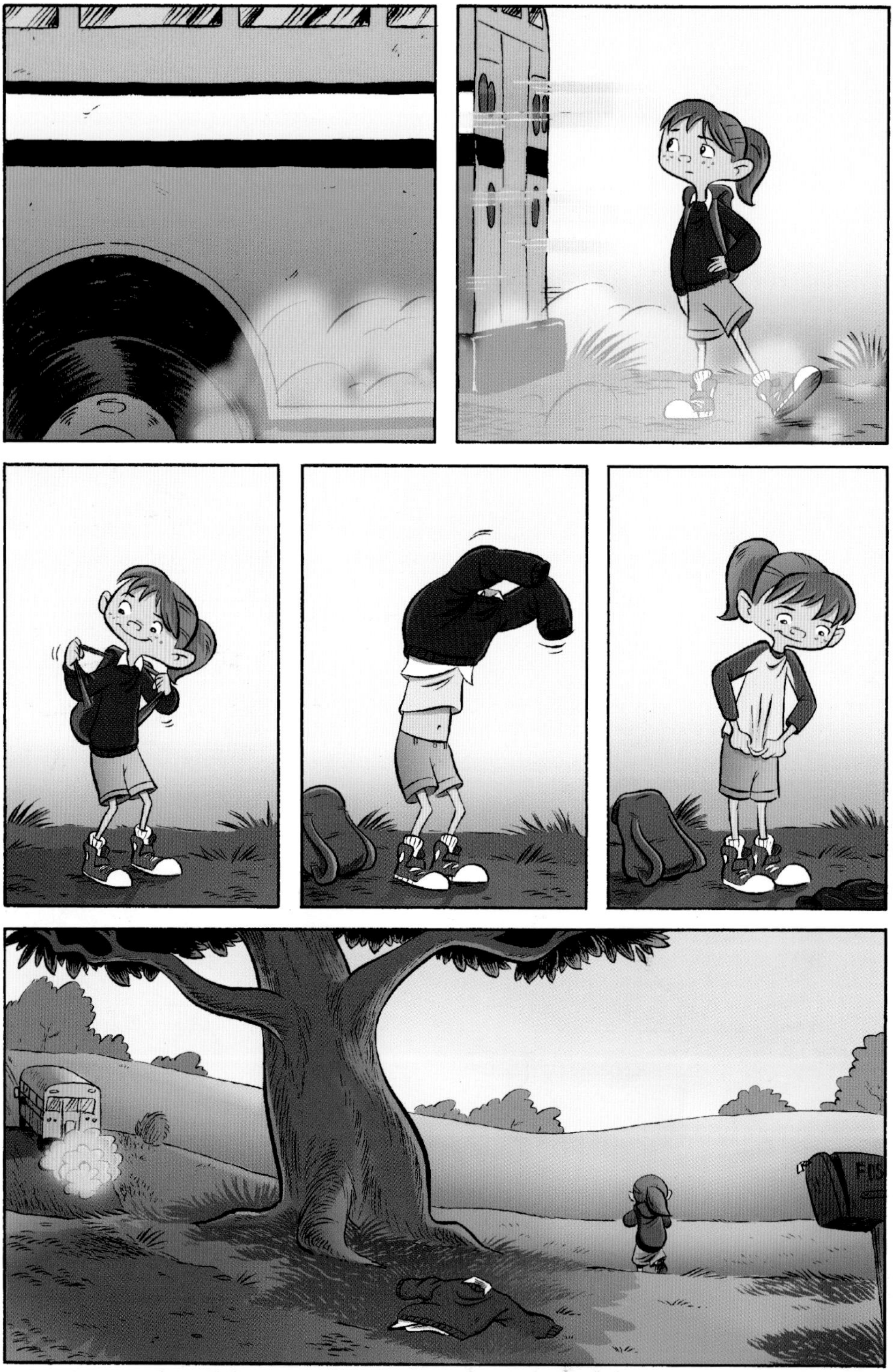

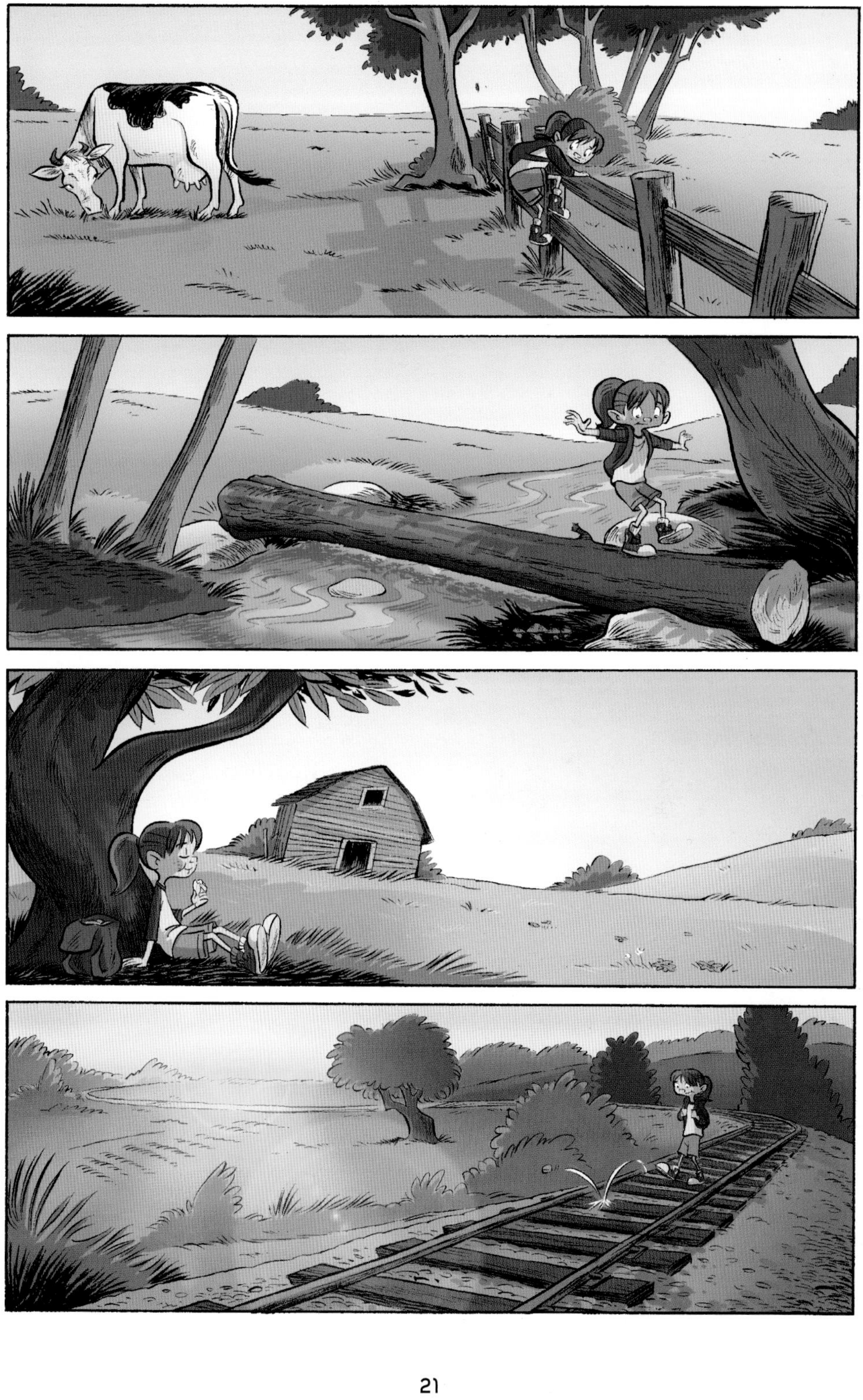

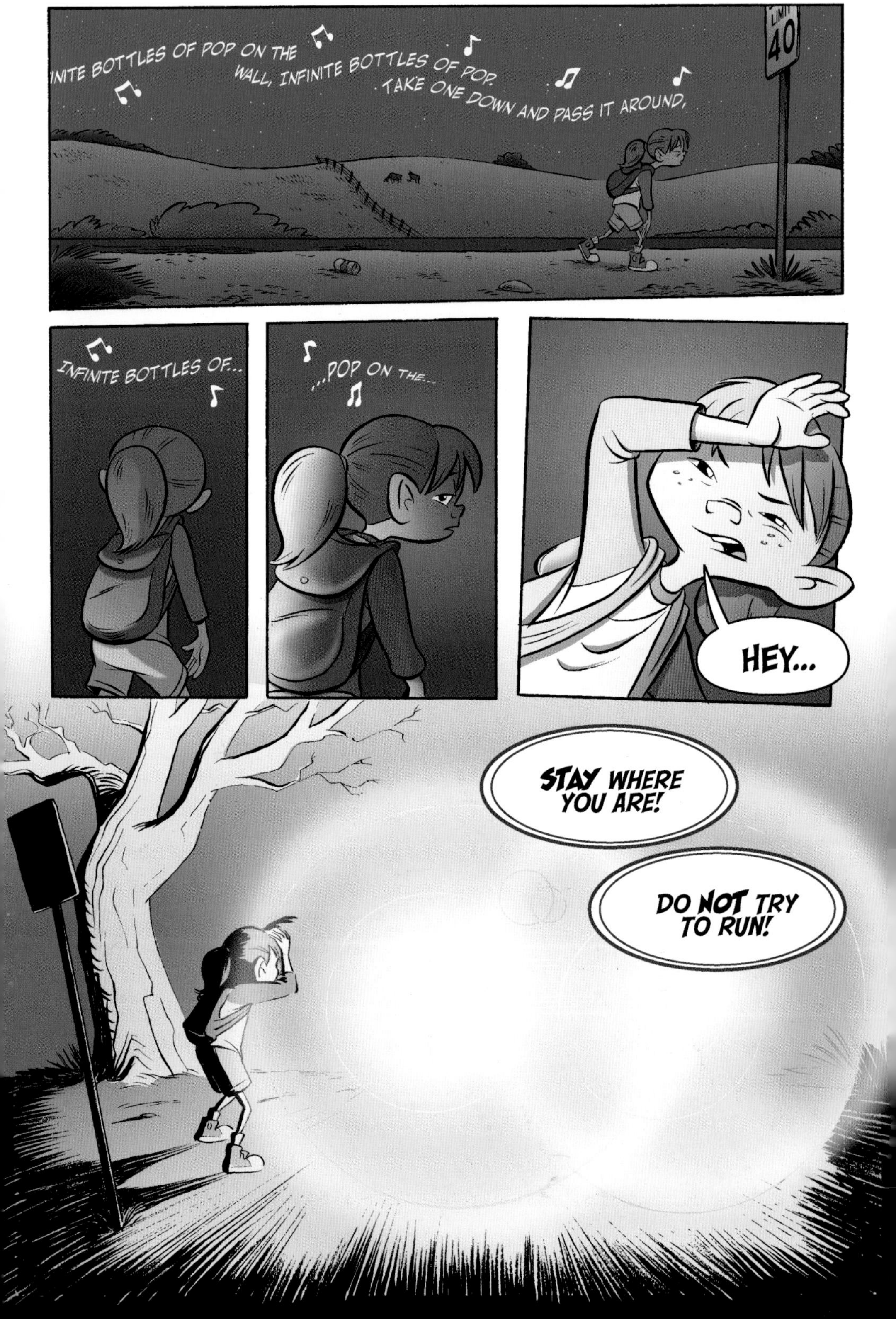
INITE BOTTLES OF POP ON THE
WALL, INFINITE BOTTLES OF POP.
TAKE ONE DOWN AND PASS IT AROUND,
LIMIT 40
INFINITE BOTTLES OF...
...POP ON THE...
HEY...
STAY WHERE YOU ARE!
DO NOT TRY TO RUN!

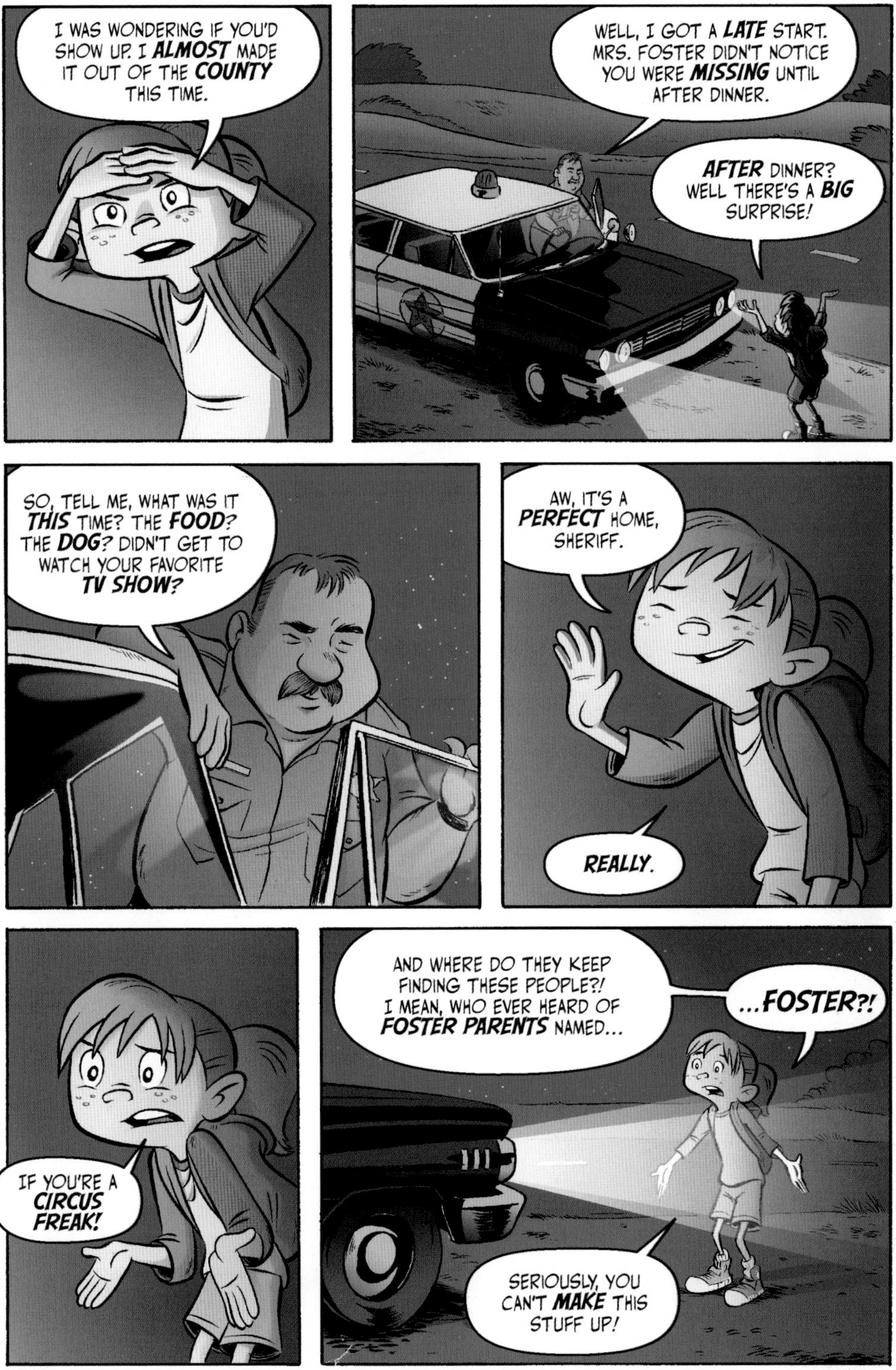
I WAS WONDERING IF YOU'D SHOW UP. I ALMOST MADE IT OUT OF THE COUNTY THIS TIME.
WELL, I GOT A LATE START. MRS. FOSTER DIDN'T NOTICE YOU WERE MISSING UNTIL AFTER DINNER.
AFTER DINNER? WELL THERE'S A BIG SURPRISE!
SO, TELL ME, WHAT WAS IT THIS TIME? THE FOOD? THE DOG? DIDN'T GET TO WATCH YOUR FAVORITE TV SHOW?
AW, IT'S A PERFECT HOME, SHERIFF.
REALLY.
AND WHERE DO THEY KEEP FINDING THESE PEOPLE?! I MEAN, WHO EVER HEARD OF FOSTER PARENTS NAMED...
...FOSTER?!
IF YOU'RE A CIRCUS FREAK!
SERIOUSLY, YOU CAN'T MAKE THIS STUFF UP!

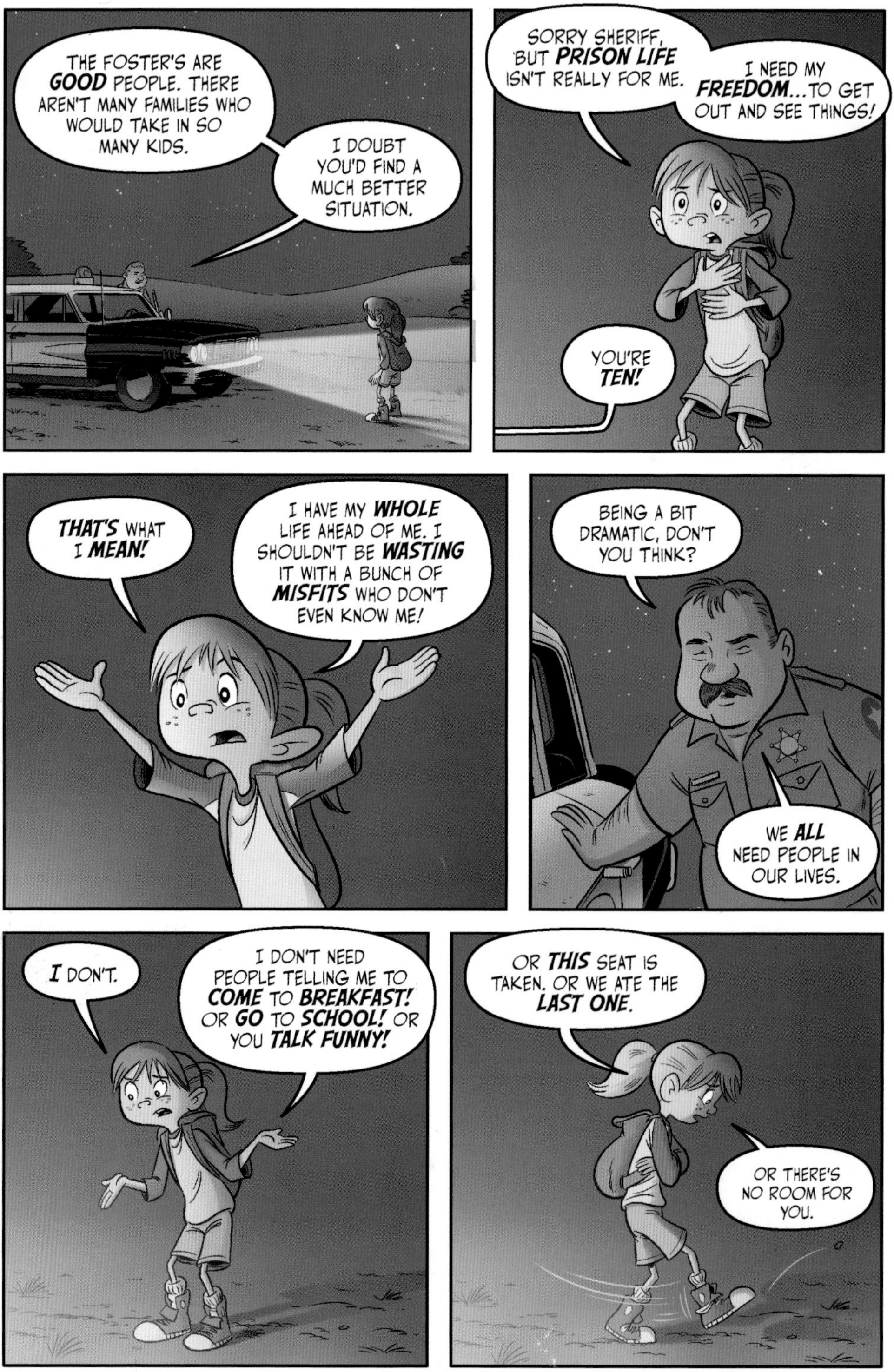
THE FOSTER'S ARE **GOOD** PEOPLE. THERE AREN'T MANY FAMILIES WHO WOULD TAKE IN SO MANY KIDS.
I DOUBT YOU'D FIND A MUCH BETTER SITUATION.
SORRY SHERIFF, BUT **PRISON LIFE** ISN'T REALLY FOR ME.
I NEED MY **FREEDOM**...TO GET OUT AND SEE THINGS!
YOU'RE **TEN!**
THAT'S WHAT I **MEAN!**
I HAVE MY **WHOLE** LIFE AHEAD OF ME. I SHOULDN'T BE **WASTING** IT WITH A BUNCH OF **MISFITS** WHO DON'T EVEN KNOW ME!
BEING A BIT DRAMATIC, DON'T YOU THINK?
WE **ALL** NEED PEOPLE IN OUR LIVES.
I DON'T.
I DON'T NEED PEOPLE TELLING ME TO **COME** TO **BREAKFAST!** OR **GO** TO **SCHOOL!** OR YOU **TALK FUNNY!**
OR **THIS** SEAT IS TAKEN. OR WE ATE THE **LAST ONE**.
OR THERE'S NO ROOM FOR YOU.

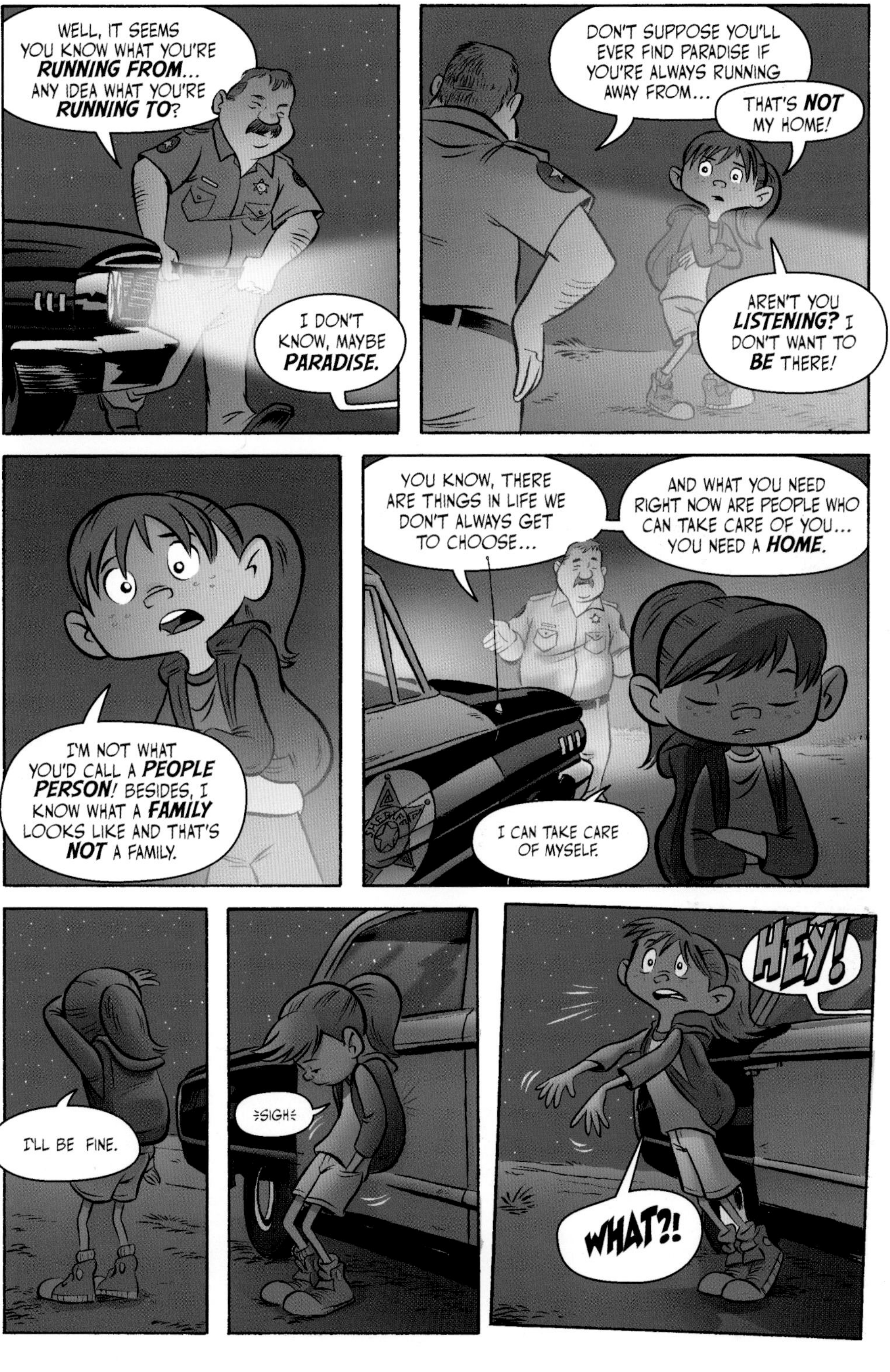
WELL, IT SEEMS YOU KNOW WHAT YOU'RE RUNNING FROM... ANY IDEA WHAT YOU'RE RUNNING TO?
I DON'T KNOW, MAYBE PARADISE.
DON'T SUPPOSE YOU'LL EVER FIND PARADISE IF YOU'RE ALWAYS RUNNING AWAY FROM...
THAT'S NOT MY HOME!
AREN'T YOU LISTENING? I DON'T WANT TO BE THERE!
I'M NOT WHAT YOU'D CALL A PEOPLE PERSON! BESIDES, I KNOW WHAT A FAMILY LOOKS LIKE AND THAT'S NOT A FAMILY.
YOU KNOW, THERE ARE THINGS IN LIFE WE DON'T ALWAYS GET TO CHOOSE...
AND WHAT YOU NEED RIGHT NOW ARE PEOPLE WHO CAN TAKE CARE OF YOU... YOU NEED A HOME.
I CAN TAKE CARE OF MYSELF.
SHERIFF
I'LL BE FINE.
SIGH
HEY!
WHAT?!

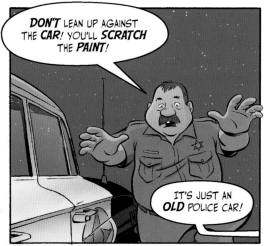

DON'T LEAN UP AGAINST THE *CAR*! YOU'LL *SCRATCH* THE *PAINT*!

IT'S JUST AN *OLD* POLICE CAR!

THIS IS NOT JUST *ANY* OLD CAR!

IT'S A *NEW* OLD CAR! A *COLLECTIBLE*!

A *1964* FORD GALAXIE 500. WITH A 250-HP THUNDERBIRD V-8, CRUISE-O-MATIC TRANSMISSION AND ONLY 42,000 *ORIGINAL* MILES.

FULLY RESTORED IN GLORIOUS *BLACK* AND *WHITE*! JUST LIKE THE ONE *ANDY GRIFFITH* DROVE DOWN THE STREETS OF *MAYBERRY*.

BEFORE *BARNEY* LEFT AND ANDY BECAME BITTER AND IRRITATED *ALL* THE TIME.

MY *GRANDMOTHER* DROVE A CAR *EXACTLY* LIKE THAT.

THIS IS *NOT* YOUR GRANDMOTHER'S CAR.

NO, *REALLY*, THAT'S *HER* CAR!

SHUT UP AND GET IN!

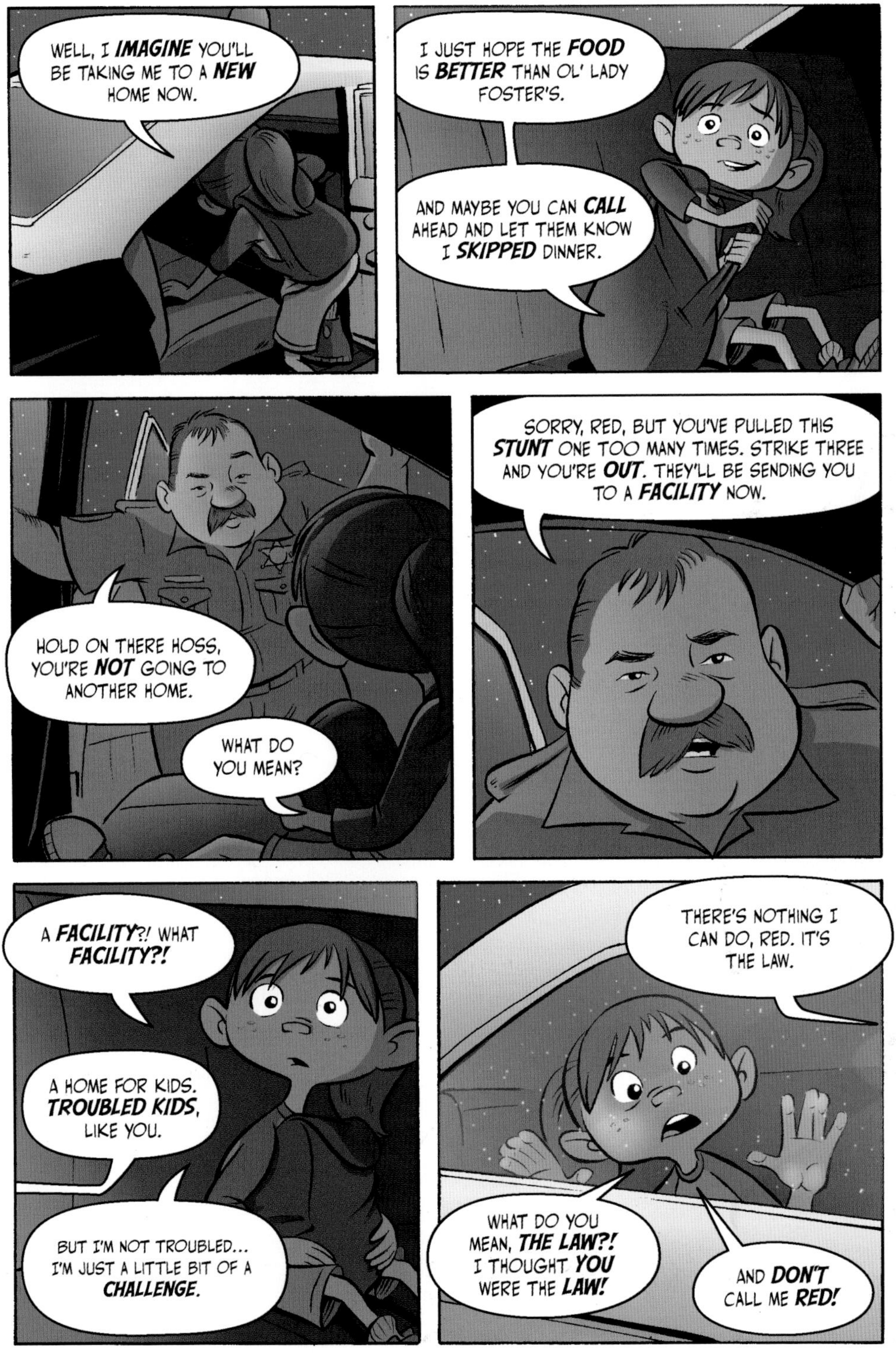
WELL, I IMAGINE YOU'LL BE TAKING ME TO A NEW HOME NOW.
I JUST HOPE THE FOOD IS BETTER THAN OL' LADY FOSTER'S.
AND MAYBE YOU CAN CALL AHEAD AND LET THEM KNOW I SKIPPED DINNER.
HOLD ON THERE HOSS, YOU'RE NOT GOING TO ANOTHER HOME.
WHAT DO YOU MEAN?
SORRY, RED, BUT YOU'VE PULLED THIS STUNT ONE TOO MANY TIMES. STRIKE THREE AND YOU'RE OUT. THEY'LL BE SENDING YOU TO A FACILITY NOW.
A FACILITY?! WHAT FACILITY?!
A HOME FOR KIDS. TROUBLED KIDS, LIKE YOU.
BUT I'M NOT TROUBLED... I'M JUST A LITTLE BIT OF A CHALLENGE.
THERE'S NOTHING I CAN DO, RED. IT'S THE LAW.
WHAT DO YOU MEAN, THE LAW?! I THOUGHT YOU WERE THE LAW!
AND DON'T CALL ME RED!

DEPUTY ONE TO SHERIFF RAMSEY!

THIS IS DEPUTY ONE TO SHERIFF RAMSEY! COME IN SHERIFF!

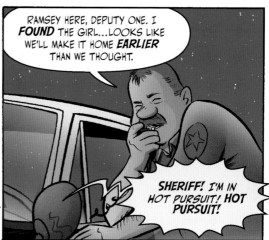

RAMSEY HERE, DEPUTY ONE. I FOUND THE GIRL...LOOKS LIKE WE'LL MAKE IT HOME EARLIER THAN WE THOUGHT.

SHERIFF! I'M IN HOT PURSUIT! HOT PURSUIT!

CALM DOWN THERE, JOSH. NOW WHAT EXACTLY ARE YOU IN "HOT PURSUIT" OF?

YOU KNOW THOSE HOTRODS THAT HAVE BEEN STREET RACING THROUGH MANCHESTER? WELL, LOOKS LIKE WE GOT US ONE, SHERIFF!

HOLY SMOKES! WELL, IT LOOKS LIKE I'M JUST ABOUT DONE HERE IF YOU NEED ANY ASSISTANCE.

WHAT'S YOUR 20?

ZOOOOSHHHH

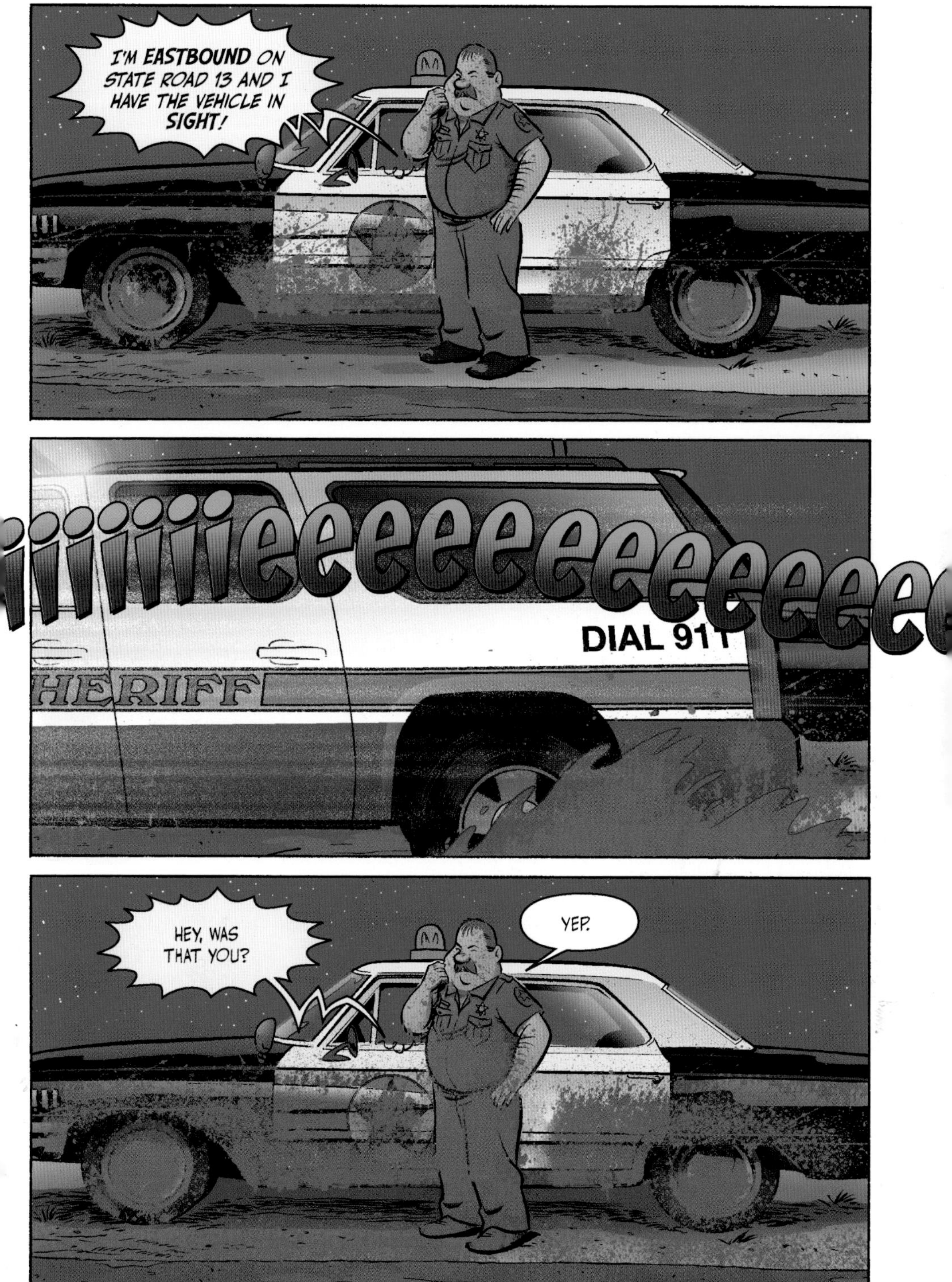
I'M **EASTBOUND** ON STATE ROAD 13 AND I HAVE THE VEHICLE IN **SIGHT**!
iiiiiiiieeeeeeeeeee
DIAL 911
HERIFF
HEY, WAS THAT YOU?
YEP.

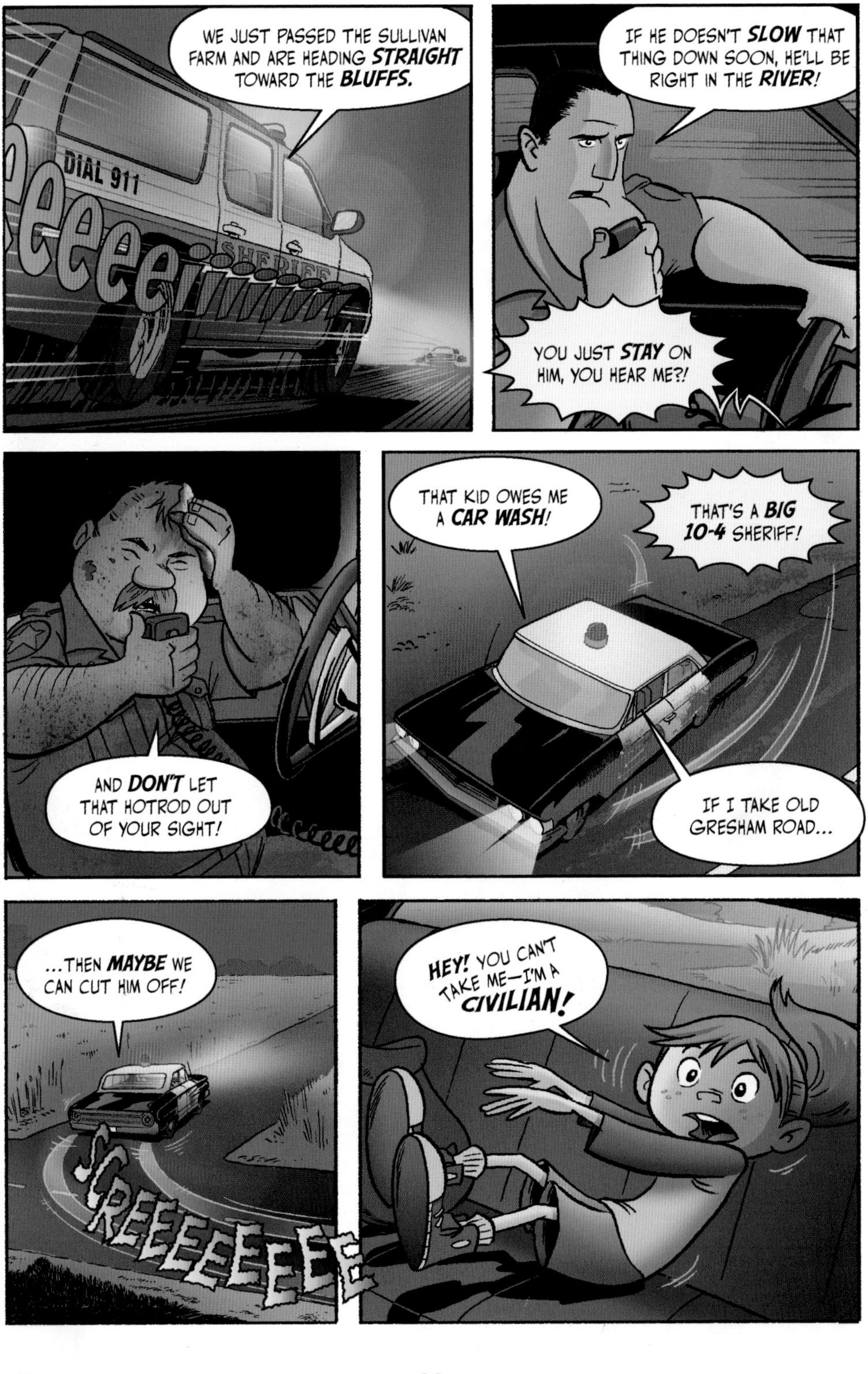
WE JUST PASSED THE SULLIVAN FARM AND ARE HEADING STRAIGHT TOWARD THE BLUFFS.
DIAL 911
SHERIFF
IF HE DOESN'T SLOW THAT THING DOWN SOON, HE'LL BE RIGHT IN THE RIVER!
YOU JUST STAY ON HIM, YOU HEAR ME?!
AND DON'T LET THAT HOTROD OUT OF YOUR SIGHT!
THAT KID OWES ME A CAR WASH!
THAT'S A BIG 10-4 SHERIFF!
IF I TAKE OLD GRESHAM ROAD...
...THEN MAYBE WE CAN CUT HIM OFF!
SCREEEEEEEEE
HEY! YOU CAN'T TAKE ME—I'M A CIVILIAN!

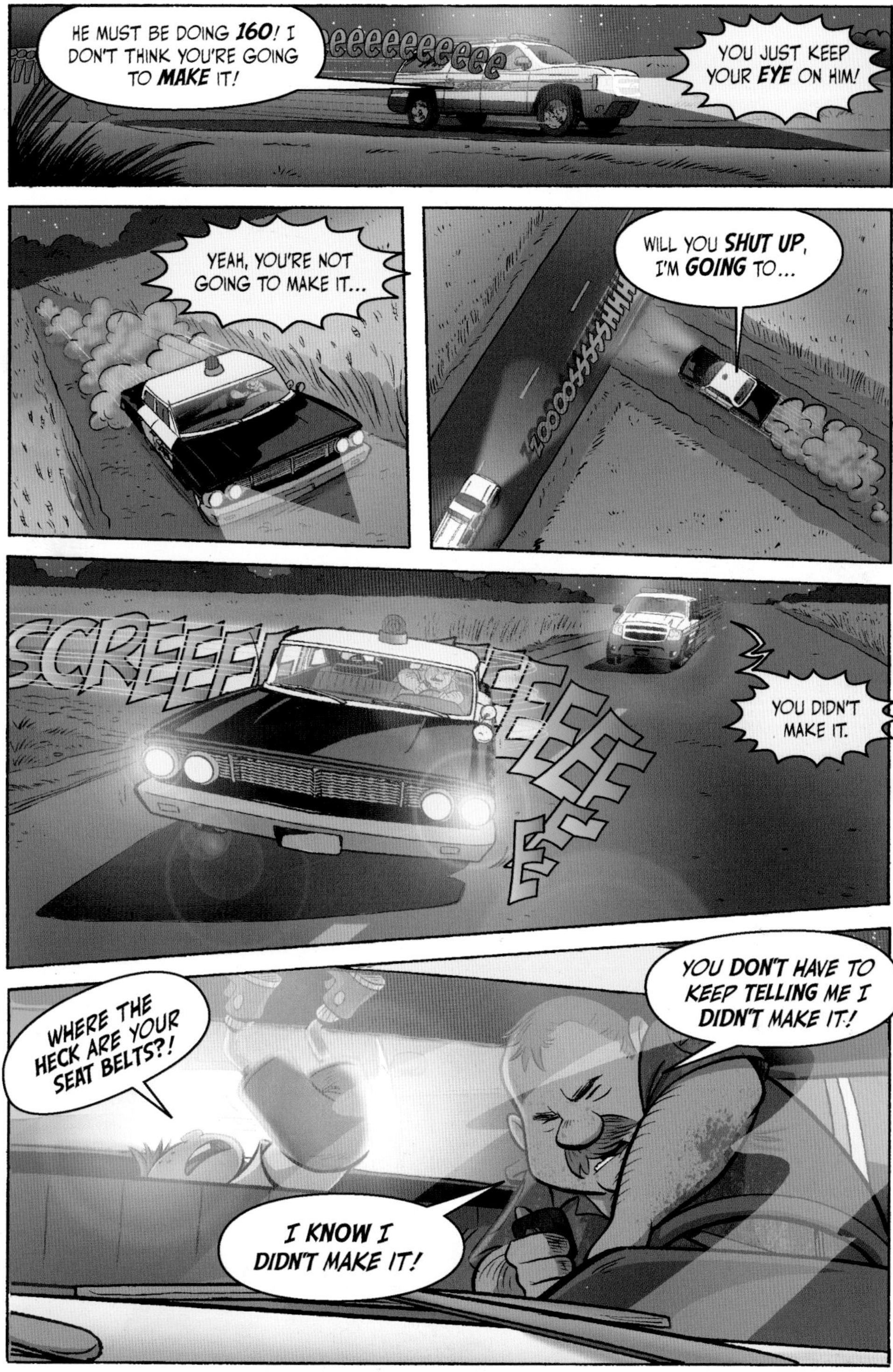
HE MUST BE DOING **160**! I DON'T THINK YOU'RE GOING TO **MAKE** IT!
YOU JUST KEEP YOUR **EYE** ON HIM!
YEAH, YOU'RE NOT GOING TO MAKE IT...
WILL YOU **SHUT UP**, I'M **GOING** TO...
ZOOOOSSSSHHH
SCREEEE
YOU DIDN'T MAKE IT.
WHERE THE HECK ARE YOUR SEAT BELTS?!
YOU **DON'T** HAVE TO KEEP **TELLING** ME I **DIDN'T** MAKE IT!
I KNOW I DIDN'T MAKE IT!

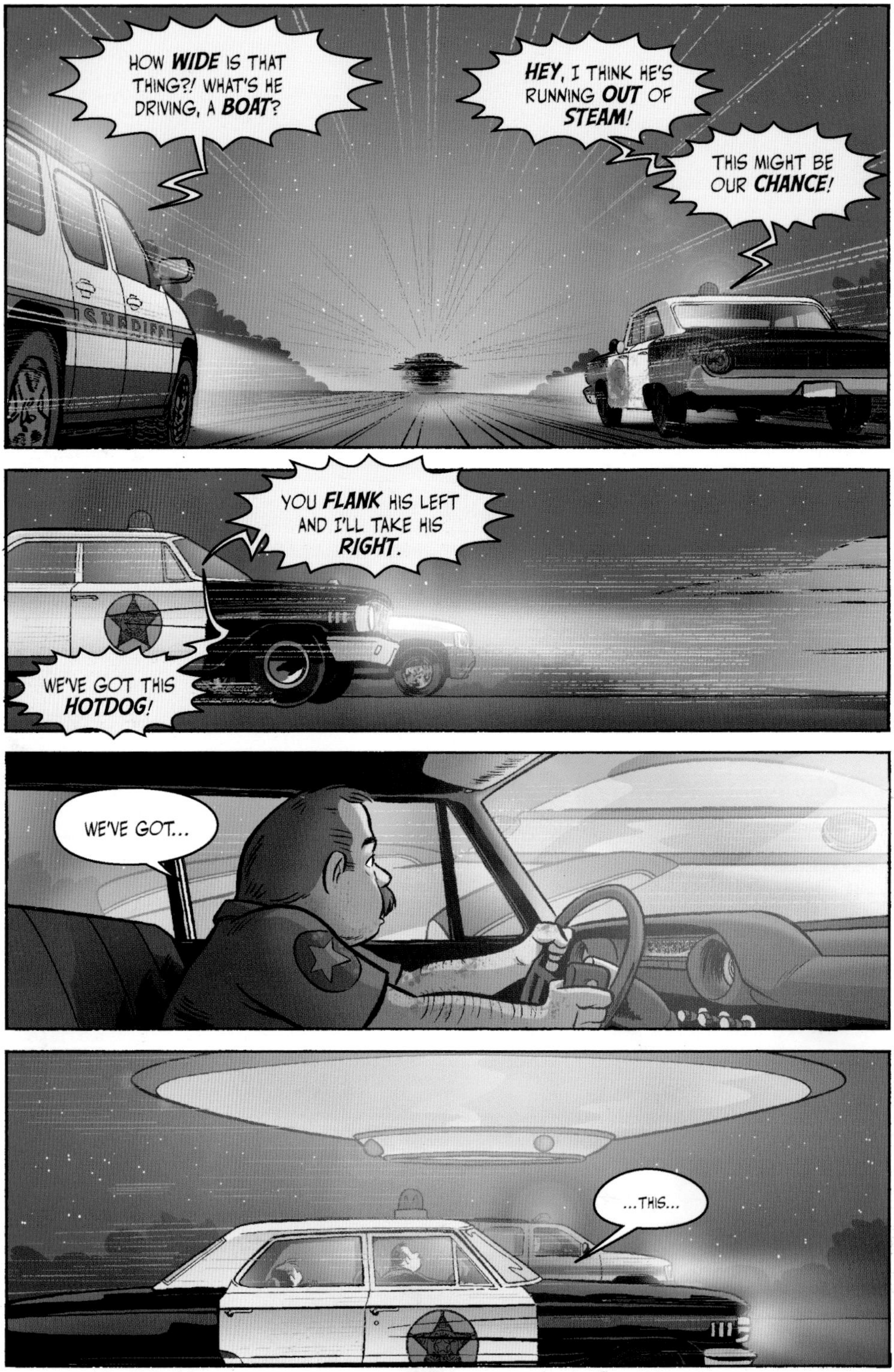
HOW WIDE IS THAT THING?! WHAT'S HE DRIVING, A BOAT?
HEY, I THINK HE'S RUNNING OUT OF STEAM!
THIS MIGHT BE OUR CHANCE!
SHERIFF
YOU FLANK HIS LEFT AND I'LL TAKE HIS RIGHT.
WE'VE GOT THIS HOTDOG!
WE'VE GOT...
...THIS...

HOLY SMOKES!

HEY, WHAT KIND OF COP CAR *IS* THIS? THERE'S *NO DOOR HANDLE?*

SLAM

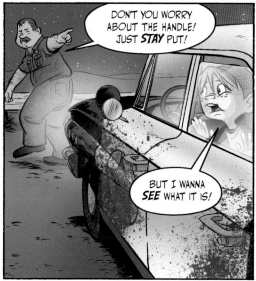

DON'T YOU WORRY ABOUT THE HANDLE! JUST *STAY* PUT!

BUT I WANNA *SEE* WHAT IT IS!

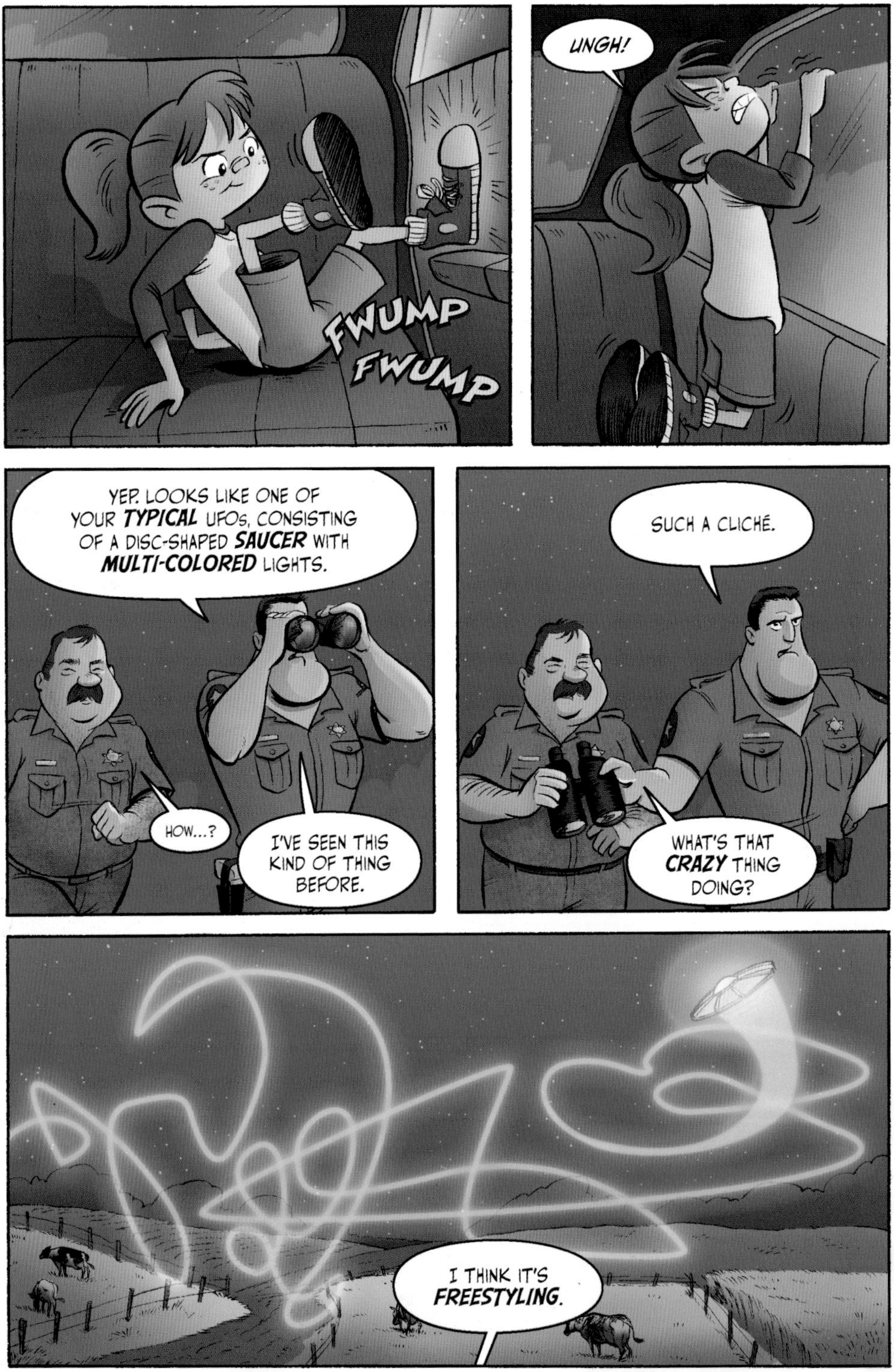
FWUMP
FWUMP
UNGH!
YEP. LOOKS LIKE ONE OF YOUR TYPICAL UFOs, CONSISTING OF A DISC-SHAPED SAUCER WITH MULTI-COLORED LIGHTS.
HOW...?
I'VE SEEN THIS KIND OF THING BEFORE.
SUCH A CLICHÉ.
WHAT'S THAT CRAZY THING DOING?
I THINK IT'S FREESTYLING.

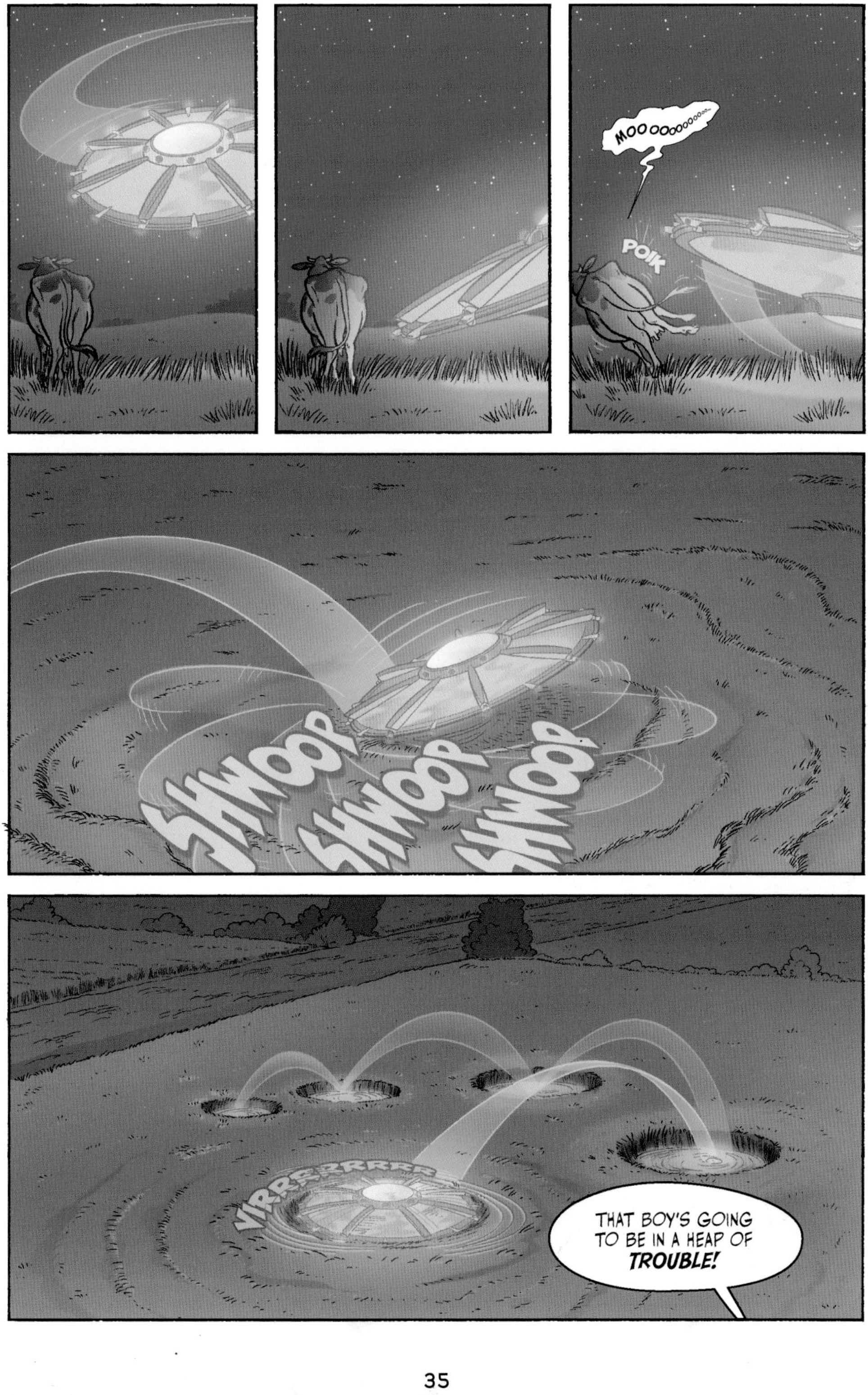
MOOOOOOOOOOOOO...
POIK
SHWOOP
SHWOOP
SHWOOP
VRRRRRRRRR
THAT BOY'S GOING TO BE IN A HEAP OF ***TROUBLE!***

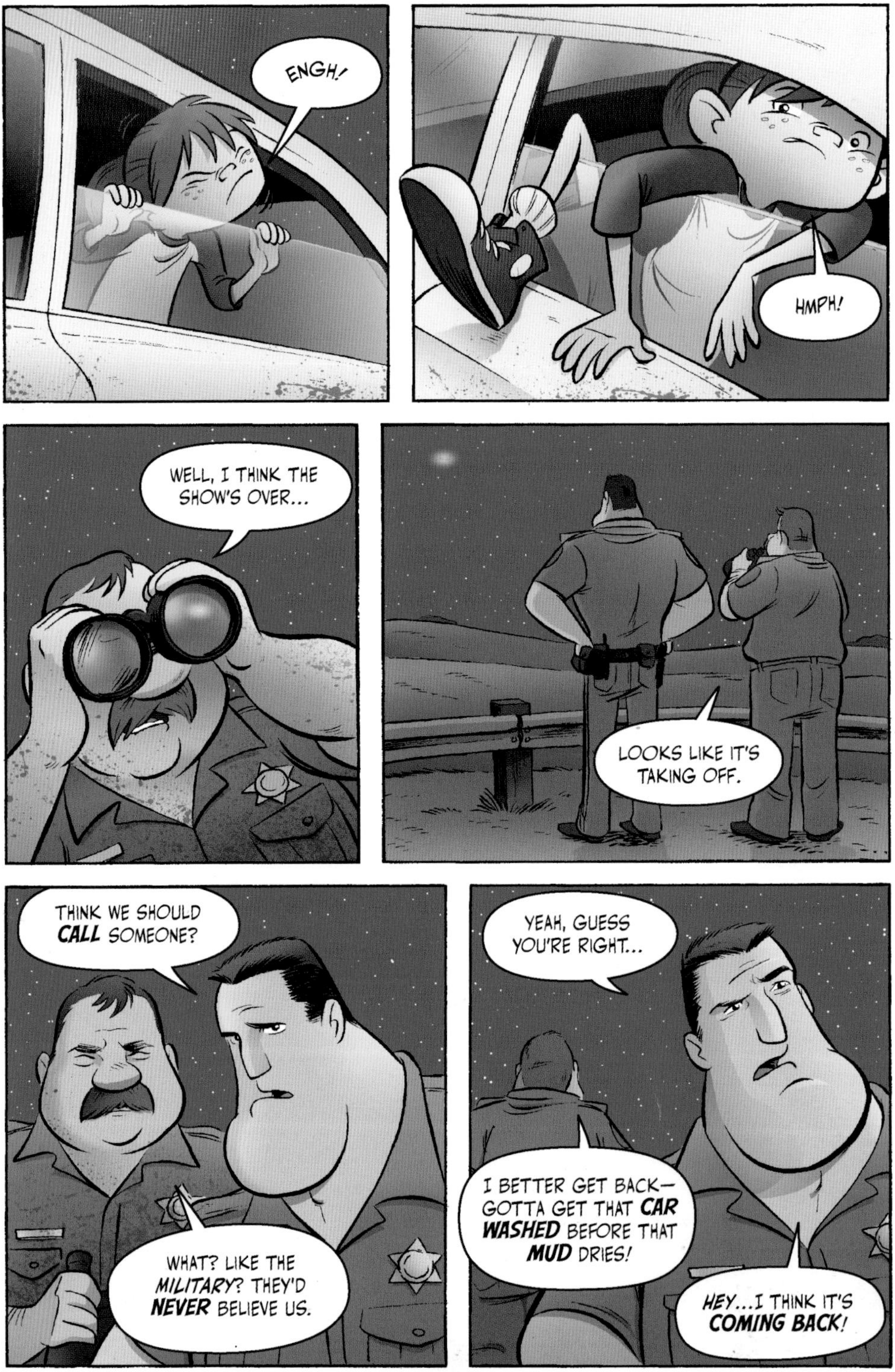
ENGH!
HMPH!
WELL, I THINK THE SHOW'S OVER...
LOOKS LIKE IT'S TAKING OFF.
THINK WE SHOULD **CALL** SOMEONE?
WHAT? LIKE THE ***MILITARY***? THEY'D ***NEVER*** BELIEVE US.
YEAH, GUESS YOU'RE RIGHT...
I BETTER GET BACK— GOTTA GET THAT ***CAR WASHED*** BEFORE THAT ***MUD*** DRIES!
HEY...I THINK IT'S ***COMING BACK!***

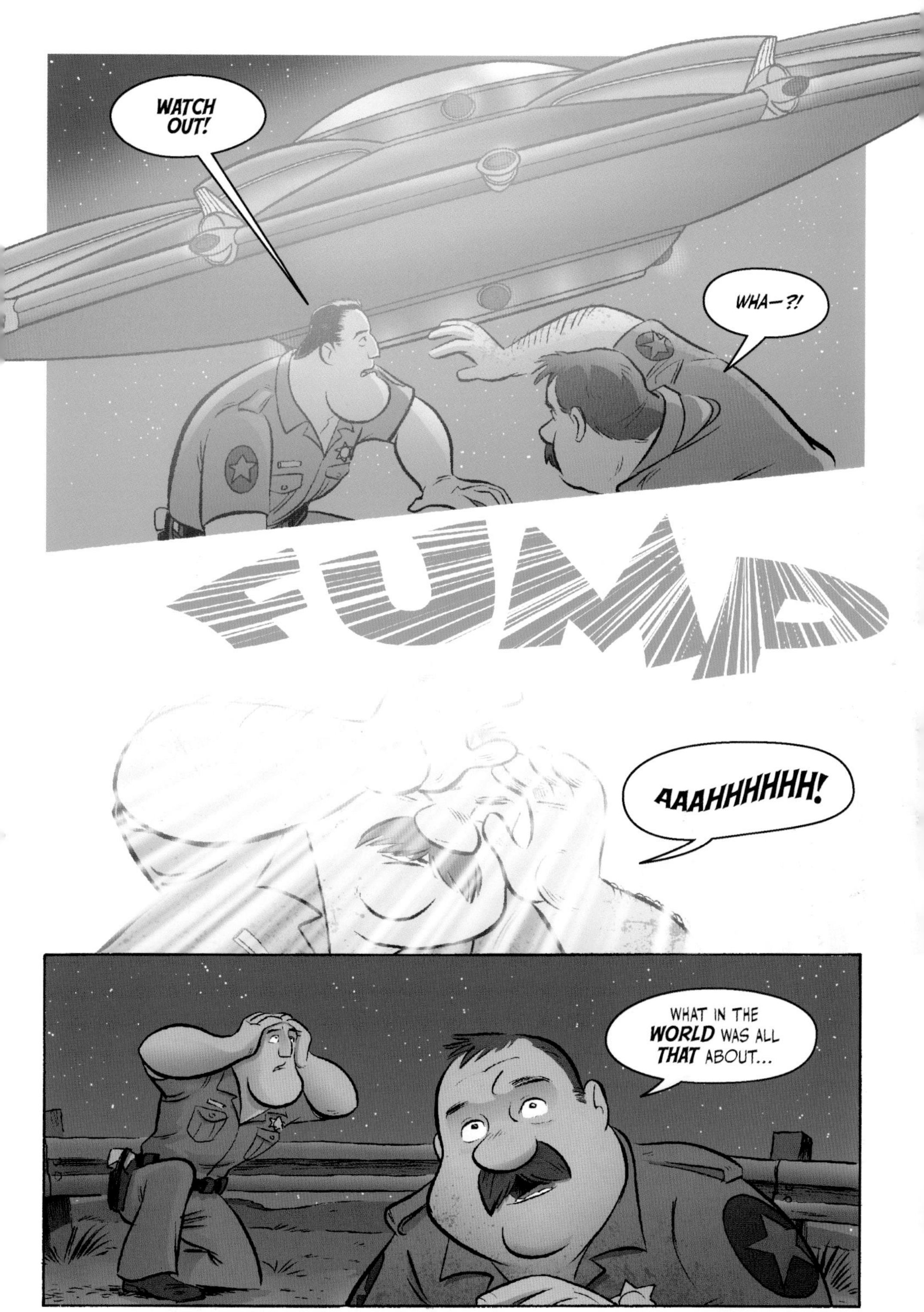
WATCH OUT!
WHA—?!
AAAHHHHH!
WHAT IN THE WORLD WAS ALL THAT ABOUT...

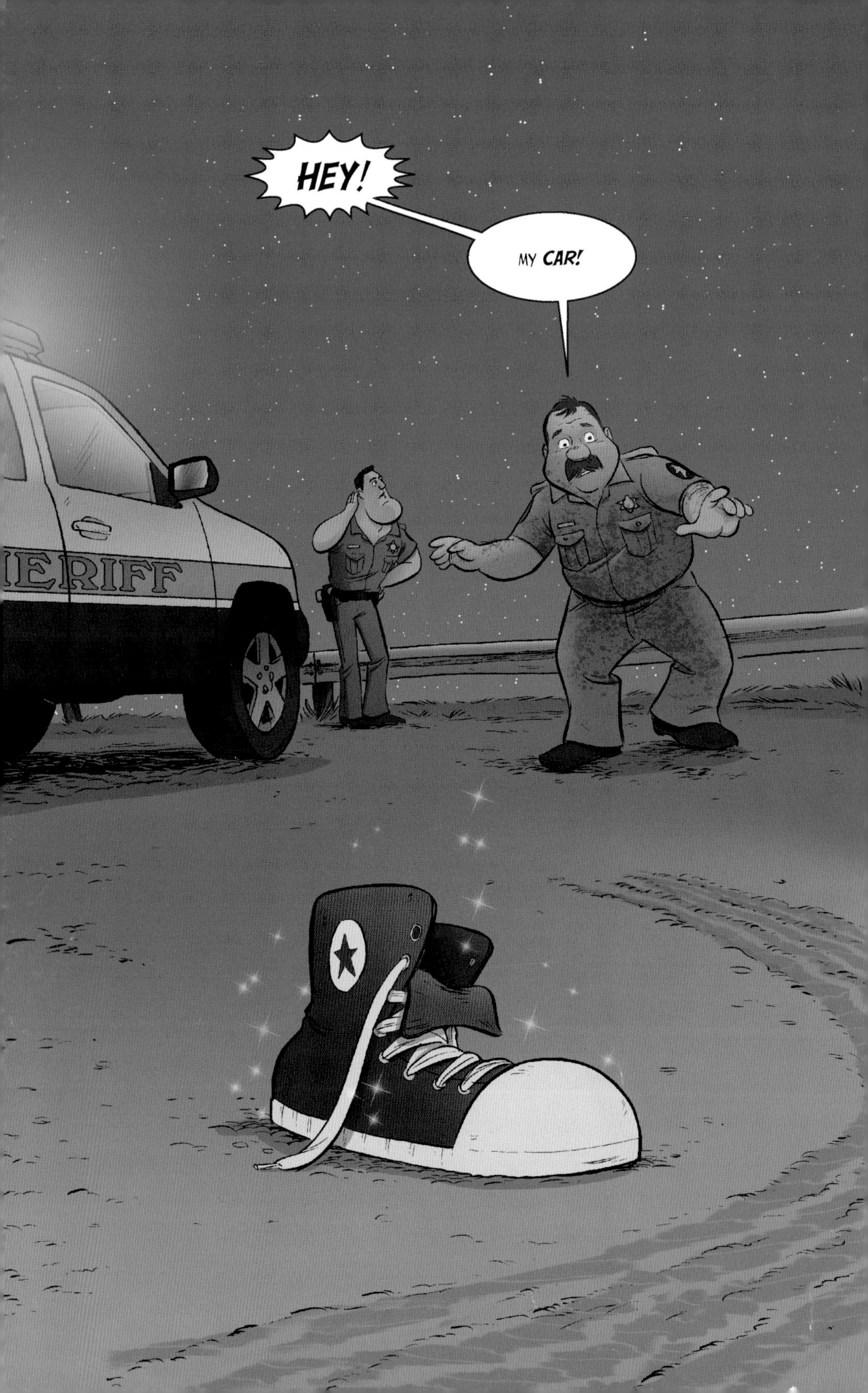
HEY!
MY CAR!
SHERIFF

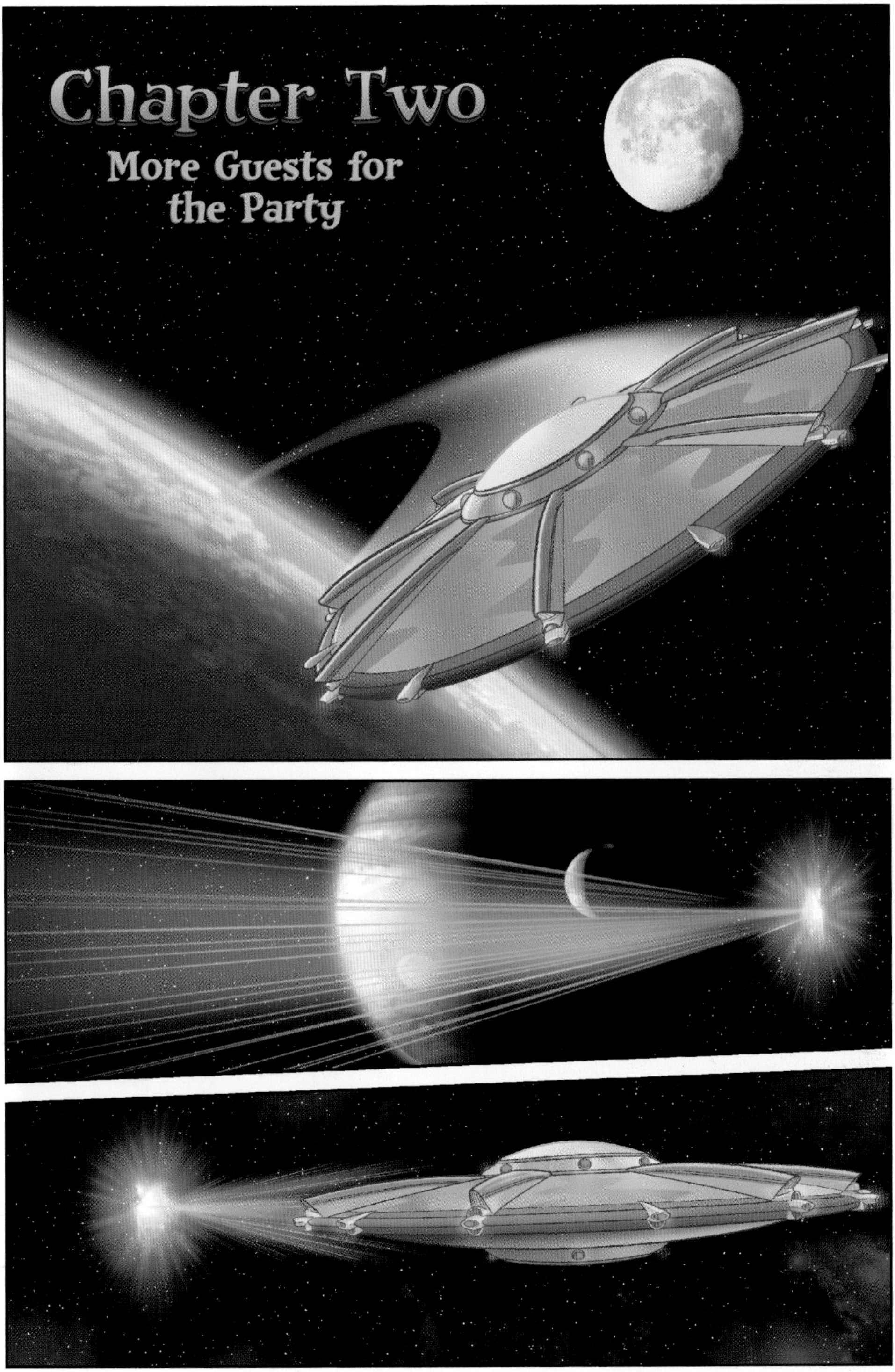
Chapter Two
More Guests for the Party

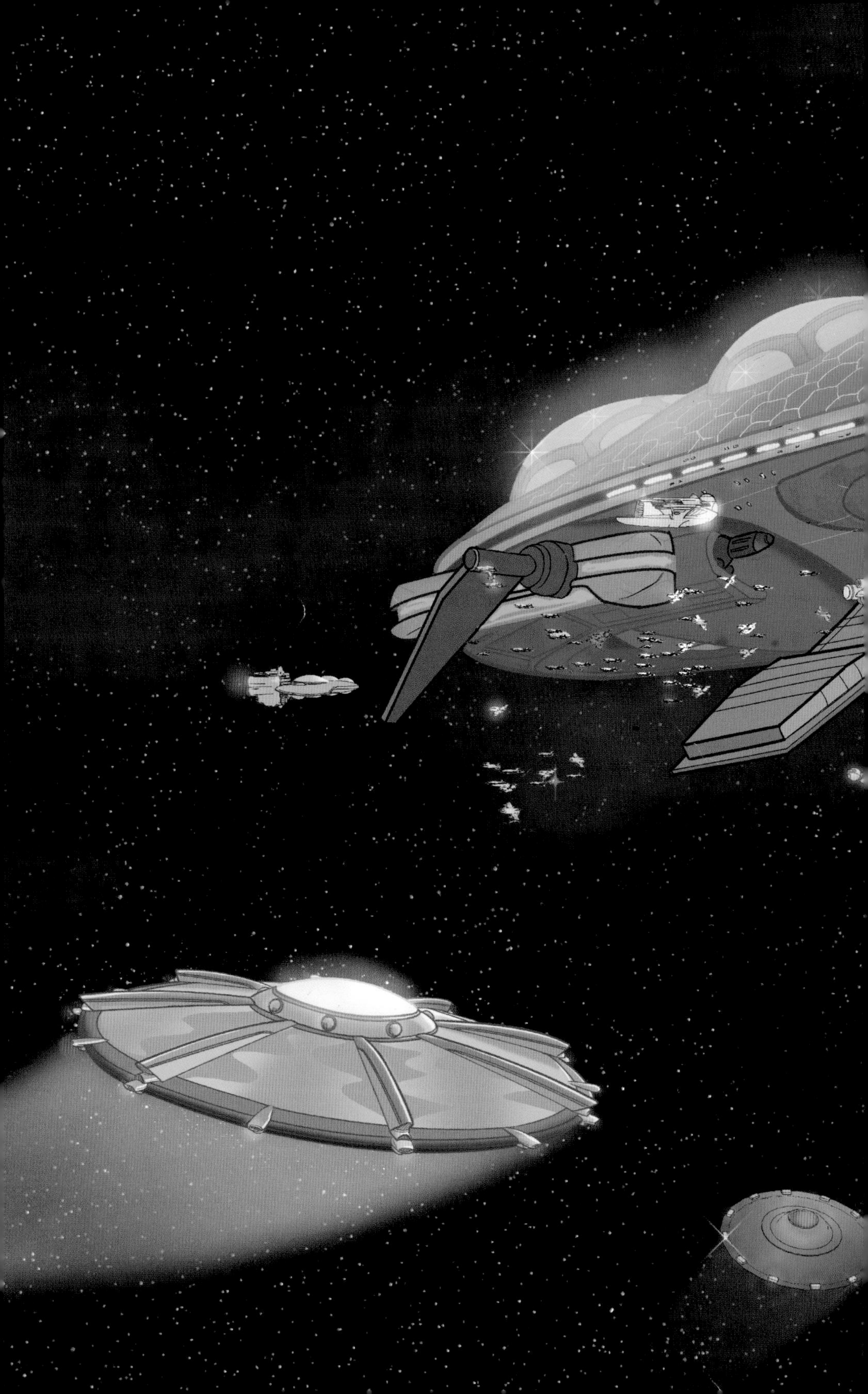

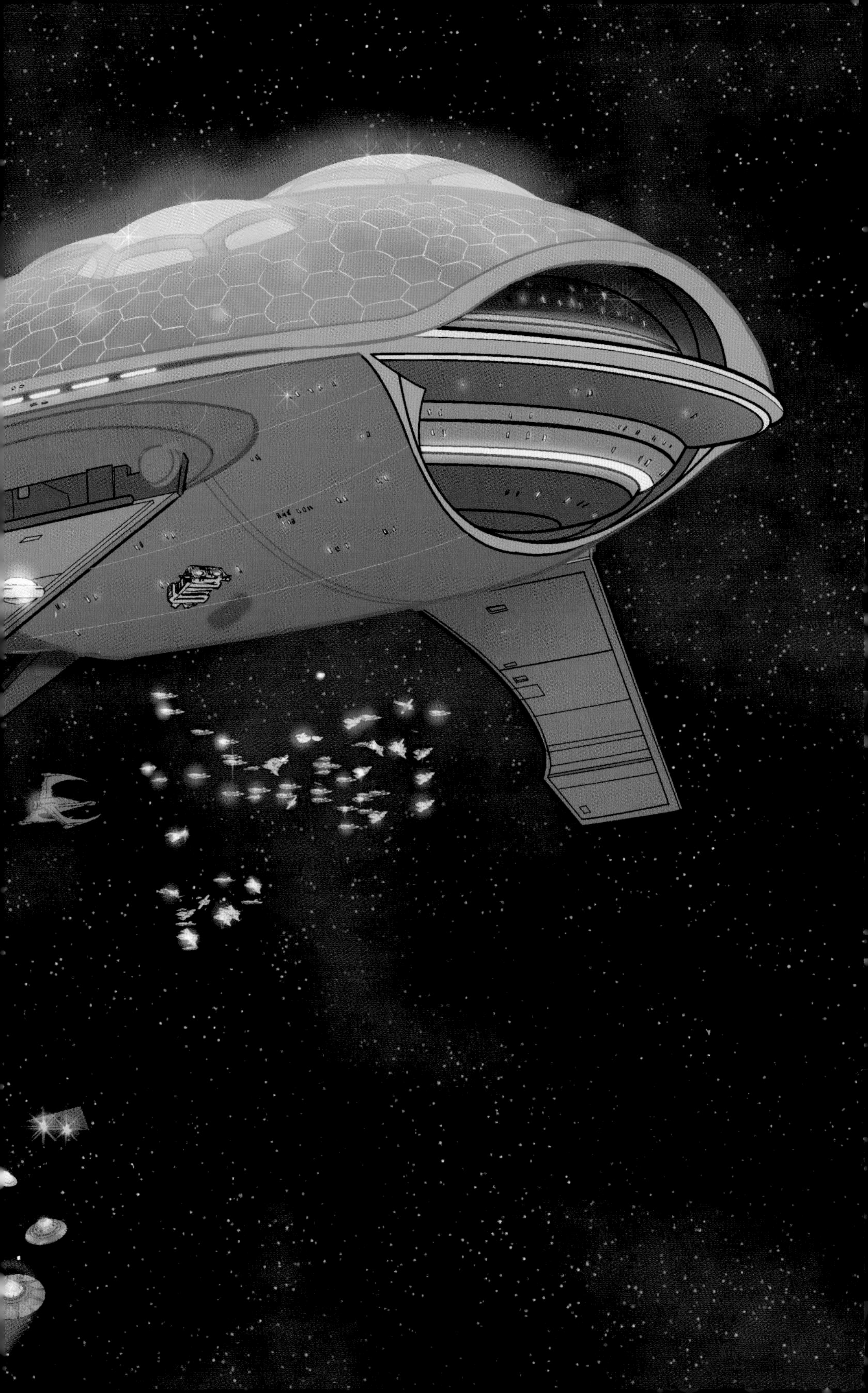

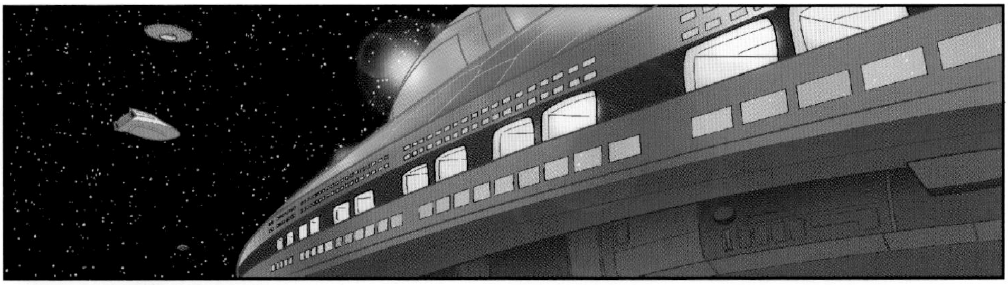

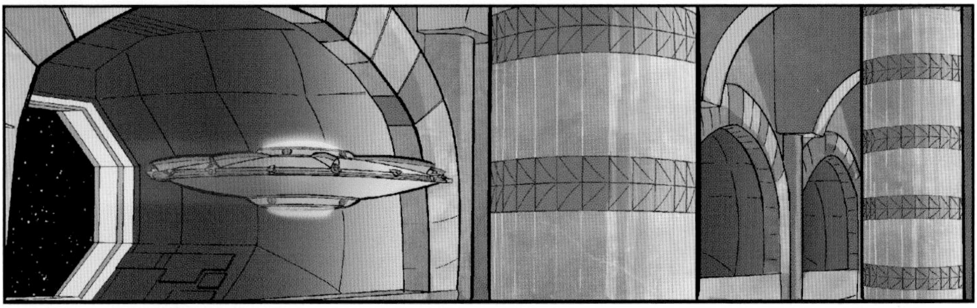

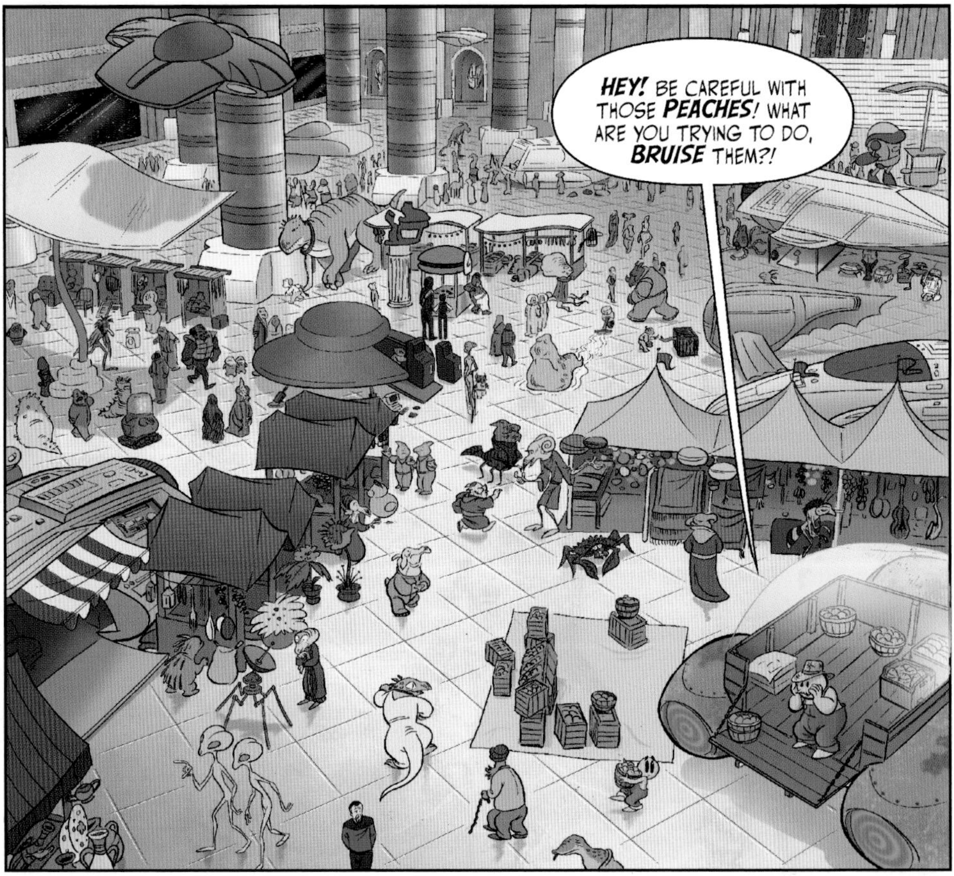
HEY! BE CAREFUL WITH THOSE PEACHES! WHAT ARE YOU TRYING TO DO, BRUISE THEM?!

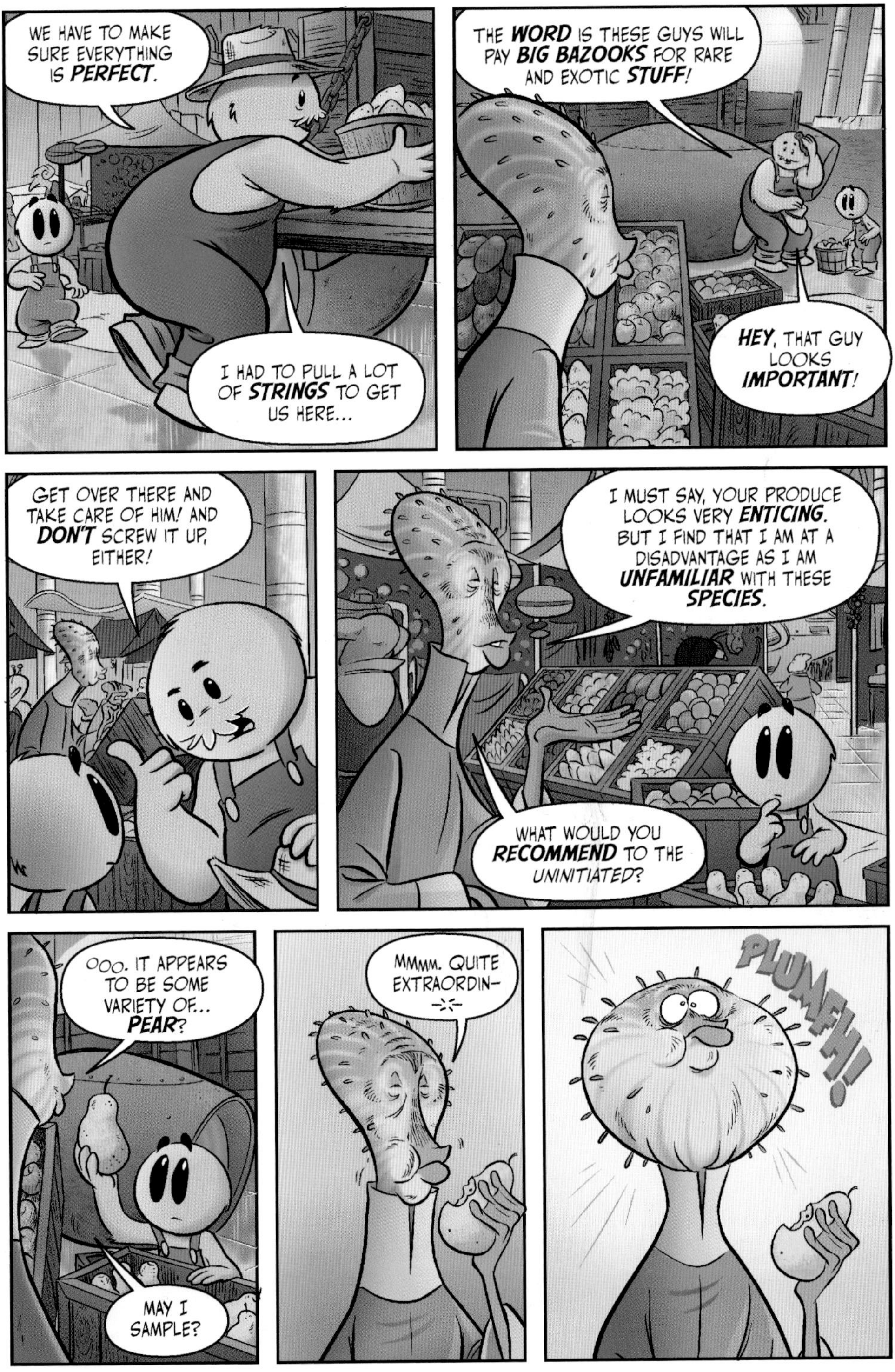
WE HAVE TO MAKE SURE EVERYTHING IS PERFECT.
I HAD TO PULL A LOT OF STRINGS TO GET US HERE...
THE WORD IS THESE GUYS WILL PAY BIG BAZOOKS FOR RARE AND EXOTIC STUFF!
HEY, THAT GUY LOOKS IMPORTANT!
GET OVER THERE AND TAKE CARE OF HIM! AND DON'T SCREW IT UP, EITHER!
I MUST SAY, YOUR PRODUCE LOOKS VERY ENTICING. BUT I FIND THAT I AM AT A DISADVANTAGE AS I AM UNFAMILIAR WITH THESE SPECIES.
WHAT WOULD YOU RECOMMEND TO THE UNINITIATED?
OOO. IT APPEARS TO BE SOME VARIETY OF... PEAR?
MAY I SAMPLE?
MMMM. QUITE EXTRAORDIN-
PLUMFH!

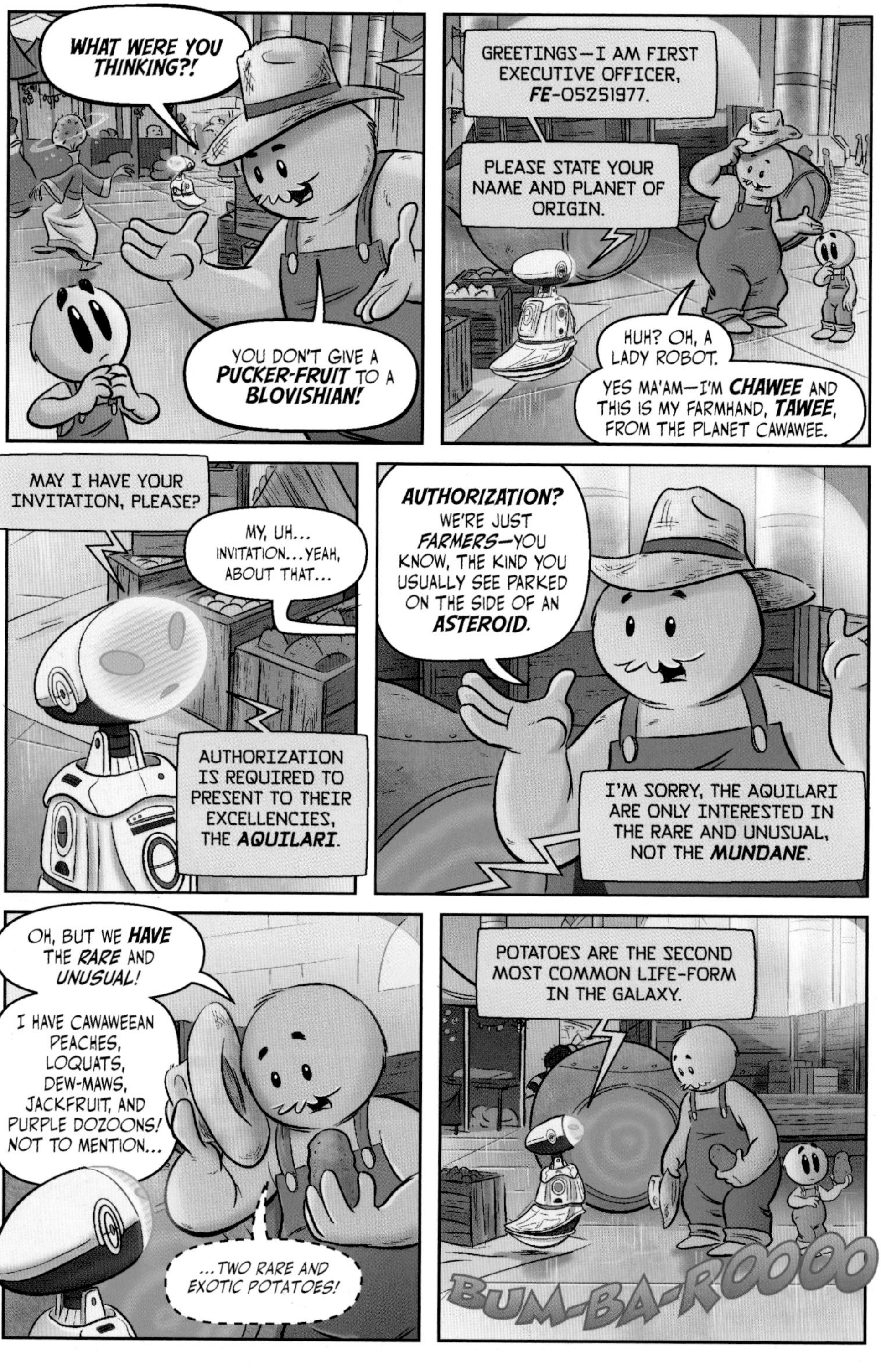
WHAT WERE YOU THINKING?!
YOU DON'T GIVE A PUCKER-FRUIT TO A BLOVISHIAN!
GREETINGS—I AM FIRST EXECUTIVE OFFICER, FE-05251977.
PLEASE STATE YOUR NAME AND PLANET OF ORIGIN.
HUH? OH, A LADY ROBOT.
YES MA'AM—I'M CHAWEE AND THIS IS MY FARMHAND, TAWEE, FROM THE PLANET CAWAWEE.
MAY I HAVE YOUR INVITATION, PLEASE?
MY, UH... INVITATION...YEAH, ABOUT THAT...
AUTHORIZATION IS REQUIRED TO PRESENT TO THEIR EXCELLENCIES, THE AQUILARI.
AUTHORIZATION? WE'RE JUST FARMERS—YOU KNOW, THE KIND YOU USUALLY SEE PARKED ON THE SIDE OF AN ASTEROID.
I'M SORRY, THE AQUILARI ARE ONLY INTERESTED IN THE RARE AND UNUSUAL, NOT THE MUNDANE.
OH, BUT WE HAVE THE RARE AND UNUSUAL!
I HAVE CAWAWEEAN PEACHES, LOQUATS, DEW-MAWS, JACKFRUIT, AND PURPLE DOZOONS! NOT TO MENTION...
...TWO RARE AND EXOTIC POTATOES!
POTATOES ARE THE SECOND MOST COMMON LIFE-FORM IN THE GALAXY.
BUM-BA-ROOOO

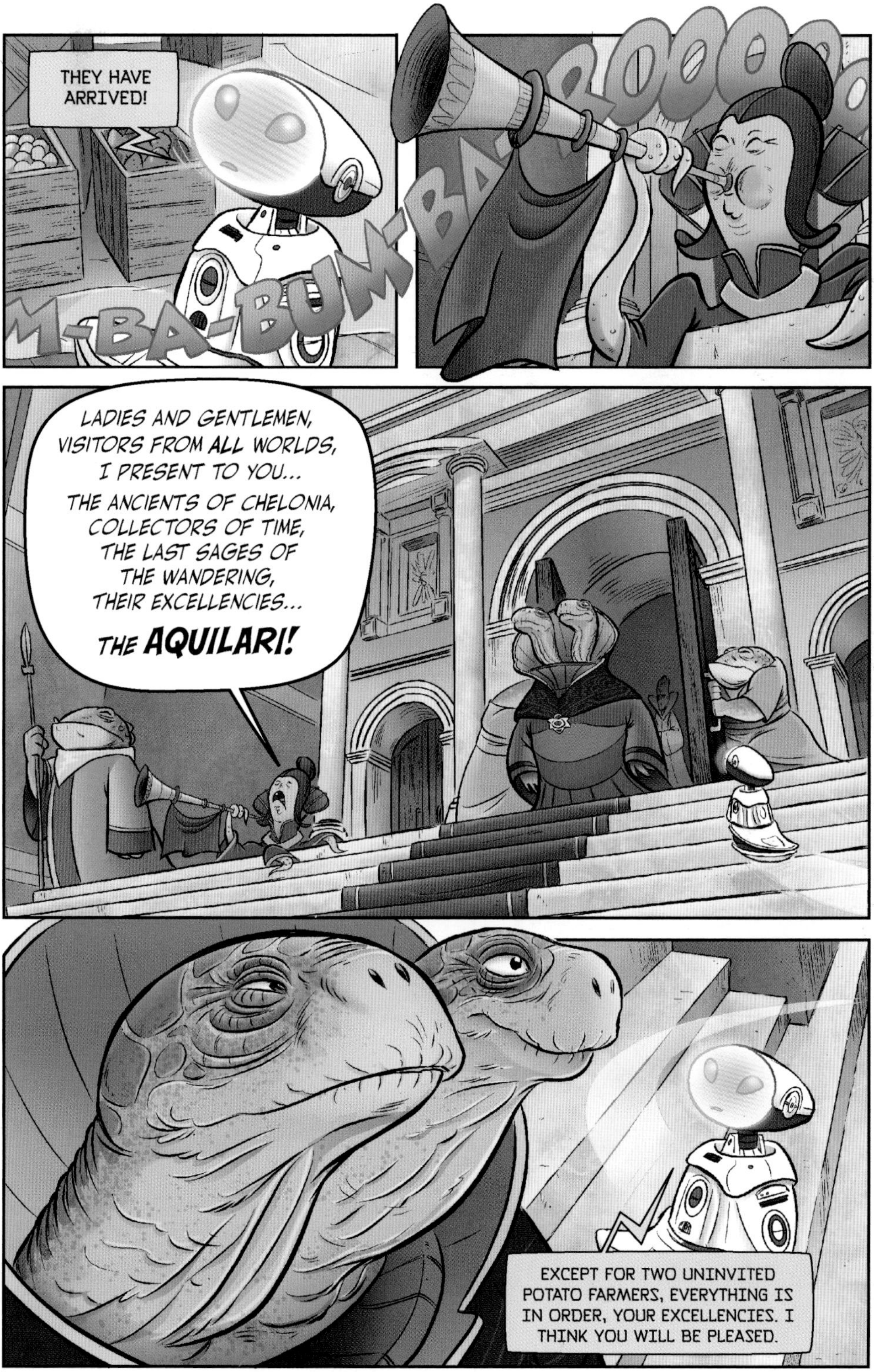
THEY HAVE ARRIVED!
M-BA-BUM-BA
ROOOOO
LADIES AND GENTLEMEN, VISITORS FROM ALL WORLDS, I PRESENT TO YOU... THE ANCIENTS OF CHELONIA, COLLECTORS OF TIME, THE LAST SAGES OF THE WANDERING, THEIR EXCELLENCIES... THE AQUILARI!
EXCEPT FOR TWO UNINVITED POTATO FARMERS, EVERYTHING IS IN ORDER, YOUR EXCELLENCIES. I THINK YOU WILL BE PLEASED.

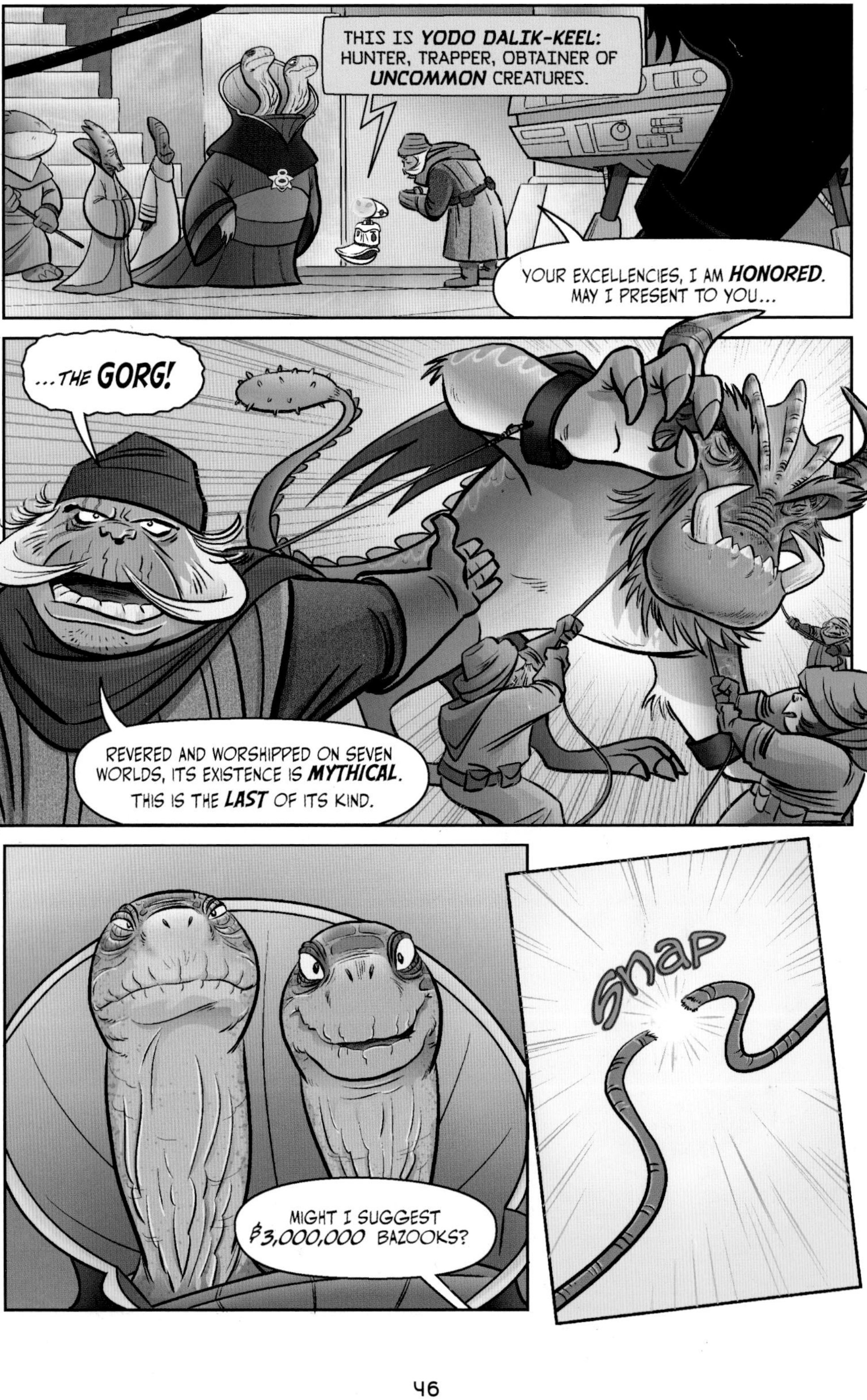
THIS IS YODO DALIK-KEEL: HUNTER, TRAPPER, OBTAINER OF UNCOMMON CREATURES.
YOUR EXCELLENCIES, I AM HONORED. MAY I PRESENT TO YOU...
...THE GORG!
REVERED AND WORSHIPPED ON SEVEN WORLDS, ITS EXISTENCE IS MYTHICAL. THIS IS THE LAST OF ITS KIND.
MIGHT I SUGGEST $3,000,000 BAZOOKS?
SNAP

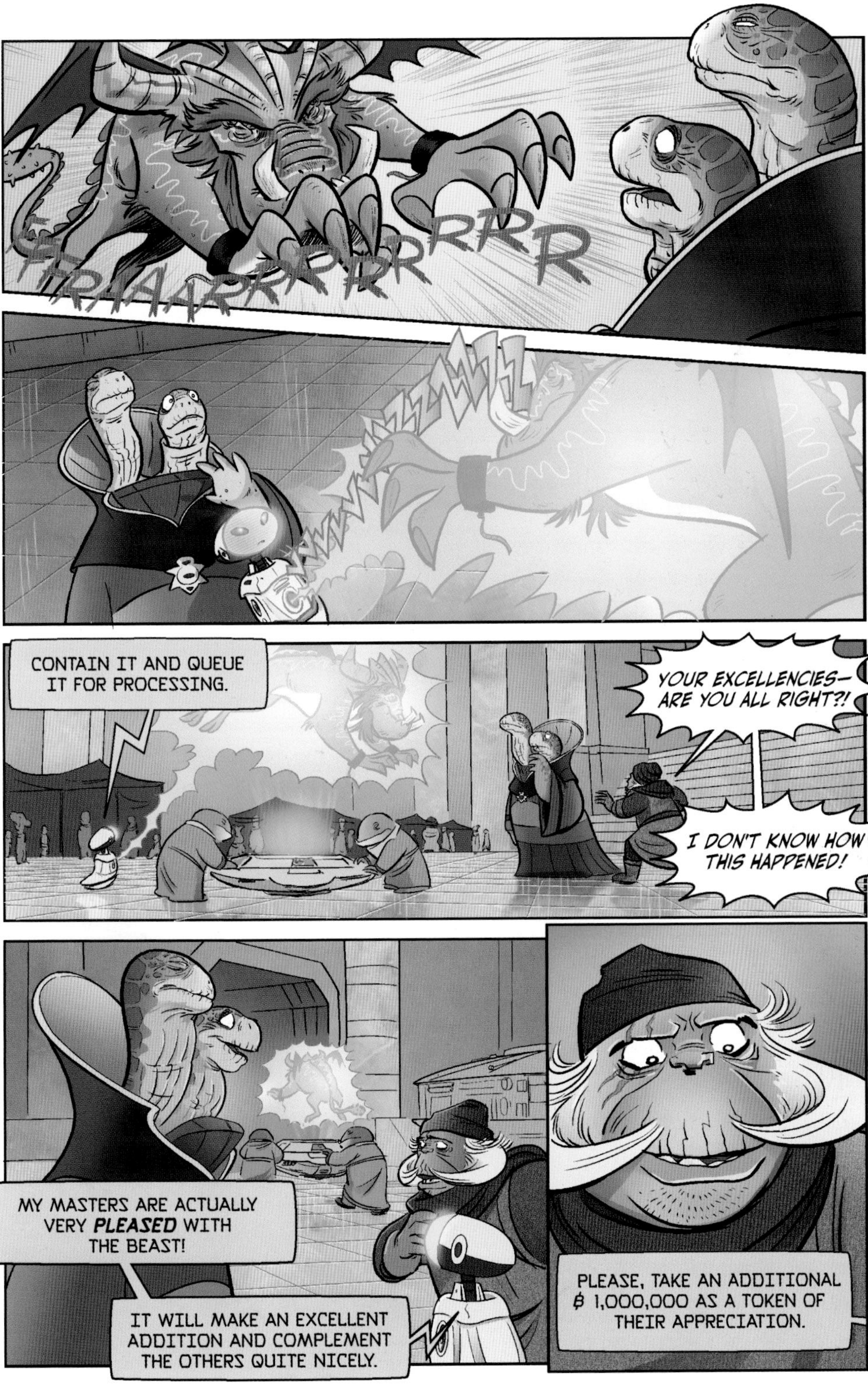
FRHAARRRRRRRRRRR
CONTAIN IT AND QUEUE IT FOR PROCESSING.
YOUR EXCELLENCIES— ARE YOU ALL RIGHT?!
I DON'T KNOW HOW THIS HAPPENED!
MY MASTERS ARE ACTUALLY VERY PLEASED WITH THE BEAST!
IT WILL MAKE AN EXCELLENT ADDITION AND COMPLEMENT THE OTHERS QUITE NICELY.
PLEASE, TAKE AN ADDITIONAL ฿ 1,000,000 AS A TOKEN OF THEIR APPRECIATION.

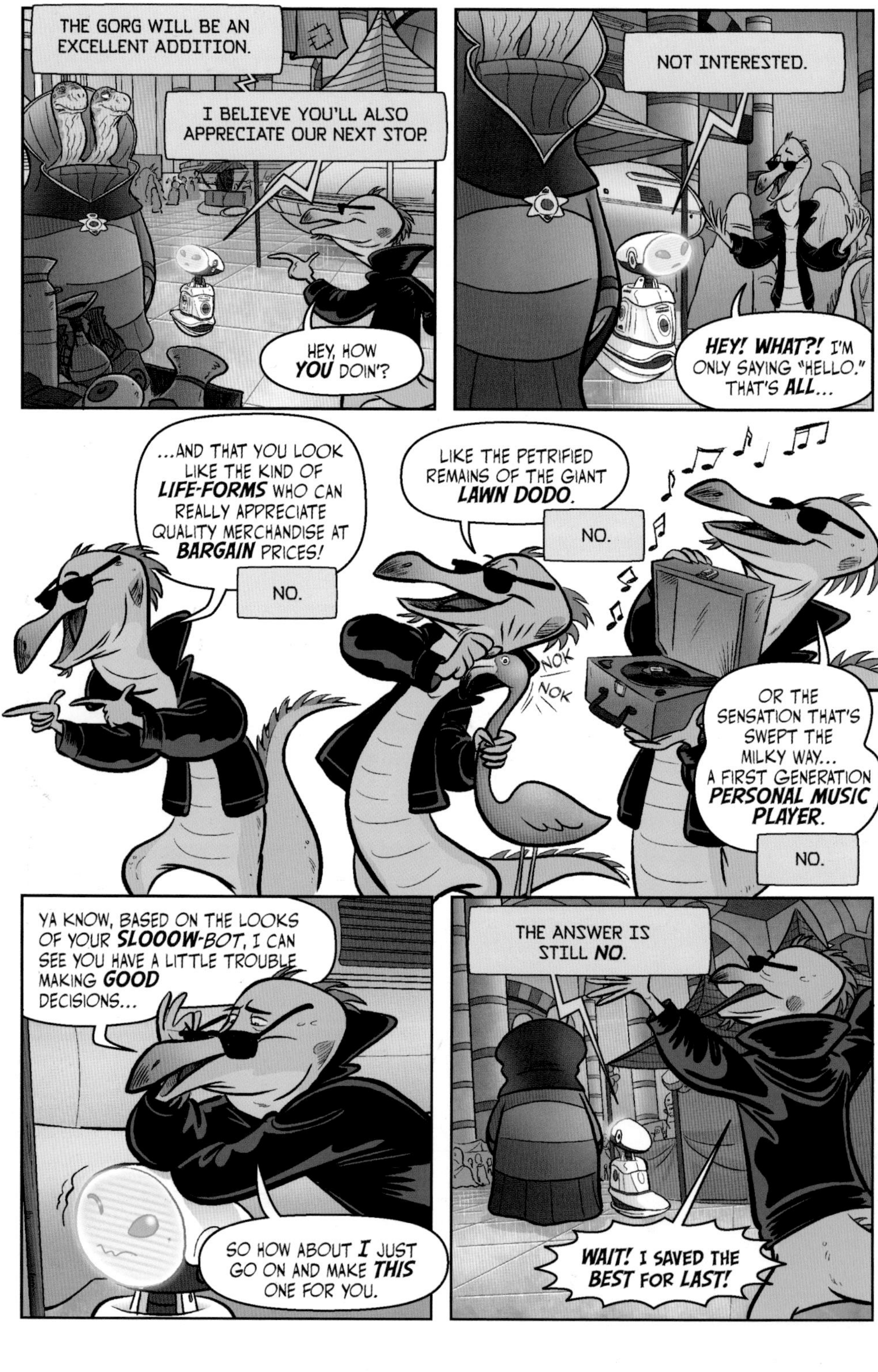
THE GORG WILL BE AN EXCELLENT ADDITION.
I BELIEVE YOU'LL ALSO APPRECIATE OUR NEXT STOP.
HEY, HOW YOU DOIN'?
NOT INTERESTED.
HEY! WHAT?! I'M ONLY SAYING "HELLO." THAT'S ALL...
...AND THAT YOU LOOK LIKE THE KIND OF LIFE-FORMS WHO CAN REALLY APPRECIATE QUALITY MERCHANDISE AT BARGAIN PRICES!
NO.
LIKE THE PETRIFIED REMAINS OF THE GIANT LAWN DODO.
NOK NOK
NO.
OR THE SENSATION THAT'S SWEPT THE MILKY WAY... A FIRST GENERATION PERSONAL MUSIC PLAYER.
NO.
YA KNOW, BASED ON THE LOOKS OF YOUR SLOOOW-BOT, I CAN SEE YOU HAVE A LITTLE TROUBLE MAKING GOOD DECISIONS...
SO HOW ABOUT I JUST GO ON AND MAKE THIS ONE FOR YOU.
THE ANSWER IS STILL NO.
WAIT! I SAVED THE BEST FOR LAST!

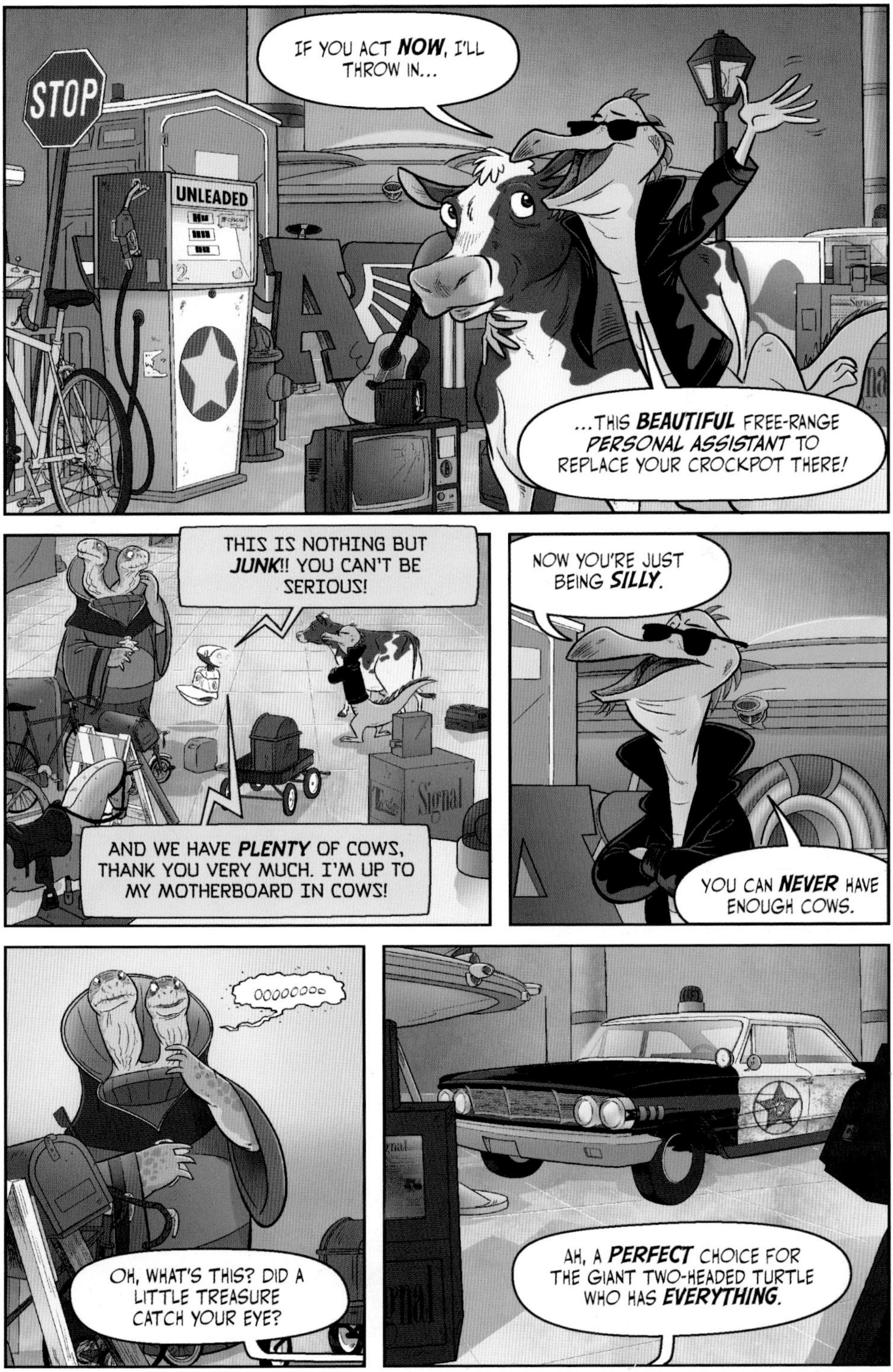
IF YOU ACT NOW, I'LL THROW IN...
...THIS BEAUTIFUL FREE-RANGE PERSONAL ASSISTANT TO REPLACE YOUR CROCKPOT THERE!
STOP
UNLEADED
THIS IS NOTHING BUT JUNK!! YOU CAN'T BE SERIOUS!
AND WE HAVE PLENTY OF COWS, THANK YOU VERY MUCH. I'M UP TO MY MOTHERBOARD IN COWS!
NOW YOU'RE JUST BEING SILLY.
YOU CAN NEVER HAVE ENOUGH COWS.
OOOOOOOO
OH, WHAT'S THIS? DID A LITTLE TREASURE CATCH YOUR EYE?
AH, A PERFECT CHOICE FOR THE GIANT TWO-HEADED TURTLE WHO HAS EVERYTHING.

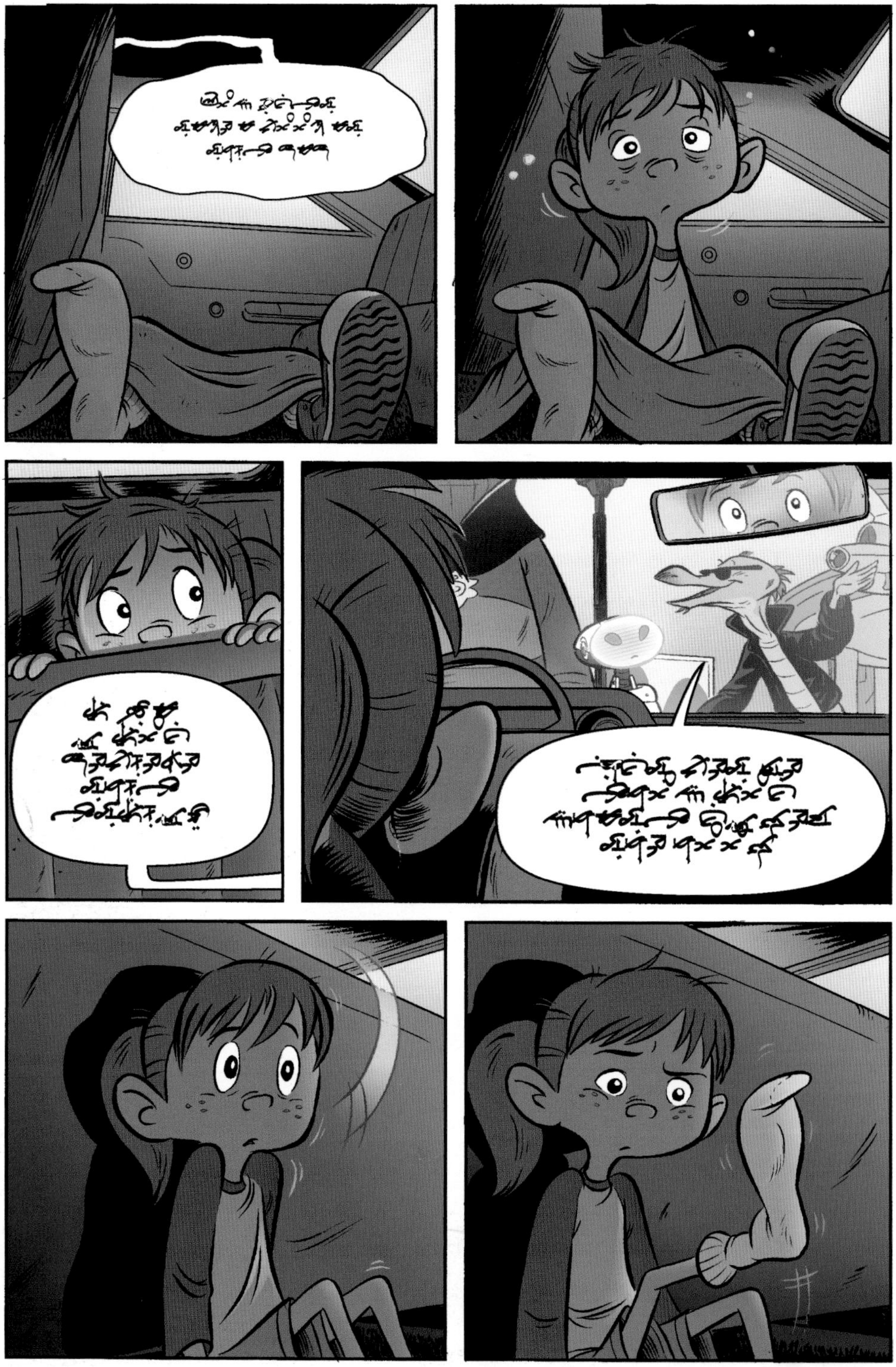

AH...YES. A *CLASSIC* INDEED. A *PRIMITIVE* COMBUSTIBLE, UH, MACHINE...ALLOY CONSTRUCTION...

AN *AUTHORITARIAN* VEHICLE...IN, UH, TRADITIONAL *FESTIVE* COLORS...

BUT *DON'T* LET ME BORE YOU WITH THE *DETAILS!*

WAIT TILL YOU *HEAR* THAT ENGINE!

IT PURRS LIKE A *HUNGRY* KITTEN.

FLIP

aaiiiieeedeeaaaai...

iiieeeee

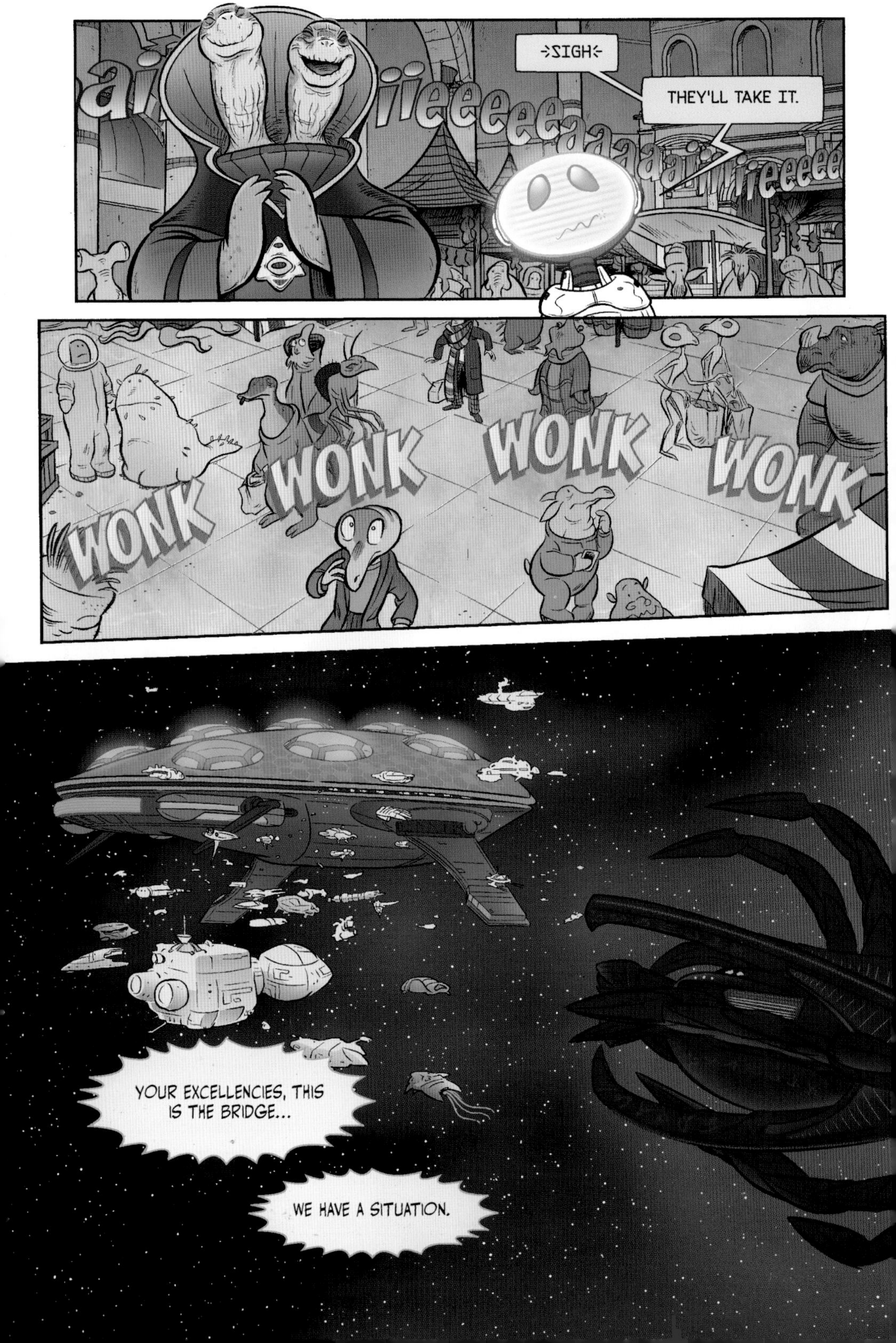
aaiiiieeeeeaaaaaaiiiiieeeeee
>SIGH<
THEY'LL TAKE IT.
WONK
WONK
WONK
WONK
YOUR EXCELLENCIES, THIS IS THE BRIDGE...
WE HAVE A SITUATION.

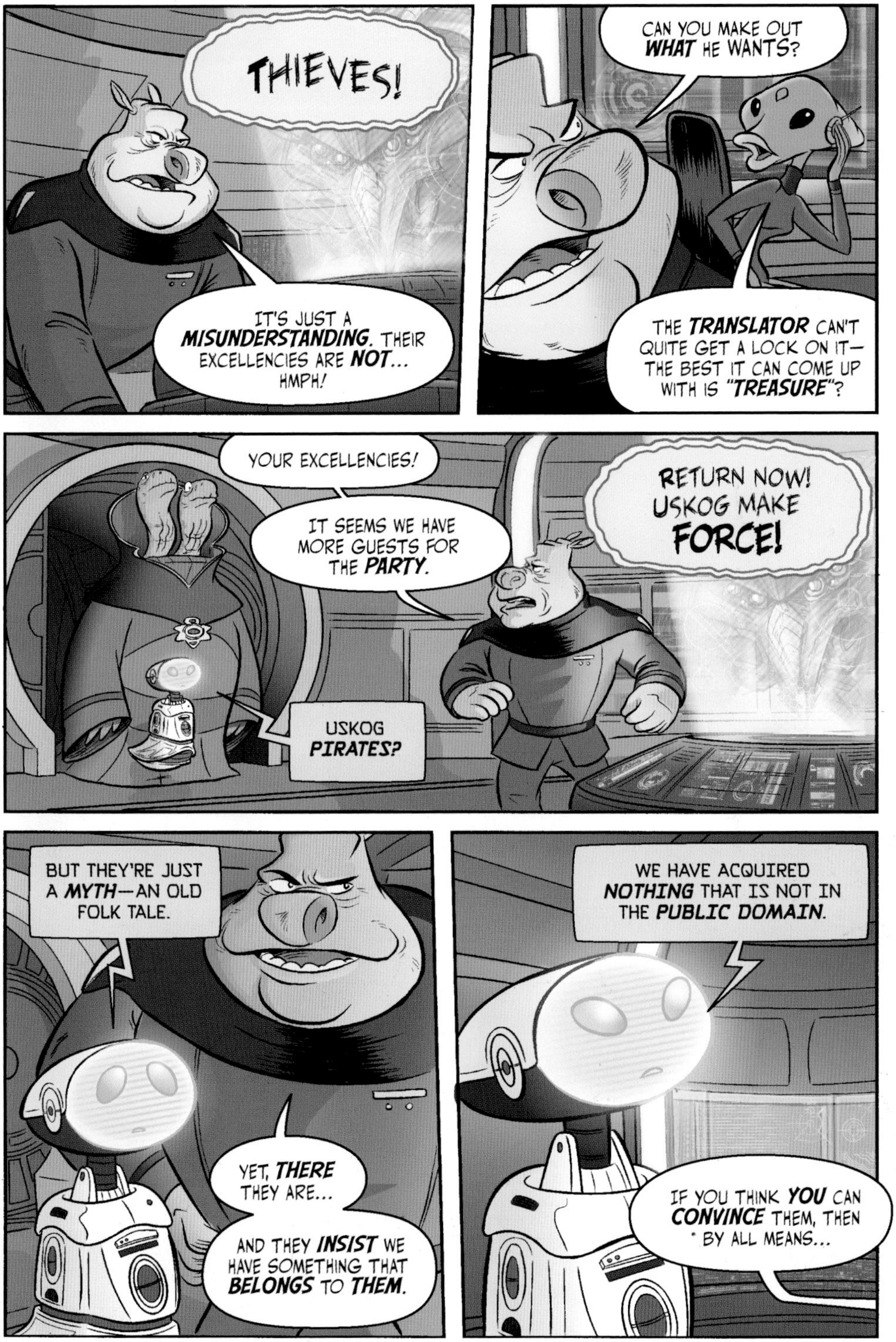
THIEVES!
IT'S JUST A MISUNDERSTANDING. THEIR EXCELLENCIES ARE NOT... HMPH!
CAN YOU MAKE OUT WHAT HE WANTS?
THE TRANSLATOR CAN'T QUITE GET A LOCK ON IT— THE BEST IT CAN COME UP WITH IS "TREASURE"?
YOUR EXCELLENCIES!
IT SEEMS WE HAVE MORE GUESTS FOR THE PARTY.
RETURN NOW! USKOG MAKE FORCE!
USKOG PIRATES?
BUT THEY'RE JUST A MYTH—AN OLD FOLK TALE.
YET, THERE THEY ARE...
AND THEY INSIST WE HAVE SOMETHING THAT BELONGS TO THEM.
WE HAVE ACQUIRED NOTHING THAT IS NOT IN THE PUBLIC DOMAIN.
IF YOU THINK YOU CAN CONVINCE THEM, THEN BY ALL MEANS...

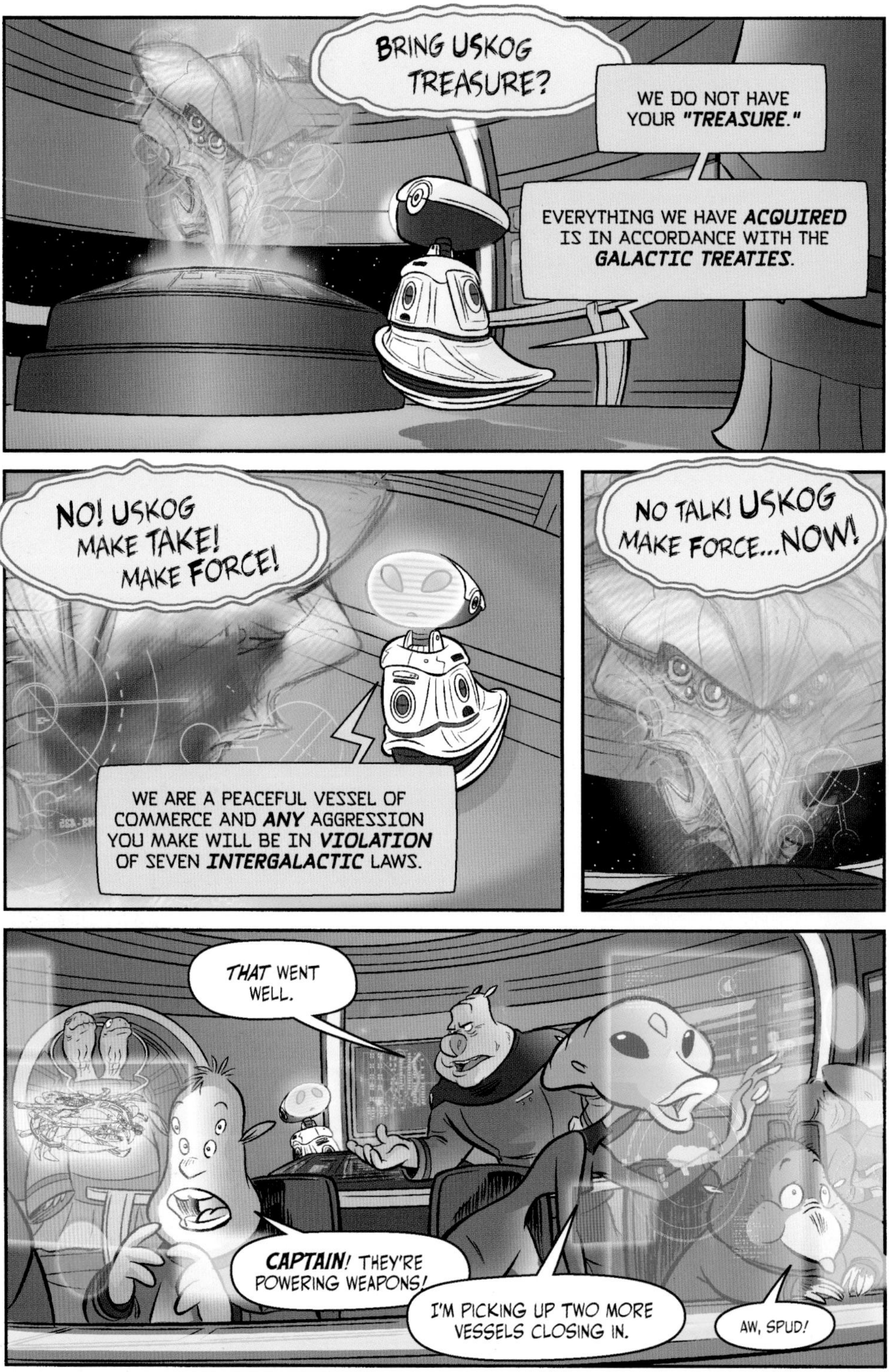

BRING USKOG TREASURE?
WE DO NOT HAVE YOUR "TREASURE."
EVERYTHING WE HAVE ACQUIRED IS IN ACCORDANCE WITH THE GALACTIC TREATIES.
NO! USKOG MAKE TAKE! MAKE FORCE!
WE ARE A PEACEFUL VESSEL OF COMMERCE AND ANY AGGRESSION YOU MAKE WILL BE IN VIOLATION OF SEVEN INTERGALACTIC LAWS.
NO TALK! USKOG MAKE FORCE...NOW!
THAT WENT WELL.
CAPTAIN! THEY'RE POWERING WEAPONS!
I'M PICKING UP TWO MORE VESSELS CLOSING IN.
AW, SPUD!

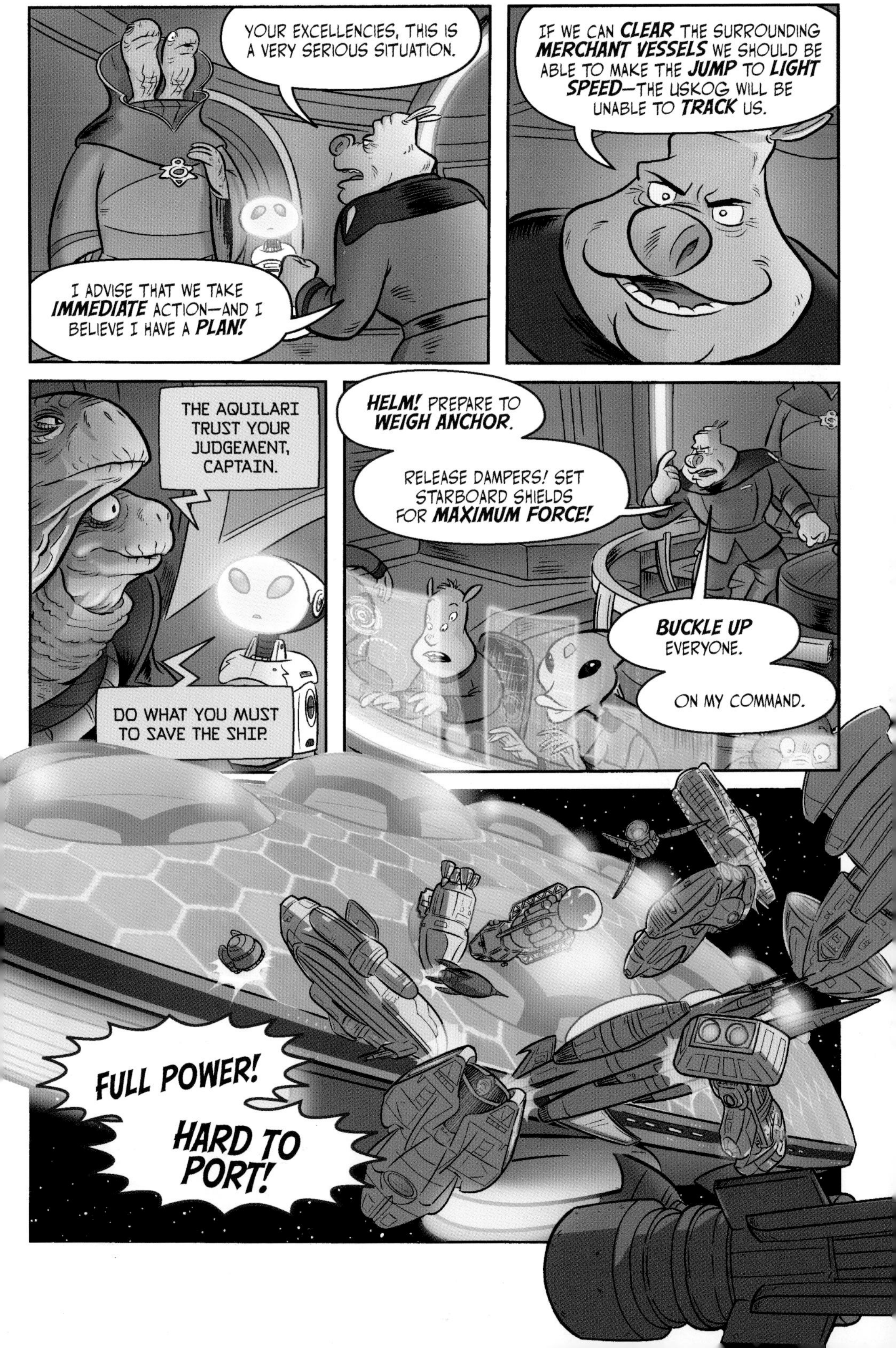
YOUR EXCELLENCIES, THIS IS A VERY SERIOUS SITUATION.
I ADVISE THAT WE TAKE IMMEDIATE ACTION—AND I BELIEVE I HAVE A PLAN!
IF WE CAN CLEAR THE SURROUNDING MERCHANT VESSELS WE SHOULD BE ABLE TO MAKE THE JUMP TO LIGHT SPEED—THE USKOG WILL BE UNABLE TO TRACK US.
THE AQUILARI TRUST YOUR JUDGEMENT, CAPTAIN.
DO WHAT YOU MUST TO SAVE THE SHIP.
HELM! PREPARE TO WEIGH ANCHOR.
RELEASE DAMPERS! SET STARBOARD SHIELDS FOR MAXIMUM FORCE!
BUCKLE UP EVERYONE.
ON MY COMMAND.
FULL POWER!
HARD TO PORT!

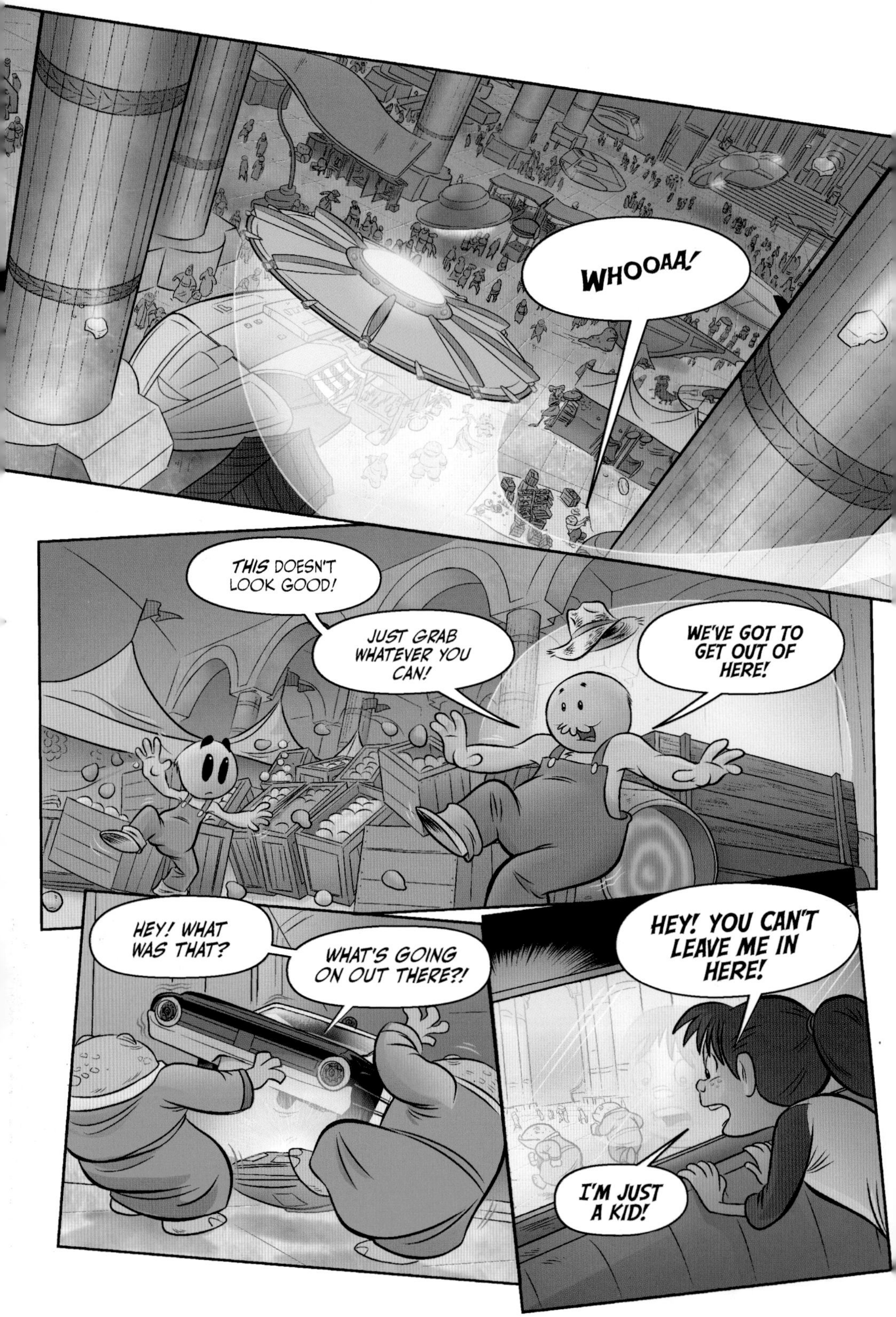
WHOOAA!
THIS DOESN'T LOOK GOOD!
JUST GRAB WHATEVER YOU CAN!
WE'VE GOT TO GET OUT OF HERE!
HEY! WHAT WAS THAT?
WHAT'S GOING ON OUT THERE?!
HEY! YOU CAN'T LEAVE ME IN HERE!
I'M JUST A KID!

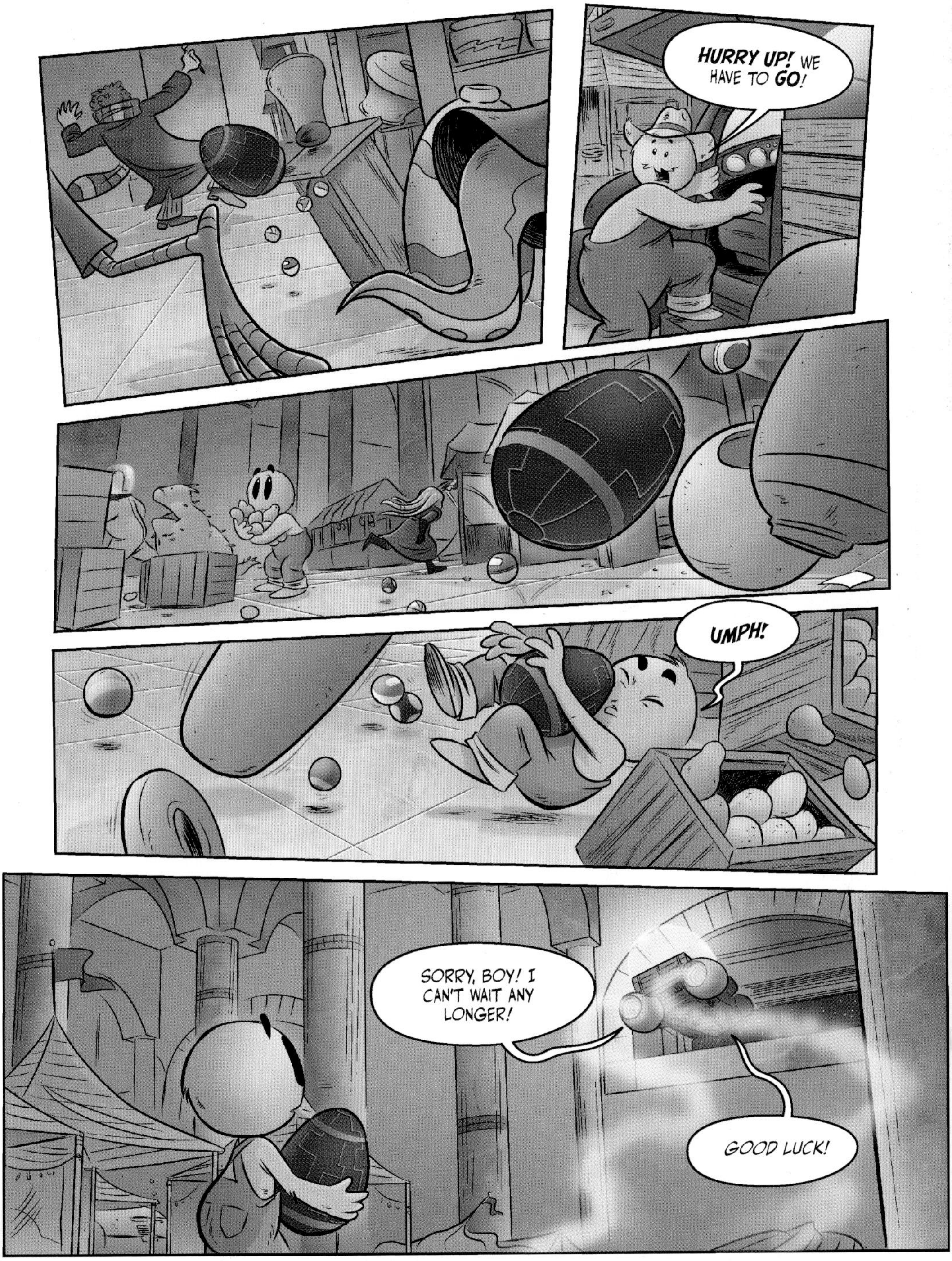
HURRY UP! WE HAVE TO GO!
UMPH!
SORRY, BOY! I CAN'T WAIT ANY LONGER!
GOOD LUCK!

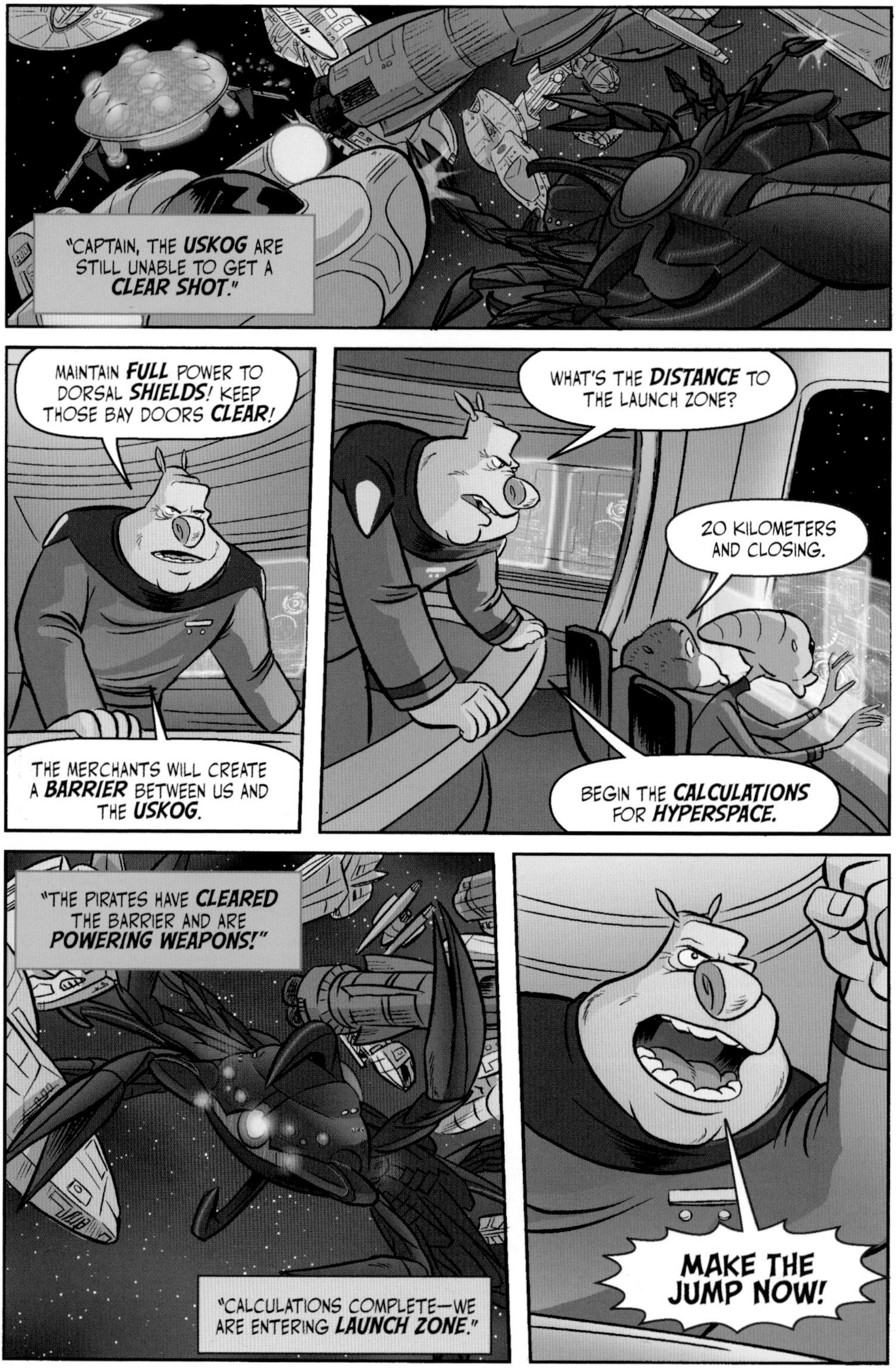
"CAPTAIN, THE USKOG ARE STILL UNABLE TO GET A CLEAR SHOT."
MAINTAIN FULL POWER TO DORSAL SHIELDS! KEEP THOSE BAY DOORS CLEAR!
THE MERCHANTS WILL CREATE A BARRIER BETWEEN US AND THE USKOG.
WHAT'S THE DISTANCE TO THE LAUNCH ZONE?
20 KILOMETERS AND CLOSING.
BEGIN THE CALCULATIONS FOR HYPERSPACE.
"THE PIRATES HAVE CLEARED THE BARRIER AND ARE POWERING WEAPONS!"
"CALCULATIONS COMPLETE—WE ARE ENTERING LAUNCH ZONE."
MAKE THE JUMP NOW!

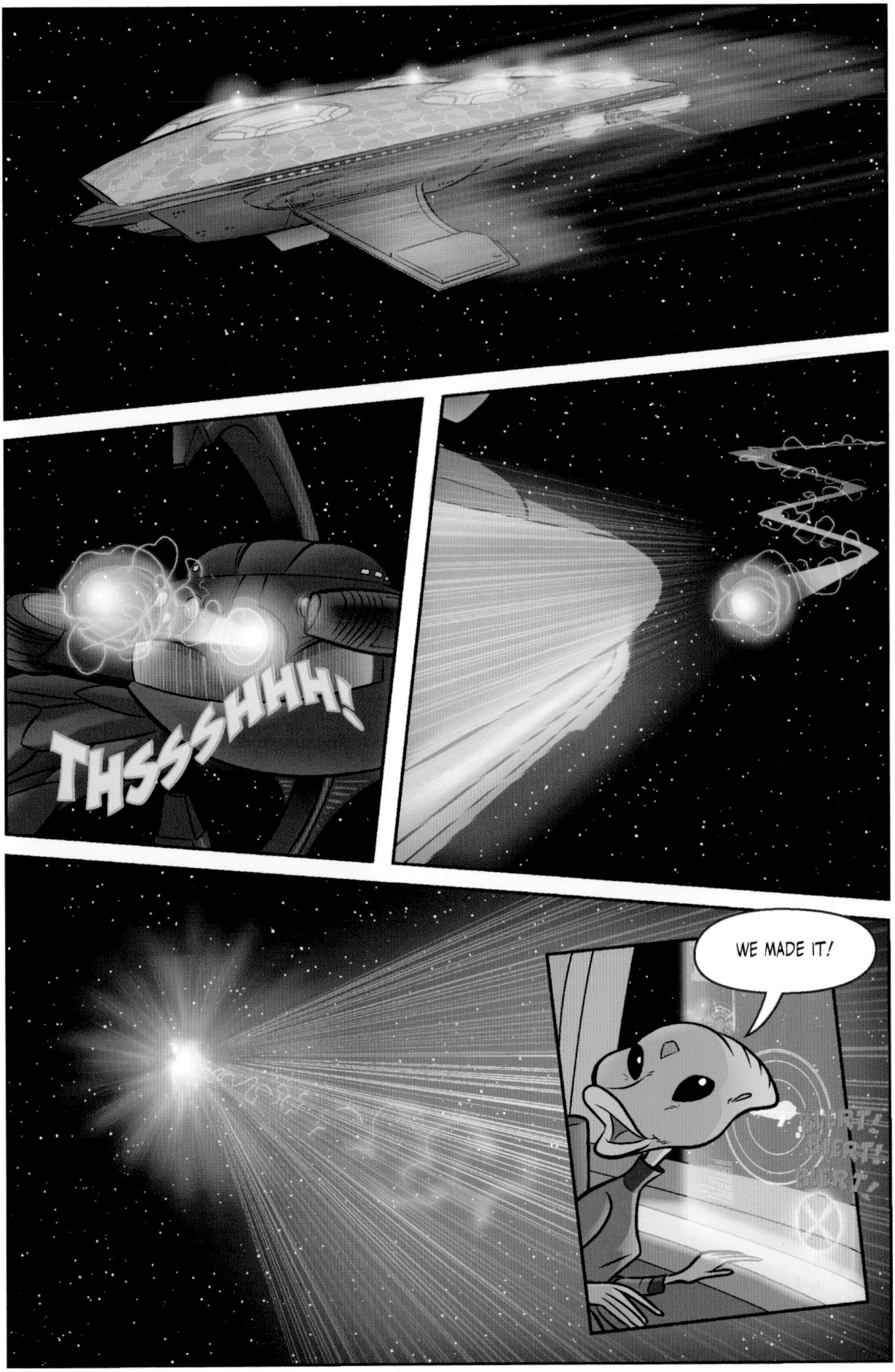
THSSSHHH!
WE MADE IT!

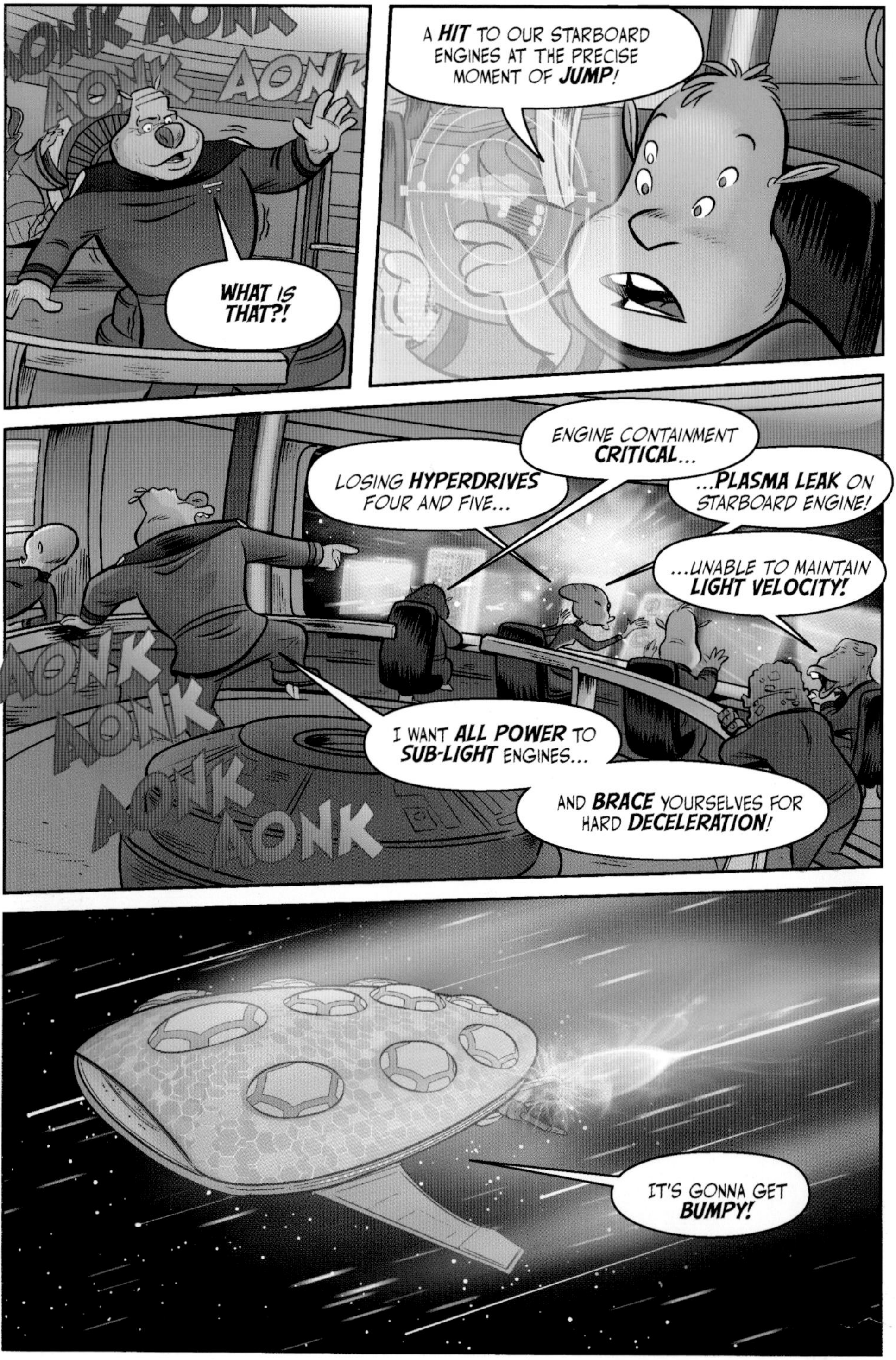
AONK AONK AONK AONK
WHAT IS THAT?!
A HIT TO OUR STARBOARD ENGINES AT THE PRECISE MOMENT OF JUMP!
LOSING HYPERDRIVES FOUR AND FIVE...
ENGINE CONTAINMENT CRITICAL...
...PLASMA LEAK ON STARBOARD ENGINE!
...UNABLE TO MAINTAIN LIGHT VELOCITY!
AONK AONK AONK AONK
I WANT ALL POWER TO SUB-LIGHT ENGINES...
AND BRACE YOURSELVES FOR HARD DECELERATION!
IT'S GONNA GET BUMPY!

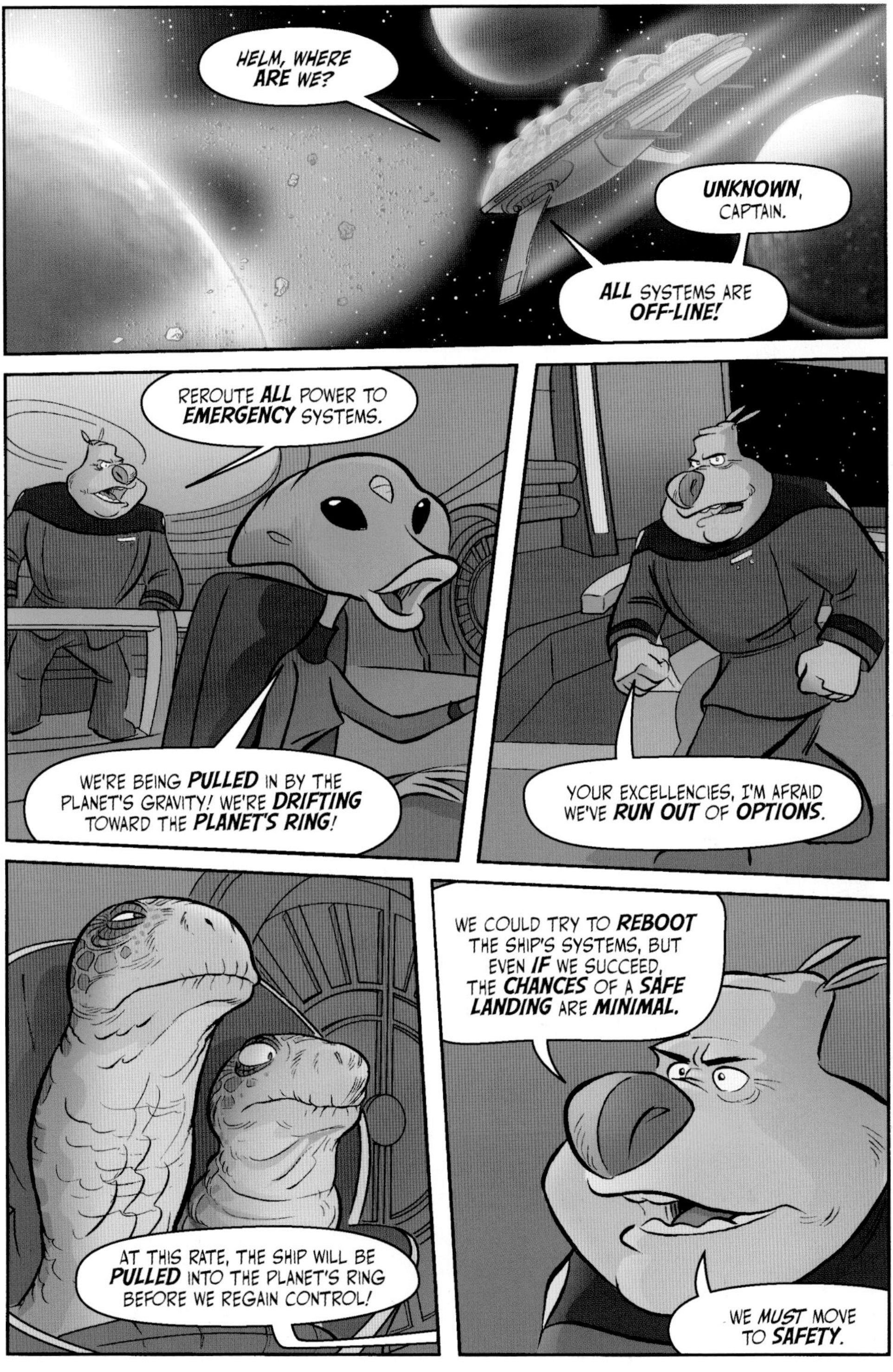
HELM, WHERE ARE WE?
UNKNOWN, CAPTAIN.
ALL SYSTEMS ARE OFF-LINE!
REROUTE ALL POWER TO EMERGENCY SYSTEMS.
WE'RE BEING PULLED IN BY THE PLANET'S GRAVITY! WE'RE DRIFTING TOWARD THE PLANET'S RING!
YOUR EXCELLENCIES, I'M AFRAID WE'VE RUN OUT OF OPTIONS.
AT THIS RATE, THE SHIP WILL BE PULLED INTO THE PLANET'S RING BEFORE WE REGAIN CONTROL!
WE COULD TRY TO REBOOT THE SHIP'S SYSTEMS, BUT EVEN IF WE SUCCEED, THE CHANCES OF A SAFE LANDING ARE MINIMAL.
WE MUST MOVE TO SAFETY.

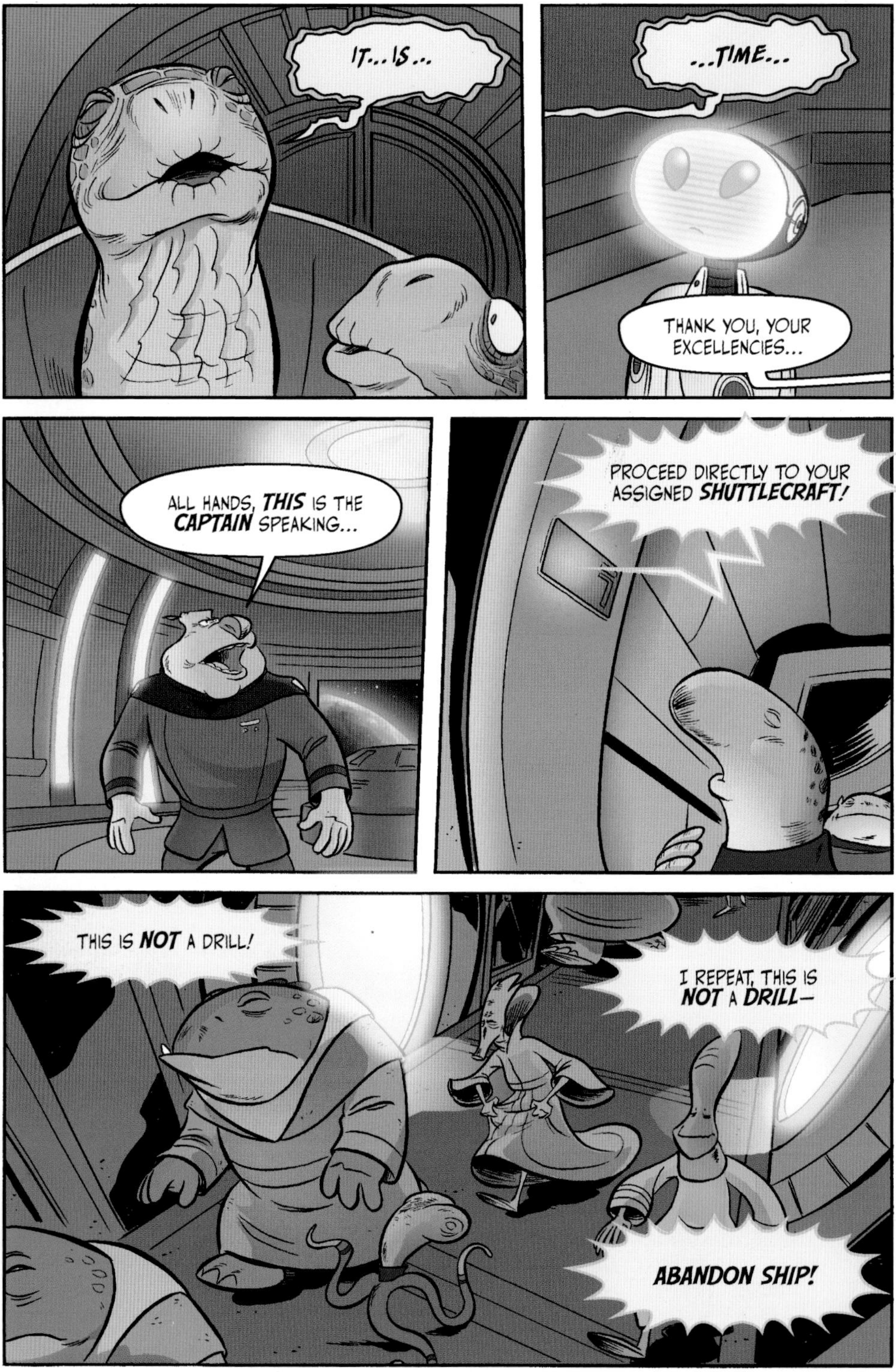
IT... IS...
...TIME...
THANK YOU, YOUR EXCELLENCIES...
ALL HANDS, **THIS** IS THE **CAPTAIN** SPEAKING...
PROCEED DIRECTLY TO YOUR ASSIGNED **SHUTTLECRAFT!**
THIS IS **NOT** A DRILL!
I REPEAT, THIS IS **NOT** A **DRILL**—
ABANDON SHIP!

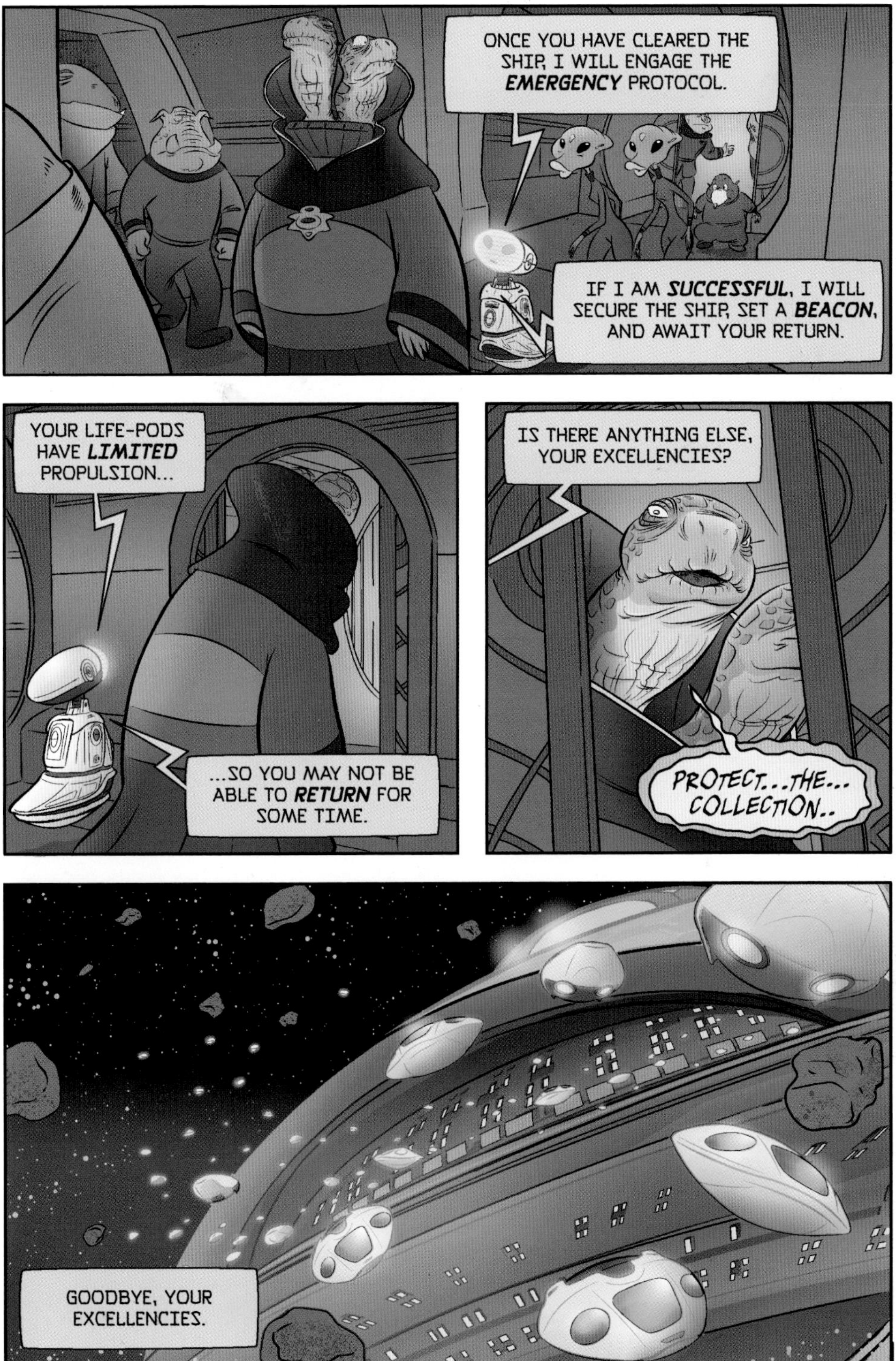
ONCE YOU HAVE CLEARED THE SHIP, I WILL ENGAGE THE EMERGENCY PROTOCOL.
IF I AM SUCCESSFUL, I WILL SECURE THE SHIP, SET A BEACON, AND AWAIT YOUR RETURN.
YOUR LIFE-PODS HAVE LIMITED PROPULSION...
...SO YOU MAY NOT BE ABLE TO RETURN FOR SOME TIME.
IS THERE ANYTHING ELSE, YOUR EXCELLENCIES?
PROTECT...THE... COLLECTION..
GOODBYE, YOUR EXCELLENCIES.

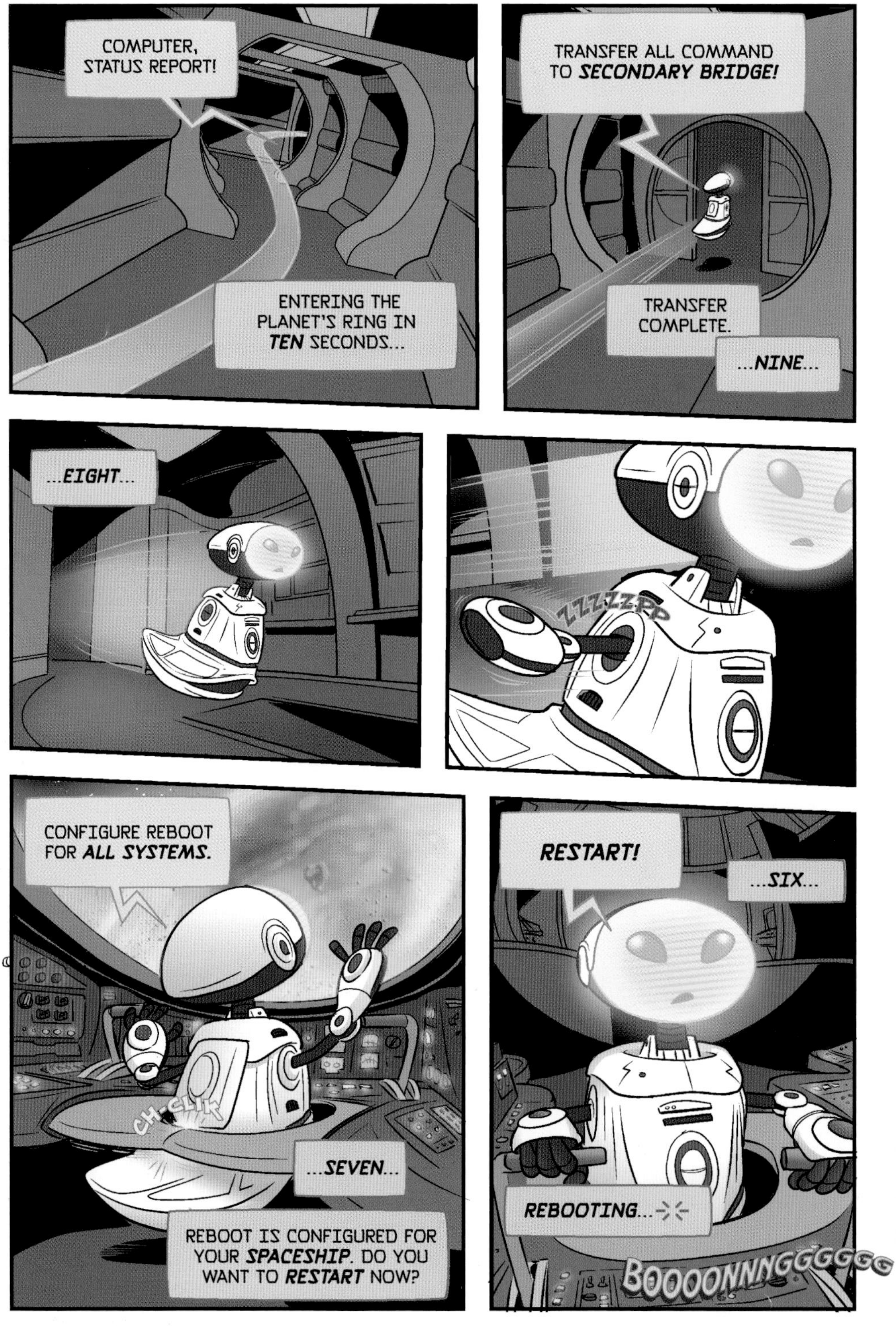
COMPUTER, STATUS REPORT!
ENTERING THE PLANET'S RING IN TEN SECONDS...
TRANSFER ALL COMMAND TO SECONDARY BRIDGE!
TRANSFER COMPLETE.
...NINE...
...EIGHT...
ZZZZZPP
CONFIGURE REBOOT FOR ALL SYSTEMS.
CH-CLIK
...SEVEN...
REBOOT IS CONFIGURED FOR YOUR SPACESHIP. DO YOU WANT TO RESTART NOW?
RESTART!
...SIX...
REBOOTING...
BOOOONNNGGGGGG

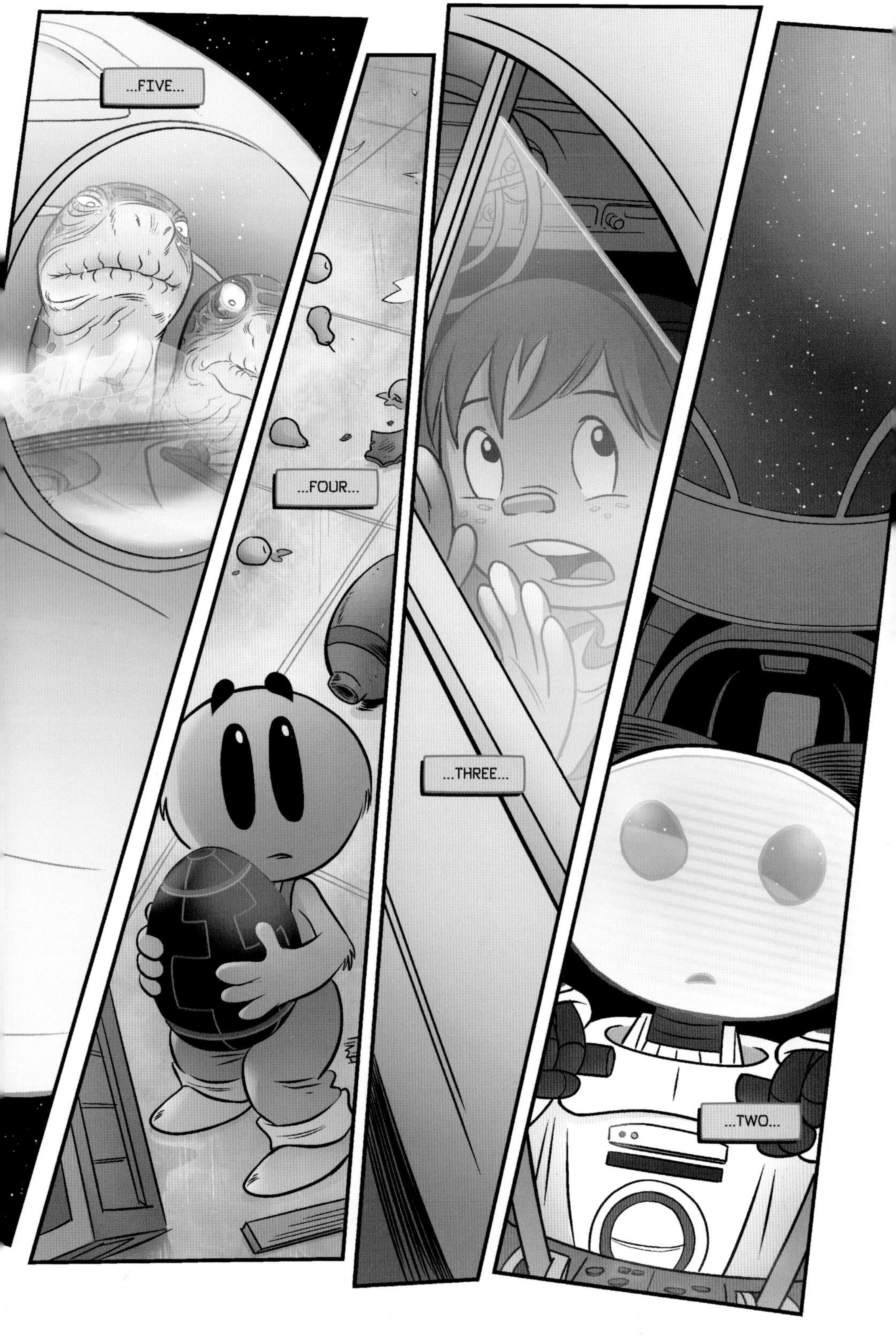
...FIVE...
...FOUR...
...THREE...
...TWO...

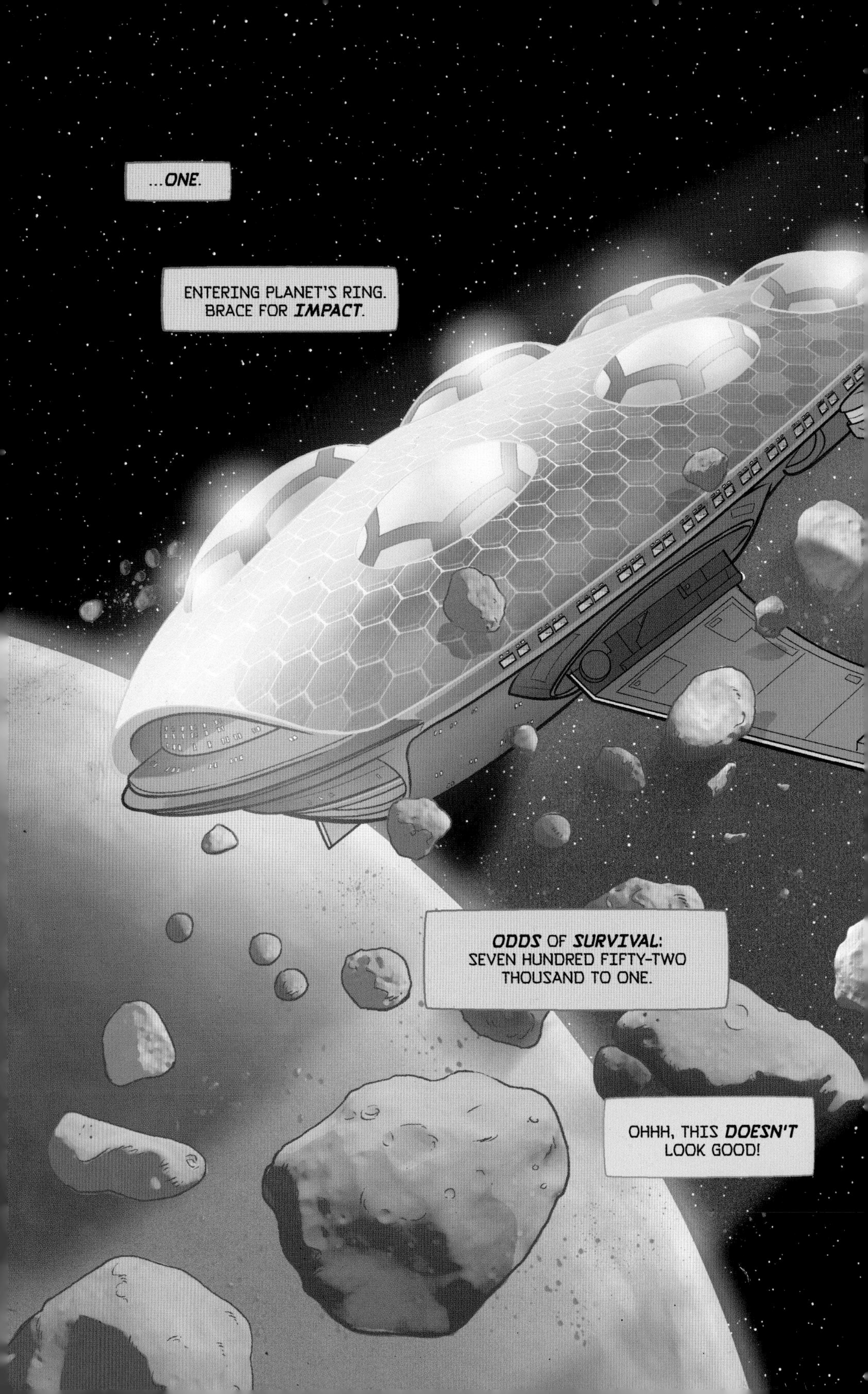
...*ONE*.
ENTERING PLANET'S RING. BRACE FOR ***IMPACT***.
ODDS OF ***SURVIVAL***: SEVEN HUNDRED FIFTY-TWO THOUSAND TO ONE.
OHHH, THIS ***DOESN'T*** LOOK GOOD!

Chapter Three

Aliens are Bad, Bad People

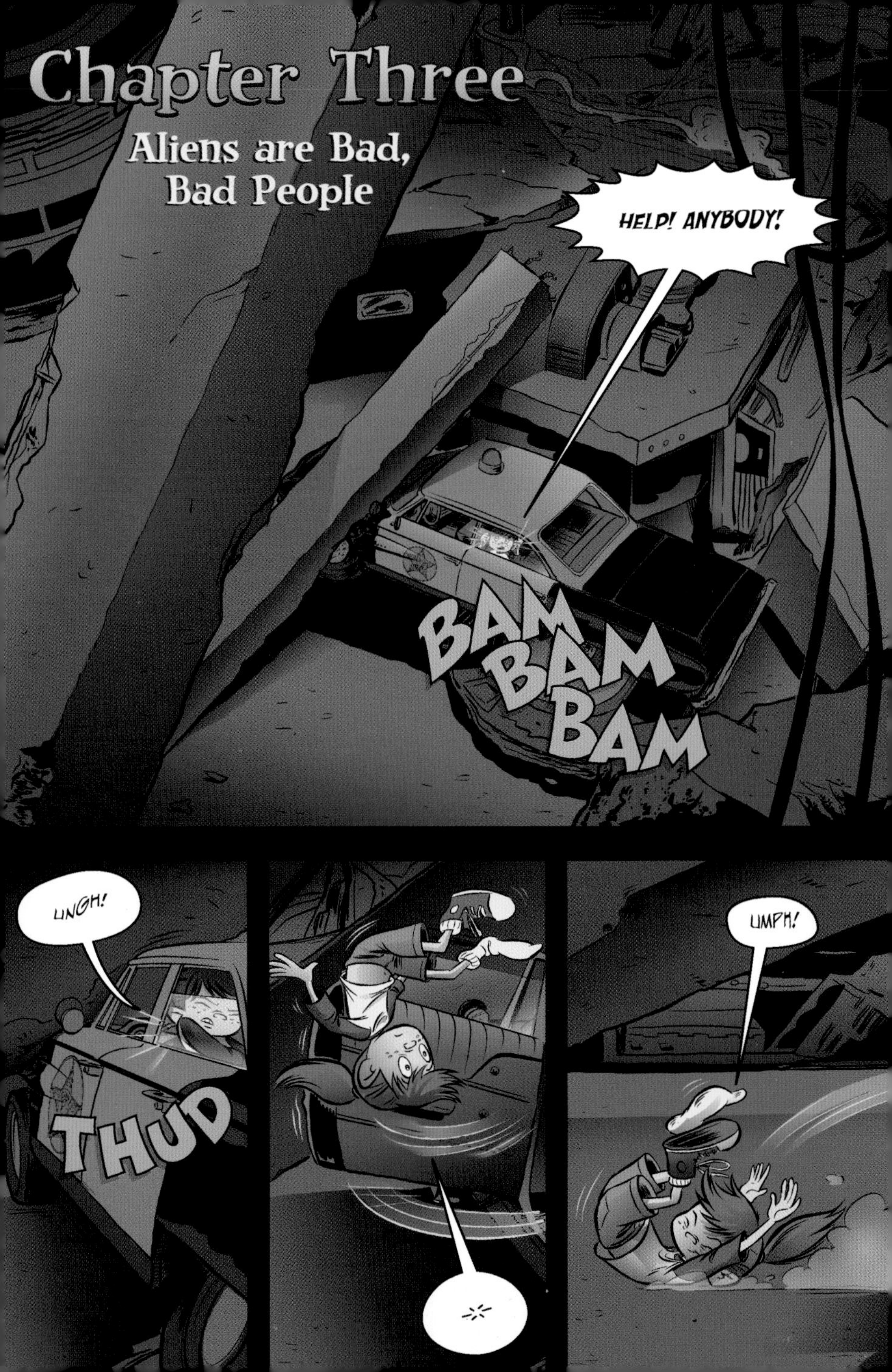
HELP! ANYBODY!
BAM
BAM
BAM
UNGH!
THUD
UMPH!

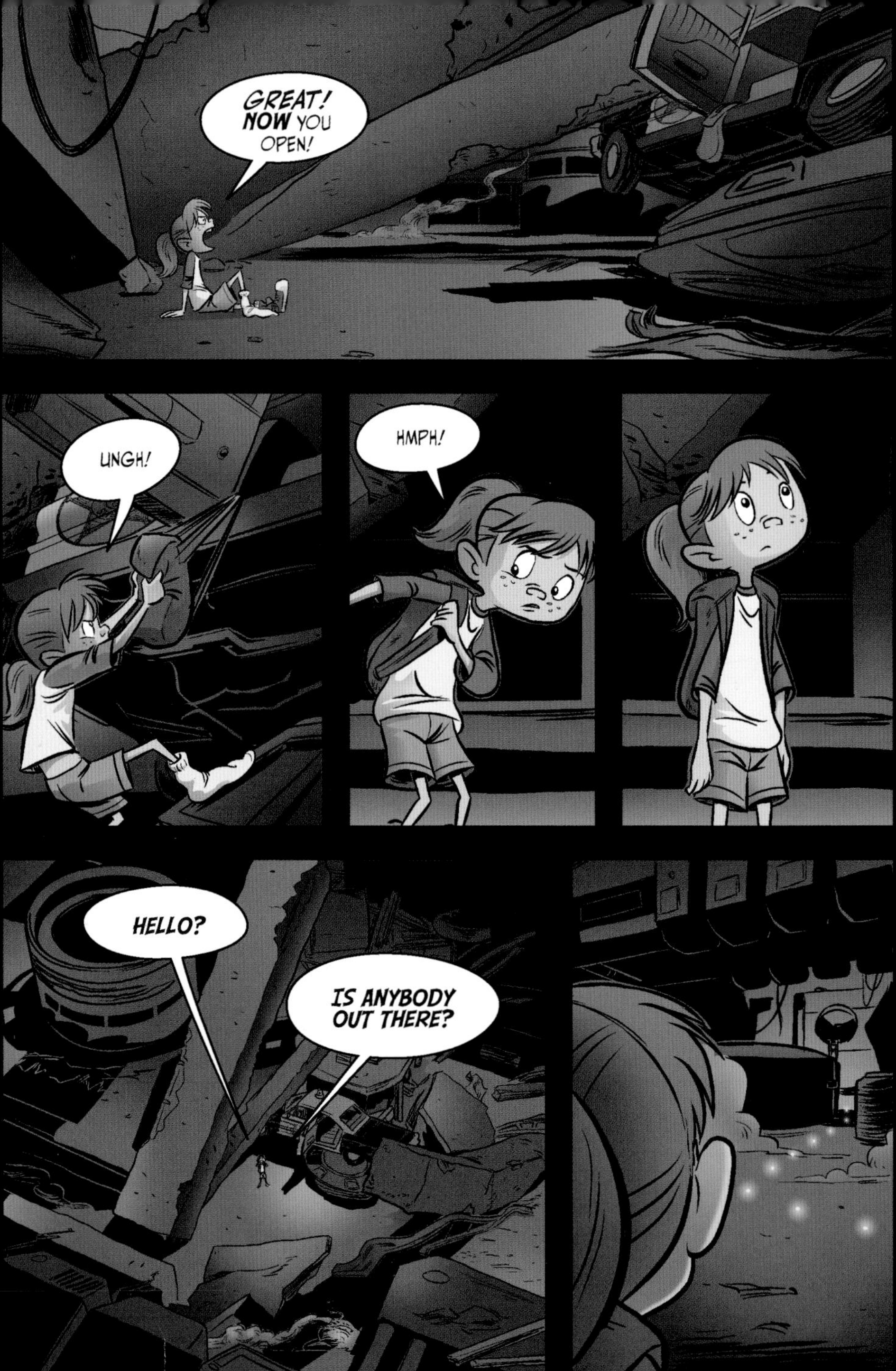
GREAT! NOW YOU OPEN!
UNGH!
HMPH!
HELLO?
IS ANYBODY OUT THERE?

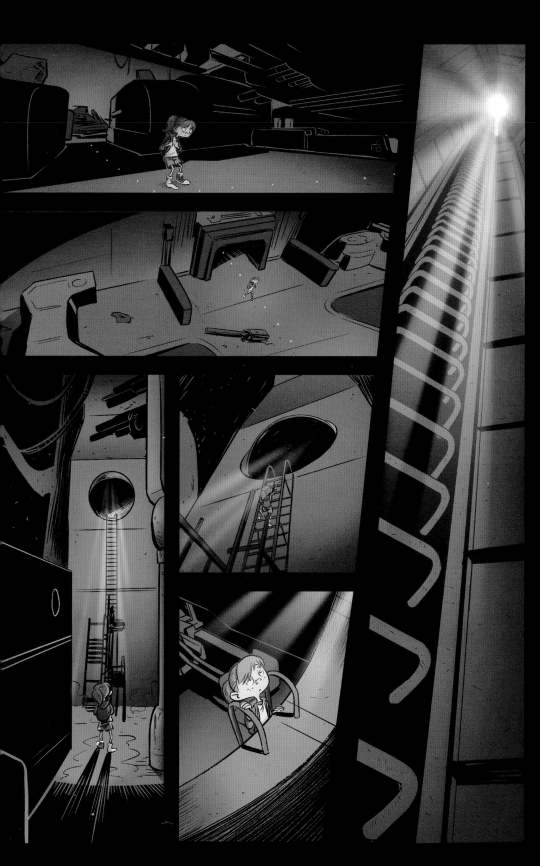

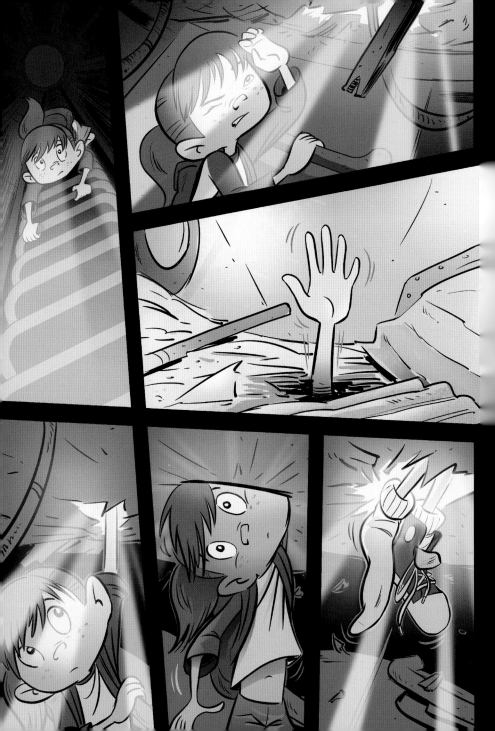

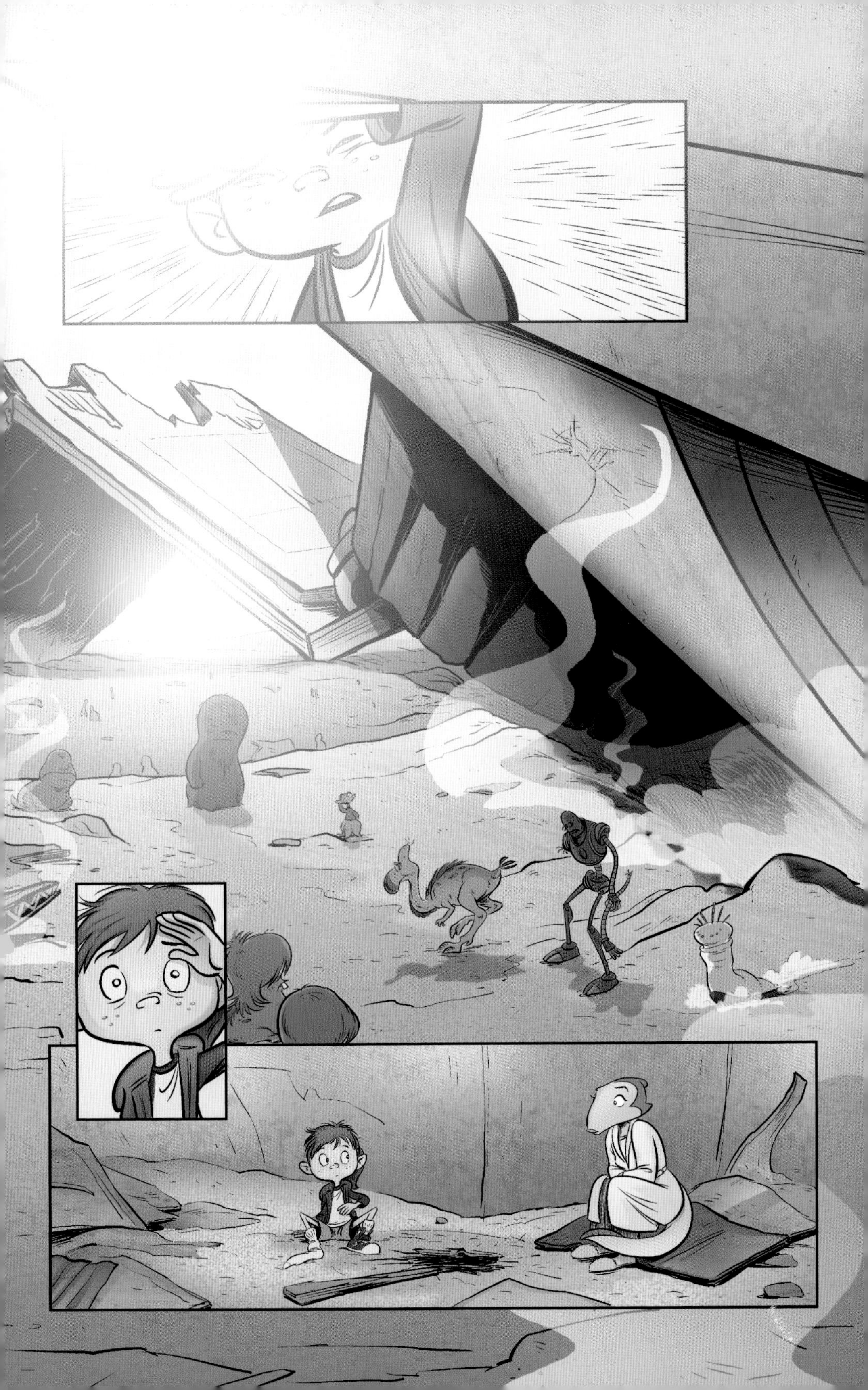

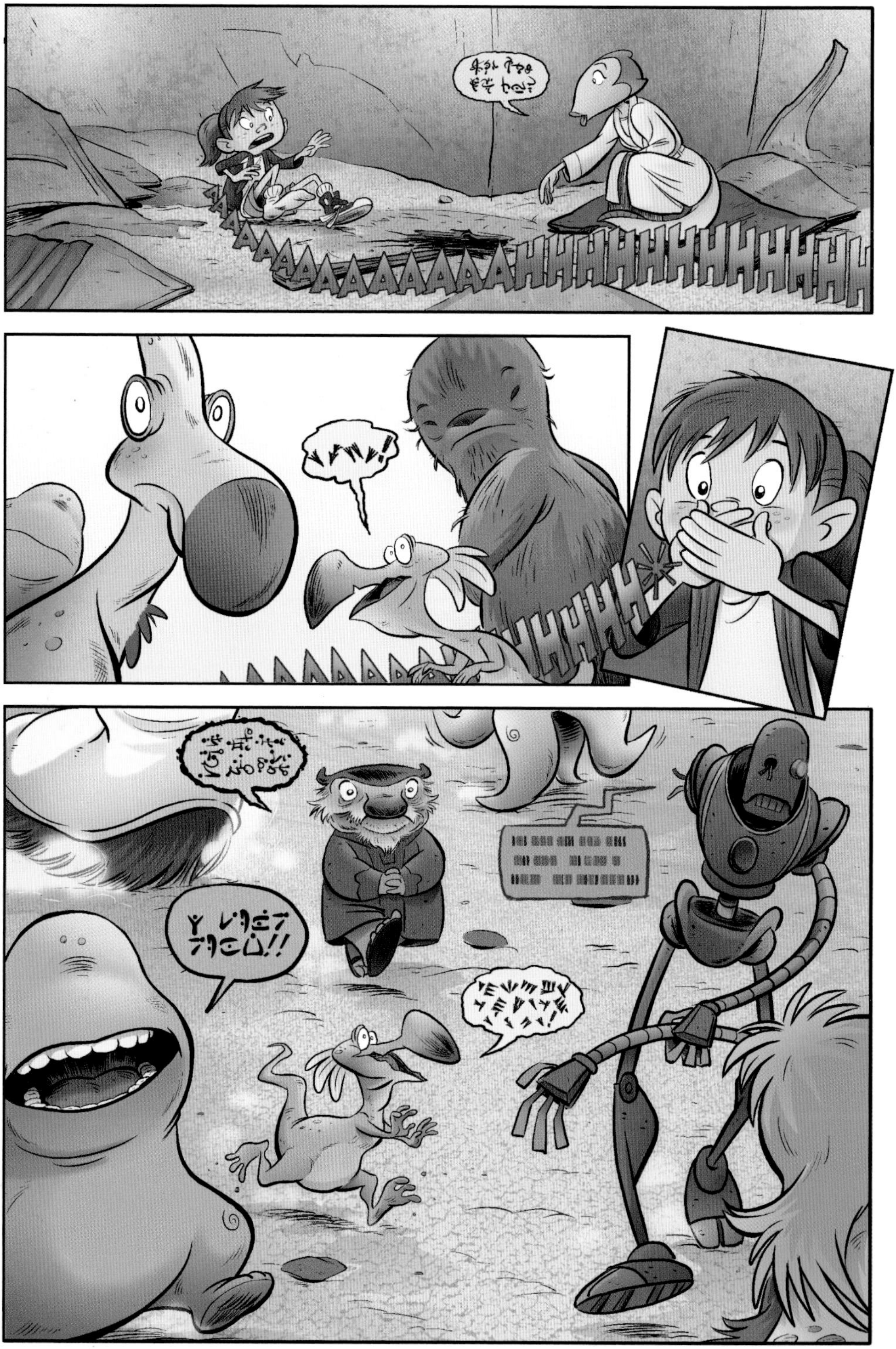
AAAAAAAAAAAAAAAHHHHHHHHHHHH
AAAAAAAHHHHHH

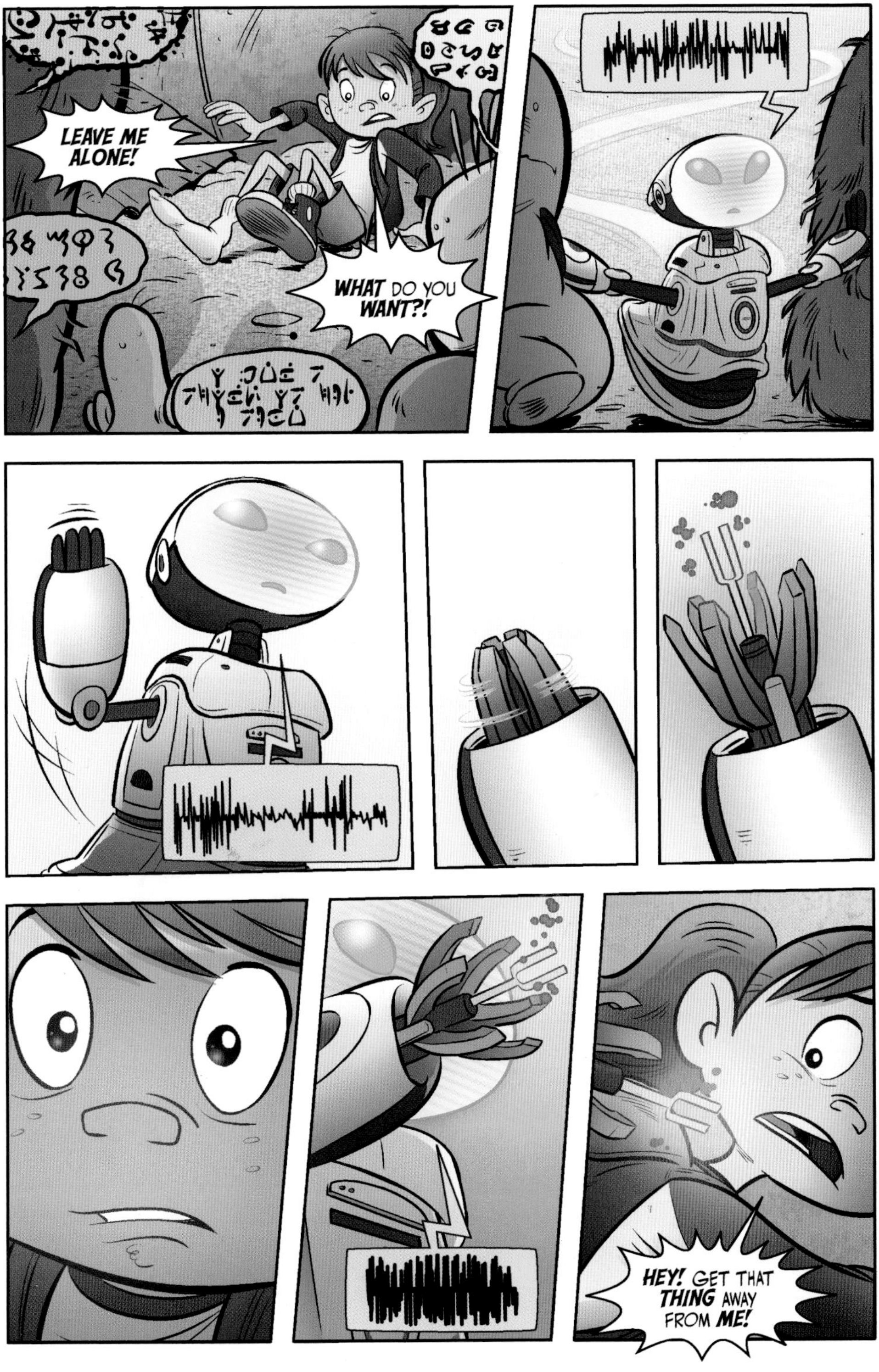
LEAVE ME ALONE!
WHAT DO YOU WANT?!
HEY! GET THAT THING AWAY FROM ME!

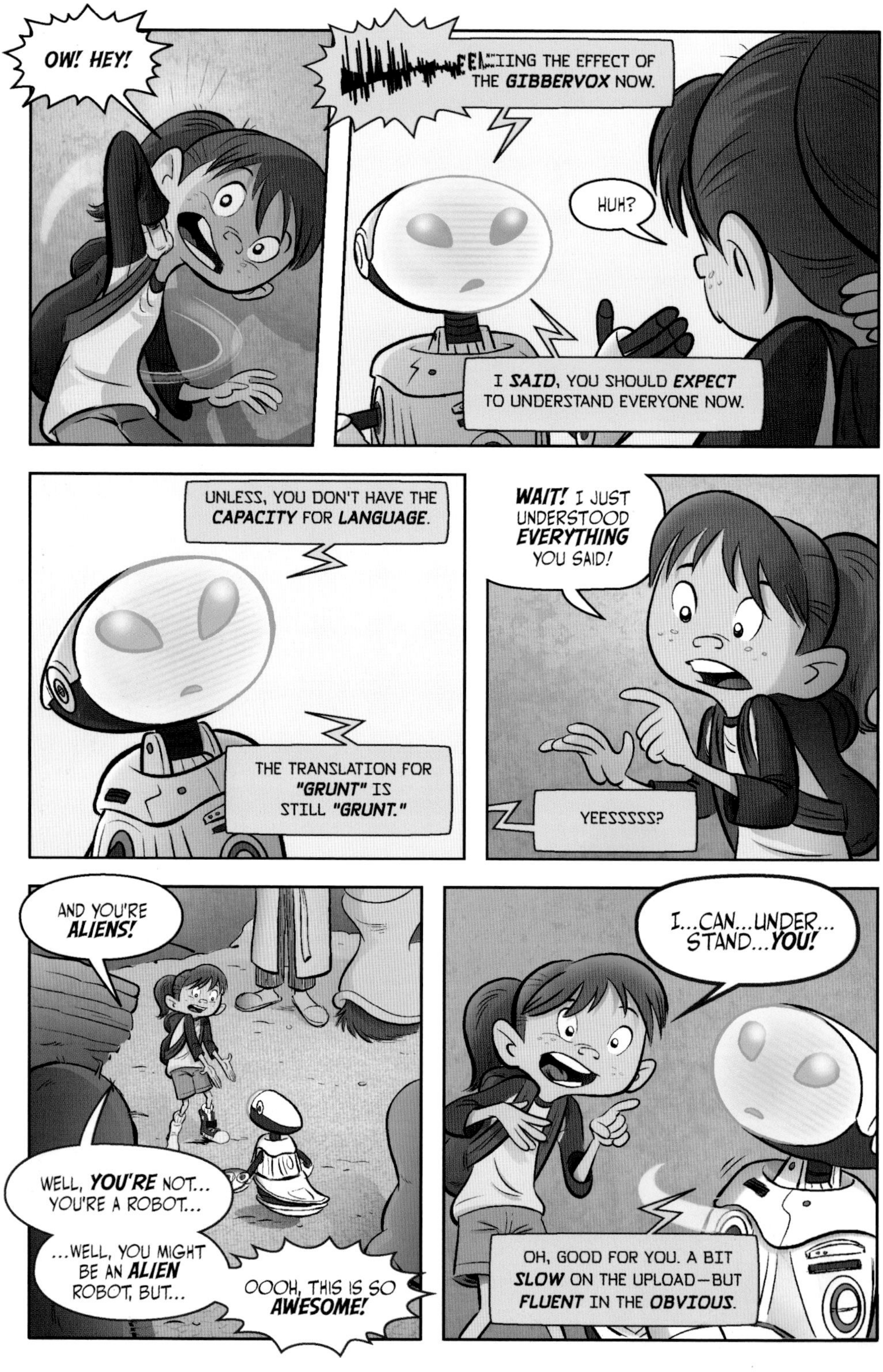
OW! HEY!
...ING THE EFFECT OF THE GIBBERVOX NOW.
HUH?
I SAID, YOU SHOULD EXPECT TO UNDERSTAND EVERYONE NOW.
UNLESS, YOU DON'T HAVE THE CAPACITY FOR LANGUAGE.
THE TRANSLATION FOR "GRUNT" IS STILL "GRUNT."
WAIT! I JUST UNDERSTOOD EVERYTHING YOU SAID!
YEESSSSS?
AND YOU'RE ALIENS!
WELL, YOU'RE NOT... YOU'RE A ROBOT...
...WELL, YOU MIGHT BE AN ALIEN ROBOT, BUT...
OOOH, THIS IS SO AWESOME!
I...CAN...UNDER... STAND...YOU!
OH, GOOD FOR YOU. A BIT SLOW ON THE UPLOAD—BUT FLUENT IN THE OBVIOUS.

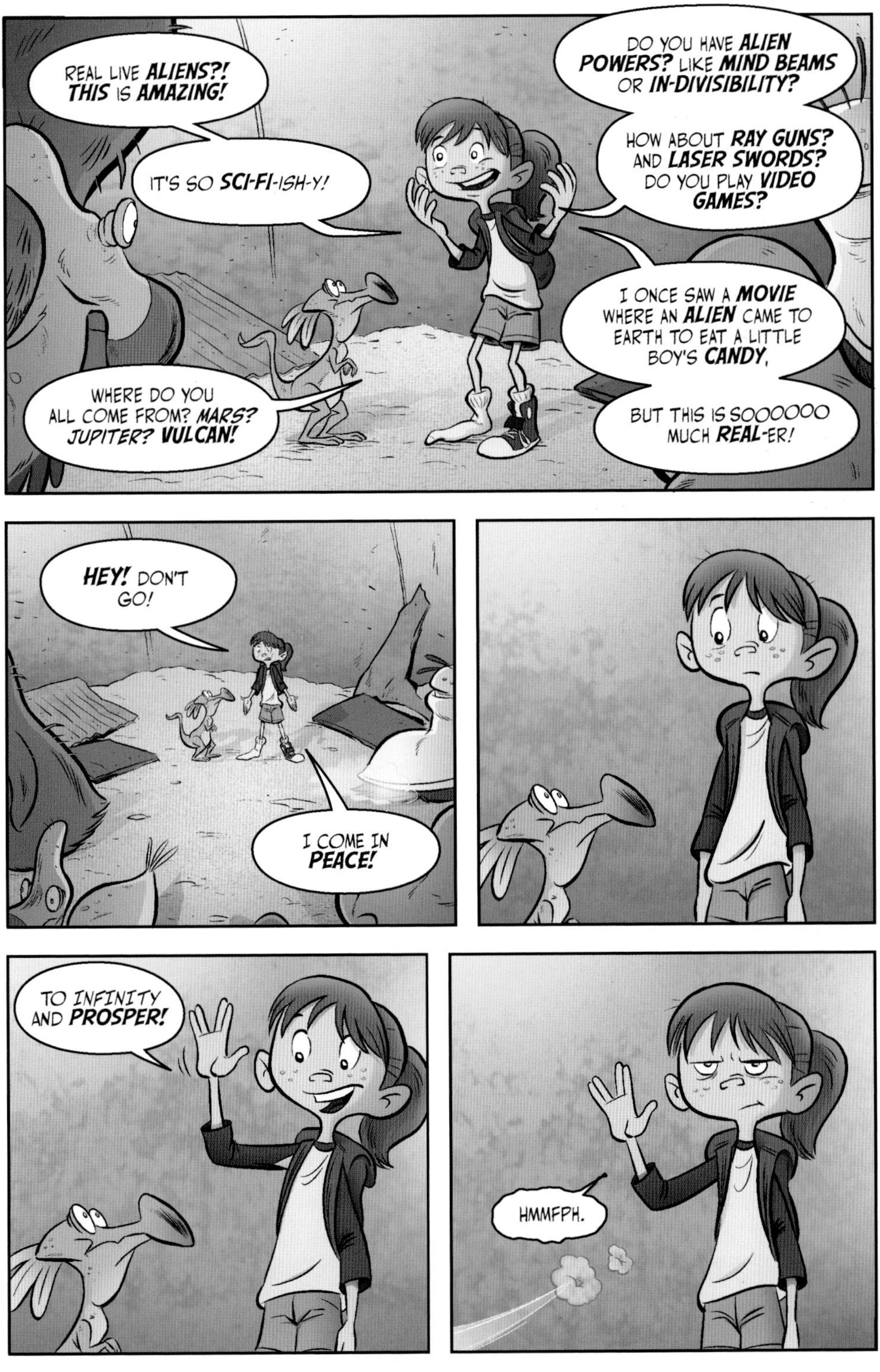

REAL LIVE ALIENS?! THIS IS AMAZING!
IT'S SO SCI-FI-ISH-Y!
DO YOU HAVE ALIEN POWERS? LIKE MIND BEAMS OR IN-DIVISIBILITY?
HOW ABOUT RAY GUNS? AND LASER SWORDS? DO YOU PLAY VIDEO GAMES?
WHERE DO YOU ALL COME FROM? MARS? JUPITER? VULCAN!
I ONCE SAW A MOVIE WHERE AN ALIEN CAME TO EARTH TO EAT A LITTLE BOY'S CANDY,
BUT THIS IS SOOOOOO MUCH REAL-ER!
HEY! DON'T GO!
I COME IN PEACE!
TO INFINITY AND PROSPER!
HMMFPH.

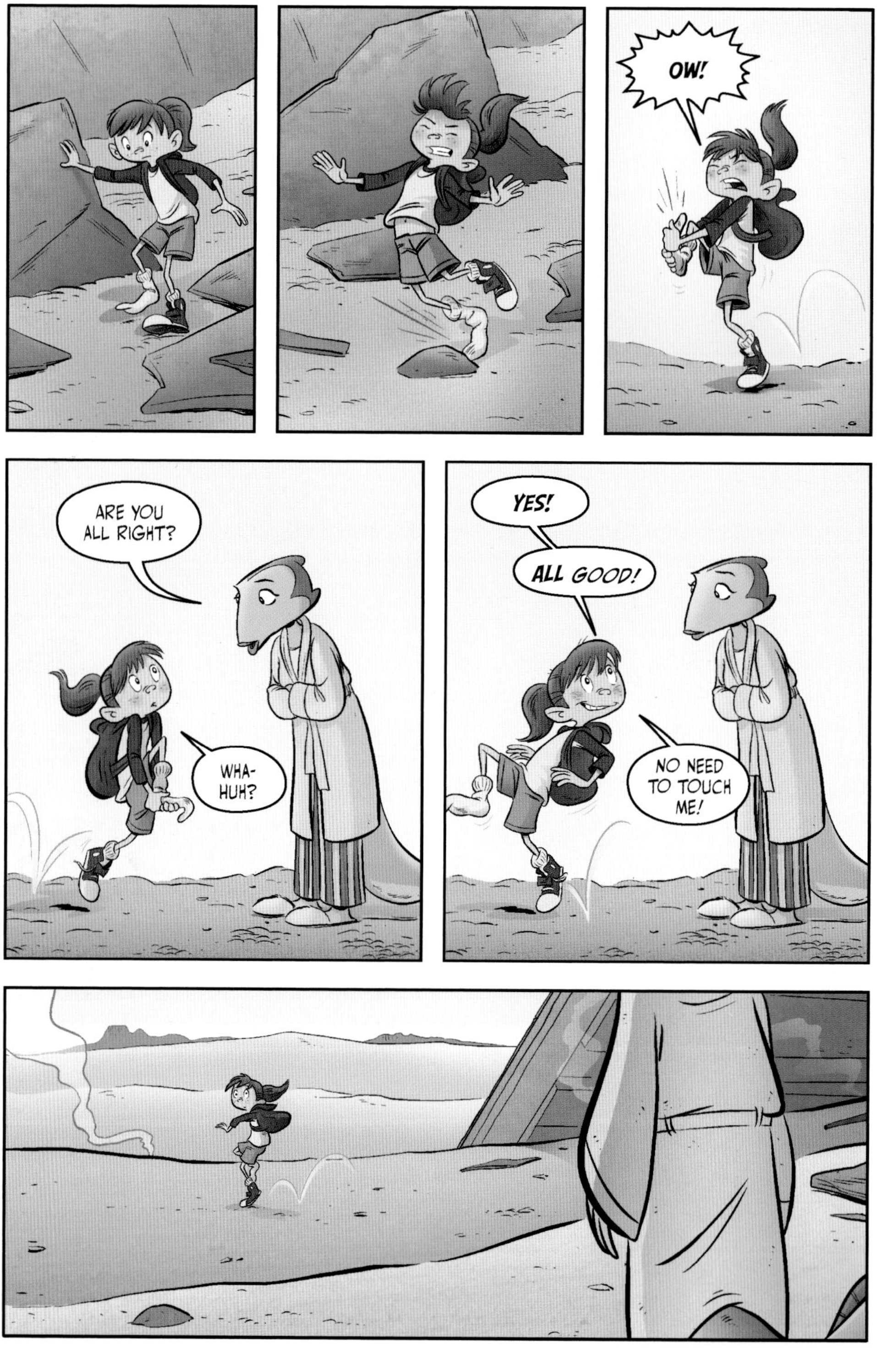
OW!
ARE YOU ALL RIGHT?
WHA-HUH?
YES!
ALL GOOD!
NO NEED TO TOUCH ME!

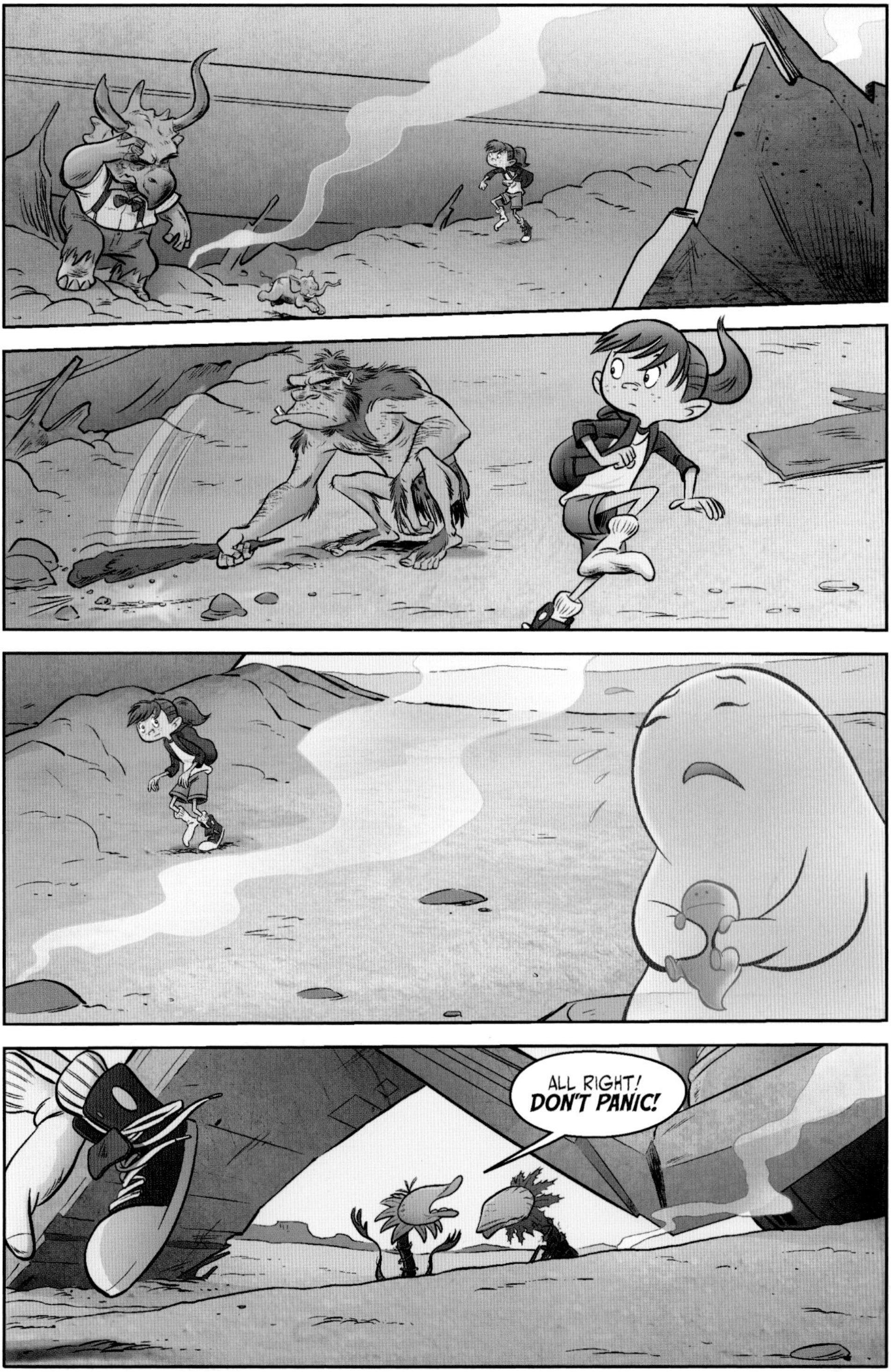
ALL RIGHT!
DON'T PANIC!

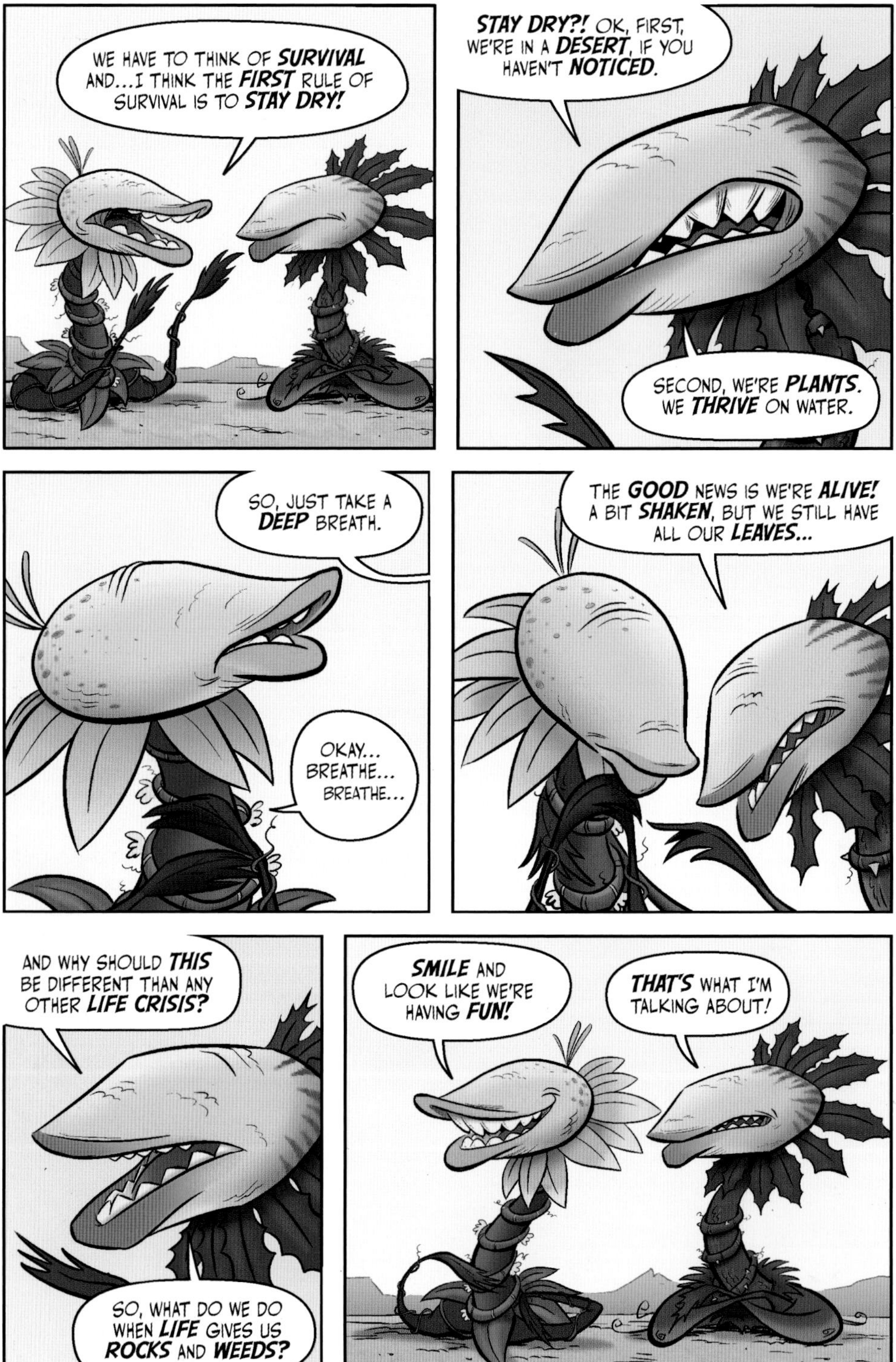
WE HAVE TO THINK OF SURVIVAL AND...I THINK THE FIRST RULE OF SURVIVAL IS TO STAY DRY!
STAY DRY?! OK, FIRST, WE'RE IN A DESERT, IF YOU HAVEN'T NOTICED.
SECOND, WE'RE PLANTS. WE THRIVE ON WATER.
SO, JUST TAKE A DEEP BREATH.
OKAY... BREATHE... BREATHE...
THE GOOD NEWS IS WE'RE ALIVE! A BIT SHAKEN, BUT WE STILL HAVE ALL OUR LEAVES...
AND WHY SHOULD THIS BE DIFFERENT THAN ANY OTHER LIFE CRISIS?
SO, WHAT DO WE DO WHEN LIFE GIVES US ROCKS AND WEEDS?
SMILE AND LOOK LIKE WE'RE HAVING FUN!
THAT'S WHAT I'M TALKING ABOUT!

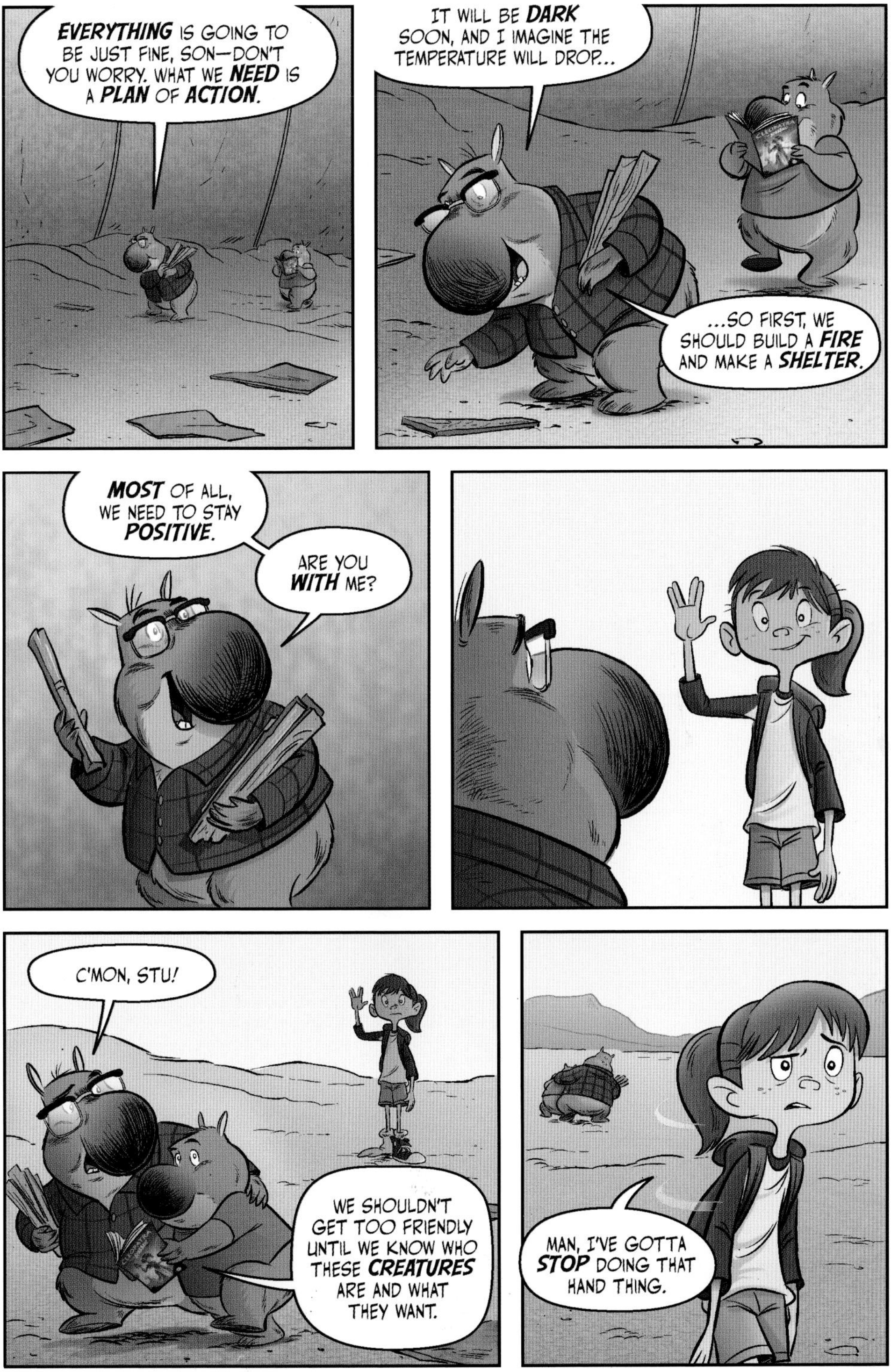
EVERYTHING IS GOING TO BE JUST FINE, SON—DON'T YOU WORRY. WHAT WE NEED IS A PLAN OF ACTION.
IT WILL BE DARK SOON, AND I IMAGINE THE TEMPERATURE WILL DROP...
...SO FIRST, WE SHOULD BUILD A FIRE AND MAKE A SHELTER.
MOST OF ALL, WE NEED TO STAY POSITIVE.
ARE YOU WITH ME?
C'MON, STU!
WE SHOULDN'T GET TOO FRIENDLY UNTIL WE KNOW WHO THESE CREATURES ARE AND WHAT THEY WANT.
MAN, I'VE GOTTA STOP DOING THAT HAND THING.

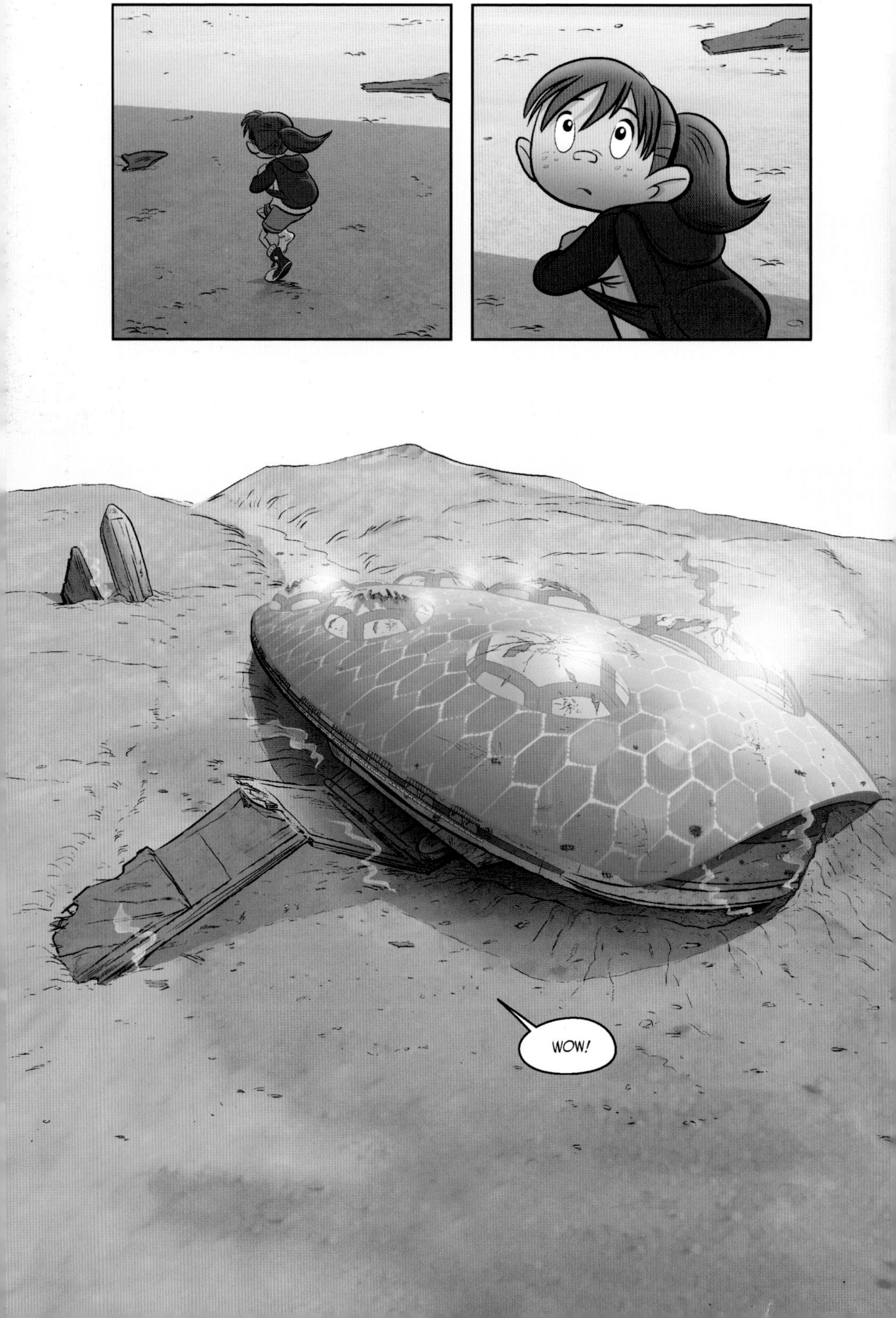
WOW!

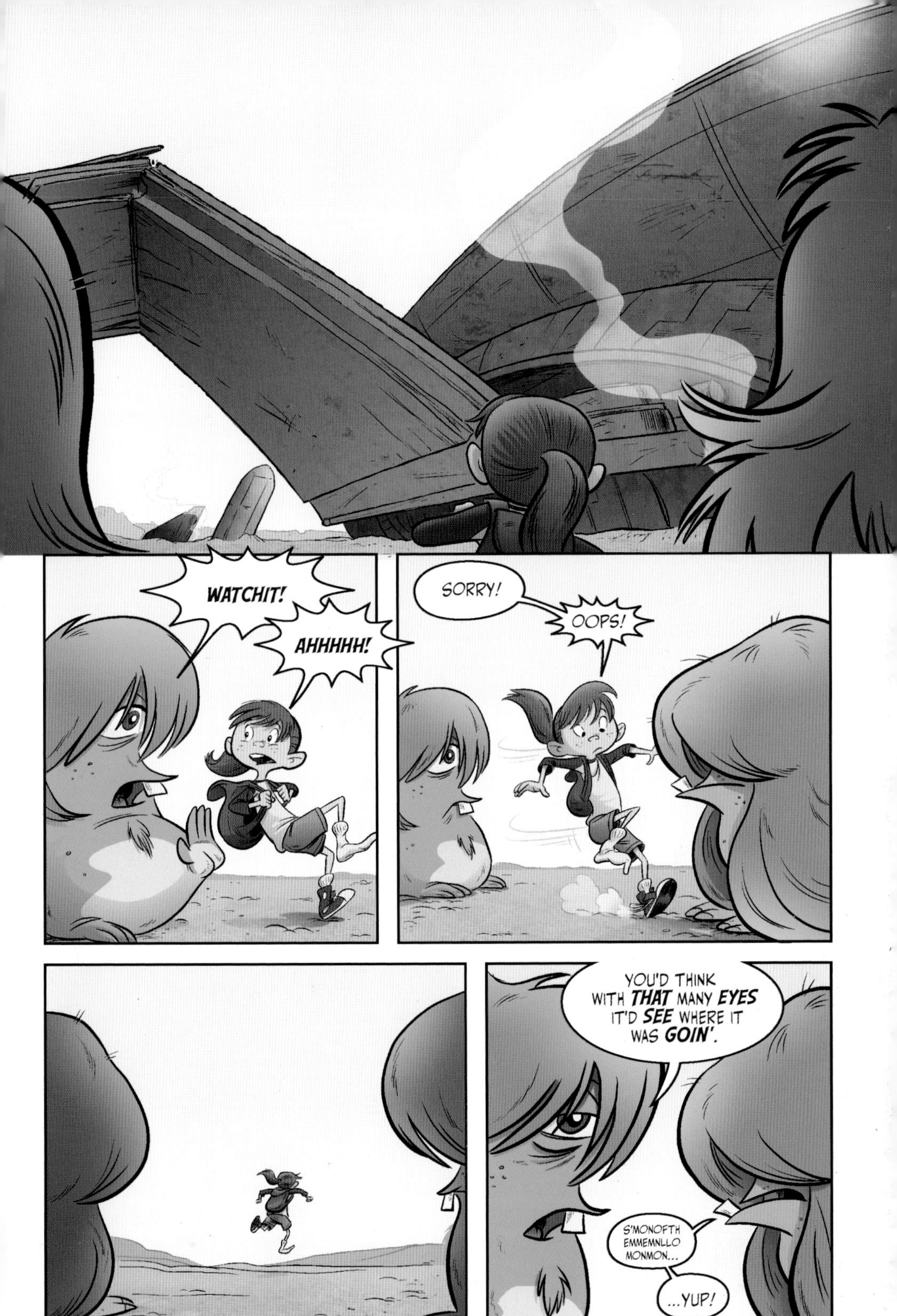
WATCHIT!
AHHHHH!
SORRY!
OOPS!
YOU'D THINK WITH **THAT** MANY **EYES** IT'D **SEE** WHERE IT WAS **GOIN'**.
S'MONOFTH EMMEMNLLO MONMON...
...YUP!

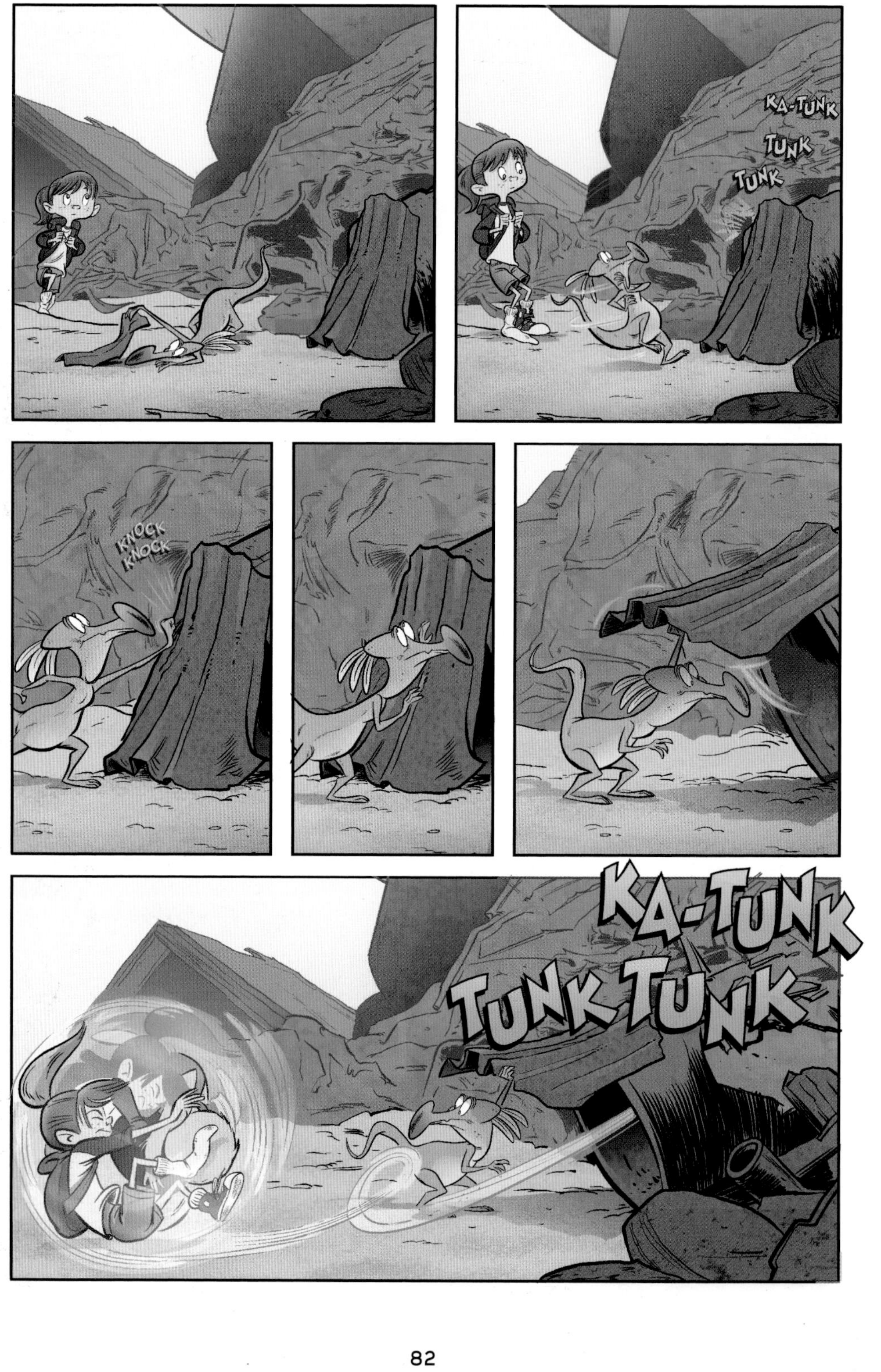
KA-TUNK
TUNK
TUNK
KNOCK
KNOCK
KA-TUNK
TUNK TUNK

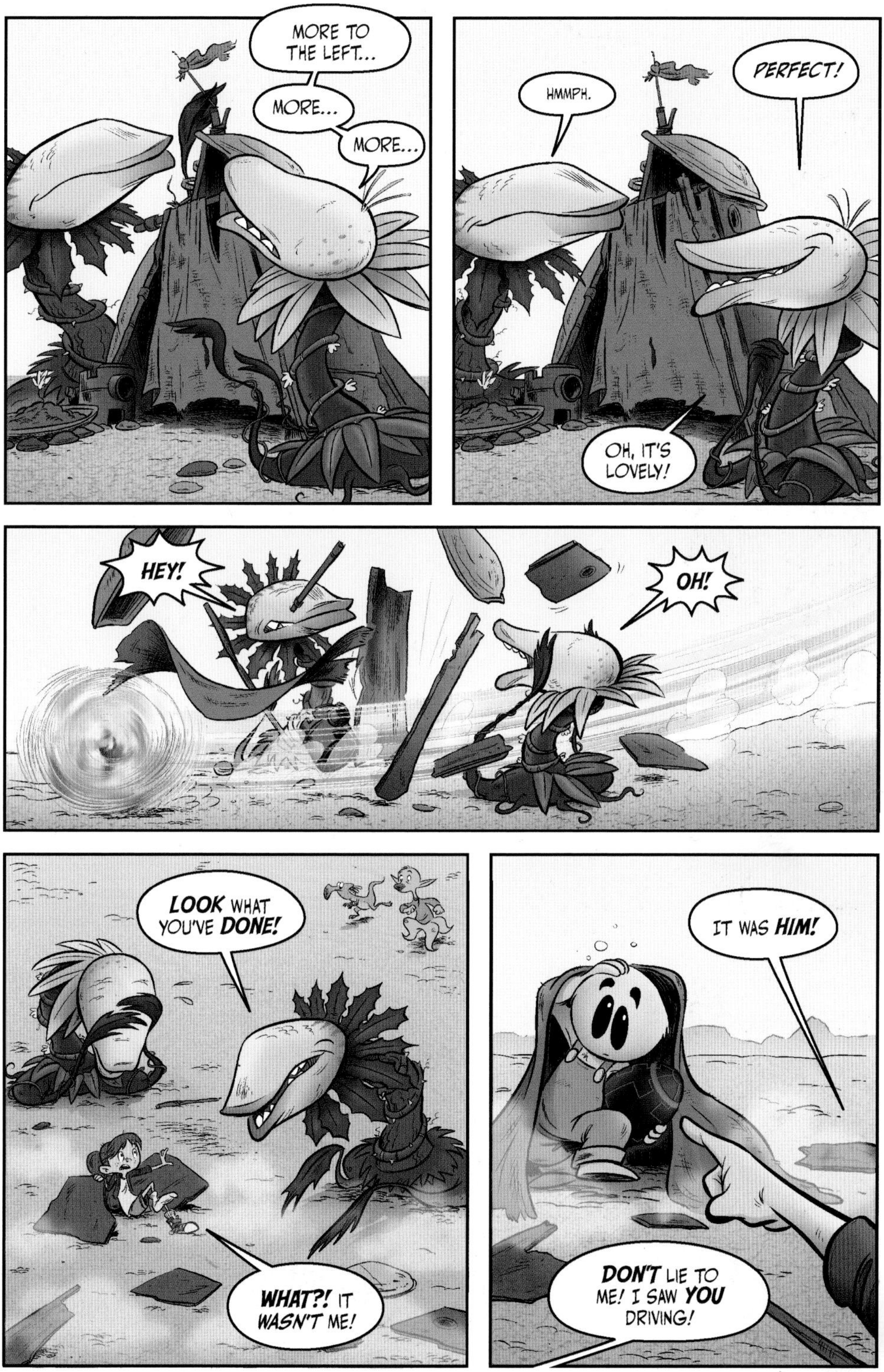
MORE TO THE LEFT...
MORE...
MORE...
HMMPH.
PERFECT!
OH, IT'S LOVELY!
HEY!
OH!
LOOK WHAT YOU'VE DONE!
WHAT?! IT WASN'T ME!
IT WAS HIM!
DON'T LIE TO ME! I SAW YOU DRIVING!

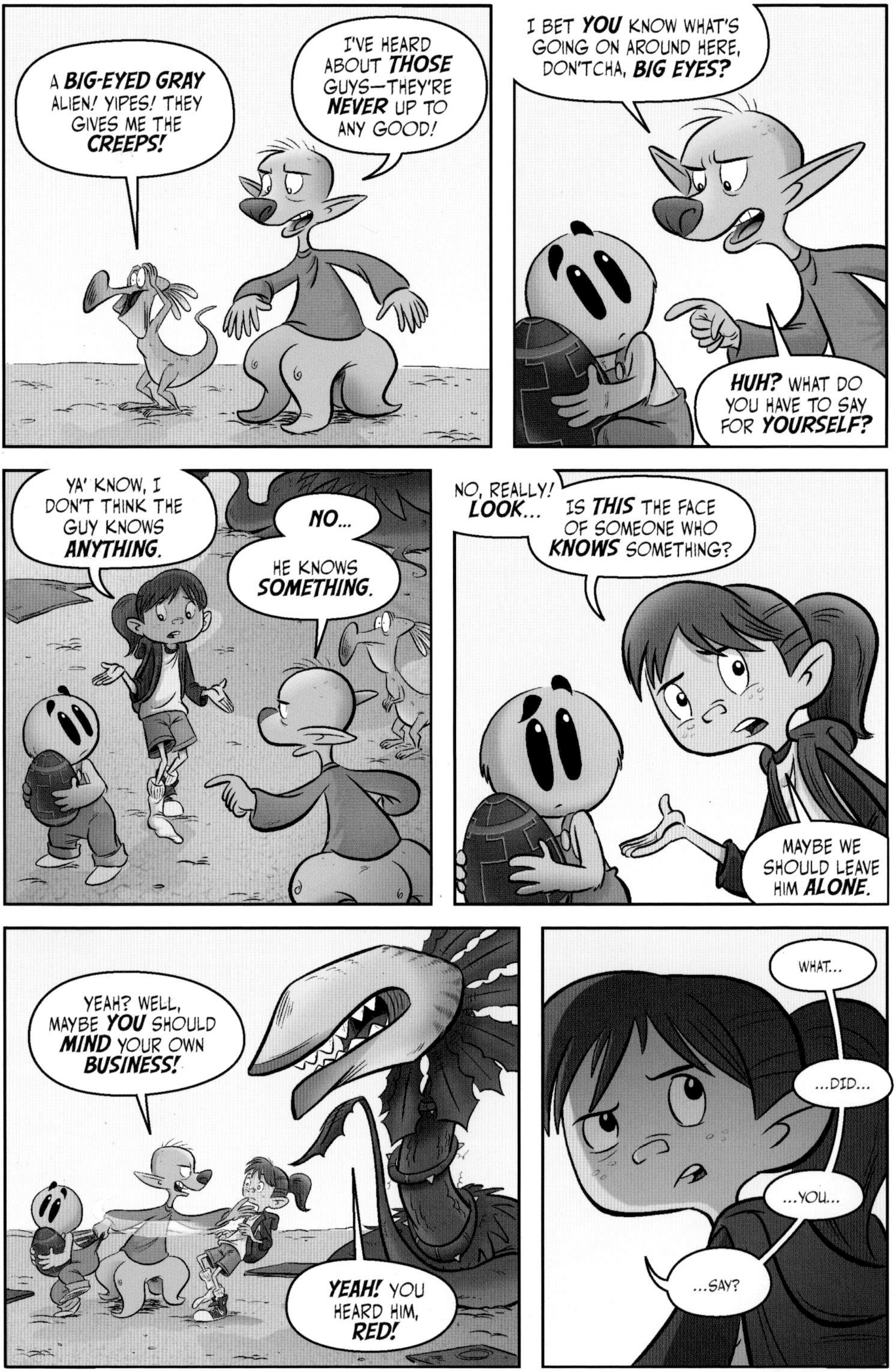
A BIG-EYED GRAY ALIEN! YIPES! THEY GIVES ME THE CREEPS!
I'VE HEARD ABOUT THOSE GUYS—THEY'RE NEVER UP TO ANY GOOD!
I BET YOU KNOW WHAT'S GOING ON AROUND HERE, DON'TCHA, BIG EYES?
HUH? WHAT DO YOU HAVE TO SAY FOR YOURSELF?
YA' KNOW, I DON'T THINK THE GUY KNOWS ANYTHING.
NO...
HE KNOWS SOMETHING.
NO, REALLY! LOOK...
IS THIS THE FACE OF SOMEONE WHO KNOWS SOMETHING?
MAYBE WE SHOULD LEAVE HIM ALONE.
YEAH? WELL, MAYBE YOU SHOULD MIND YOUR OWN BUSINESS!
YEAH! YOU HEARD HIM, RED!
WHAT...
...DID...
...YOU...
...SAY?

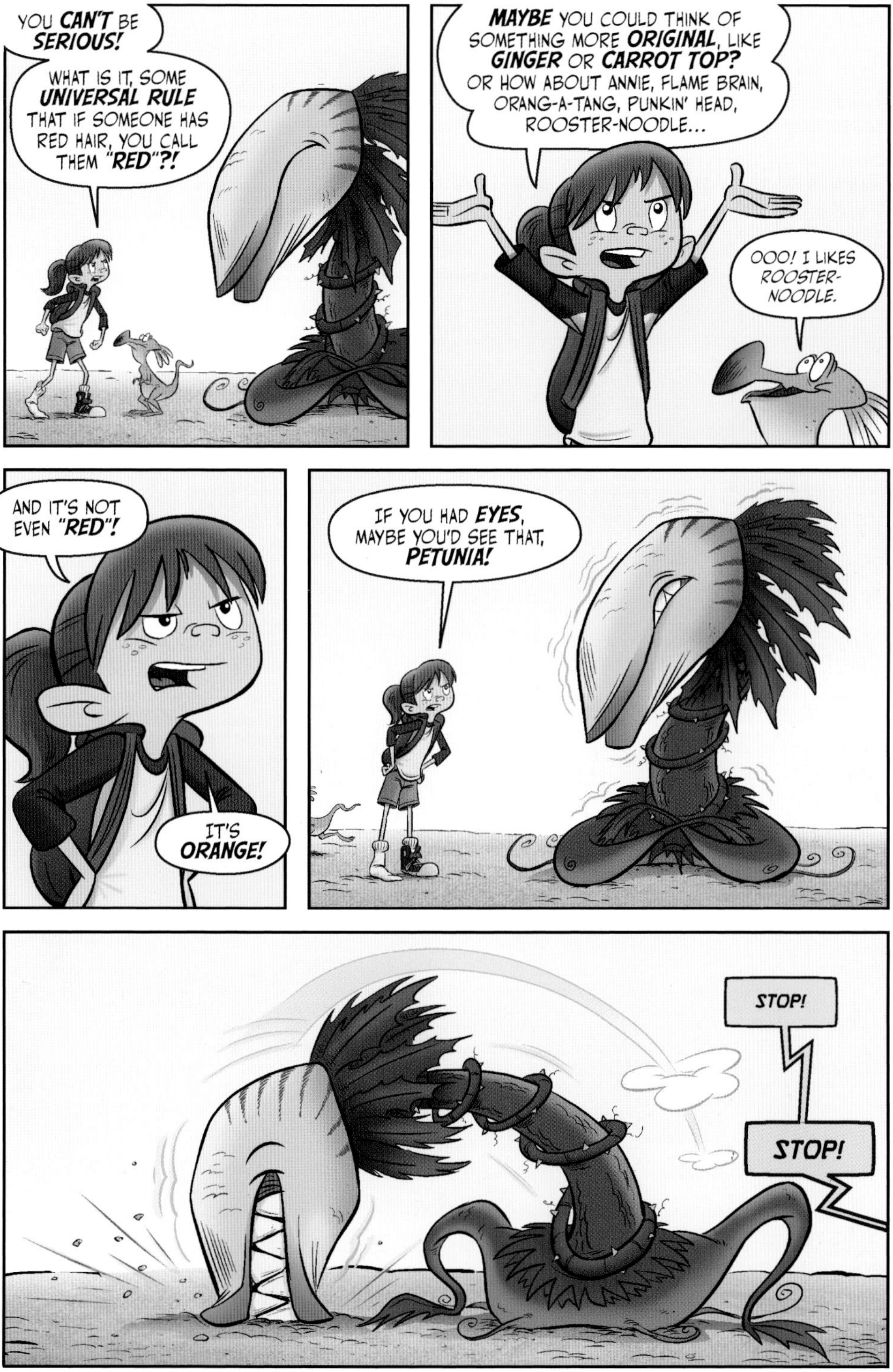

YOU **CAN'T** BE **SERIOUS!**
WHAT IS IT, SOME **UNIVERSAL RULE** THAT IF SOMEONE HAS RED HAIR, YOU CALL THEM **"RED"?!**
MAYBE YOU COULD THINK OF SOMETHING MORE **ORIGINAL**, LIKE **GINGER** OR **CARROT TOP?** OR HOW ABOUT ANNIE, FLAME BRAIN, ORANG-A-TANG, PUNKIN' HEAD, ROOSTER-NOODLE...
OOO! I LIKES ROOSTER-NOODLE.
AND IT'S NOT EVEN **"RED"!**
IT'S **ORANGE!**
IF YOU HAD **EYES**, MAYBE YOU'D SEE THAT, **PETUNIA!**
STOP!
STOP!

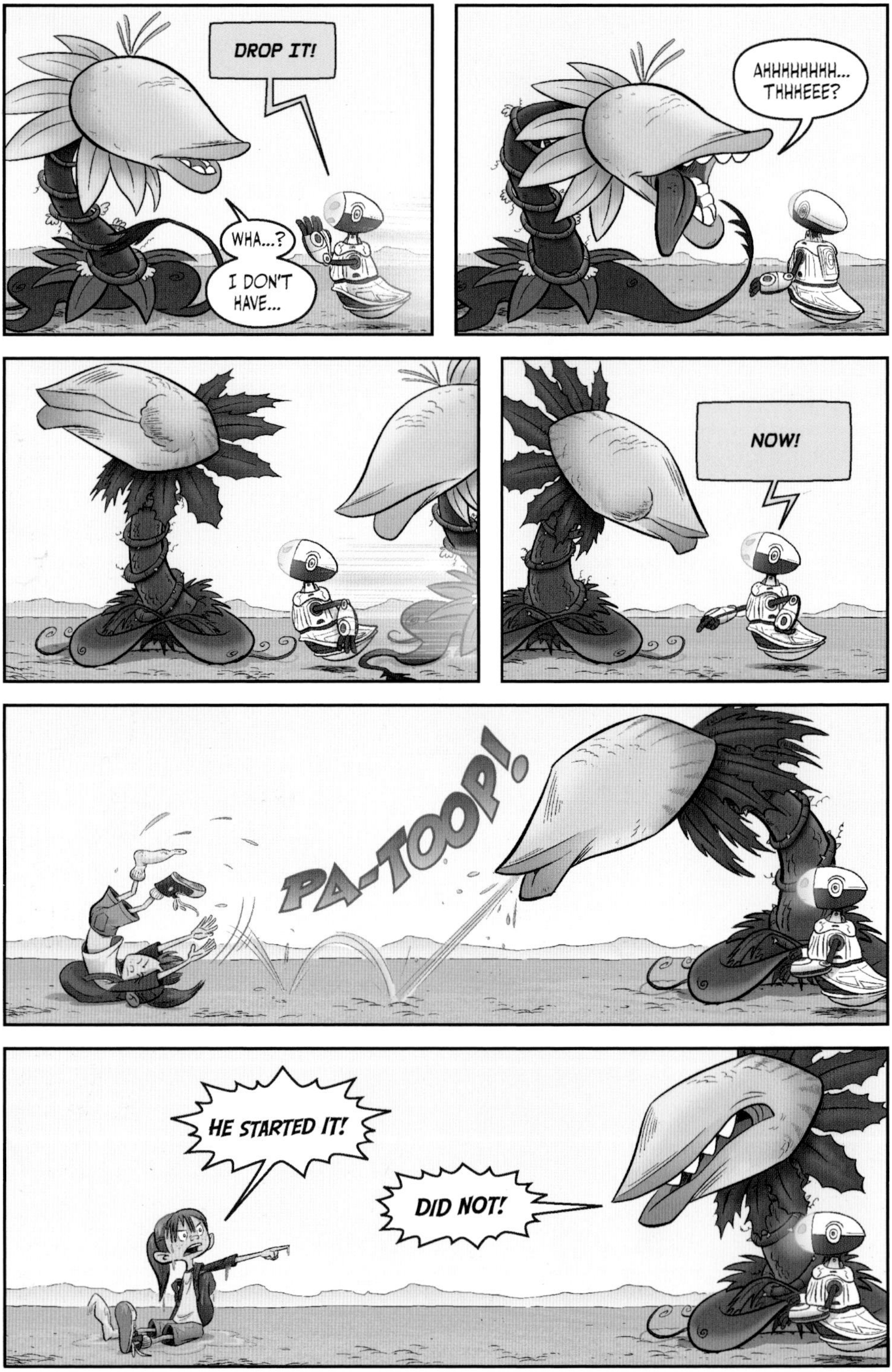
DROP IT!
WHA...?
I DON'T HAVE...
AHHHHHHHH... THHHEEE?
NOW!
PA-TOOP!
HE STARTED IT!
DID NOT!

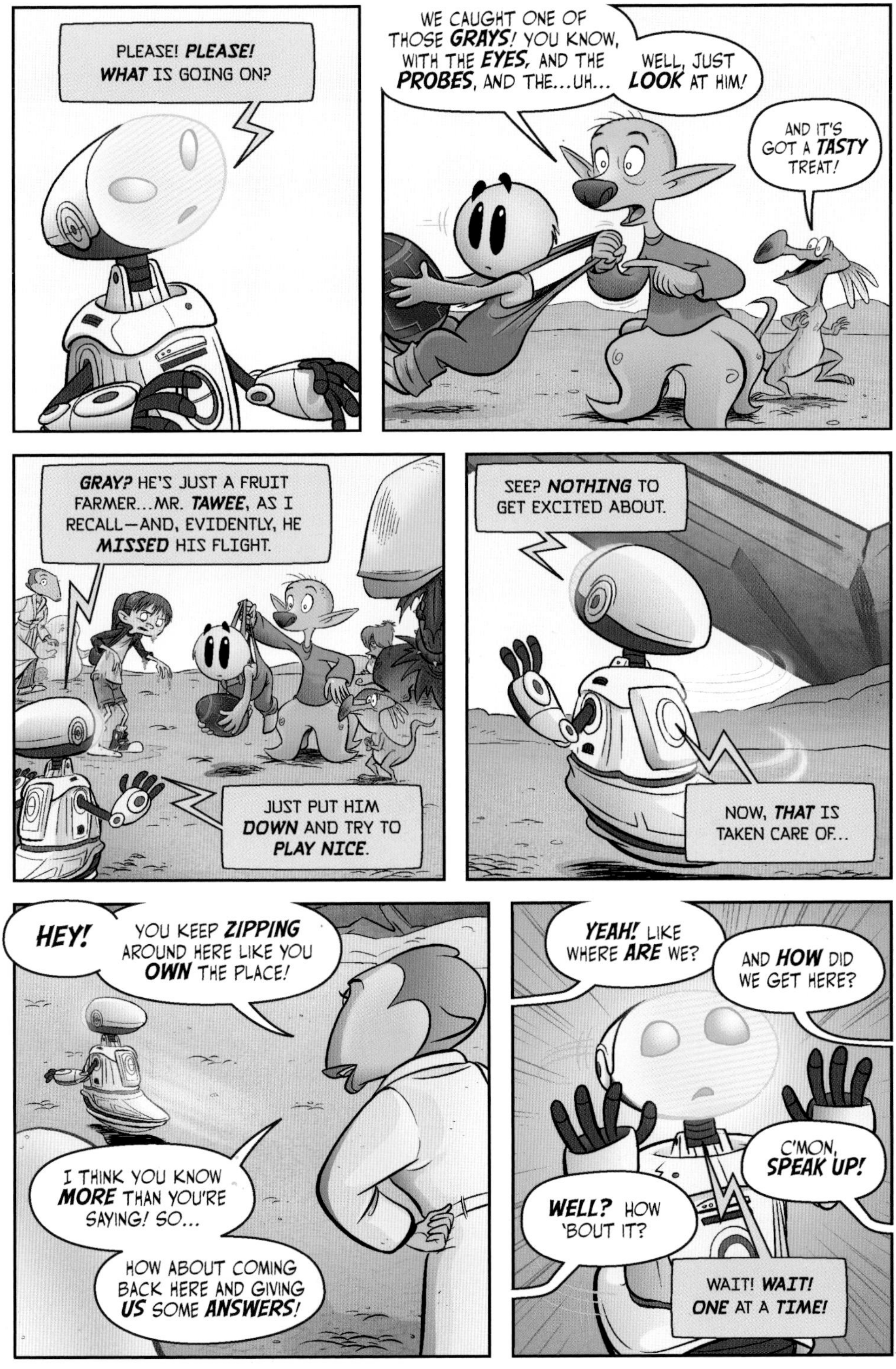
PLEASE! PLEASE! WHAT IS GOING ON?
WE CAUGHT ONE OF THOSE GRAYS! YOU KNOW, WITH THE EYES, AND THE PROBES, AND THE...UH...
WELL, JUST LOOK AT HIM!
AND IT'S GOT A TASTY TREAT!
GRAY? HE'S JUST A FRUIT FARMER...MR. TAWEE, AS I RECALL—AND, EVIDENTLY, HE MISSED HIS FLIGHT.
JUST PUT HIM DOWN AND TRY TO PLAY NICE.
SEE? NOTHING TO GET EXCITED ABOUT.
NOW, THAT IS TAKEN CARE OF...
HEY!
YOU KEEP ZIPPING AROUND HERE LIKE YOU OWN THE PLACE!
I THINK YOU KNOW MORE THAN YOU'RE SAYING! SO...
HOW ABOUT COMING BACK HERE AND GIVING US SOME ANSWERS!
YEAH! LIKE WHERE ARE WE?
AND HOW DID WE GET HERE?
C'MON, SPEAK UP!
WELL? HOW 'BOUT IT?
WAIT! WAIT! ONE AT A TIME!

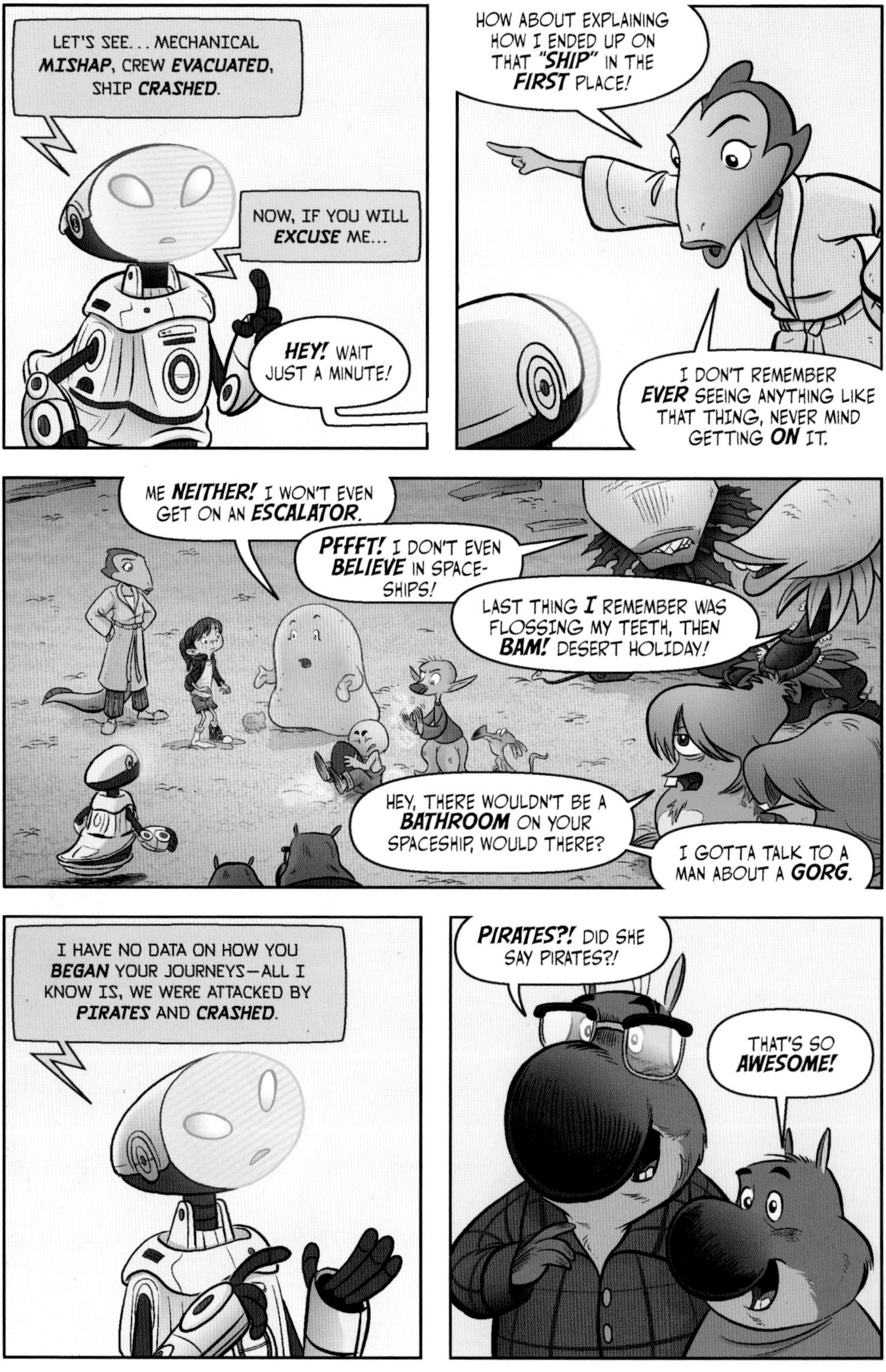
LET'S SEE... MECHANICAL MISHAP, CREW EVACUATED, SHIP CRASHED.
NOW, IF YOU WILL EXCUSE ME...
HEY! WAIT JUST A MINUTE!
HOW ABOUT EXPLAINING HOW I ENDED UP ON THAT "SHIP" IN THE FIRST PLACE!
I DON'T REMEMBER EVER SEEING ANYTHING LIKE THAT THING, NEVER MIND GETTING ON IT.
ME NEITHER! I WON'T EVEN GET ON AN ESCALATOR.
PFFFT! I DON'T EVEN BELIEVE IN SPACE-SHIPS!
LAST THING I REMEMBER WAS FLOSSING MY TEETH, THEN BAM! DESERT HOLIDAY!
HEY, THERE WOULDN'T BE A BATHROOM ON YOUR SPACESHIP, WOULD THERE?
I GOTTA TALK TO A MAN ABOUT A GORG.
I HAVE NO DATA ON HOW YOU BEGAN YOUR JOURNEYS—ALL I KNOW IS, WE WERE ATTACKED BY PIRATES AND CRASHED.
PIRATES?! DID SHE SAY PIRATES?!
THAT'S SO AWESOME!

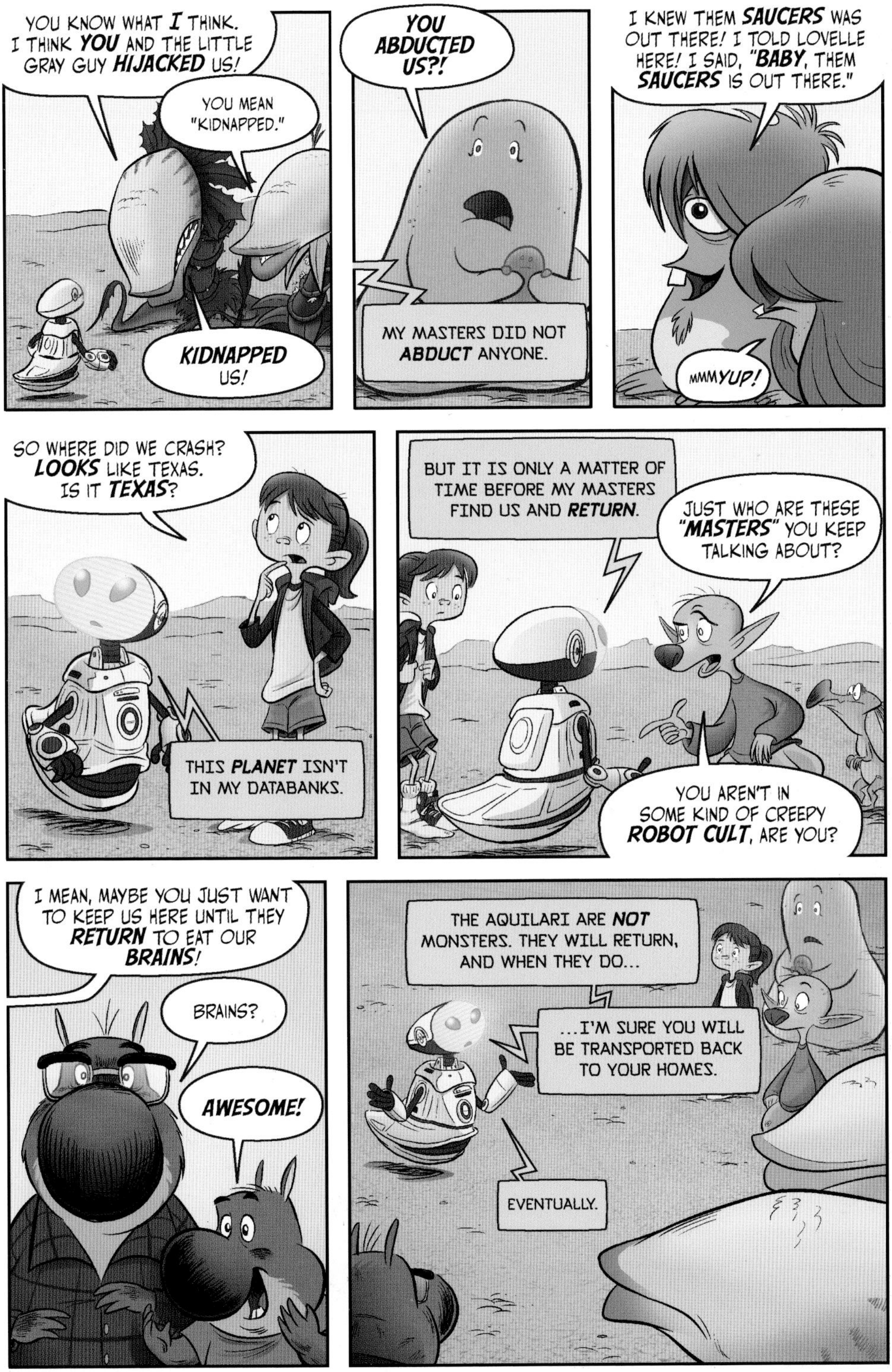

YOU KNOW WHAT I THINK. I THINK YOU AND THE LITTLE GRAY GUY HIJACKED US!
YOU MEAN "KIDNAPPED."
KIDNAPPED US!
YOU ABDUCTED US?!
MY MASTERS DID NOT ABDUCT ANYONE.
I KNEW THEM SAUCERS WAS OUT THERE! I TOLD LOVELLE HERE! I SAID, "BABY, THEM SAUCERS IS OUT THERE."
MMMYUP!
SO WHERE DID WE CRASH? LOOKS LIKE TEXAS. IS IT TEXAS?
THIS PLANET ISN'T IN MY DATABANKS.
BUT IT IS ONLY A MATTER OF TIME BEFORE MY MASTERS FIND US AND RETURN.
JUST WHO ARE THESE "MASTERS" YOU KEEP TALKING ABOUT?
YOU AREN'T IN SOME KIND OF CREEPY ROBOT CULT, ARE YOU?
I MEAN, MAYBE YOU JUST WANT TO KEEP US HERE UNTIL THEY RETURN TO EAT OUR BRAINS!
BRAINS?
AWESOME!
THE AQUILARI ARE NOT MONSTERS. THEY WILL RETURN, AND WHEN THEY DO...
...I'M SURE YOU WILL BE TRANSPORTED BACK TO YOUR HOMES.
EVENTUALLY.

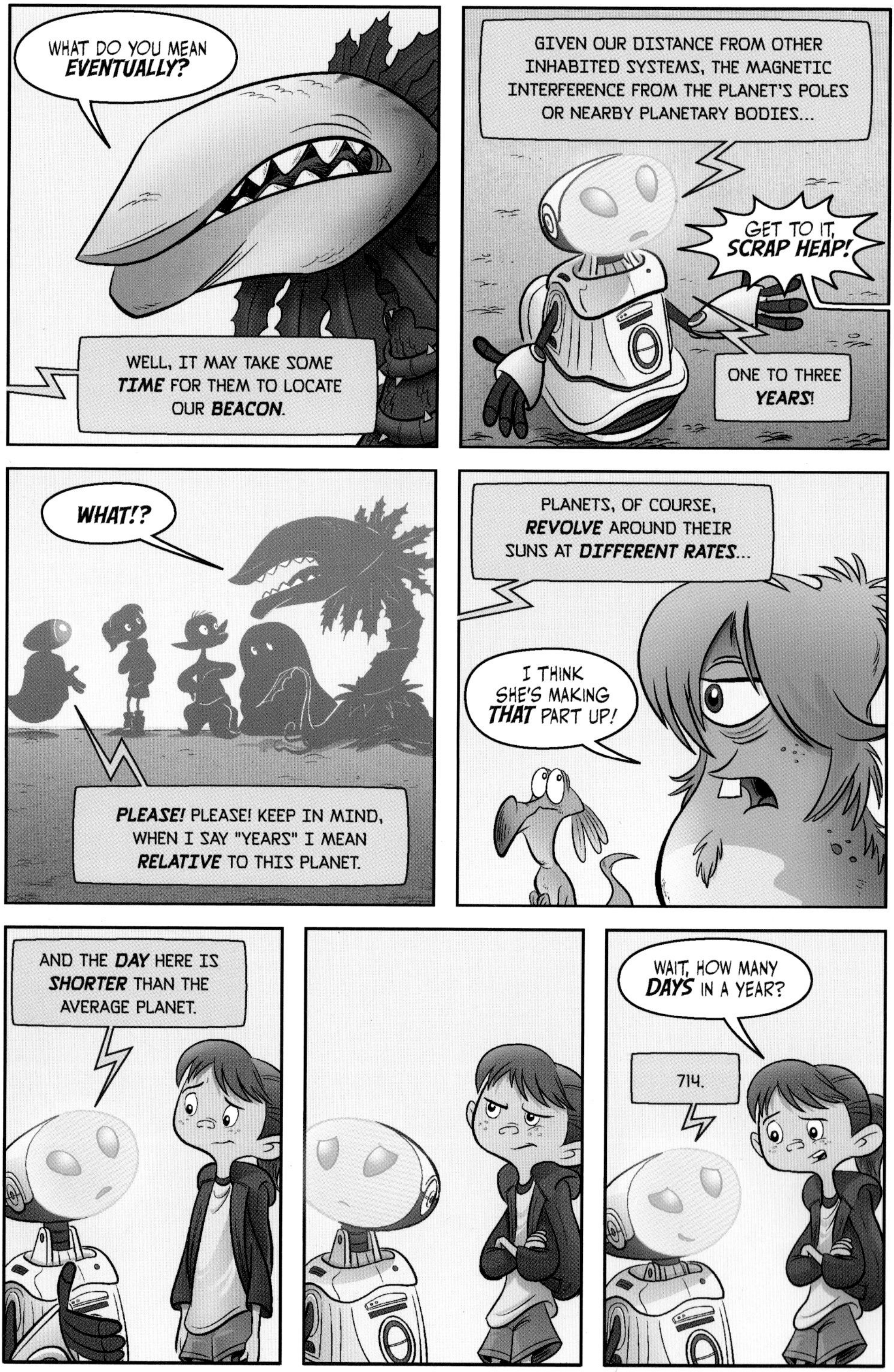

WHAT DO YOU MEAN **EVENTUALLY?**
WELL, IT MAY TAKE SOME **TIME** FOR THEM TO LOCATE OUR **BEACON**.
GIVEN OUR DISTANCE FROM OTHER INHABITED SYSTEMS, THE MAGNETIC INTERFERENCE FROM THE PLANET'S POLES OR NEARBY PLANETARY BODIES...
GET TO IT, **SCRAP HEAP!**
ONE TO THREE **YEARS**!
WHAT!?
PLEASE! PLEASE! KEEP IN MIND, WHEN I SAY "YEARS" I MEAN **RELATIVE** TO THIS PLANET.
PLANETS, OF COURSE, **REVOLVE** AROUND THEIR SUNS AT **DIFFERENT RATES**...
I THINK SHE'S MAKING **THAT** PART UP!
AND THE **DAY** HERE IS **SHORTER** THAN THE AVERAGE PLANET.
WAIT, HOW MANY **DAYS** IN A YEAR?
714.

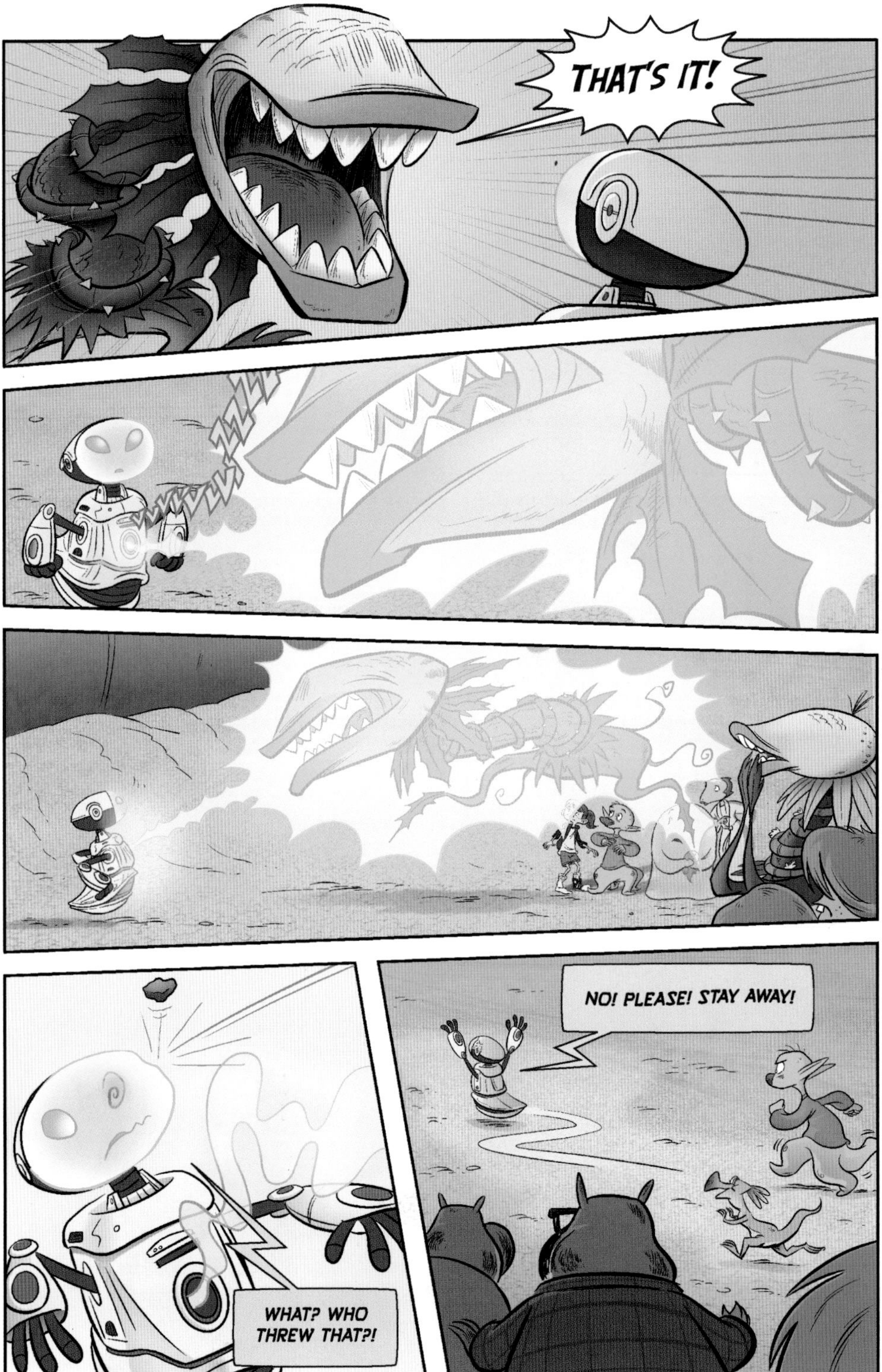
THAT'S IT!
NO! PLEASE! STAY AWAY!
WHAT? WHO THREW THAT?!

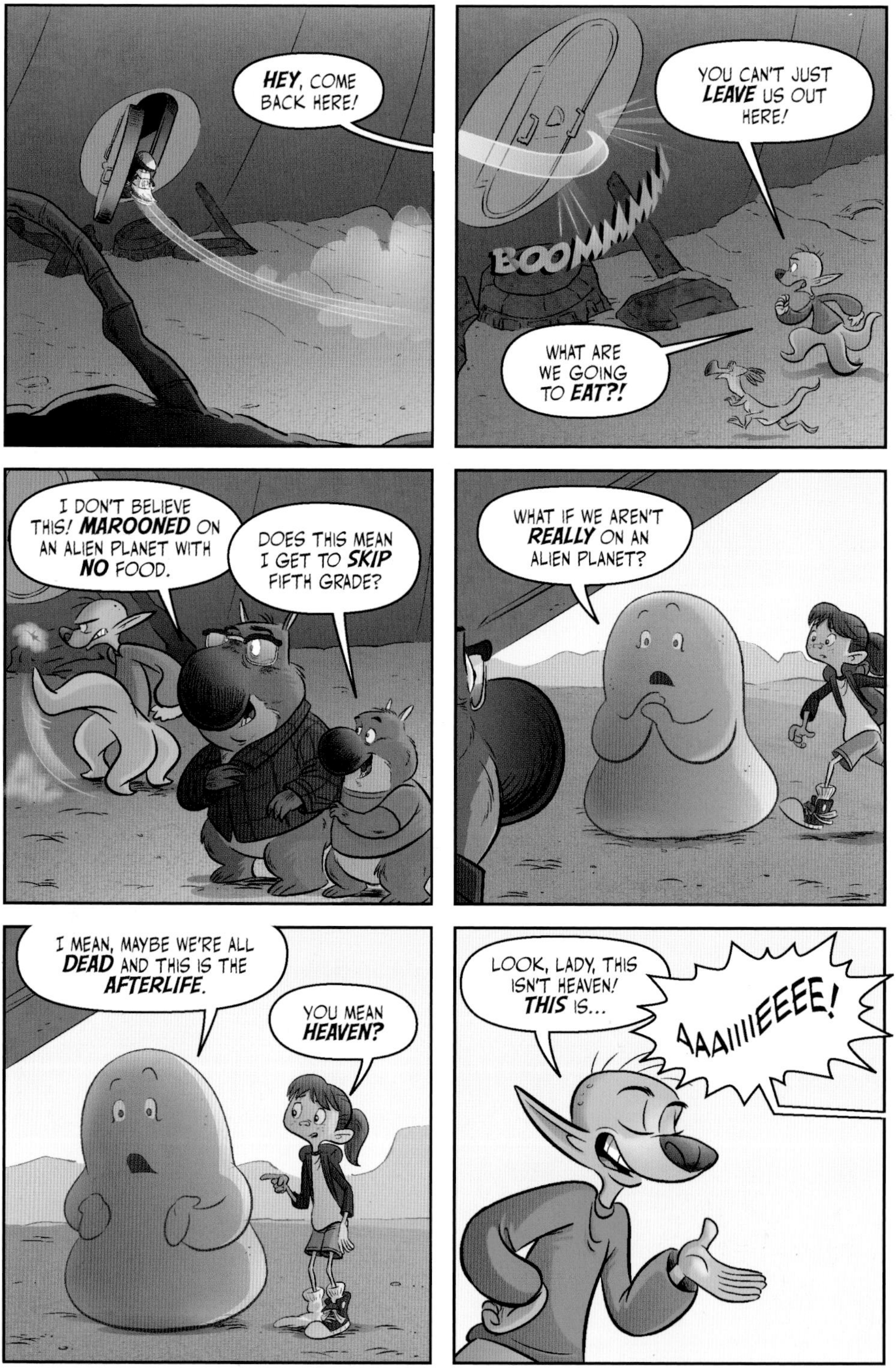
HEY, COME BACK HERE!
YOU CAN'T JUST LEAVE US OUT HERE!
BOOMMMMM
WHAT ARE WE GOING TO EAT?!
I DON'T BELIEVE THIS! MAROONED ON AN ALIEN PLANET WITH NO FOOD.
DOES THIS MEAN I GET TO SKIP FIFTH GRADE?
WHAT IF WE AREN'T REALLY ON AN ALIEN PLANET?
I MEAN, MAYBE WE'RE ALL DEAD AND THIS IS THE AFTERLIFE.
YOU MEAN HEAVEN?
LOOK, LADY, THIS ISN'T HEAVEN! THIS IS...
AAAIIIIEEEE!

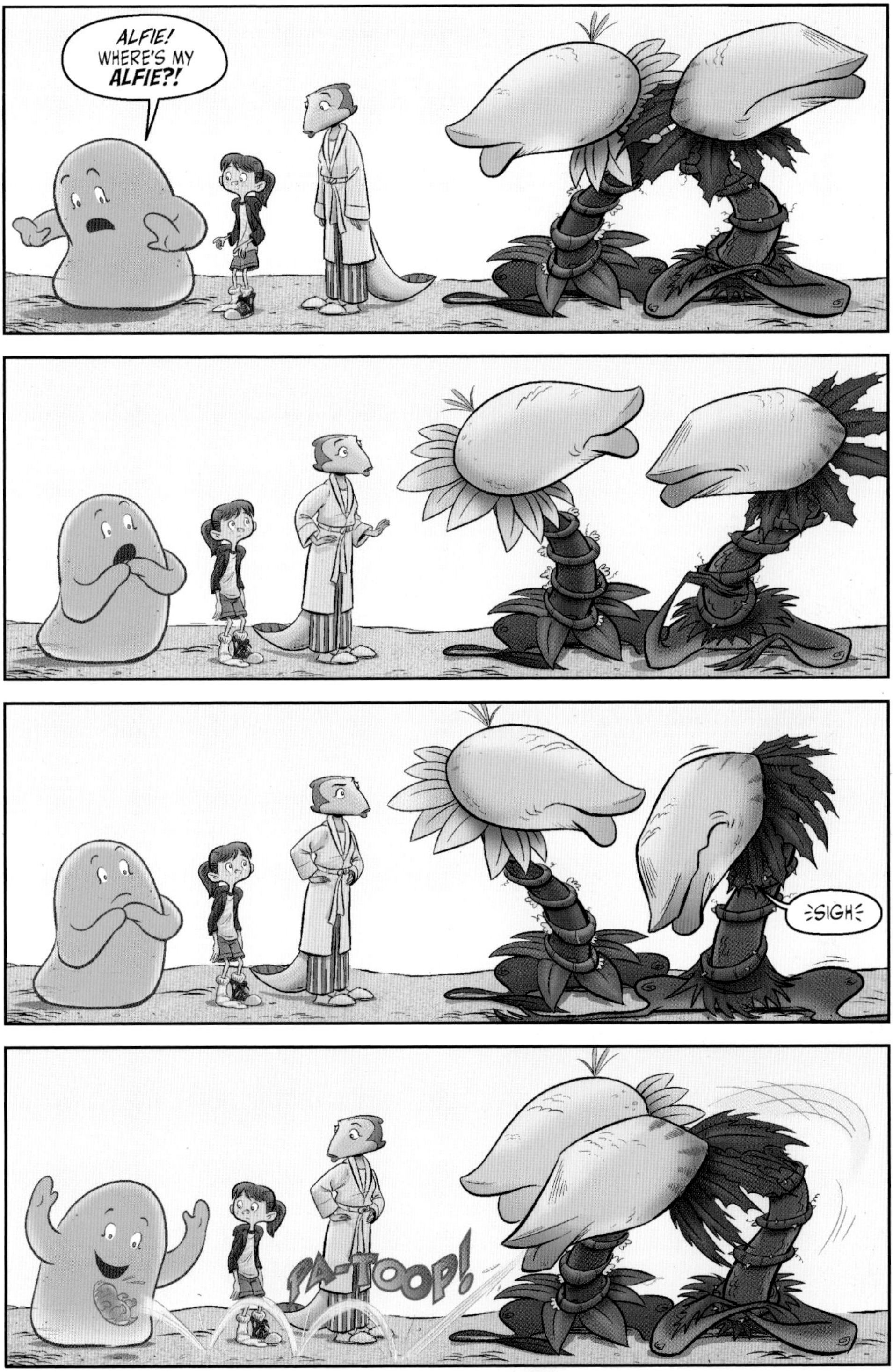
ALFIE! WHERE'S MY ALFIE?!
SIGH
PA-TOOP!

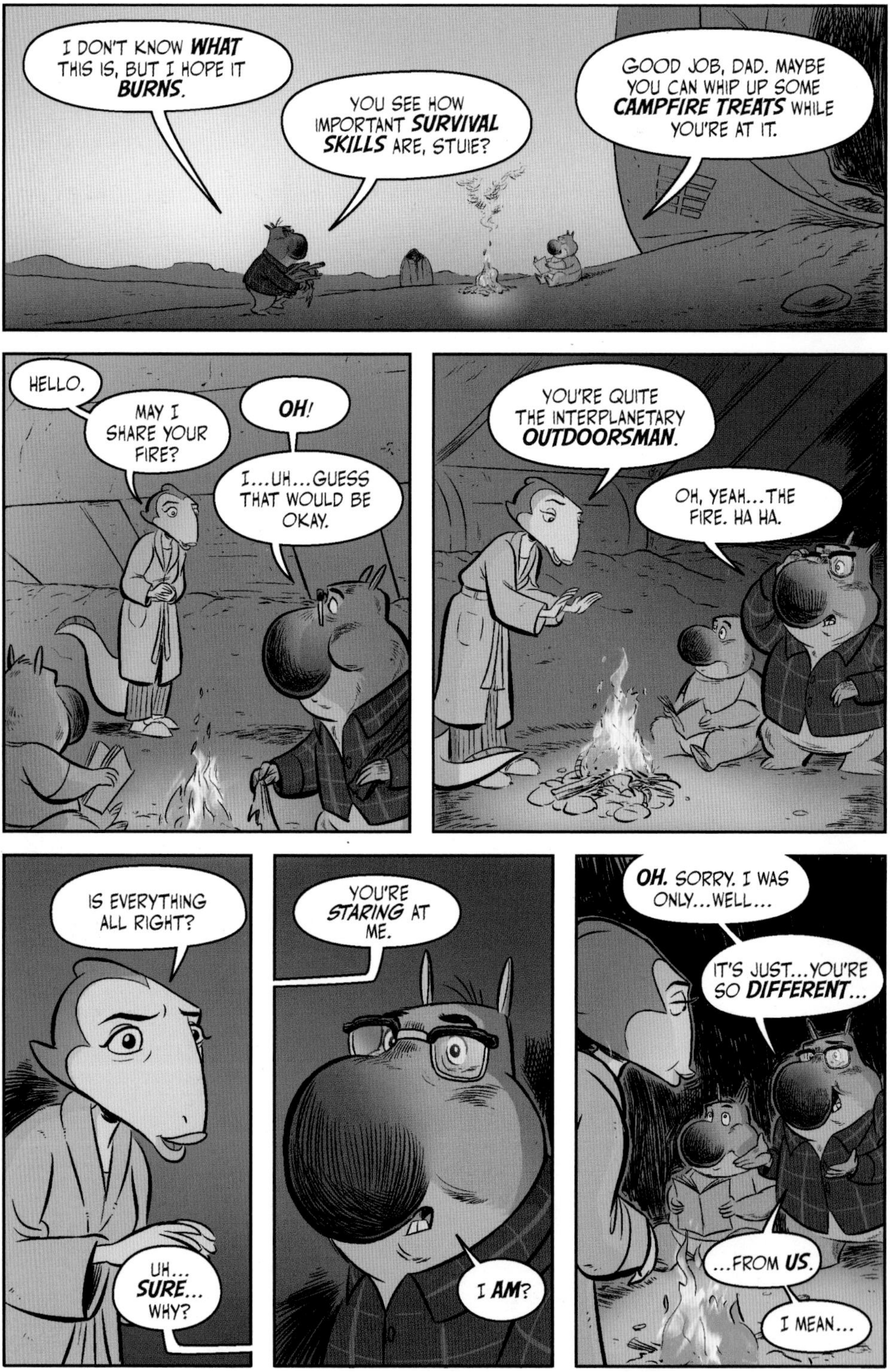
I DON'T KNOW **WHAT** THIS IS, BUT I HOPE IT **BURNS**.
YOU SEE HOW IMPORTANT **SURVIVAL SKILLS** ARE, STUIE?
GOOD JOB, DAD. MAYBE YOU CAN WHIP UP SOME **CAMPFIRE TREATS** WHILE YOU'RE AT IT.
HELLO.
MAY I SHARE YOUR FIRE?
OH!
I...UH...GUESS THAT WOULD BE OKAY.
YOU'RE QUITE THE INTERPLANETARY **OUTDOORSMAN**.
OH, YEAH...THE FIRE. HA HA.
IS EVERYTHING ALL RIGHT?
UH... **SURE**... WHY?
YOU'RE **STARING** AT ME.
I **AM**?
OH. SORRY. I WAS ONLY...WELL...
IT'S JUST...YOU'RE SO **DIFFERENT**...
...FROM **US**.
I MEAN...

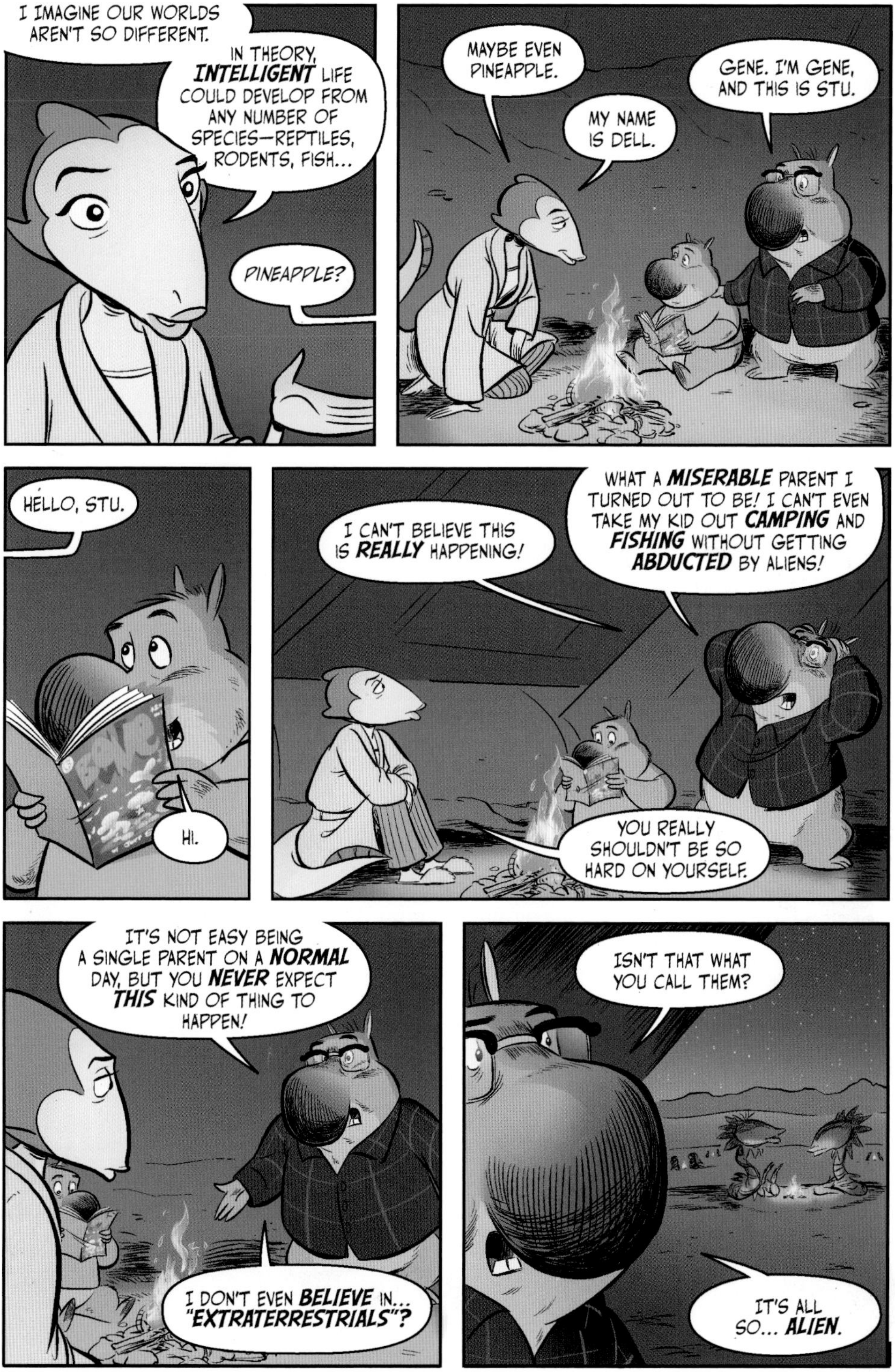
I IMAGINE OUR WORLDS AREN'T SO DIFFERENT.
IN THEORY, **INTELLIGENT** LIFE COULD DEVELOP FROM ANY NUMBER OF SPECIES—REPTILES, RODENTS, FISH...
PINEAPPLE?
MAYBE EVEN PINEAPPLE.
MY NAME IS DELL.
GENE. I'M GENE, AND THIS IS STU.
HELLO, STU.
HI.
I CAN'T BELIEVE THIS IS ***REALLY*** HAPPENING!
WHAT A ***MISERABLE*** PARENT I TURNED OUT TO BE! I CAN'T EVEN TAKE MY KID OUT ***CAMPING*** AND ***FISHING*** WITHOUT GETTING ***ABDUCTED*** BY ALIENS!
YOU REALLY SHOULDN'T BE SO HARD ON YOURSELF.
IT'S NOT EASY BEING A SINGLE PARENT ON A ***NORMAL*** DAY, BUT YOU ***NEVER*** EXPECT ***THIS*** KIND OF THING TO HAPPEN!
I DON'T EVEN ***BELIEVE*** IN... ***"EXTRATERRESTRIALS"?***
ISN'T THAT WHAT YOU CALL THEM?
IT'S ALL SO... ***ALIEN.***

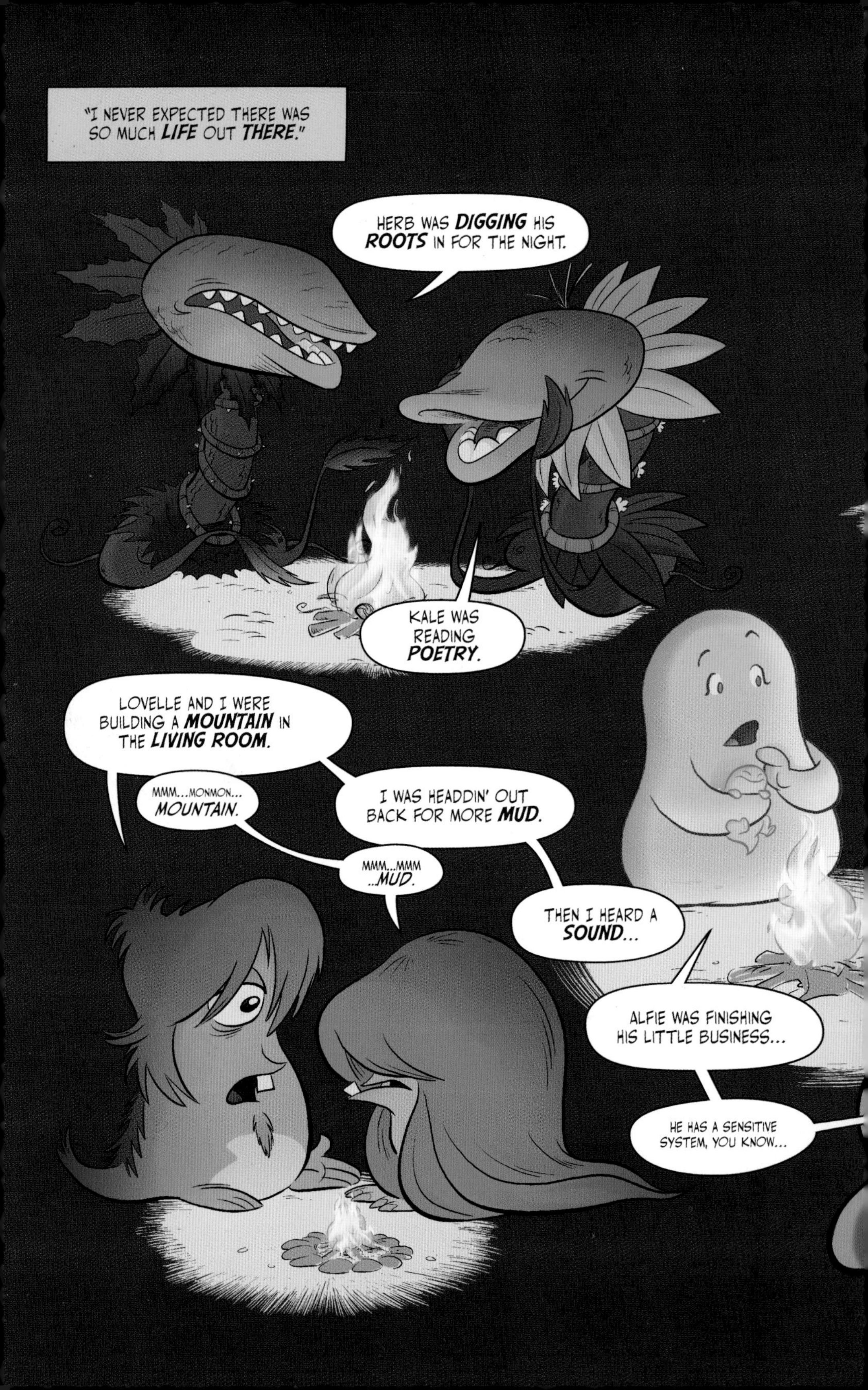
"I NEVER EXPECTED THERE WAS SO MUCH LIFE OUT THERE."
HERB WAS DIGGING HIS ROOTS IN FOR THE NIGHT.
KALE WAS READING POETRY.
LOVELLE AND I WERE BUILDING A MOUNTAIN IN THE LIVING ROOM.
MMM...MONMON... MOUNTAIN.
I WAS HEADDIN' OUT BACK FOR MORE MUD.
MMM...MMM ...MUD.
THEN I HEARD A SOUND...
ALFIE WAS FINISHING HIS LITTLE BUSINESS...
HE HAS A SENSITIVE SYSTEM, YOU KNOW...

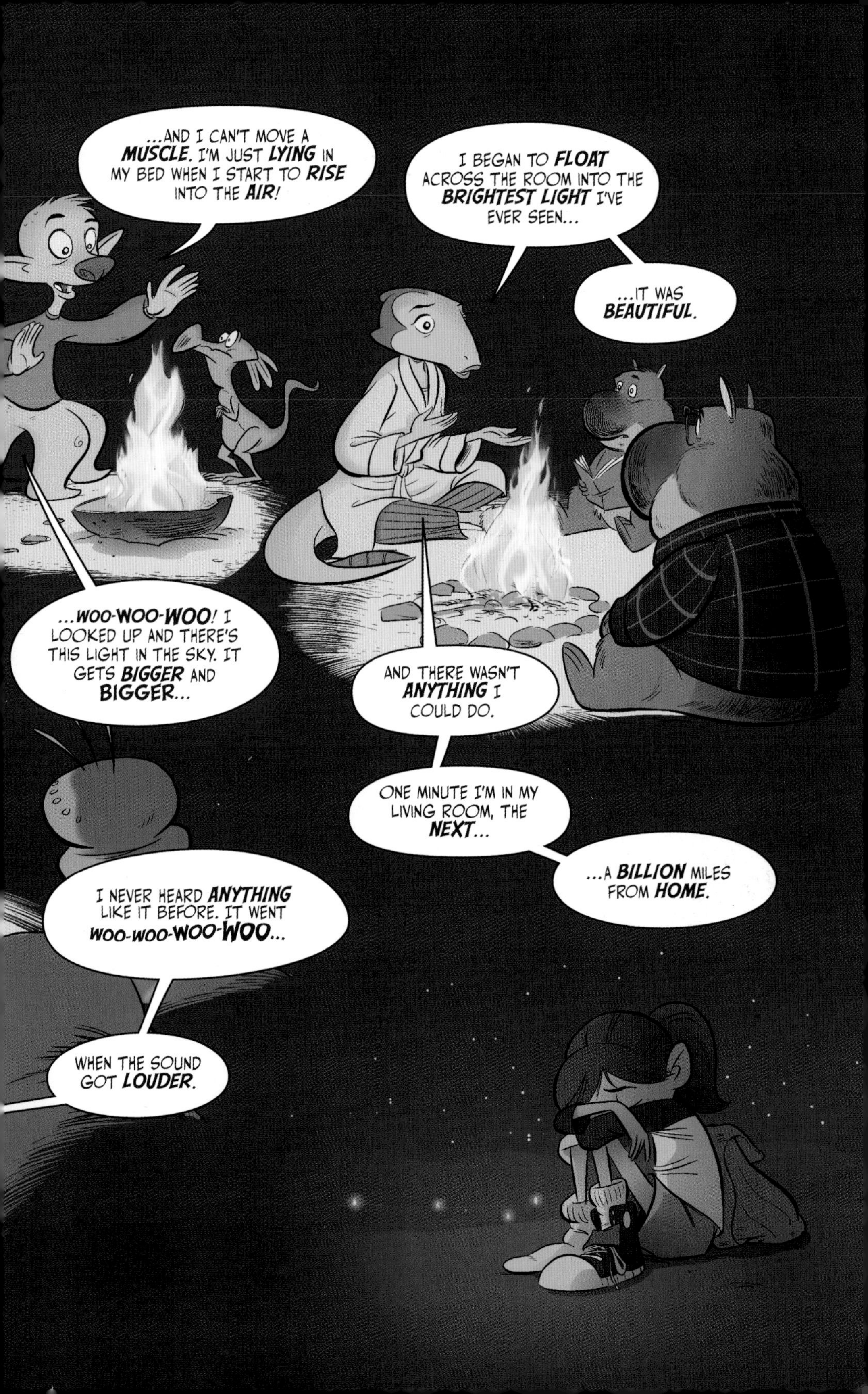
...AND I CAN'T MOVE A MUSCLE. I'M JUST LYING IN MY BED WHEN I START TO RISE INTO THE AIR!
I BEGAN TO FLOAT ACROSS THE ROOM INTO THE BRIGHTEST LIGHT I'VE EVER SEEN...
...IT WAS BEAUTIFUL.
...WOO-WOO-WOO! I LOOKED UP AND THERE'S THIS LIGHT IN THE SKY. IT GETS BIGGER AND BIGGER...
AND THERE WASN'T ANYTHING I COULD DO.
ONE MINUTE I'M IN MY LIVING ROOM, THE NEXT...
...A BILLION MILES FROM HOME.
I NEVER HEARD ANYTHING LIKE IT BEFORE. IT WENT WOO-WOO-WOO-WOO...
WHEN THE SOUND GOT LOUDER.

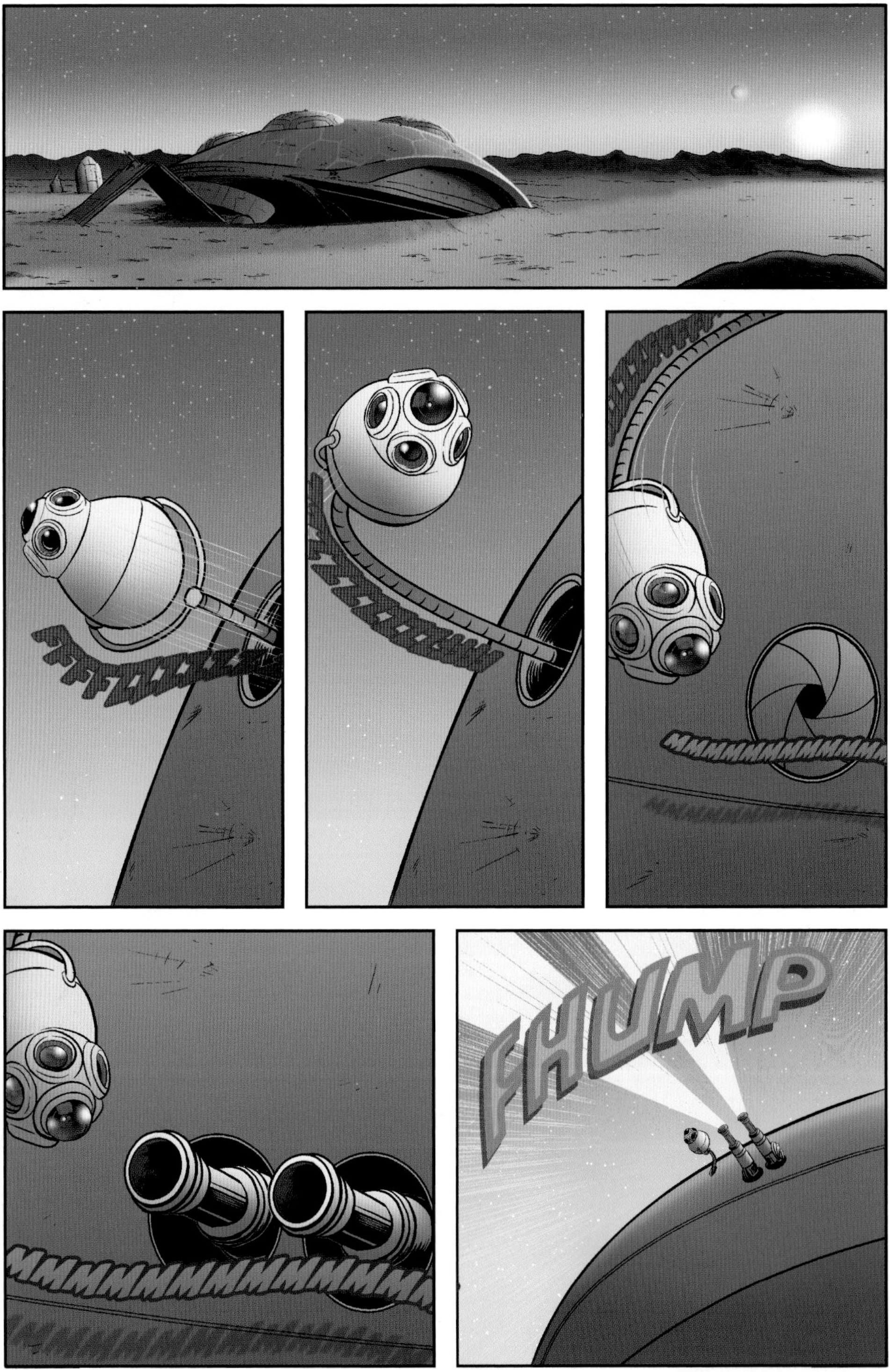
FHUMP

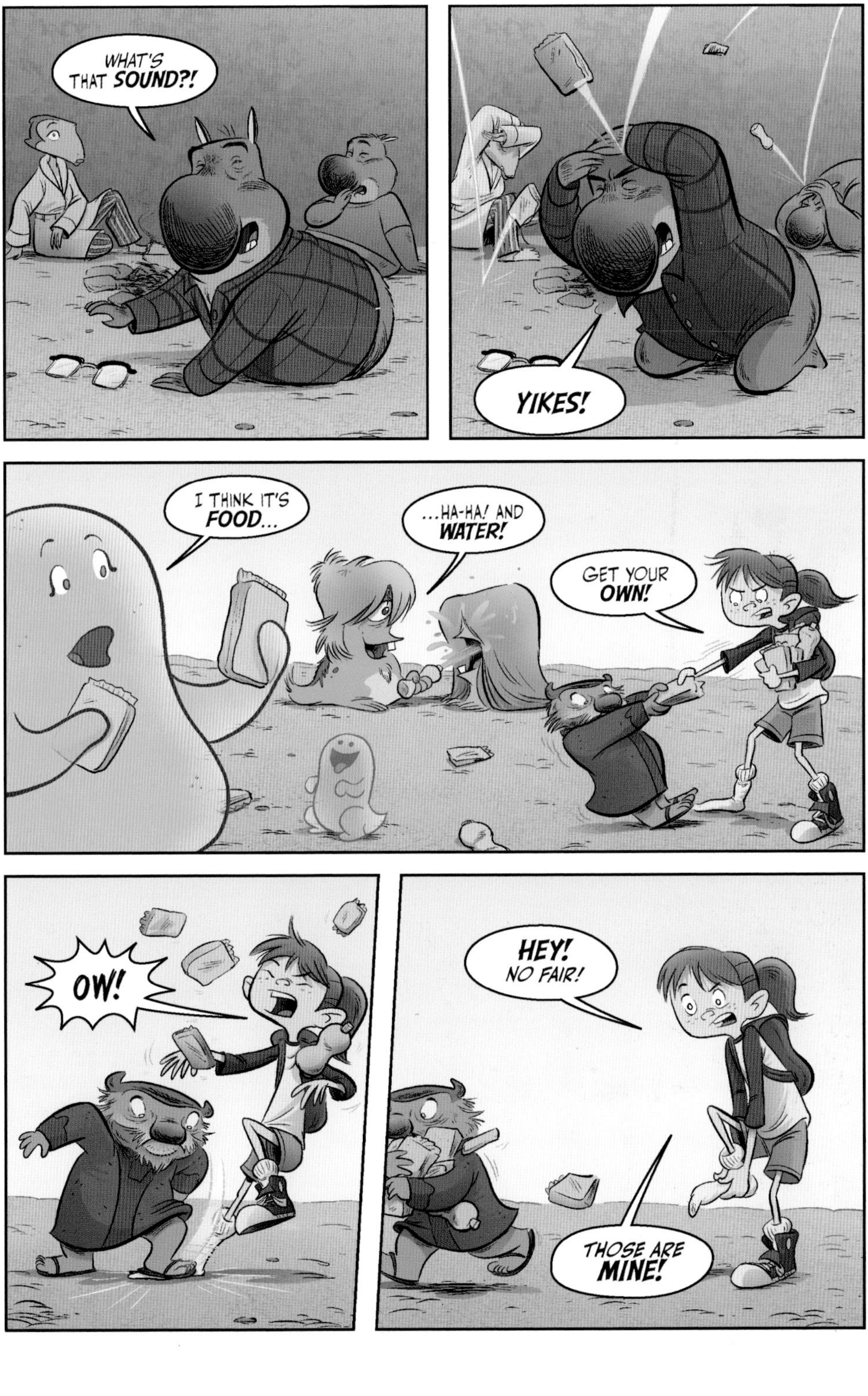
WHAT'S THAT SOUND?!
YIKES!
I THINK IT'S FOOD...
...HA-HA! AND WATER!
GET YOUR OWN!
OW!
HEY! NO FAIR!
THOSE ARE MINE!

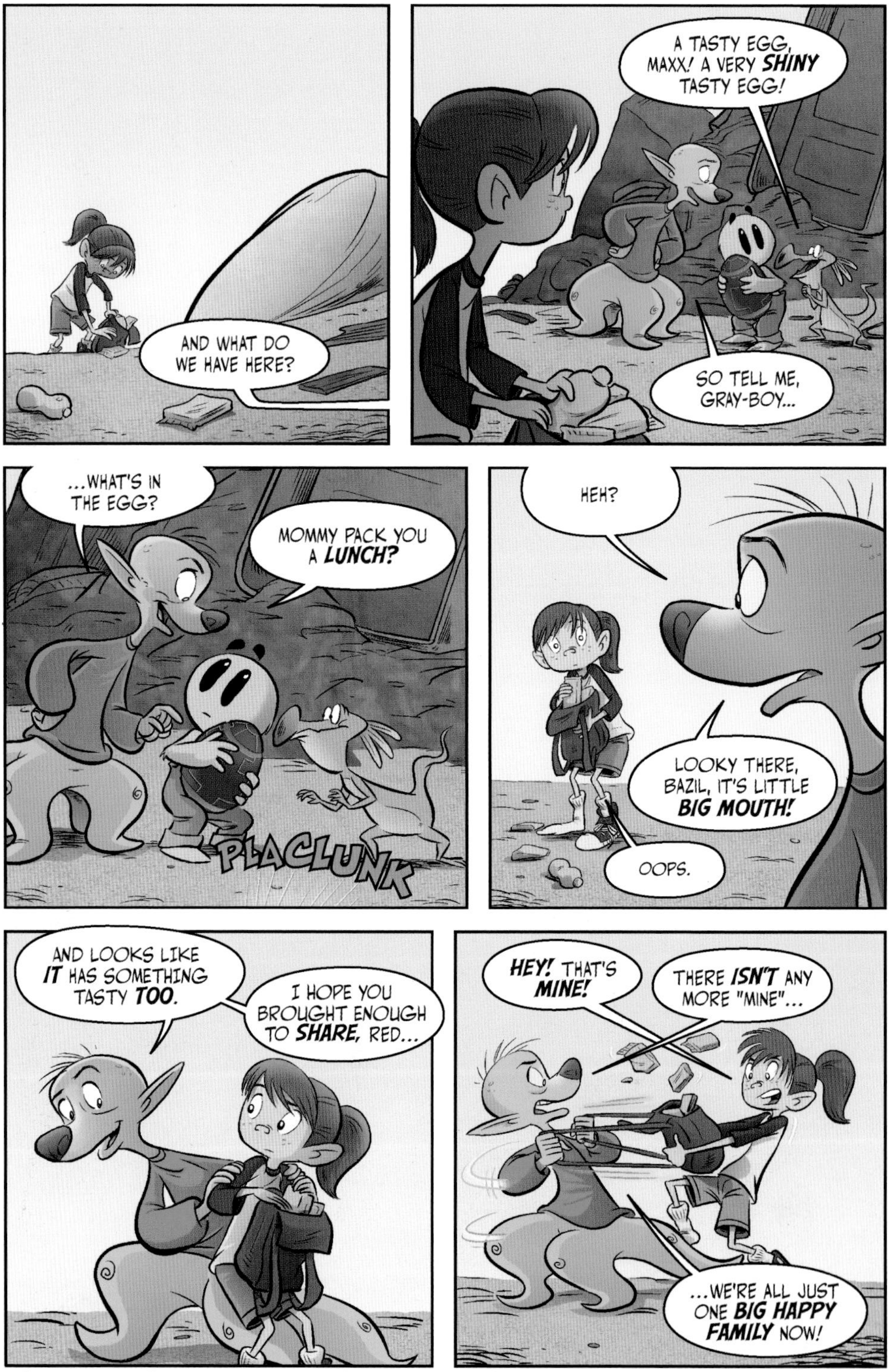
AND WHAT DO WE HAVE HERE?
A TASTY EGG, MAXX! A VERY SHINY TASTY EGG!
SO TELL ME, GRAY-BOY...
...WHAT'S IN THE EGG?
MOMMY PACK YOU A LUNCH?
PLACLUNK
HEH?
LOOKY THERE, BAZIL, IT'S LITTLE BIG MOUTH!
OOPS.
AND LOOKS LIKE IT HAS SOMETHING TASTY TOO.
I HOPE YOU BROUGHT ENOUGH TO SHARE, RED...
HEY! THAT'S MINE!
THERE ISN'T ANY MORE "MINE"...
...WE'RE ALL JUST ONE BIG HAPPY FAMILY NOW!

SNAP

OOMF!

AAAAAHHHHHHHHHHHHHHHHHHHHHHHHHHH!

FHUMP

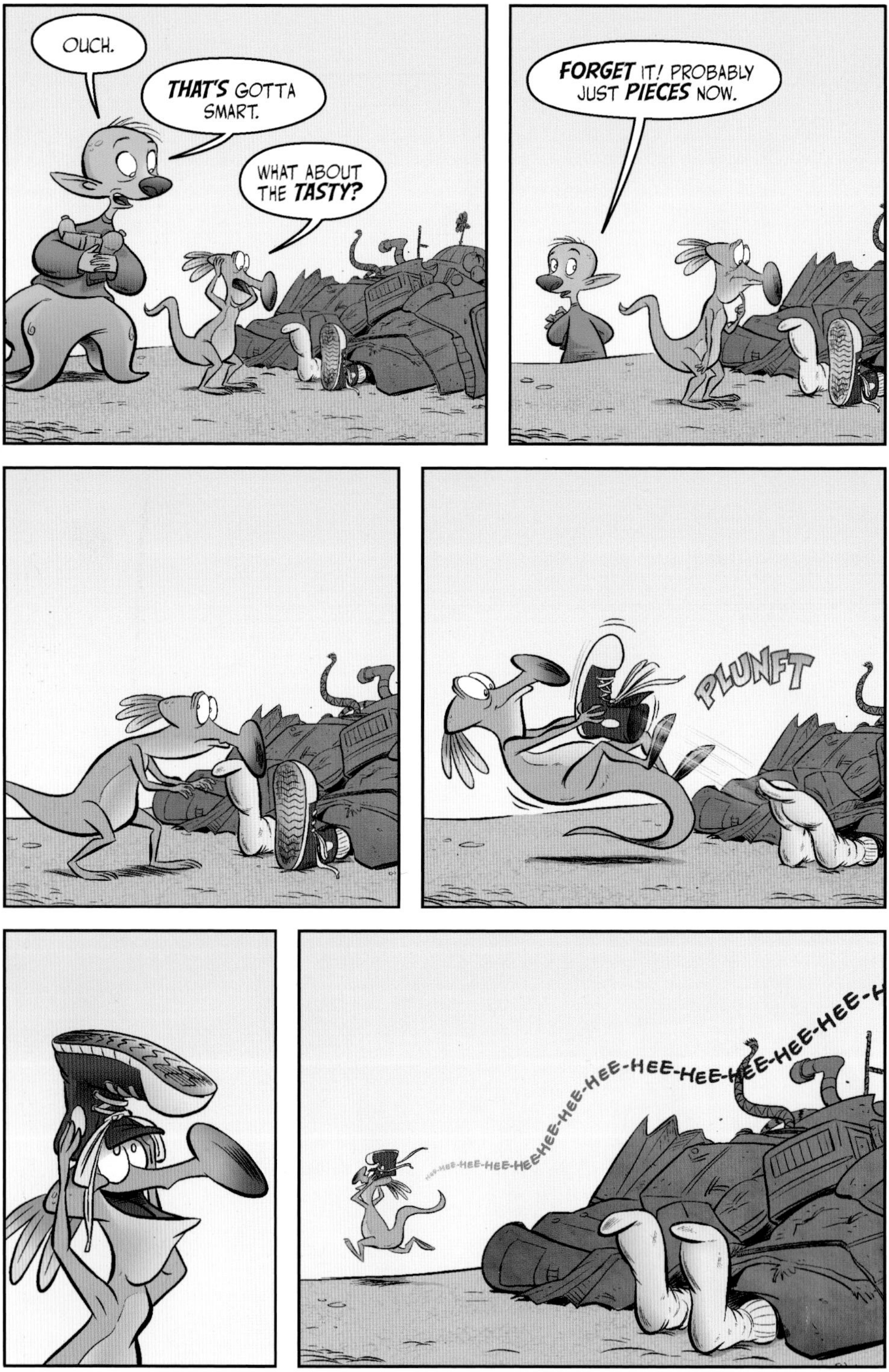
OUCH.
THAT'S GOTTA SMART.
WHAT ABOUT THE TASTY?
FORGET IT! PROBABLY JUST PIECES NOW.
PLUNFT
HEE-HEE-HEE-HEE-HEE-HEE-HEE-HEE-HEE-HEE-HEE-HEE-HEE-HEE-H

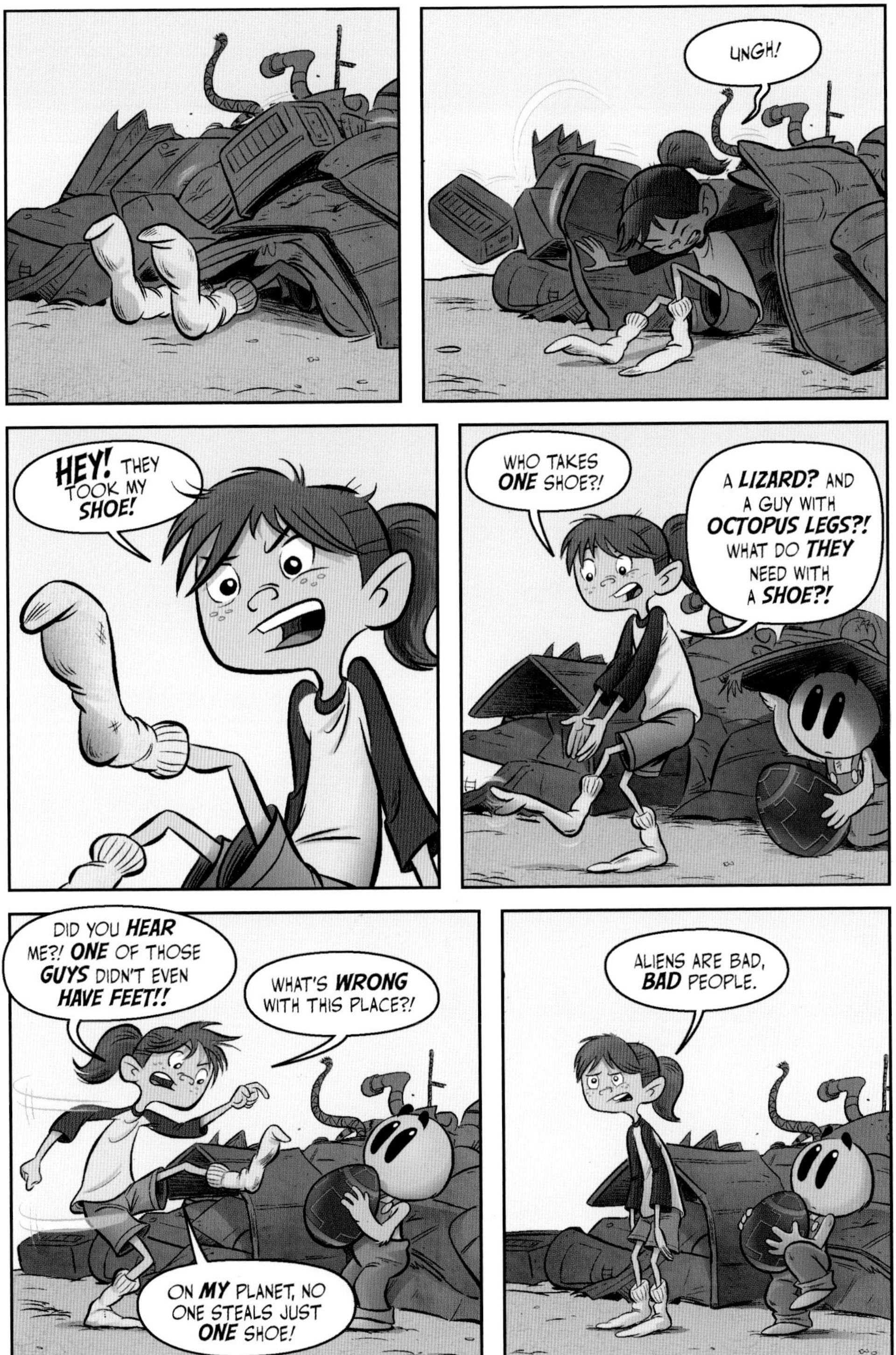
UNGH!
HEY! THEY TOOK MY SHOE!
WHO TAKES ONE SHOE?!
A LIZARD? AND A GUY WITH OCTOPUS LEGS?! WHAT DO THEY NEED WITH A SHOE?!
DID YOU HEAR ME?! ONE OF THOSE GUYS DIDN'T EVEN HAVE FEET!!
WHAT'S WRONG WITH THIS PLACE?!
ON MY PLANET, NO ONE STEALS JUST ONE SHOE!
ALIENS ARE BAD, BAD PEOPLE.

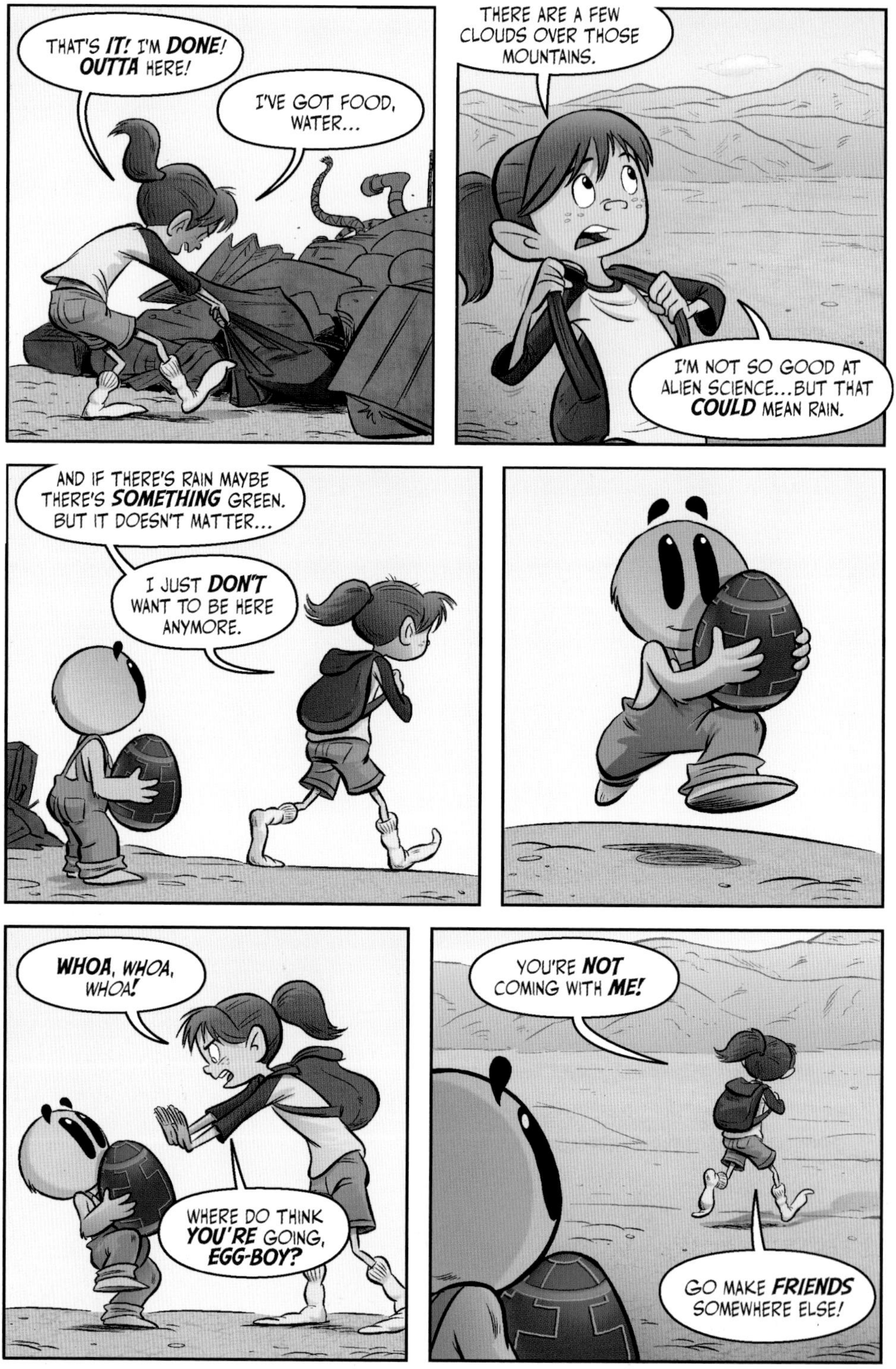
THAT'S IT! I'M DONE! OUTTA HERE!
I'VE GOT FOOD, WATER...
THERE ARE A FEW CLOUDS OVER THOSE MOUNTAINS.
I'M NOT SO GOOD AT ALIEN SCIENCE...BUT THAT COULD MEAN RAIN.
AND IF THERE'S RAIN MAYBE THERE'S SOMETHING GREEN. BUT IT DOESN'T MATTER...
I JUST DON'T WANT TO BE HERE ANYMORE.
WHOA, WHOA, WHOA!
WHERE DO THINK YOU'RE GOING, EGG-BOY?
YOU'RE NOT COMING WITH ME!
GO MAKE FRIENDS SOMEWHERE ELSE!

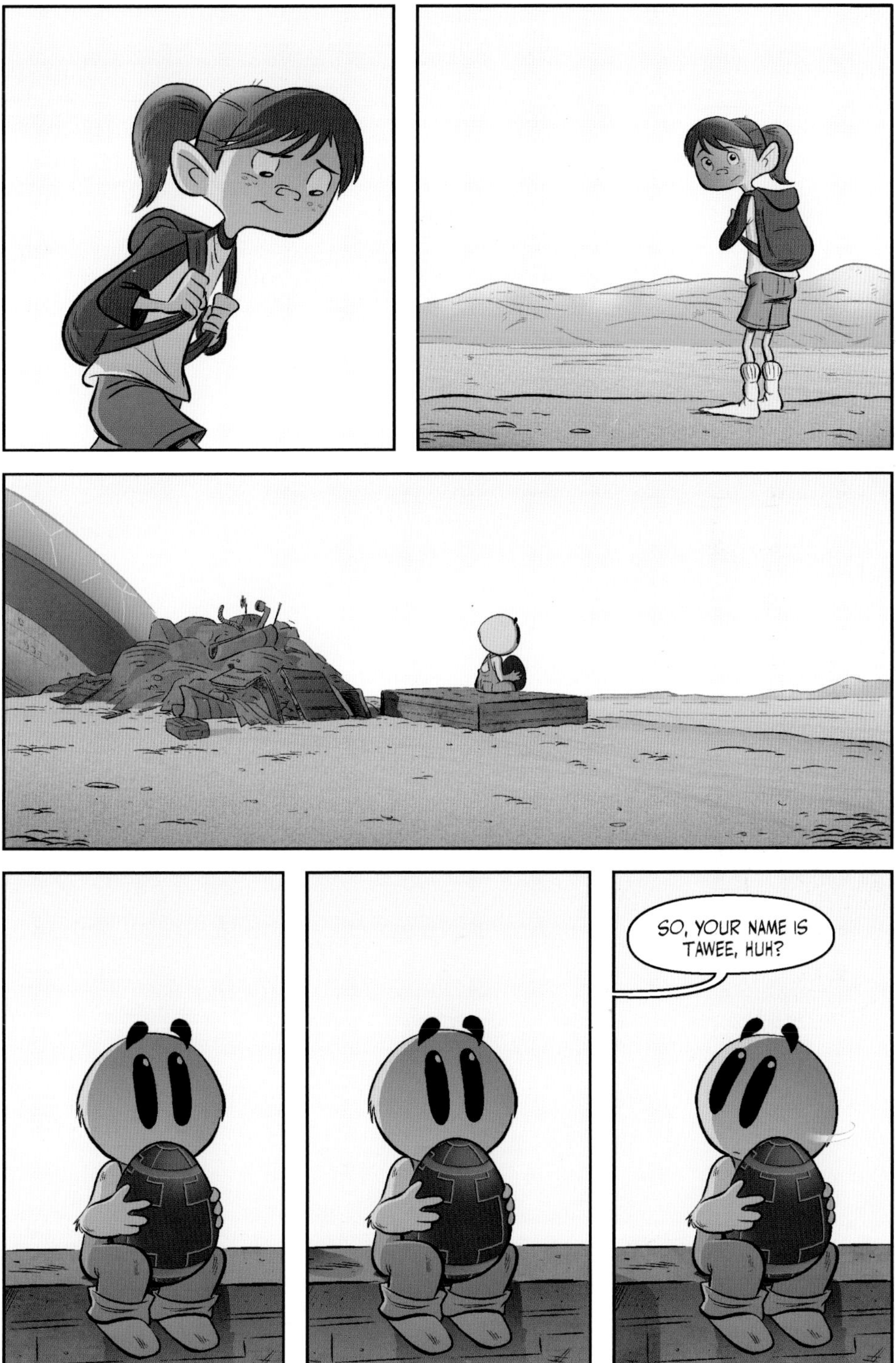
SO, YOUR NAME IS TAWEE, HUH?

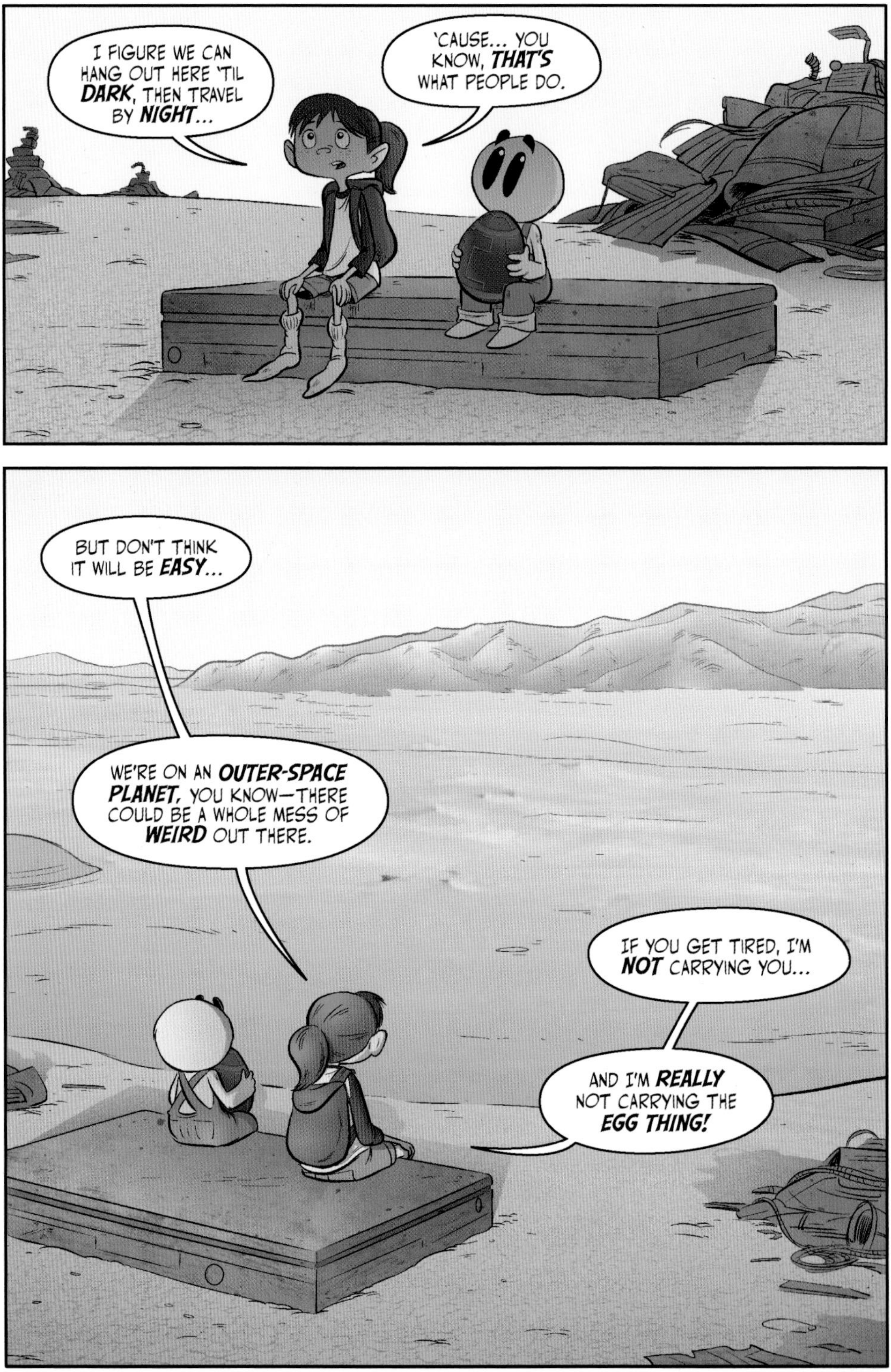
I FIGURE WE CAN HANG OUT HERE 'TIL DARK, THEN TRAVEL BY NIGHT...
'CAUSE... YOU KNOW, THAT'S WHAT PEOPLE DO.
BUT DON'T THINK IT WILL BE EASY...
WE'RE ON AN OUTER-SPACE PLANET, YOU KNOW—THERE COULD BE A WHOLE MESS OF WEIRD OUT THERE.
IF YOU GET TIRED, I'M NOT CARRYING YOU...
AND I'M REALLY NOT CARRYING THE EGG THING!

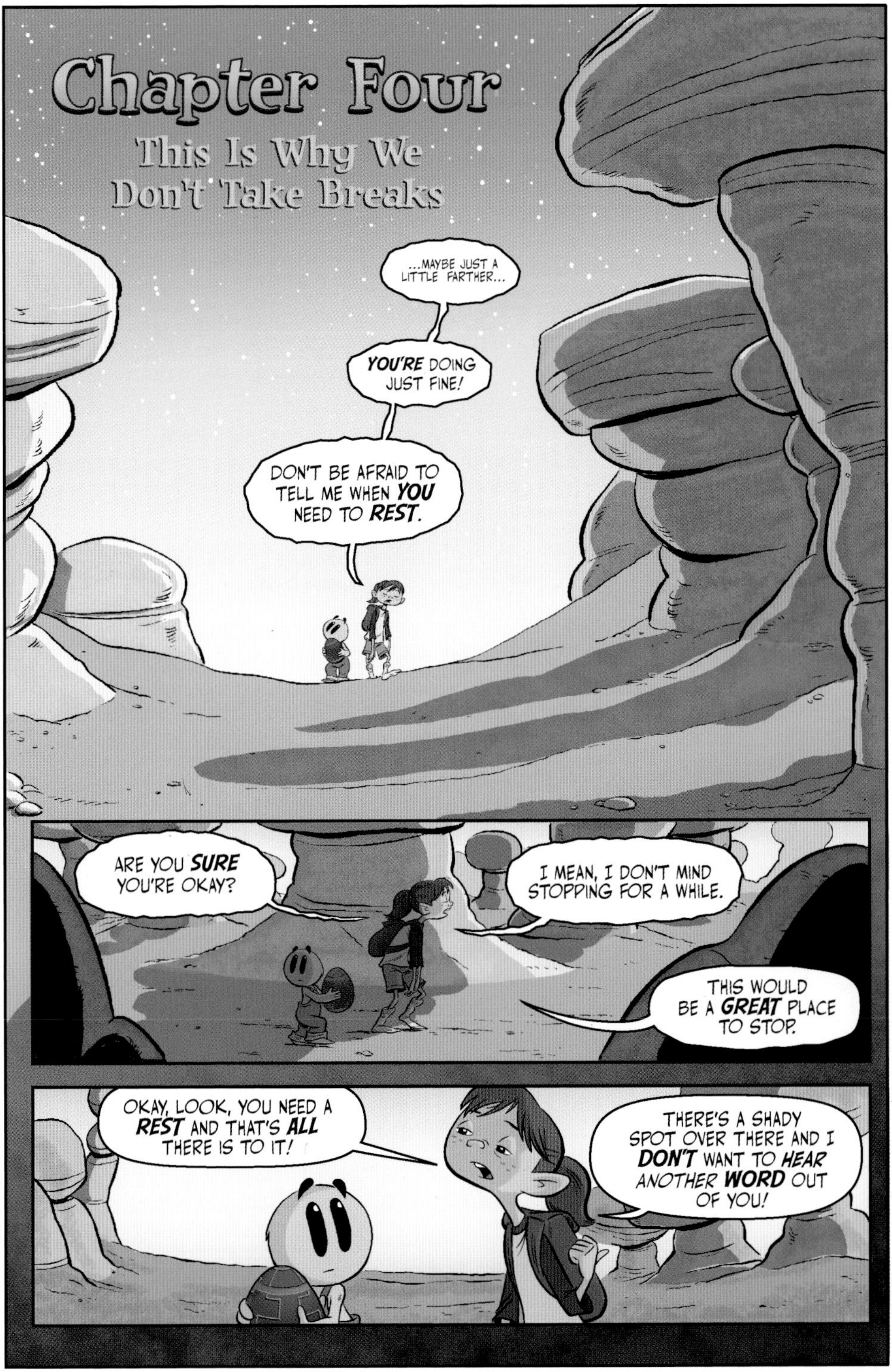
Chapter Four
This Is Why We Don't Take Breaks
...MAYBE JUST A LITTLE FARTHER...
YOU'RE DOING JUST FINE!
DON'T BE AFRAID TO TELL ME WHEN YOU NEED TO REST.
ARE YOU SURE YOU'RE OKAY?
I MEAN, I DON'T MIND STOPPING FOR A WHILE.
THIS WOULD BE A GREAT PLACE TO STOP.
OKAY, LOOK, YOU NEED A REST AND THAT'S ALL THERE IS TO IT!
THERE'S A SHADY SPOT OVER THERE AND I DON'T WANT TO HEAR ANOTHER WORD OUT OF YOU!

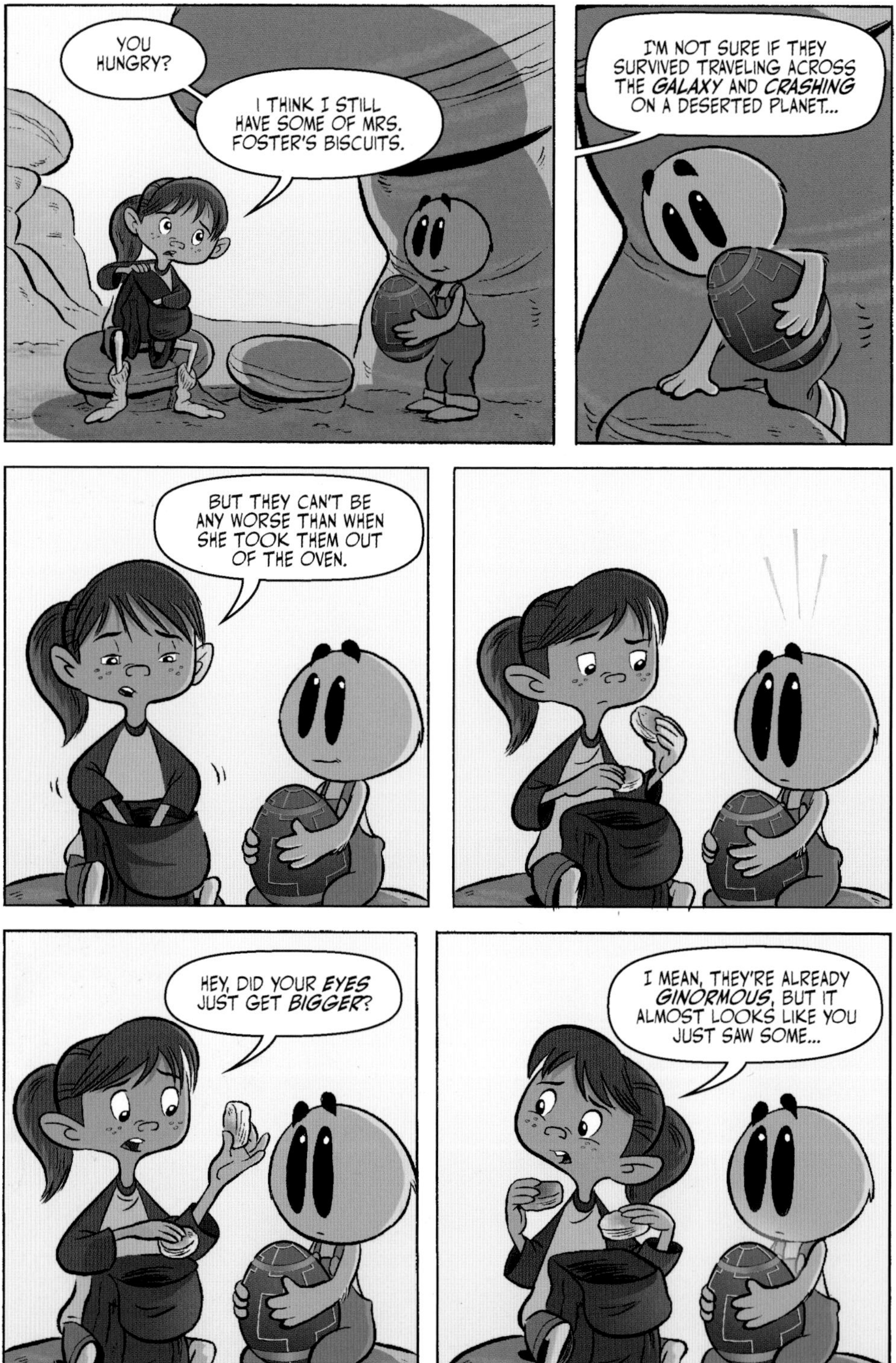
YOU HUNGRY?
I THINK I STILL HAVE SOME OF MRS. FOSTER'S BISCUITS.
I'M NOT SURE IF THEY SURVIVED TRAVELING ACROSS THE *GALAXY* AND *CRASHING* ON A DESERTED PLANET...
BUT THEY CAN'T BE ANY WORSE THAN WHEN SHE TOOK THEM OUT OF THE OVEN.
HEY, DID YOUR *EYES* JUST GET *BIGGER*?
I MEAN, THEY'RE ALREADY *GINORMOUS*, BUT IT ALMOST LOOKS LIKE YOU JUST SAW SOME...

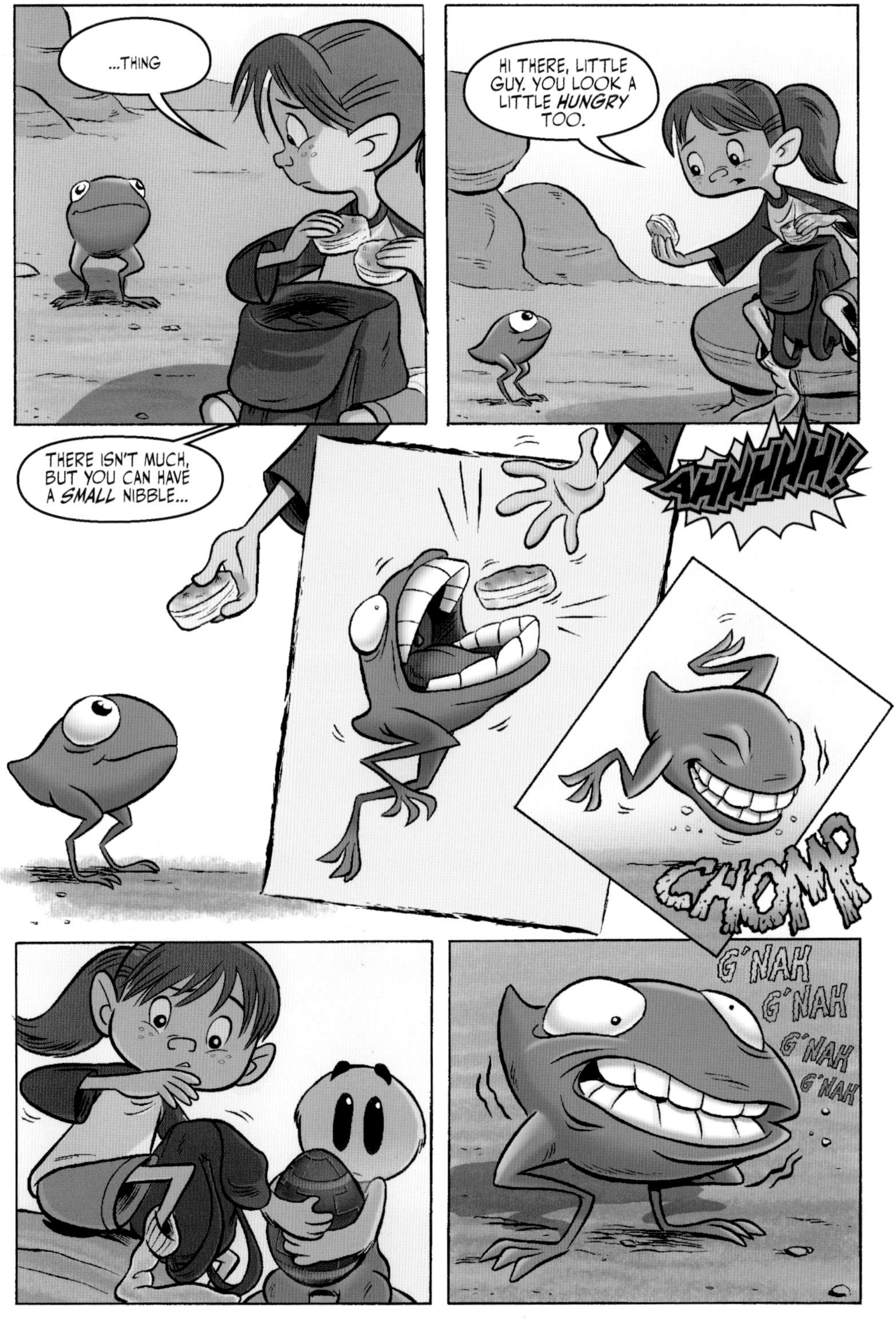
...THING
HI THERE, LITTLE GUY. YOU LOOK A LITTLE *HUNGRY* TOO.
THERE ISN'T MUCH, BUT YOU CAN HAVE A *SMALL* NIBBLE...
AHHHHHH!
CHOMP
G'NAH
G'NAH
G'NAH
G'NAH

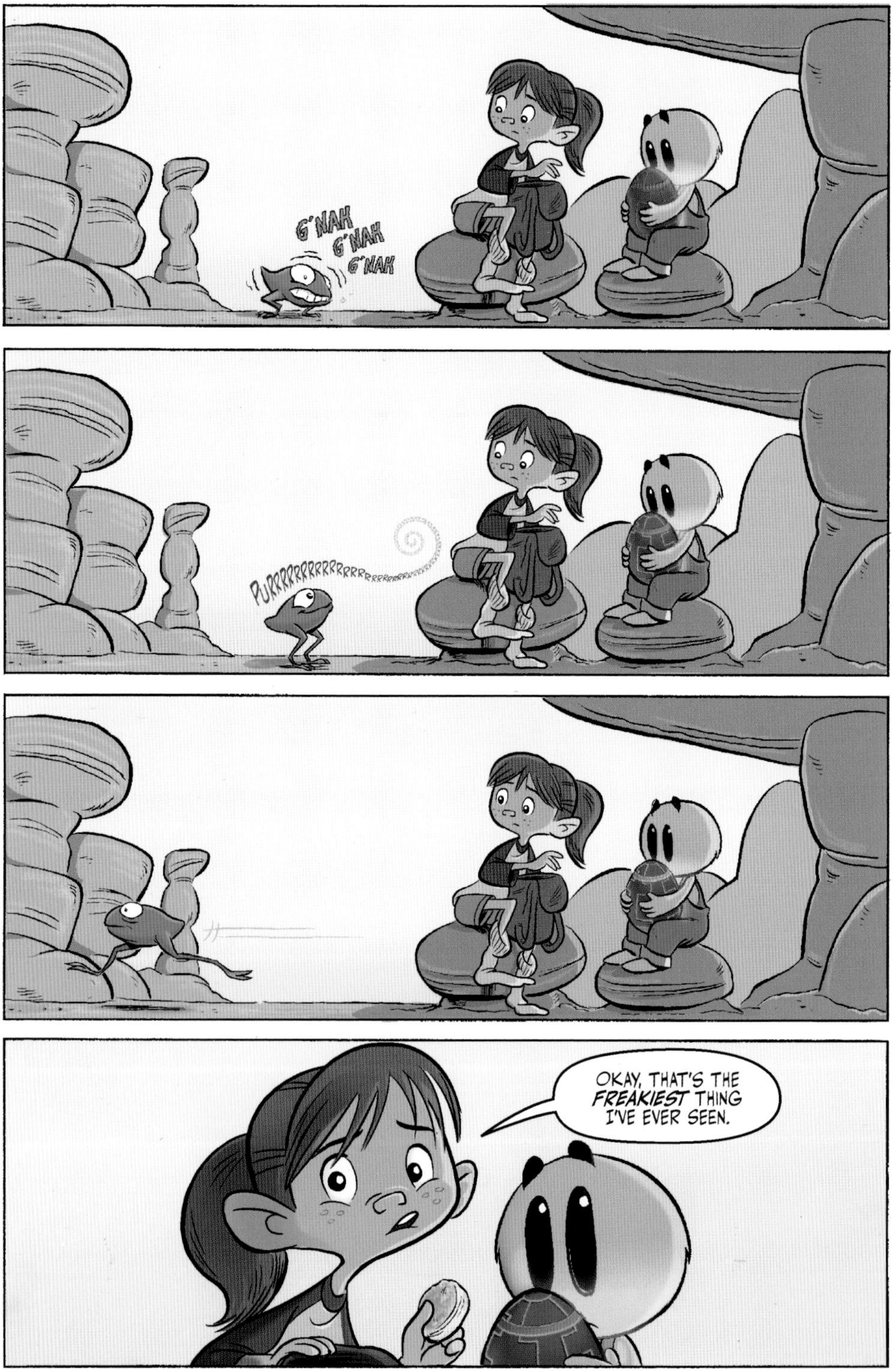
G'NAH
G'NAH
G'NAH
PURRRRRRRRRRRRRRRRRRRRRRRR
OKAY, THAT'S THE *FREAKIEST* THING I'VE EVER SEEN.

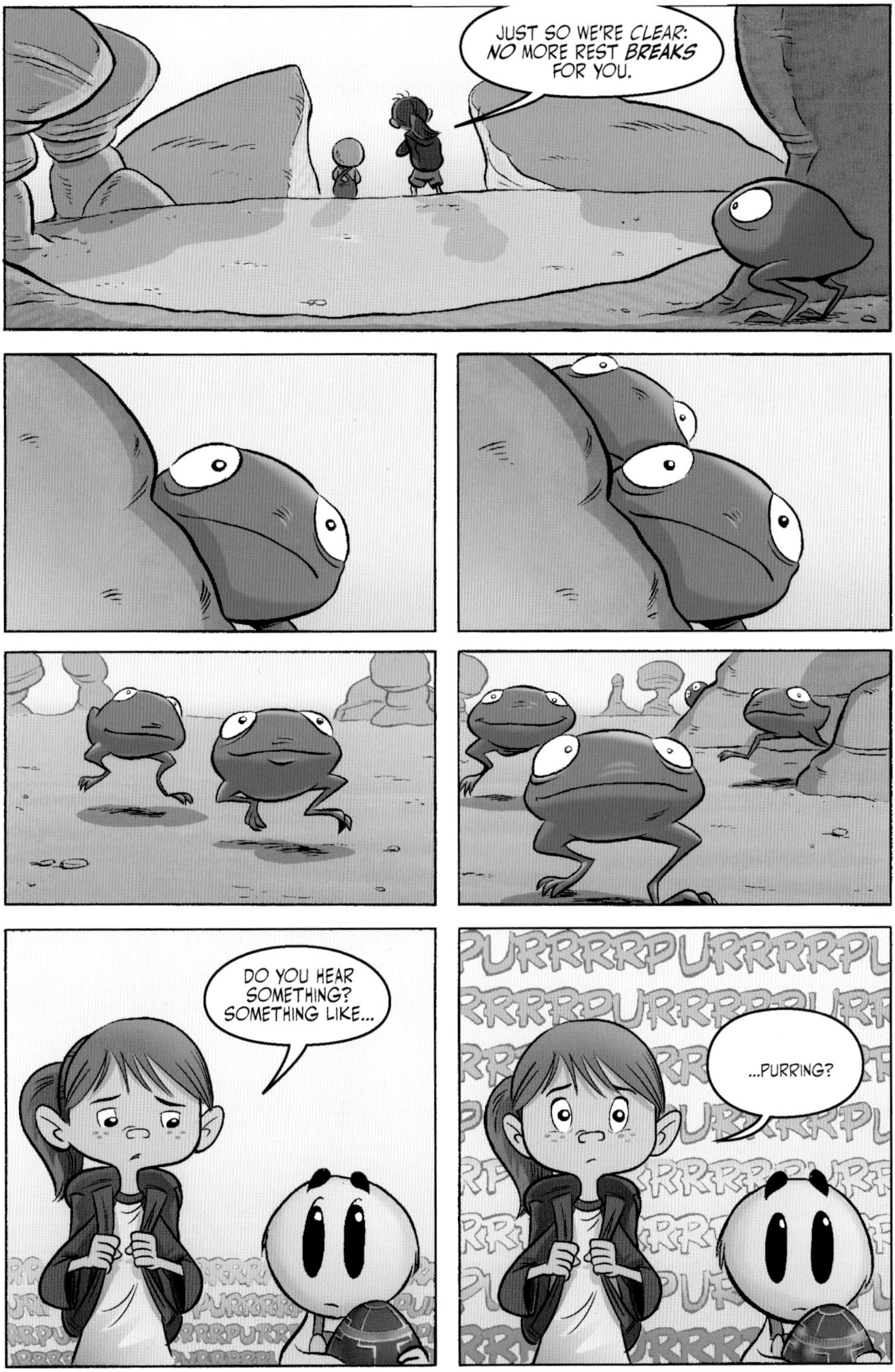
JUST SO WE'RE CLEAR: NO MORE REST BREAKS FOR YOU.
DO YOU HEAR SOMETHING? SOMETHING LIKE...
...PURRING?
PURRRRP

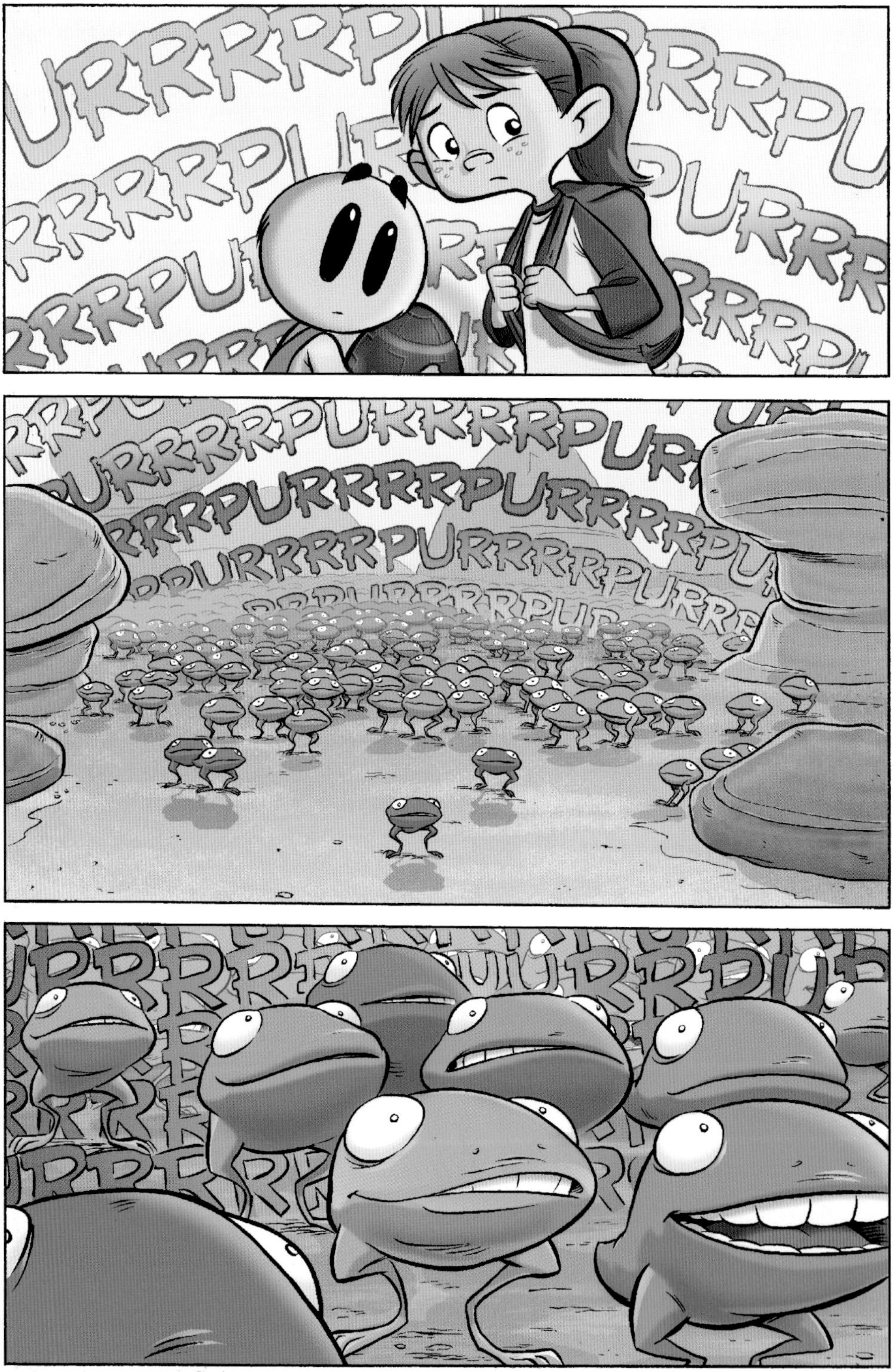
URRRRPURRRRPU
RRRRPURRRRPURRRR
PURRRRRPURRRRRPUR
RRRPURRRRRPURRRRRPU
PURRRRRPURRRRRPURR

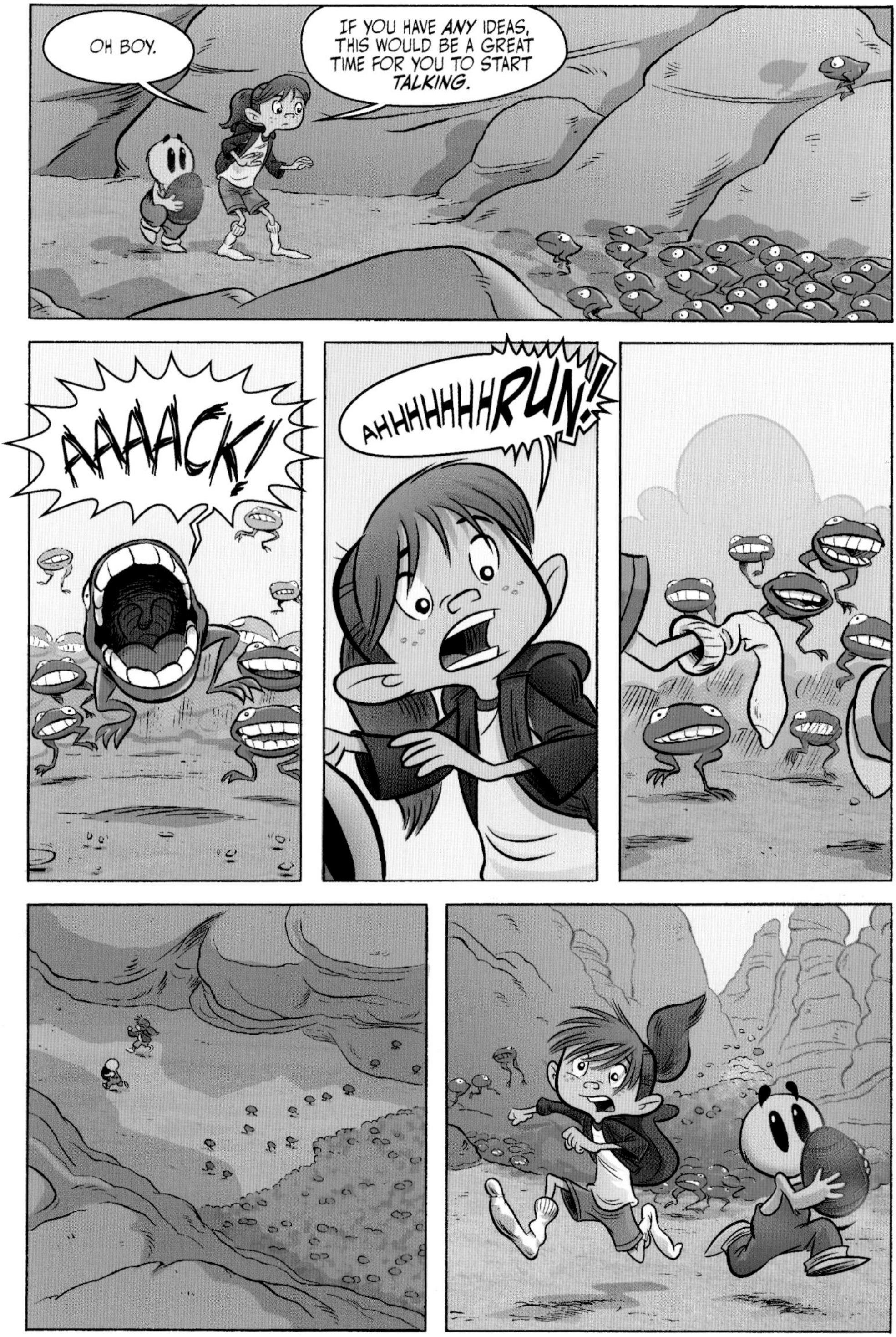
OH BOY.
IF YOU HAVE ANY IDEAS, THIS WOULD BE A GREAT TIME FOR YOU TO START TALKING.
AAAACK!
AHHHHHHHRUN!

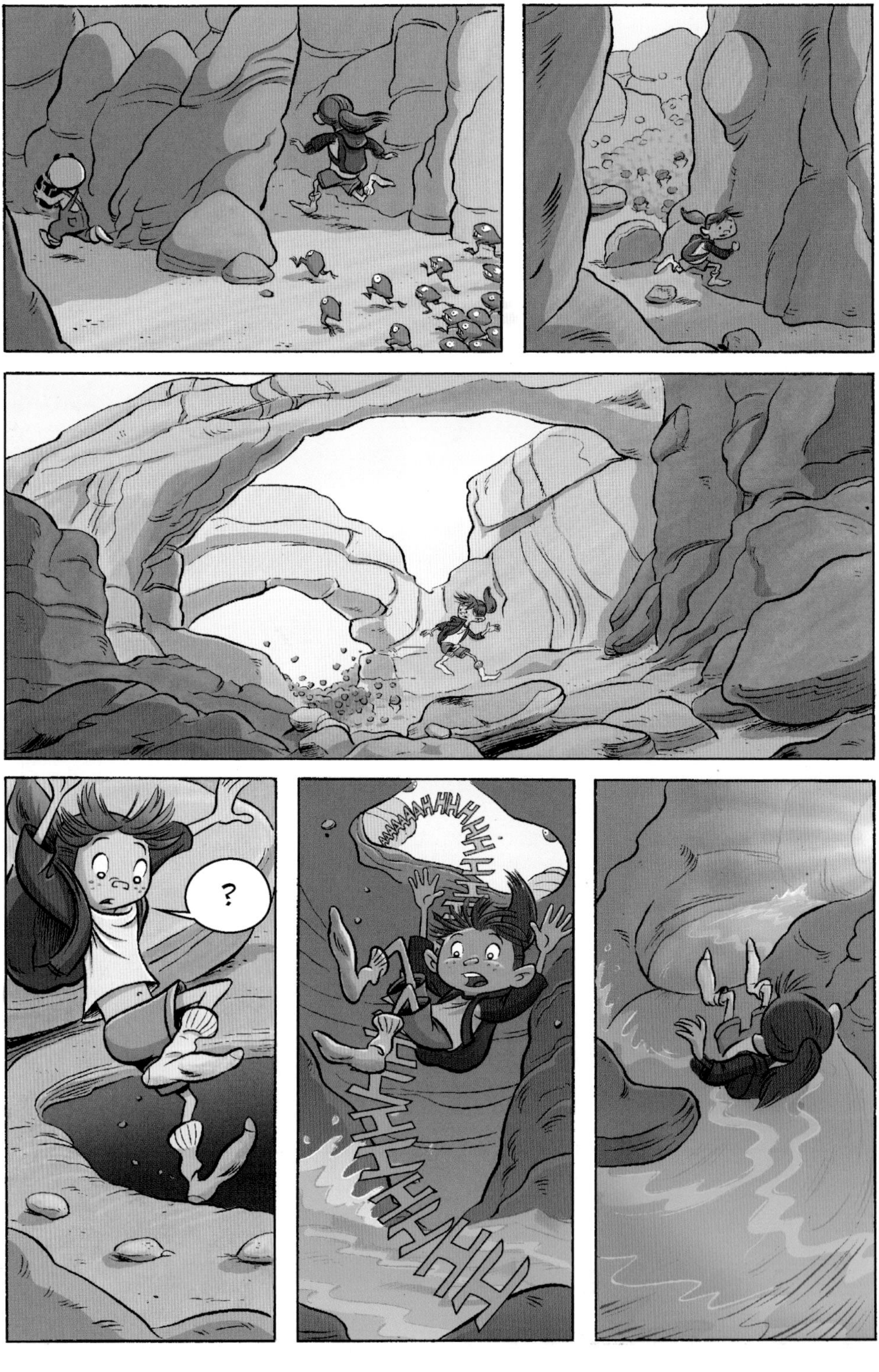
?
AAAAAAAAHHHHHHHHHHHHHHHHHHH

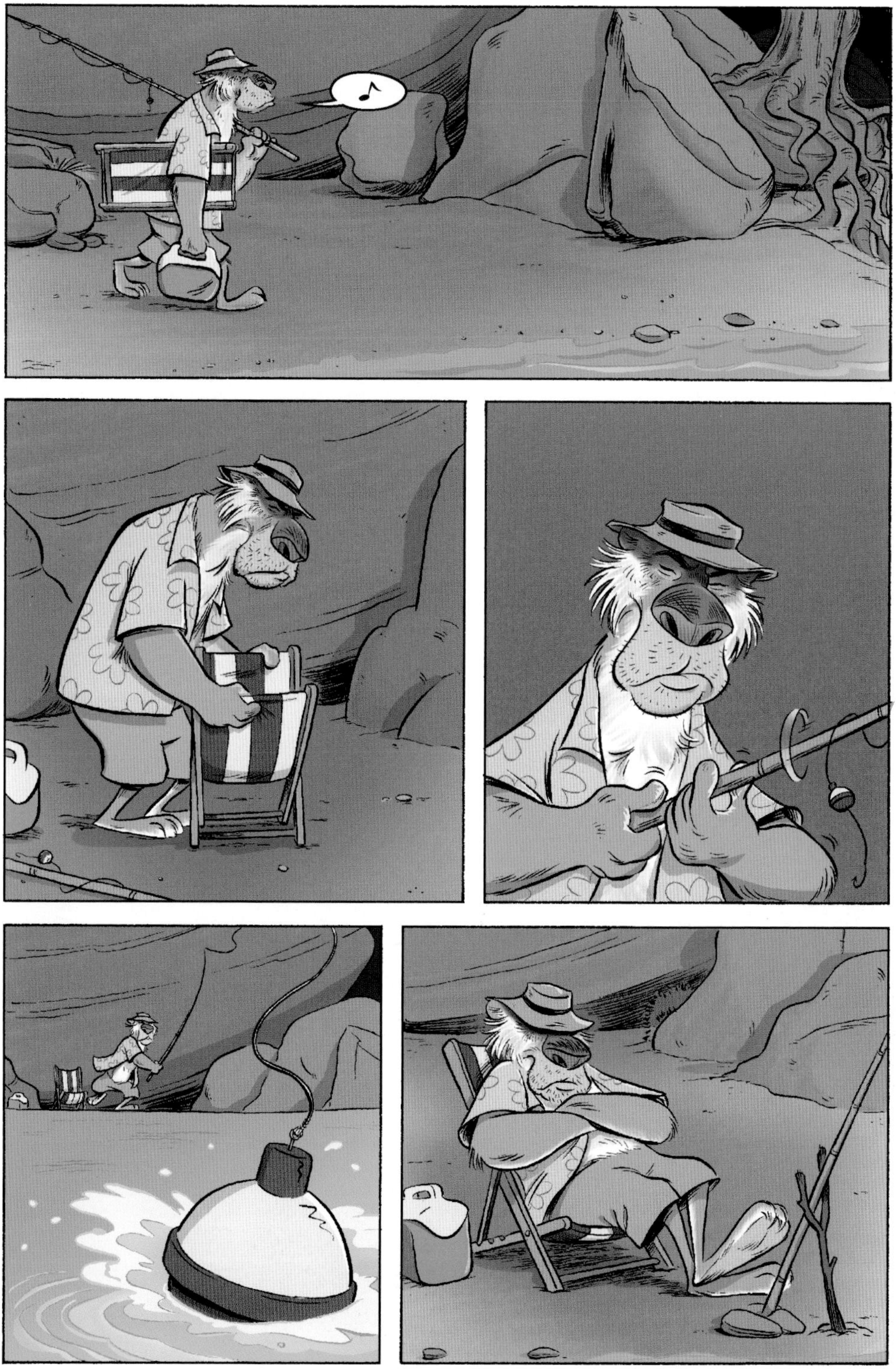

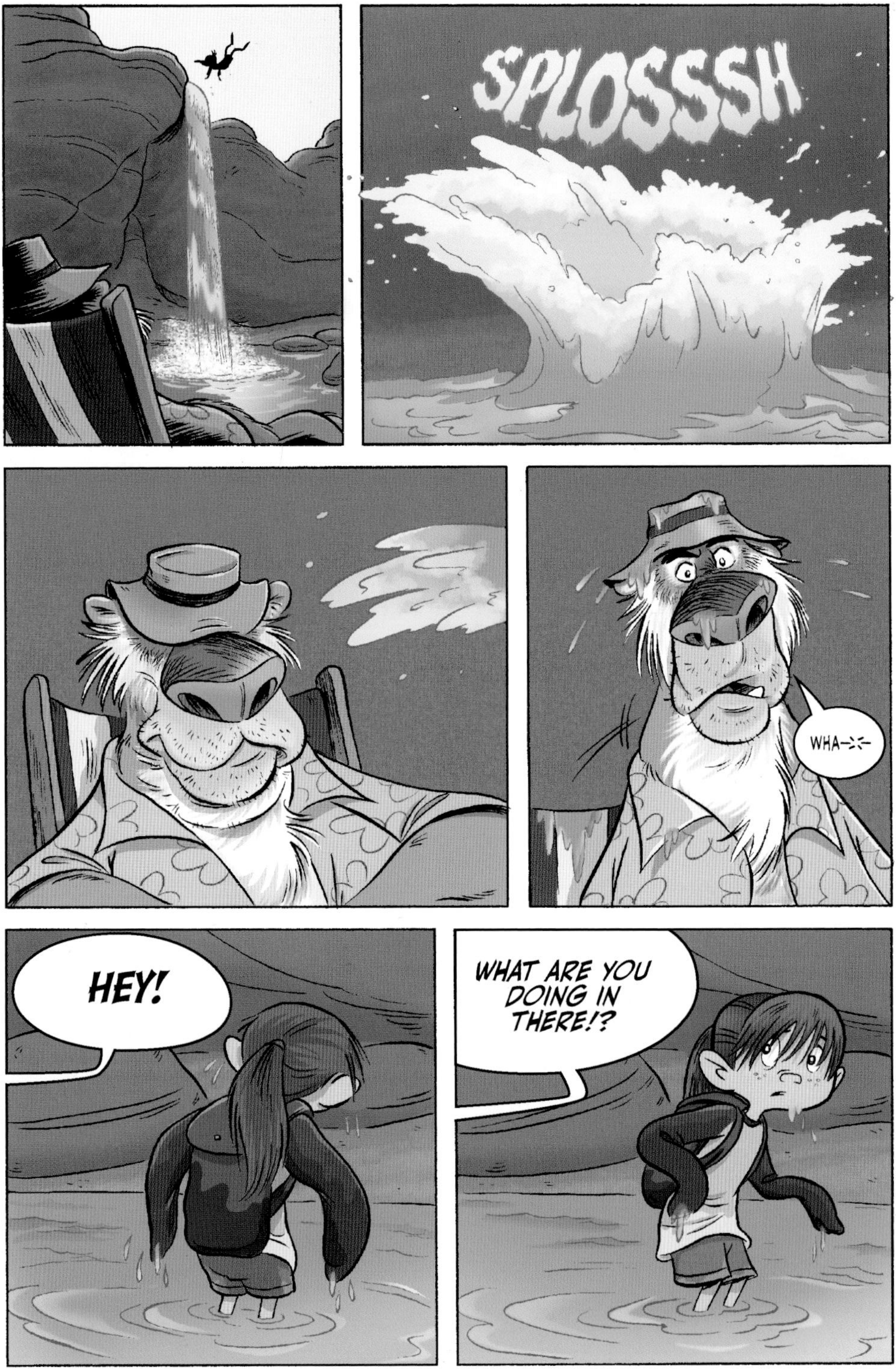
SPLOSSSH
WHA--!--
HEY!
WHAT ARE YOU DOING IN THERE!?

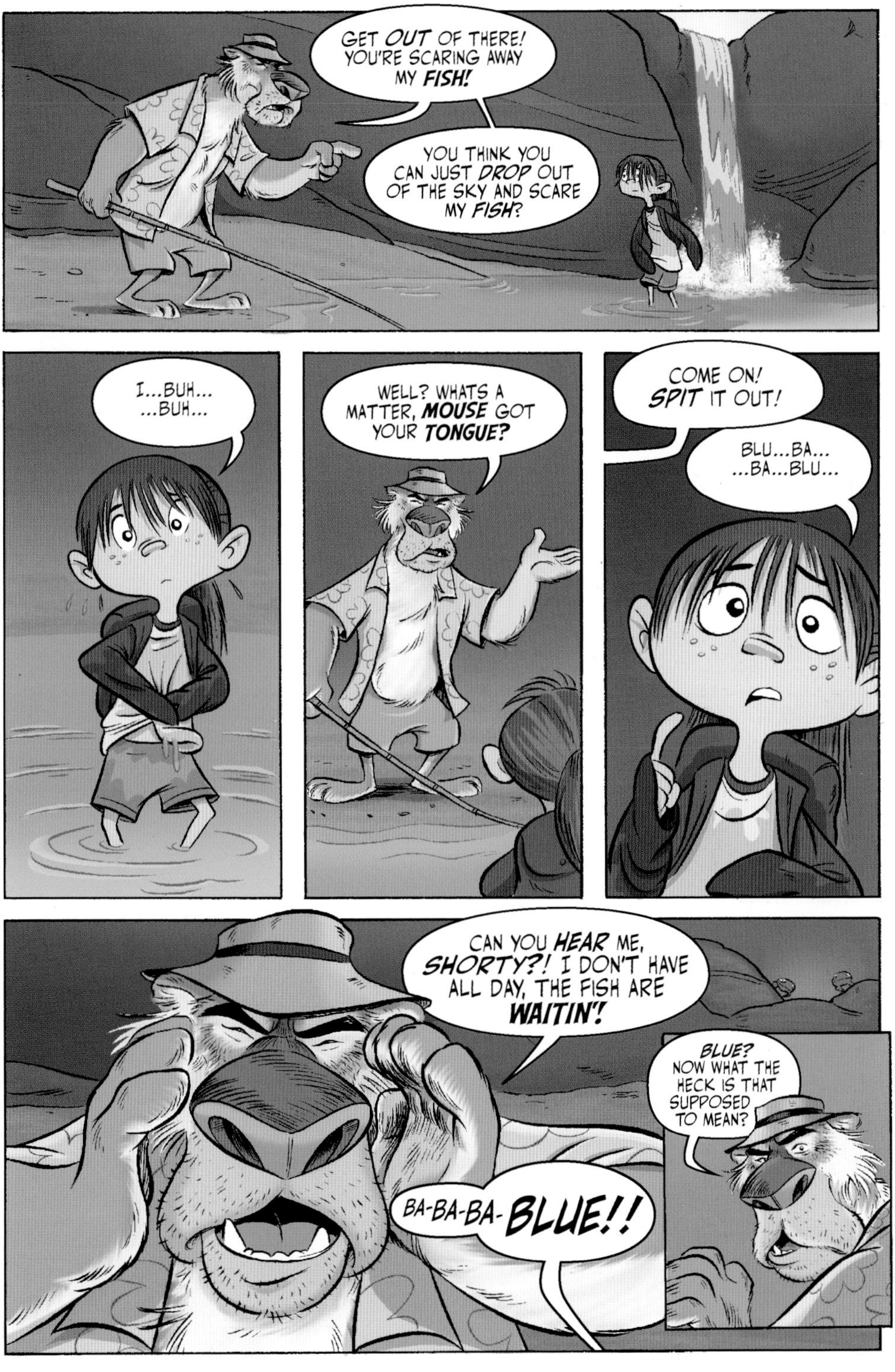
GET OUT OF THERE! YOU'RE SCARING AWAY MY FISH!
YOU THINK YOU CAN JUST DROP OUT OF THE SKY AND SCARE MY FISH?
I...BUH... ...BUH...
WELL? WHATS A MATTER, MOUSE GOT YOUR TONGUE?
COME ON! SPIT IT OUT!
BLU...BA... ...BA...BLU...
CAN YOU HEAR ME, SHORTY?! I DON'T HAVE ALL DAY, THE FISH ARE WAITIN'!
BA-BA-BA-BLUE!!
BLUE? NOW WHAT THE HECK IS THAT SUPPOSED TO MEAN?

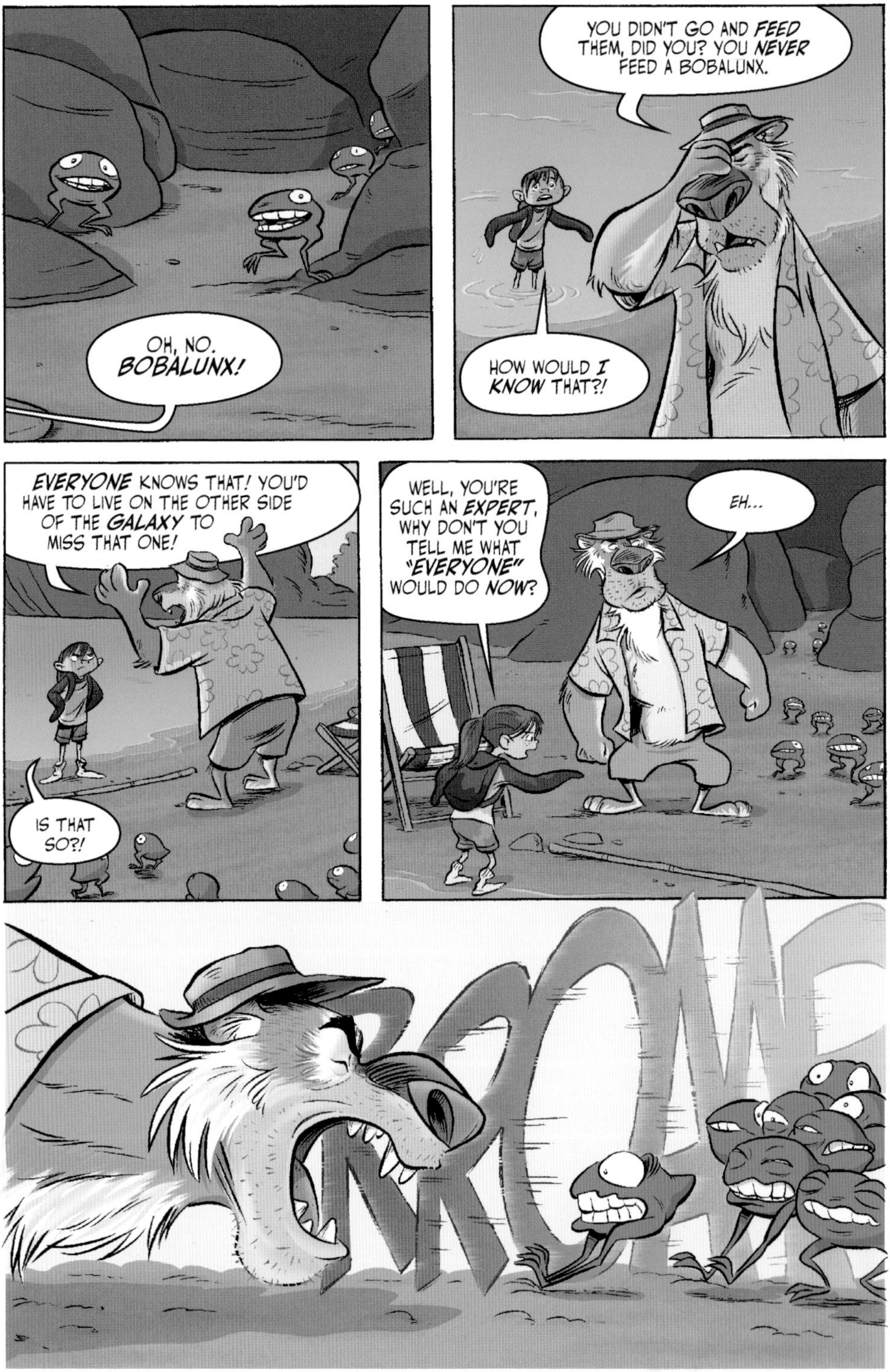
OH, NO. BOBALUNX!
YOU DIDN'T GO AND FEED THEM, DID YOU? YOU NEVER FEED A BOBALUNX.
HOW WOULD I KNOW THAT?!
EVERYONE KNOWS THAT! YOU'D HAVE TO LIVE ON THE OTHER SIDE OF THE GALAXY TO MISS THAT ONE!
IS THAT SO?!
WELL, YOU'RE SUCH AN EXPERT, WHY DON'T YOU TELL ME WHAT "EVERYONE" WOULD DO NOW?
EH...

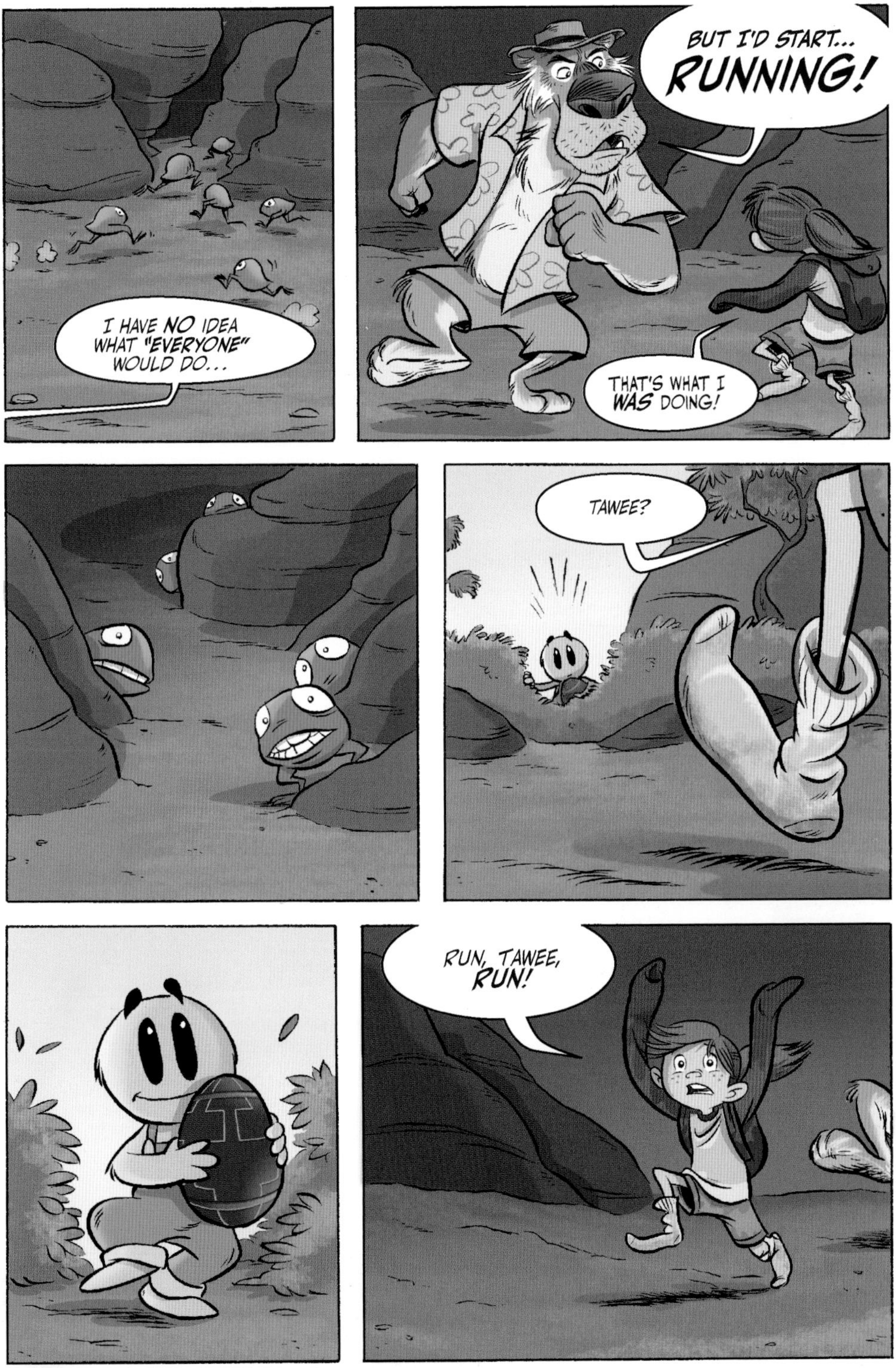
I HAVE NO IDEA WHAT "EVERYONE" WOULD DO...
BUT I'D START... RUNNING!
THAT'S WHAT I WAS DOING!
TAWEE?
RUN, TAWEE, RUN!

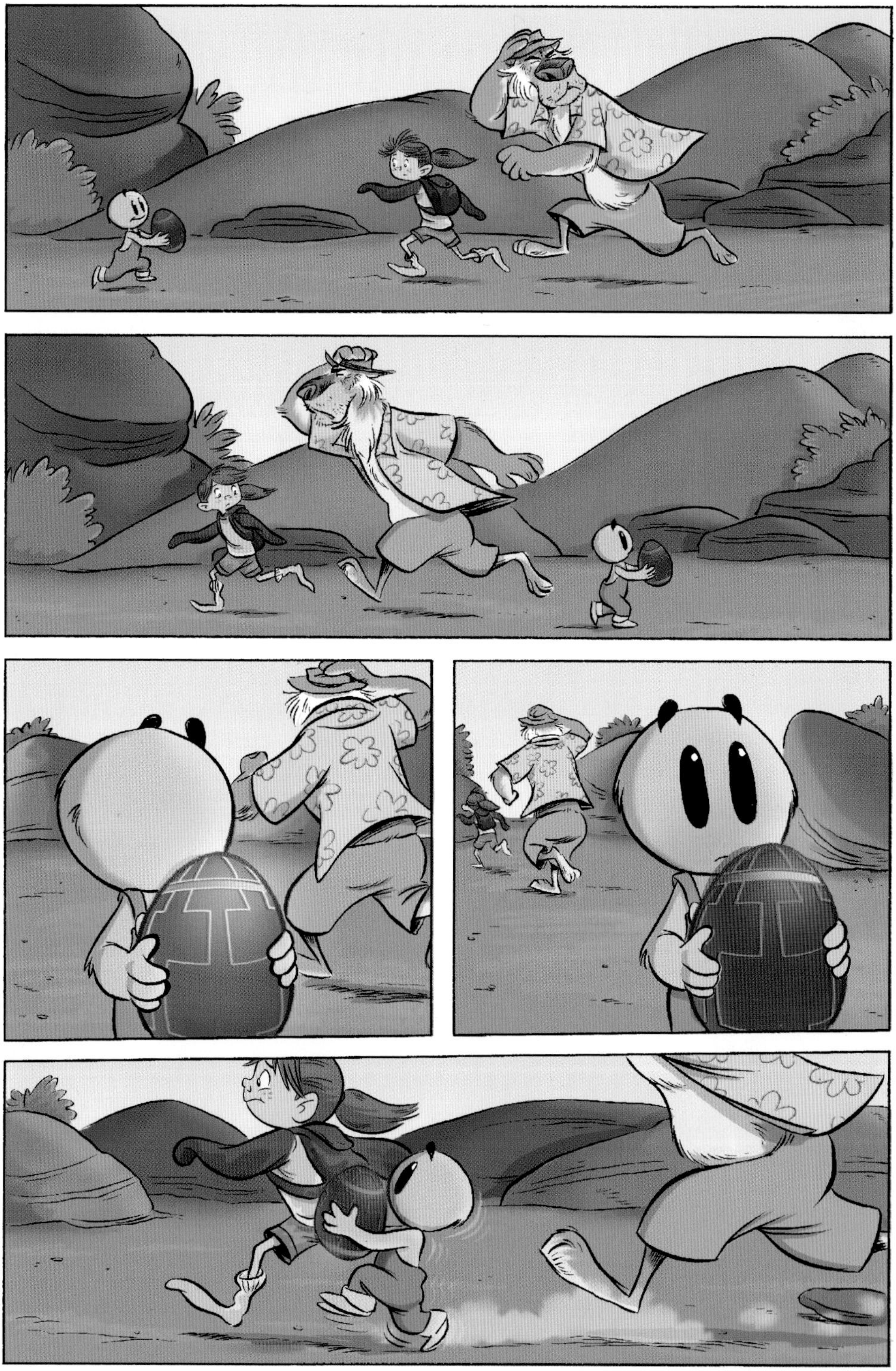

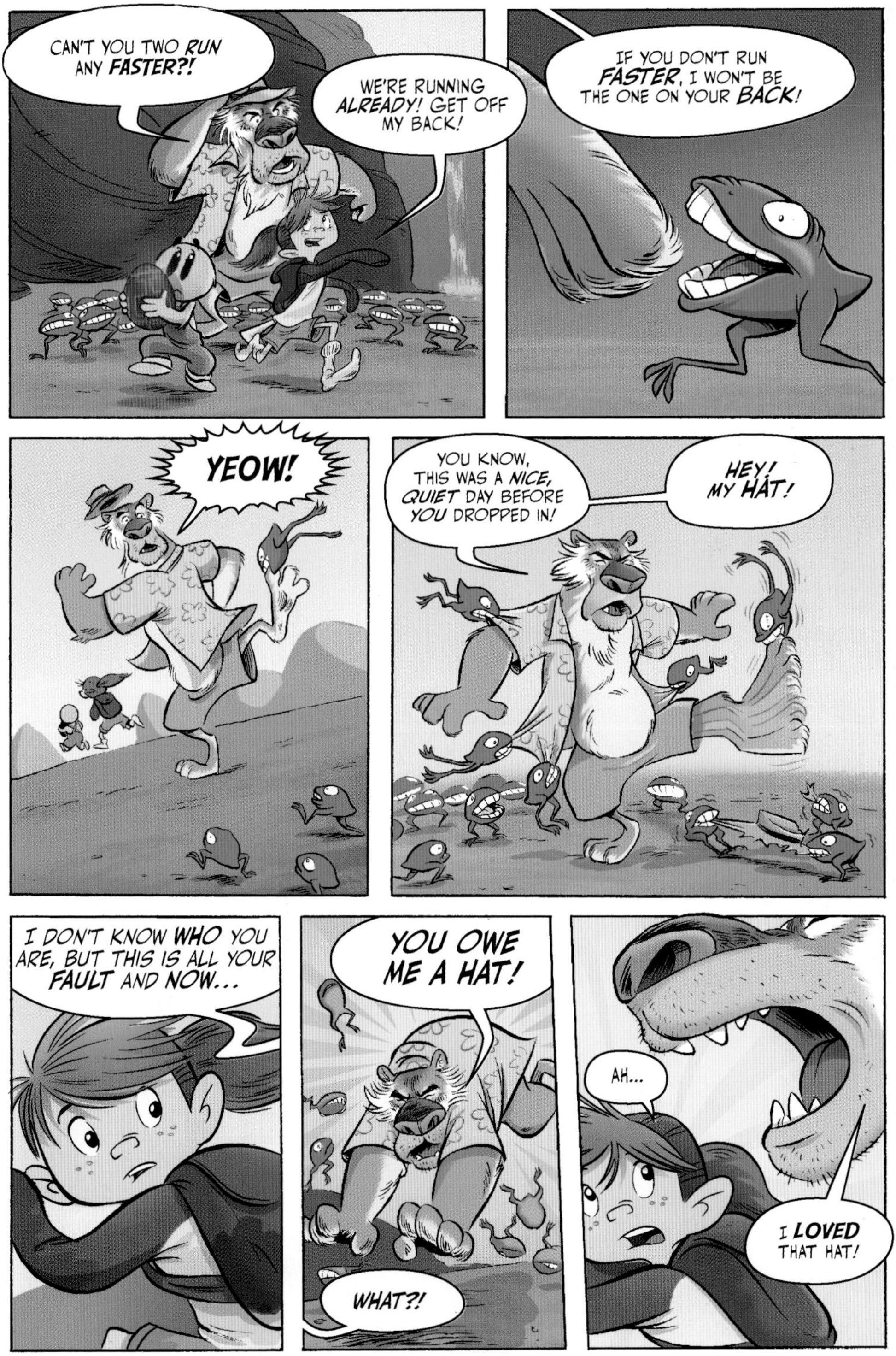
CAN'T YOU TWO RUN ANY FASTER?!
WE'RE RUNNING ALREADY! GET OFF MY BACK!
IF YOU DON'T RUN FASTER, I WON'T BE THE ONE ON YOUR BACK!
YEOW!
YOU KNOW, THIS WAS A NICE, QUIET DAY BEFORE YOU DROPPED IN!
HEY! MY HAT!
I DON'T KNOW WHO YOU ARE, BUT THIS IS ALL YOUR FAULT AND NOW...
YOU OWE ME A HAT!
WHAT?!
AH...
I LOVED THAT HAT!

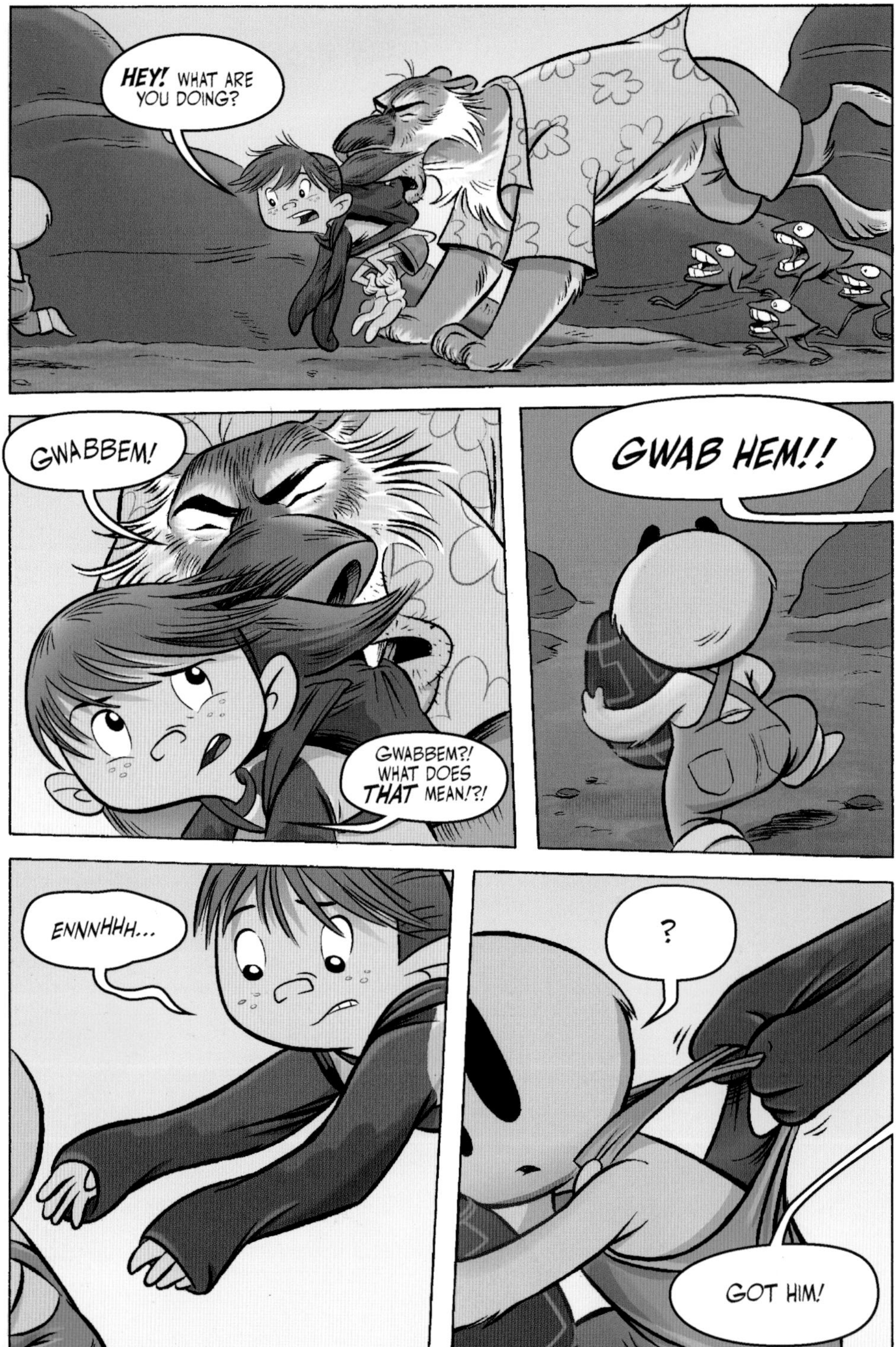
HEY! WHAT ARE YOU DOING?
GWABBEM!
GWABBEM?! WHAT DOES THAT MEAN!?!
GWAB HEM!!
ENNNHHH...
?
GOT HIM!

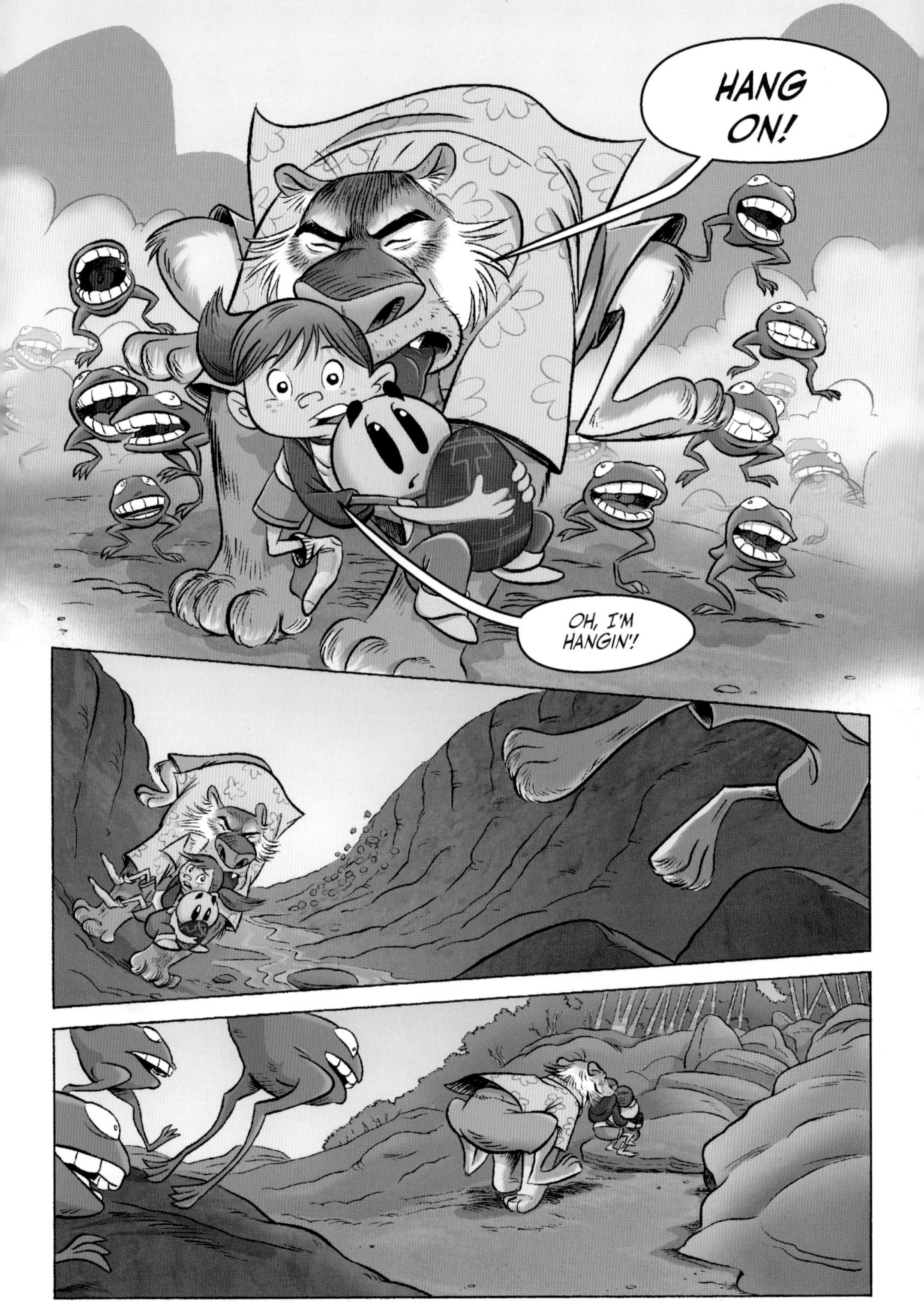
HANG ON!
OH, I'M HANGIN'!

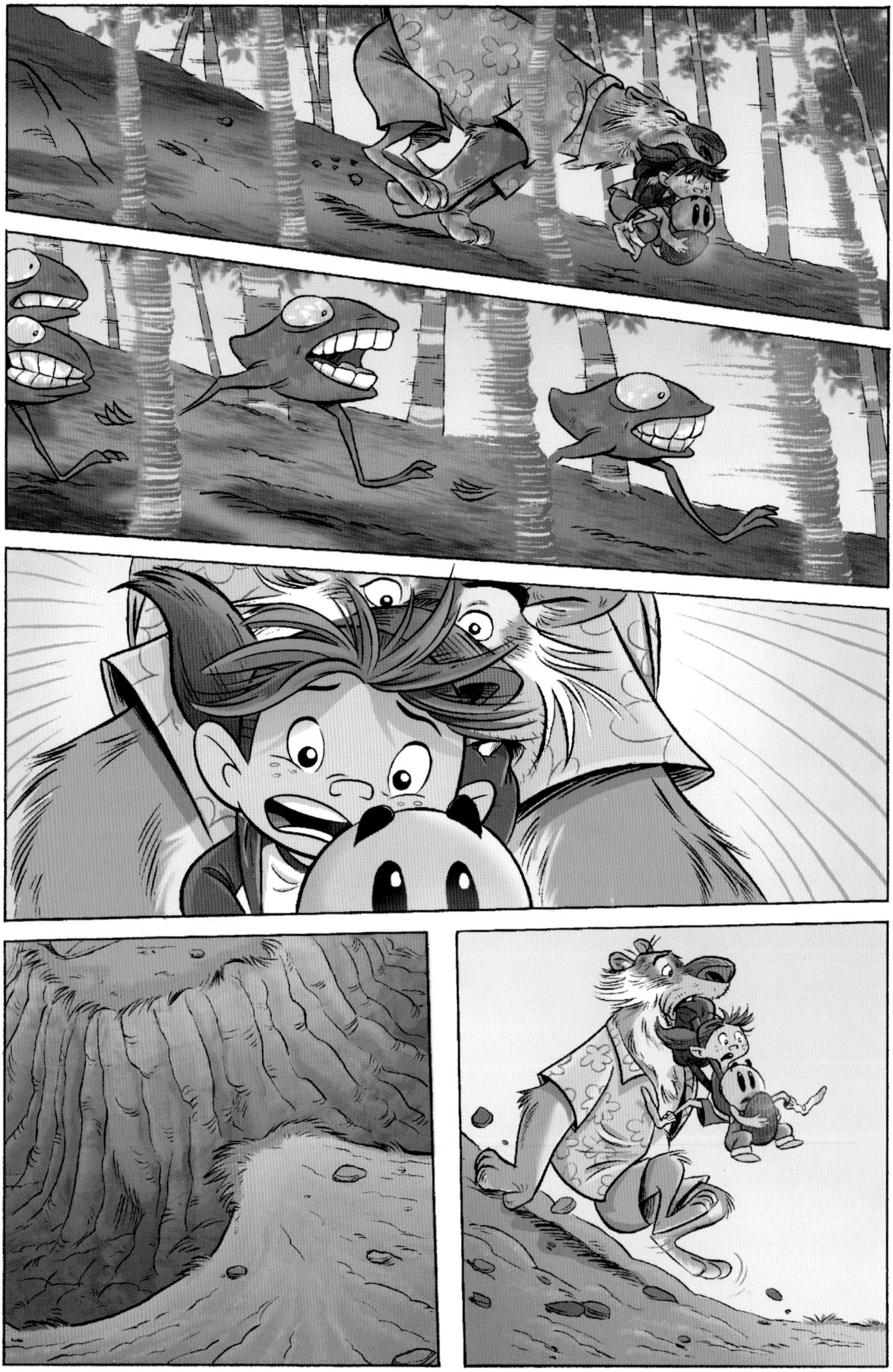

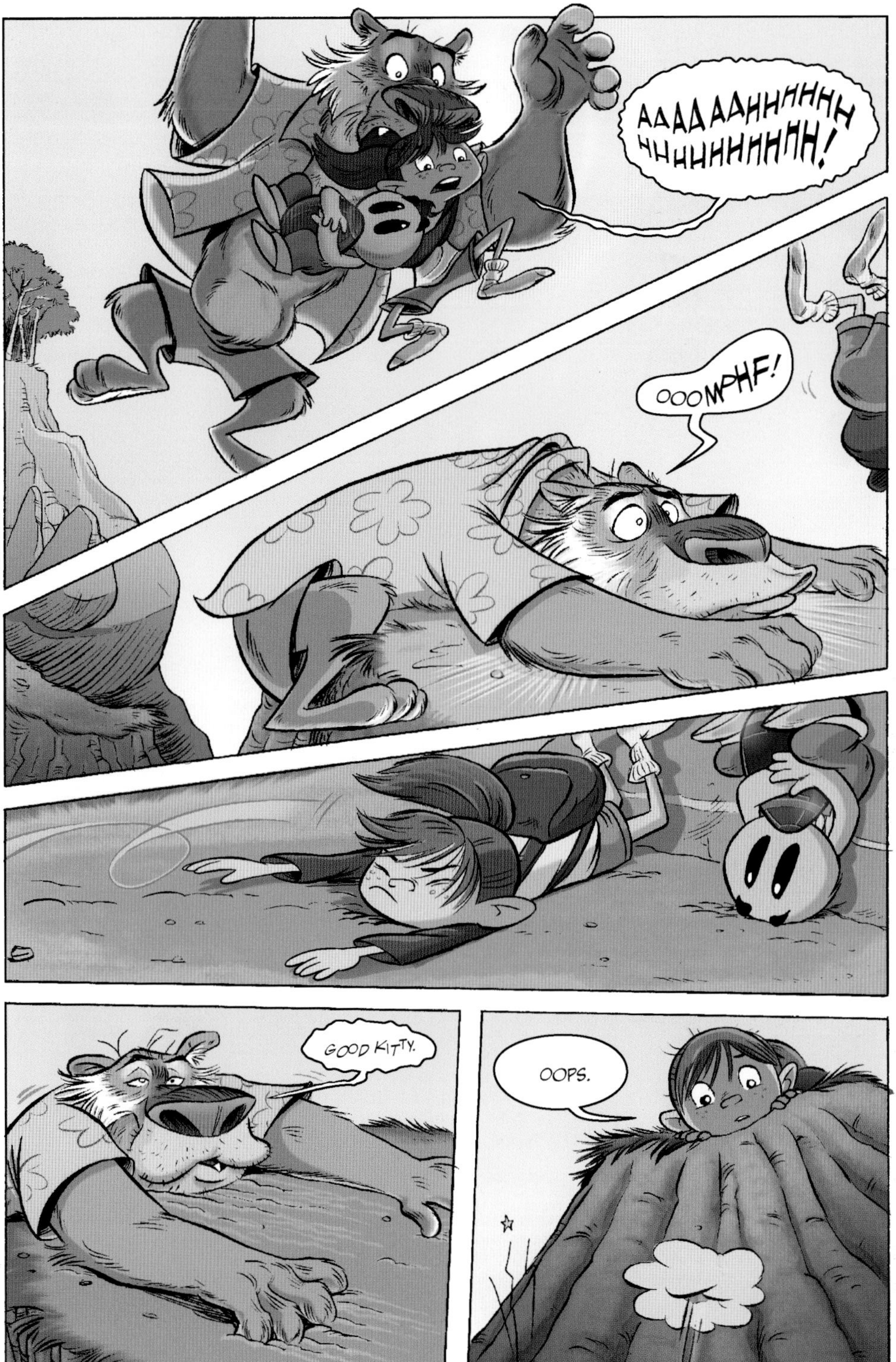
AAAAAAHHHHHHHHHHHHHHHH!
OOOMPHF!
GOOD KITTY.
OOPS.

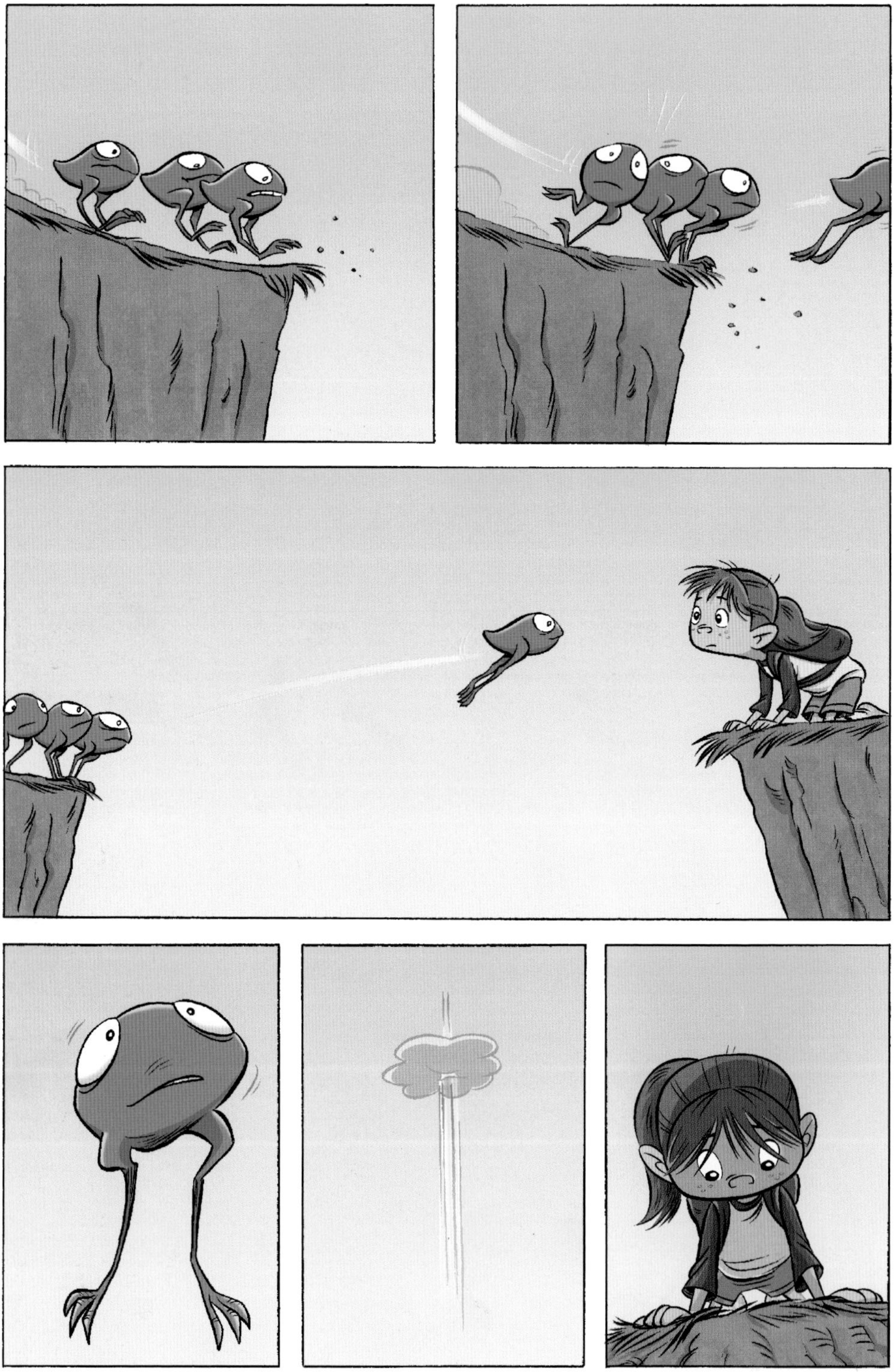

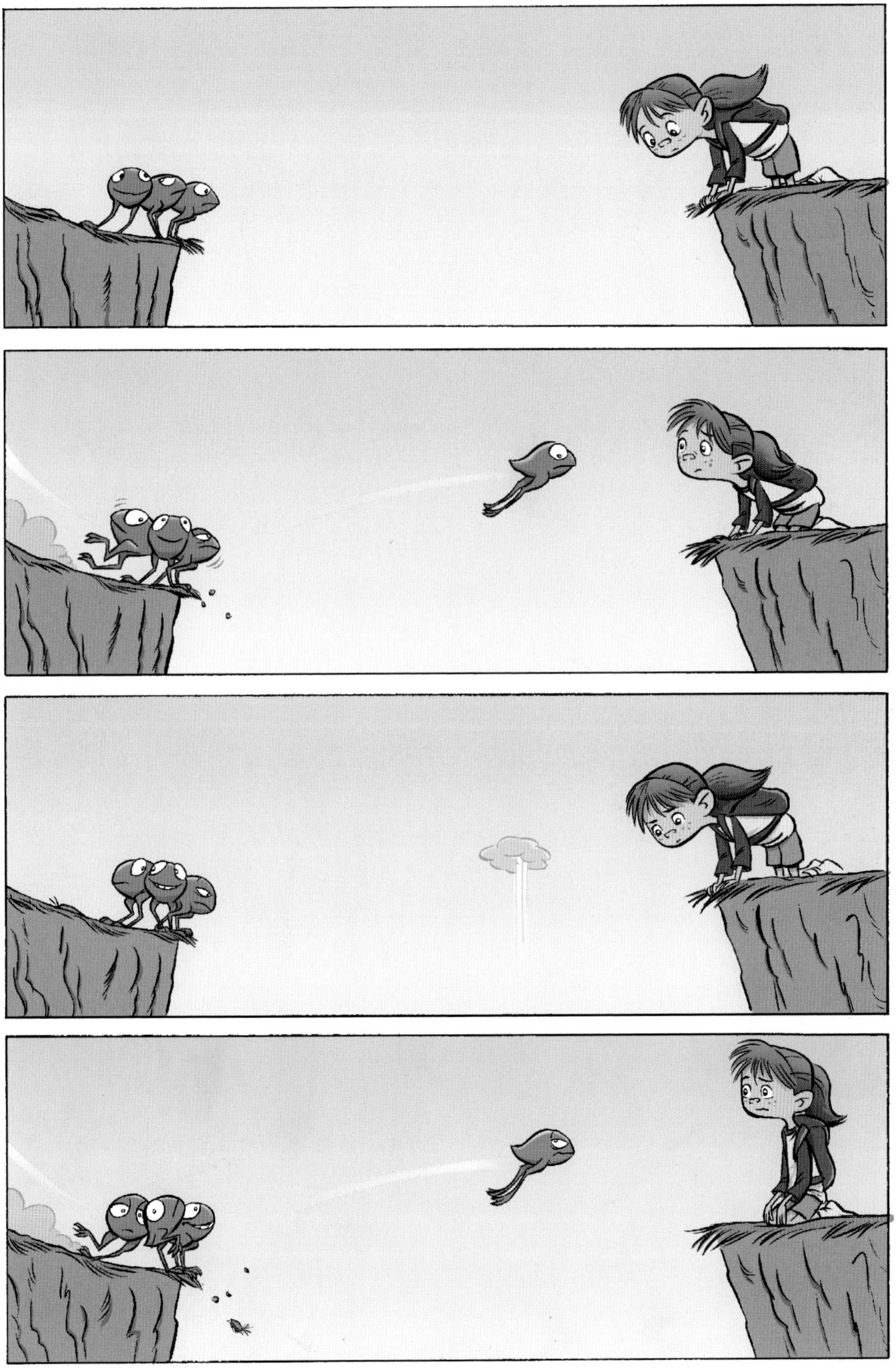

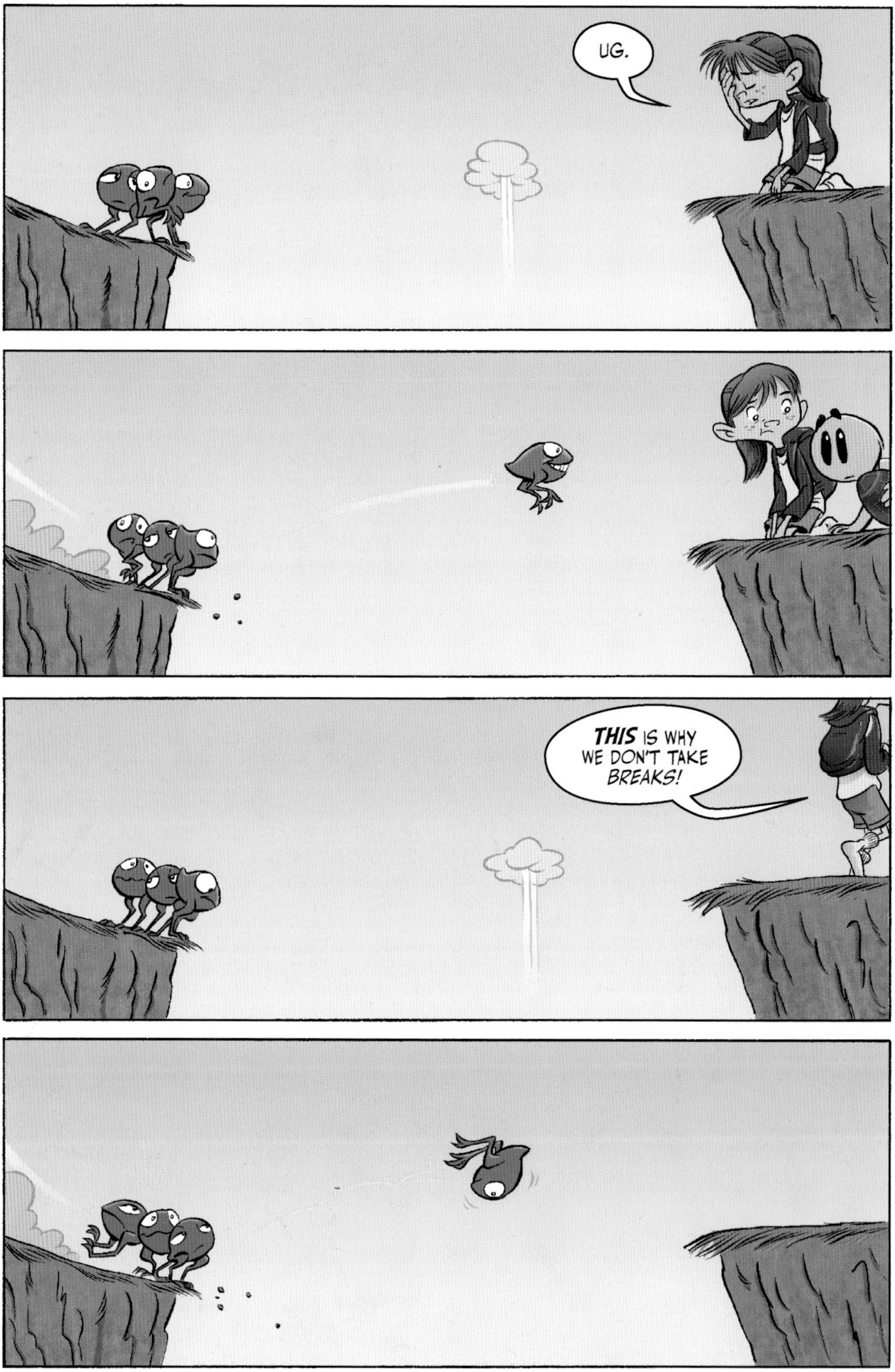
UG.
THIS IS WHY WE DON'T TAKE BREAKS!

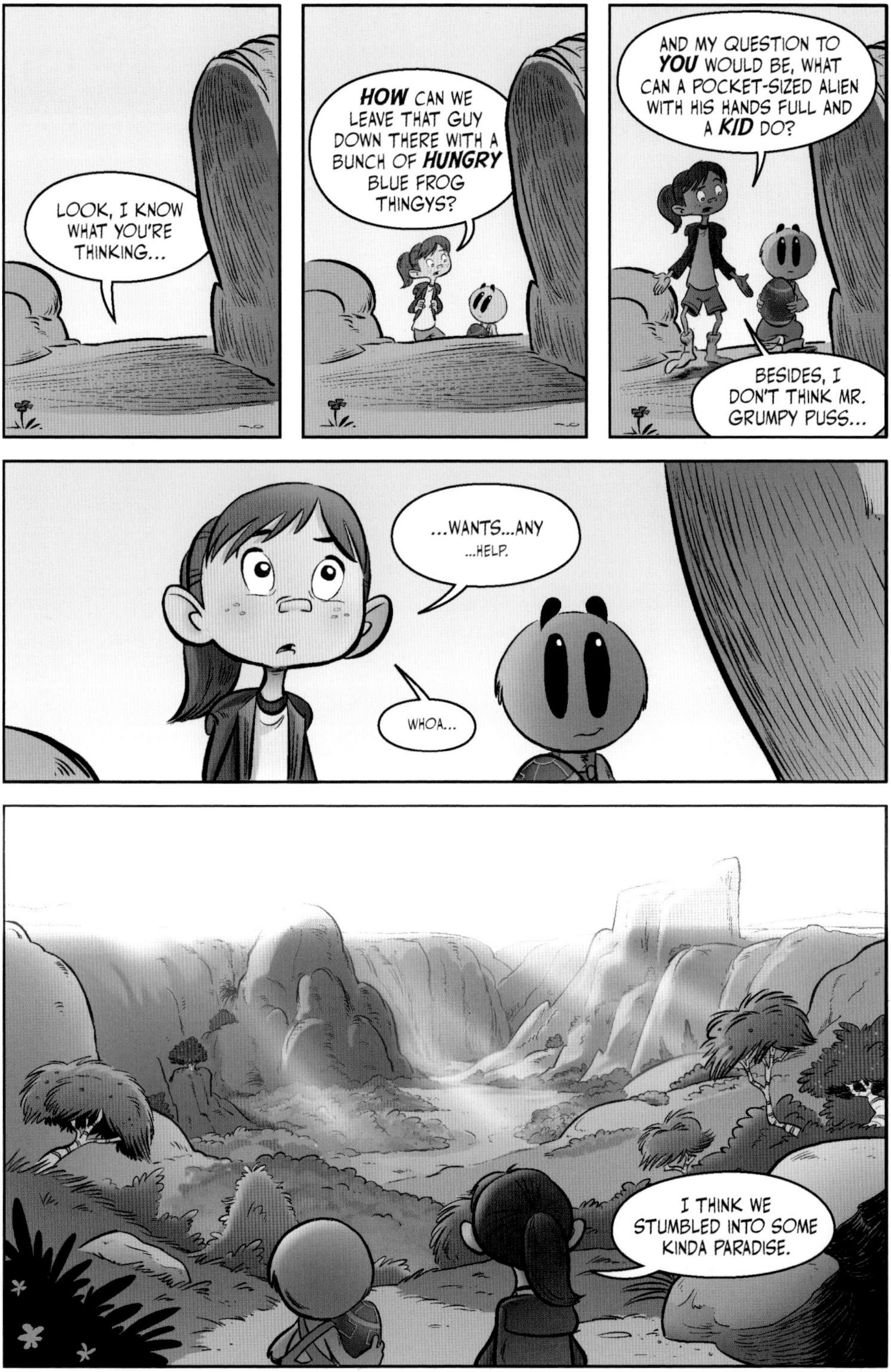
LOOK, I KNOW WHAT YOU'RE THINKING...
HOW CAN WE LEAVE THAT GUY DOWN THERE WITH A BUNCH OF HUNGRY BLUE FROG THINGYS?
AND MY QUESTION TO YOU WOULD BE, WHAT CAN A POCKET-SIZED ALIEN WITH HIS HANDS FULL AND A KID DO?
BESIDES, I DON'T THINK MR. GRUMPY PUSS...
...WANTS...ANY ...HELP.
WHOA...
I THINK WE STUMBLED INTO SOME KINDA PARADISE.

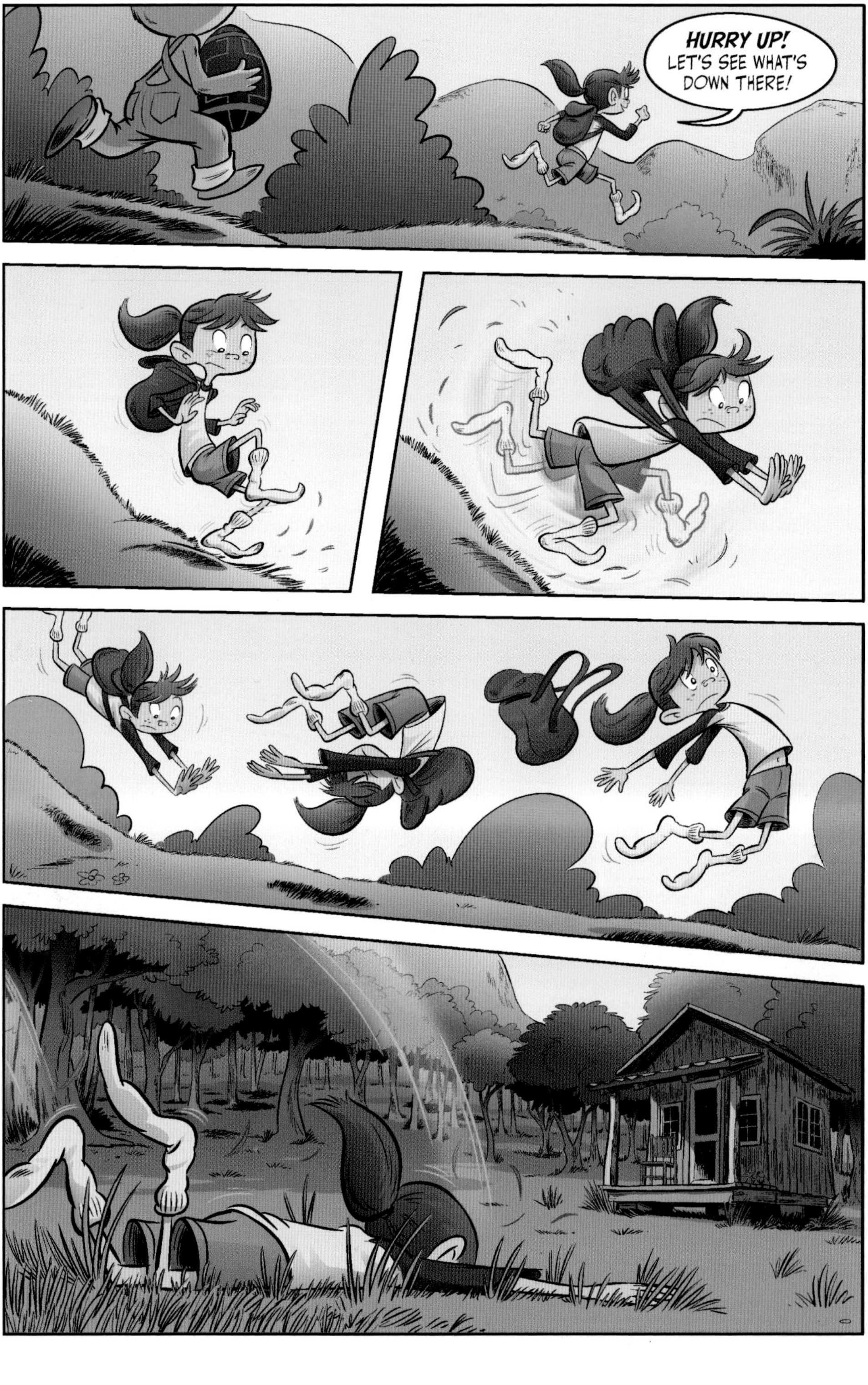
HURRY UP! LET'S SEE WHAT'S DOWN THERE!

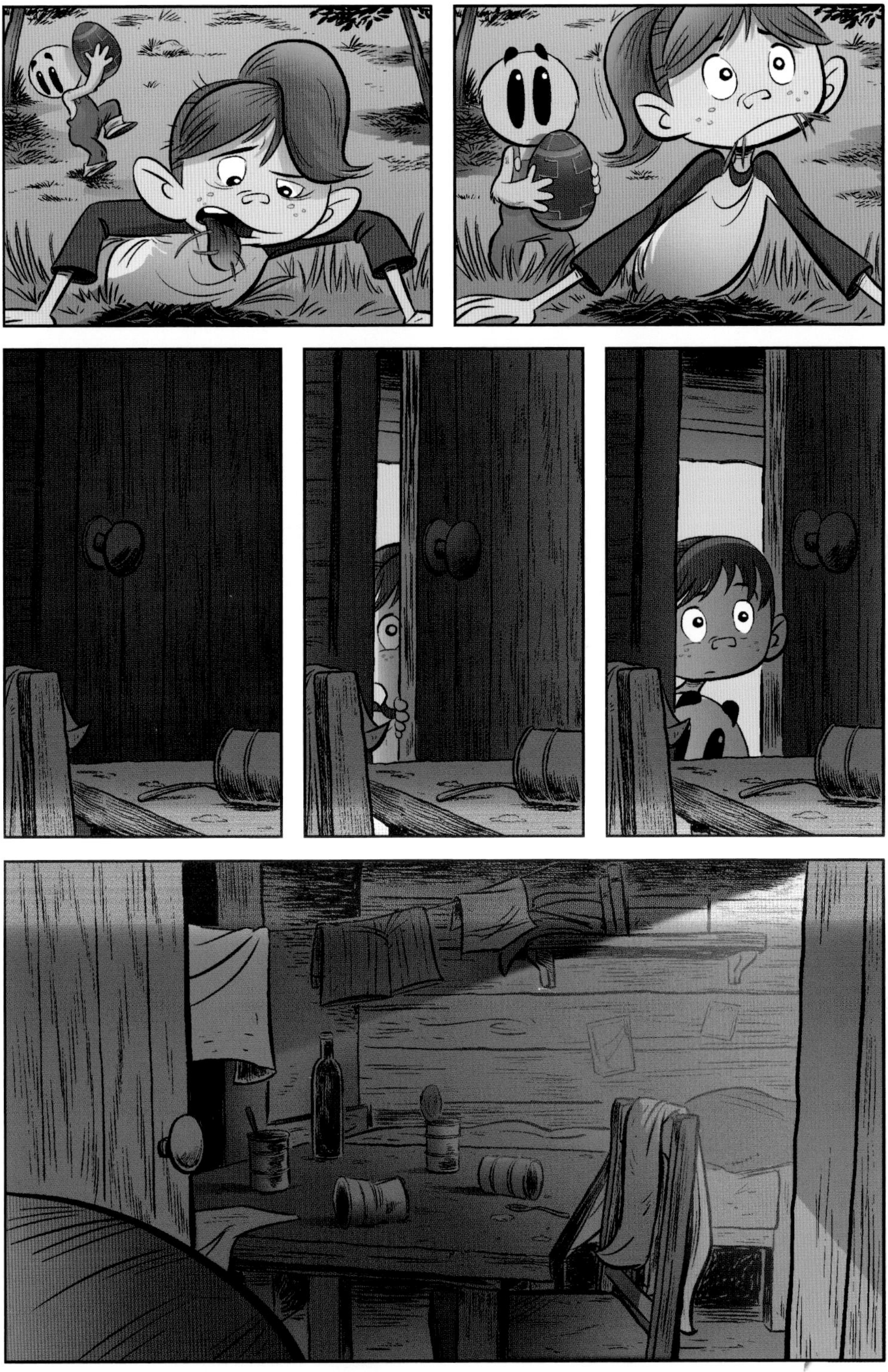

HELLO?

ANYBODY HOME?

HMM, THIS **KINDA** LOOKS LIKE **EARTH** STUFF...

BUT IT DOESN'T LOOK LIKE ANYONE'S BEEN HERE IN A **LONG** TIME.

UGH!

MAKE THAT A **VERY** LONG TIME!

HEY!

WHAT ARE YOU **DOING?!**

YOU CAN'T BE **THERE!** WHAT IF SOMEONE **DOES** LIVE HERE!

AND WHAT IF THAT SOMEONE IS AN **IT!**

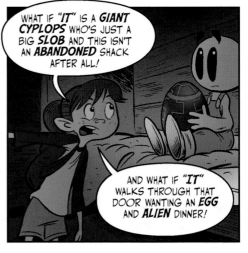

WHAT IF **"IT"** IS A **GIANT CYPLOPS** WHO'S JUST A BIG **SLOB** AND THIS ISN'T AN **ABANDONED** SHACK AFTER ALL!

AND WHAT IF **"IT"** WALKS THROUGH THAT DOOR WANTING AN **EGG** AND **ALIEN** DINNER!

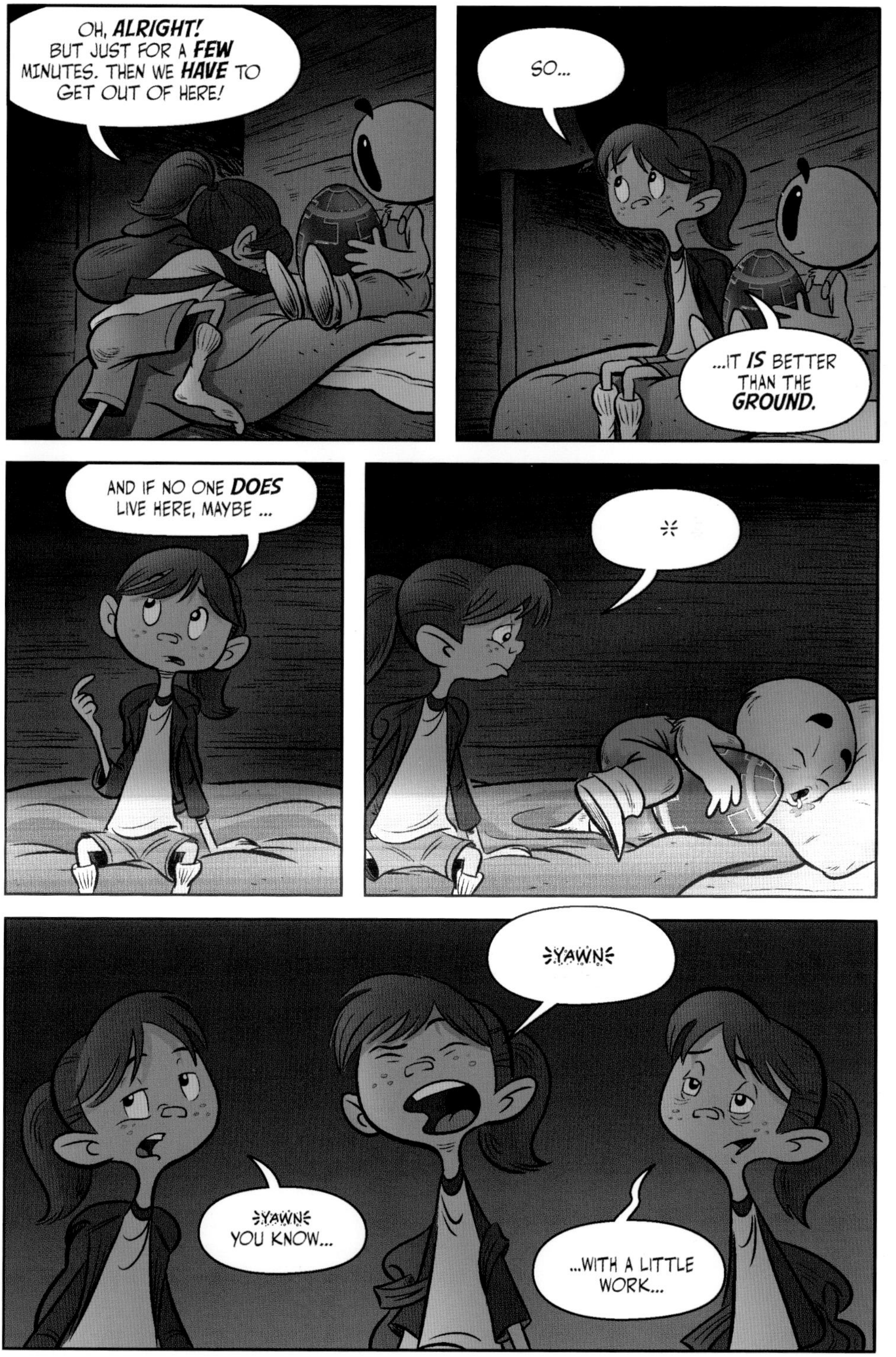
OH, **ALRIGHT!** BUT JUST FOR A **FEW** MINUTES. THEN WE **HAVE** TO GET OUT OF HERE!
SO...
...IT **IS** BETTER THAN THE **GROUND.**
AND IF NO ONE **DOES** LIVE HERE, MAYBE ...
YAWN
YAWN YOU KNOW...
...WITH A LITTLE WORK...

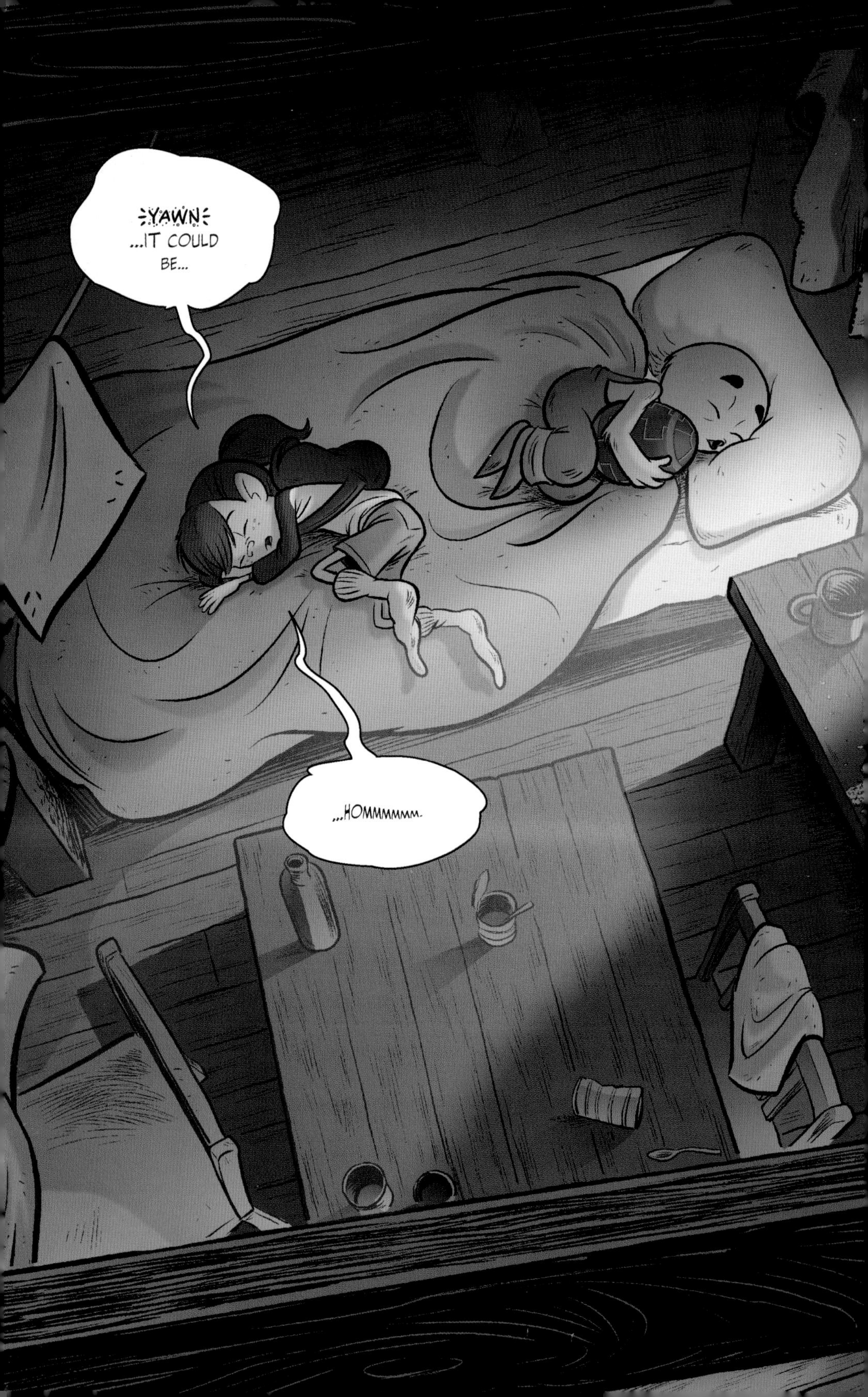
YAWN ...IT COULD BE...
...HOMMMMMM.

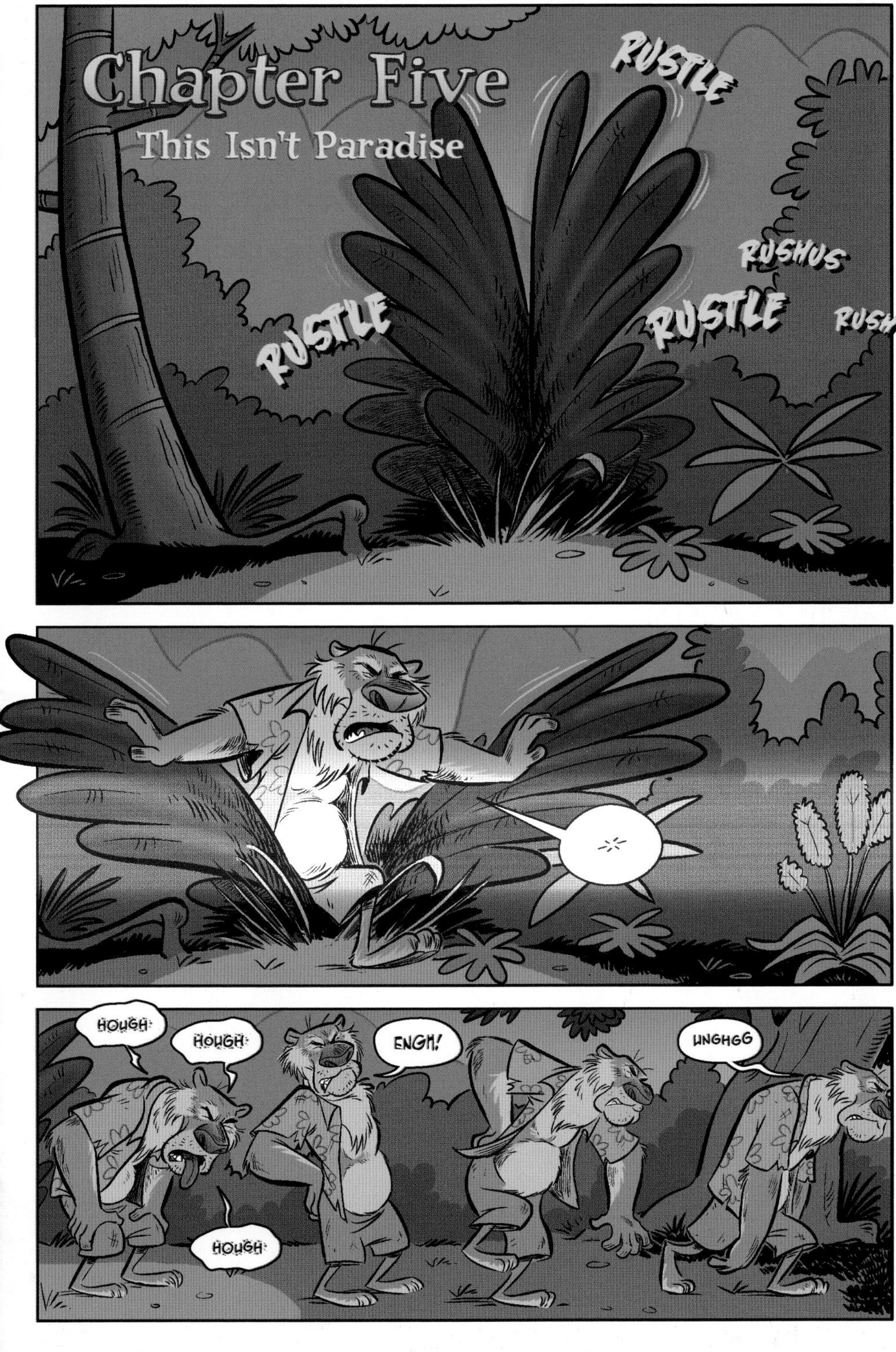
Chapter Five
This Isn't Paradise
RUSTLE
RUSHUS
RUSTLE
RUSH
RUSTLE
HOUGH
HOUGH
HOUGH
ENGH!
UNGHGG

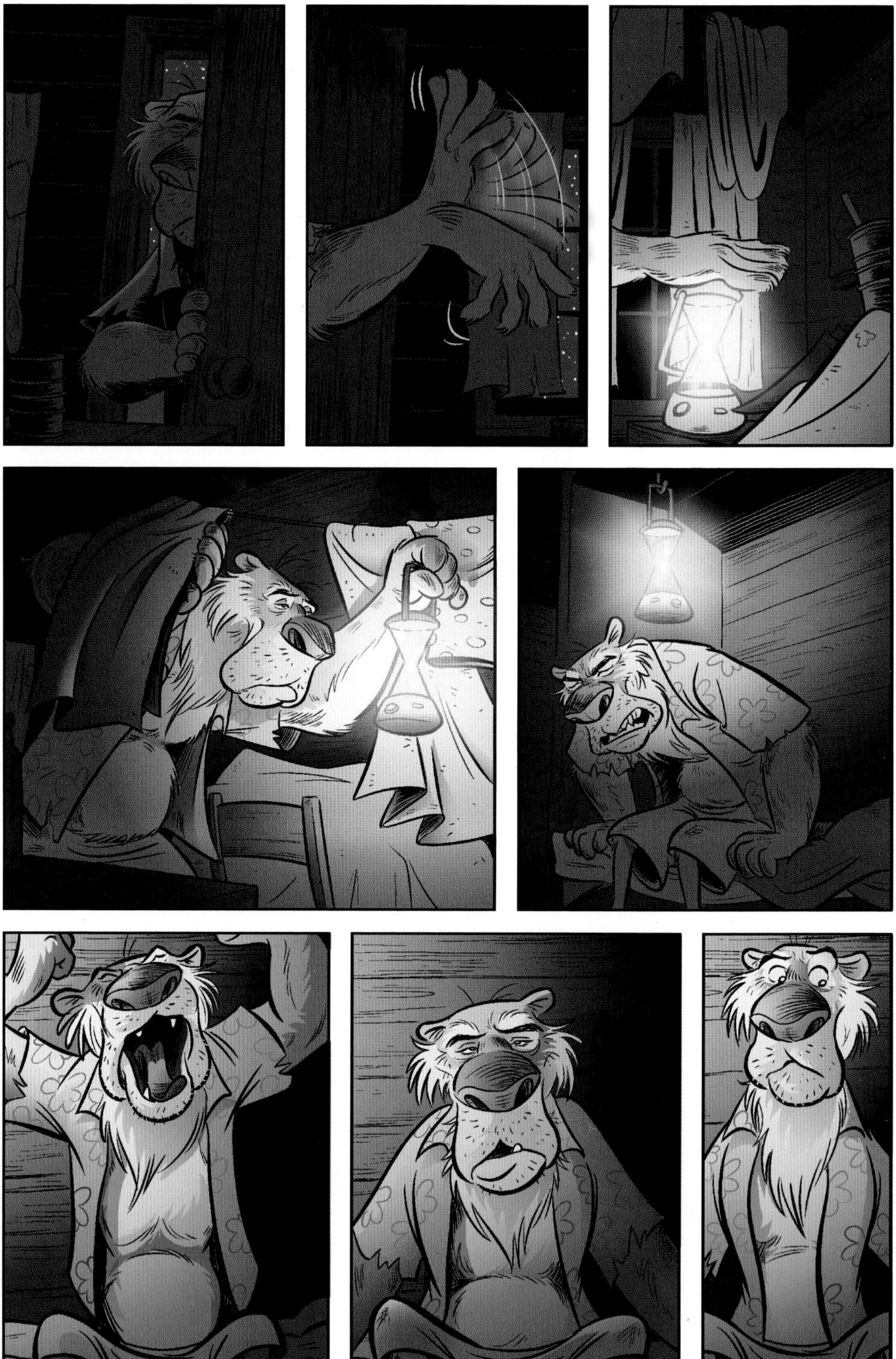

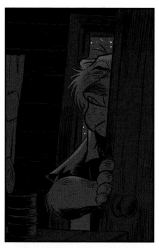

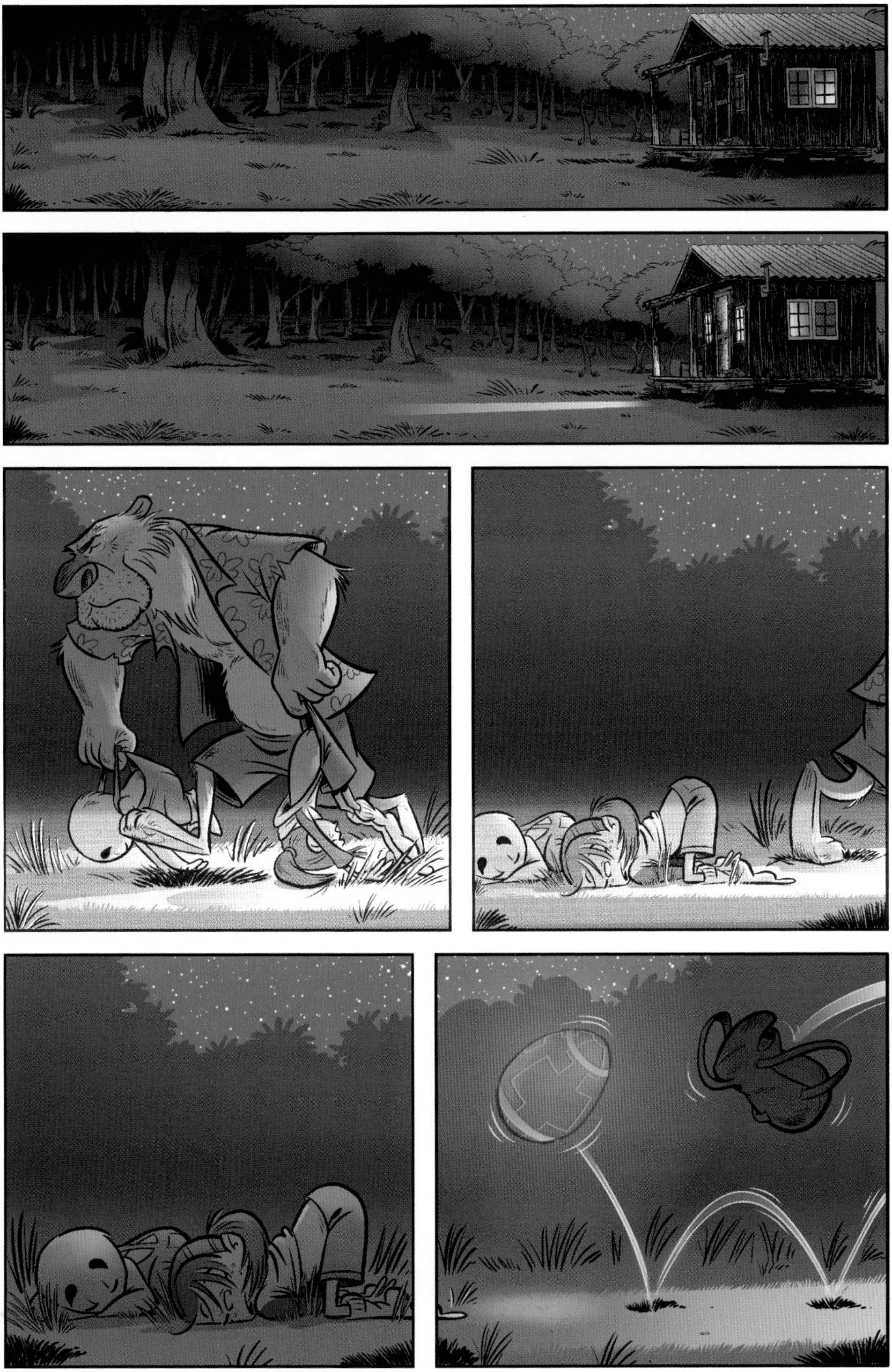

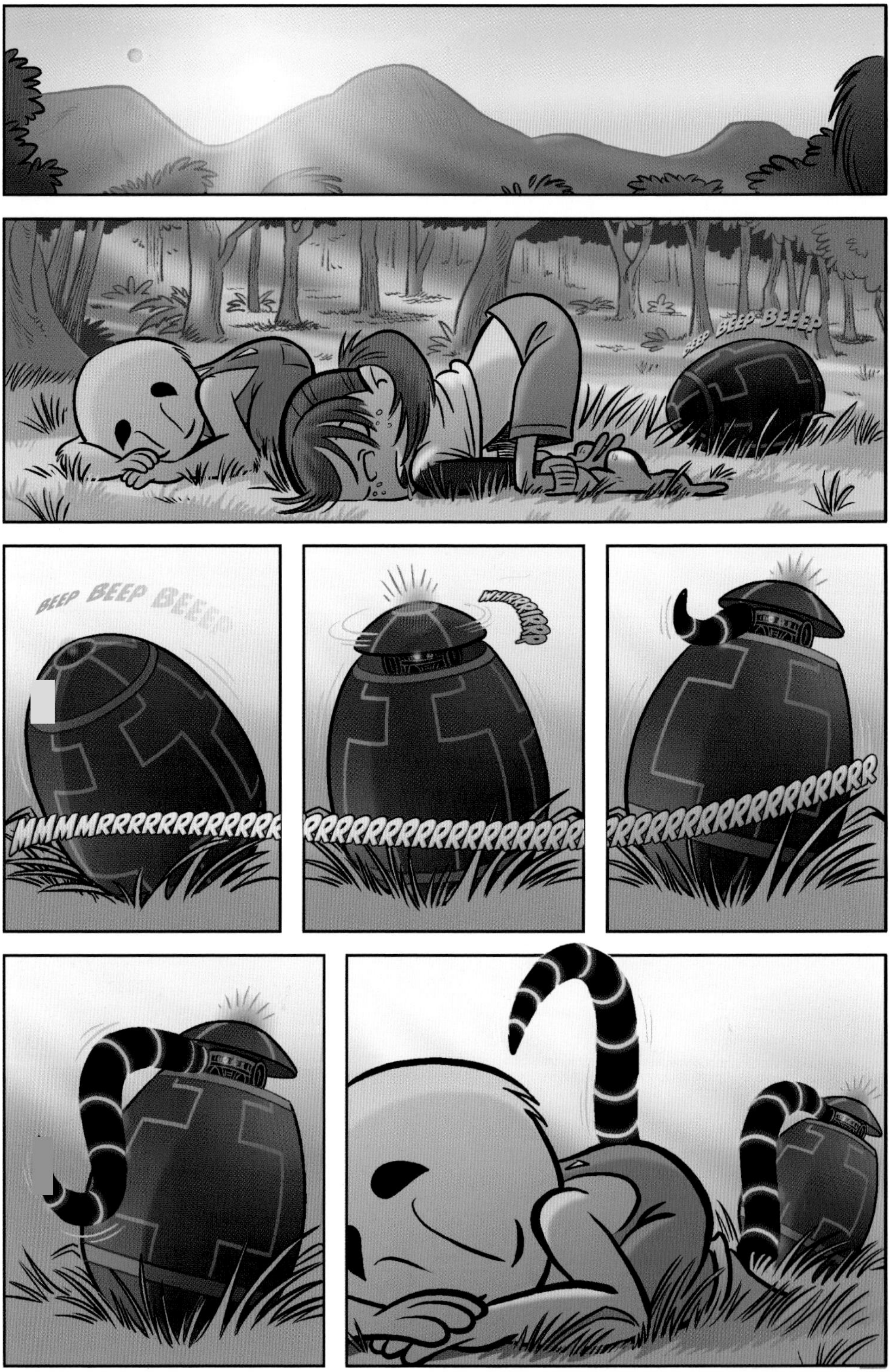
BEEP BEEP BEEEP
BEEP BEEP BEEEP
WHIRRRRRR
MMMMRRRRRRRRRRRRR
RRRRRRRRRRRRRRRRRRR
RRRRRRRRRRRRRRRRRRR

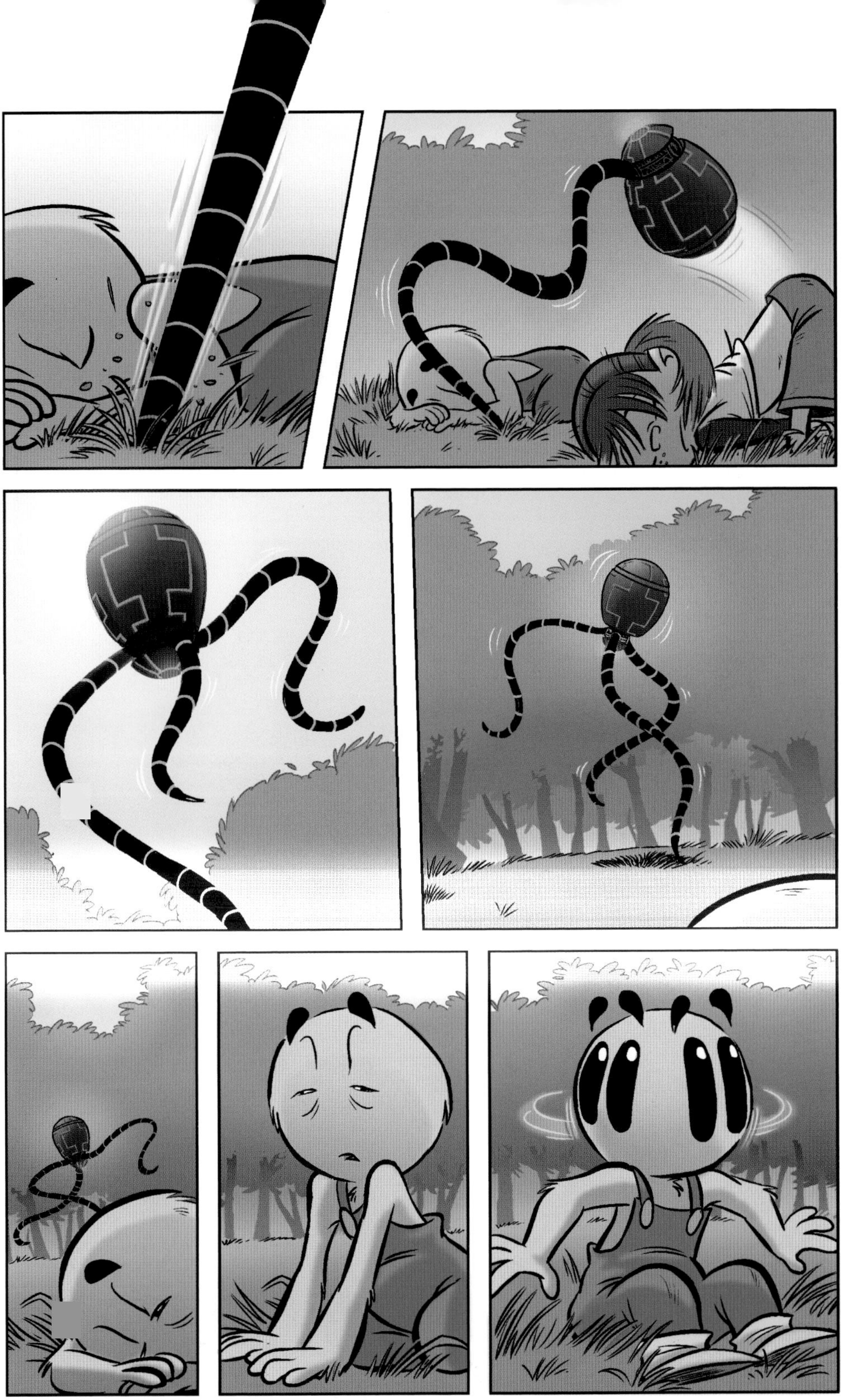

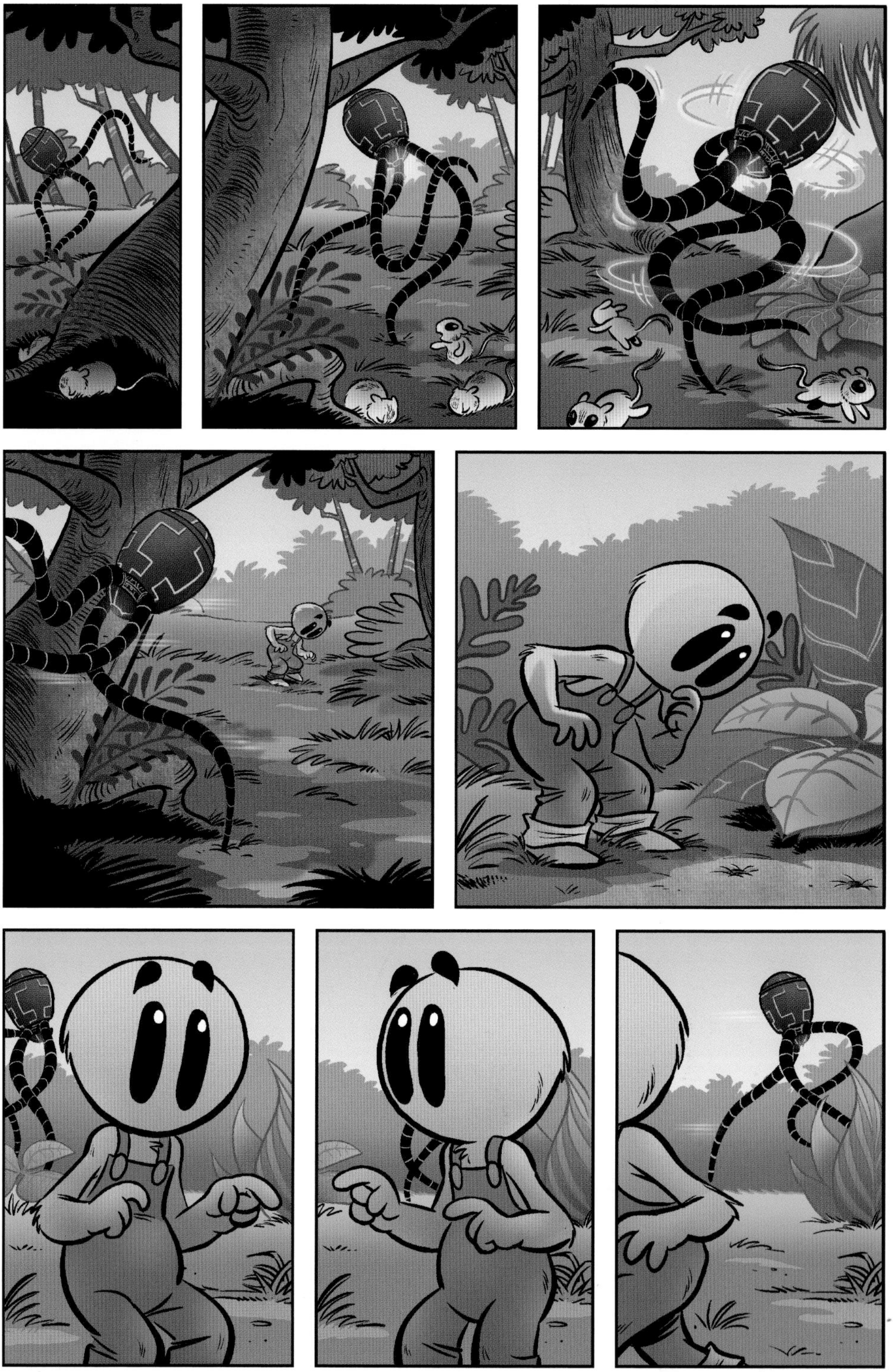

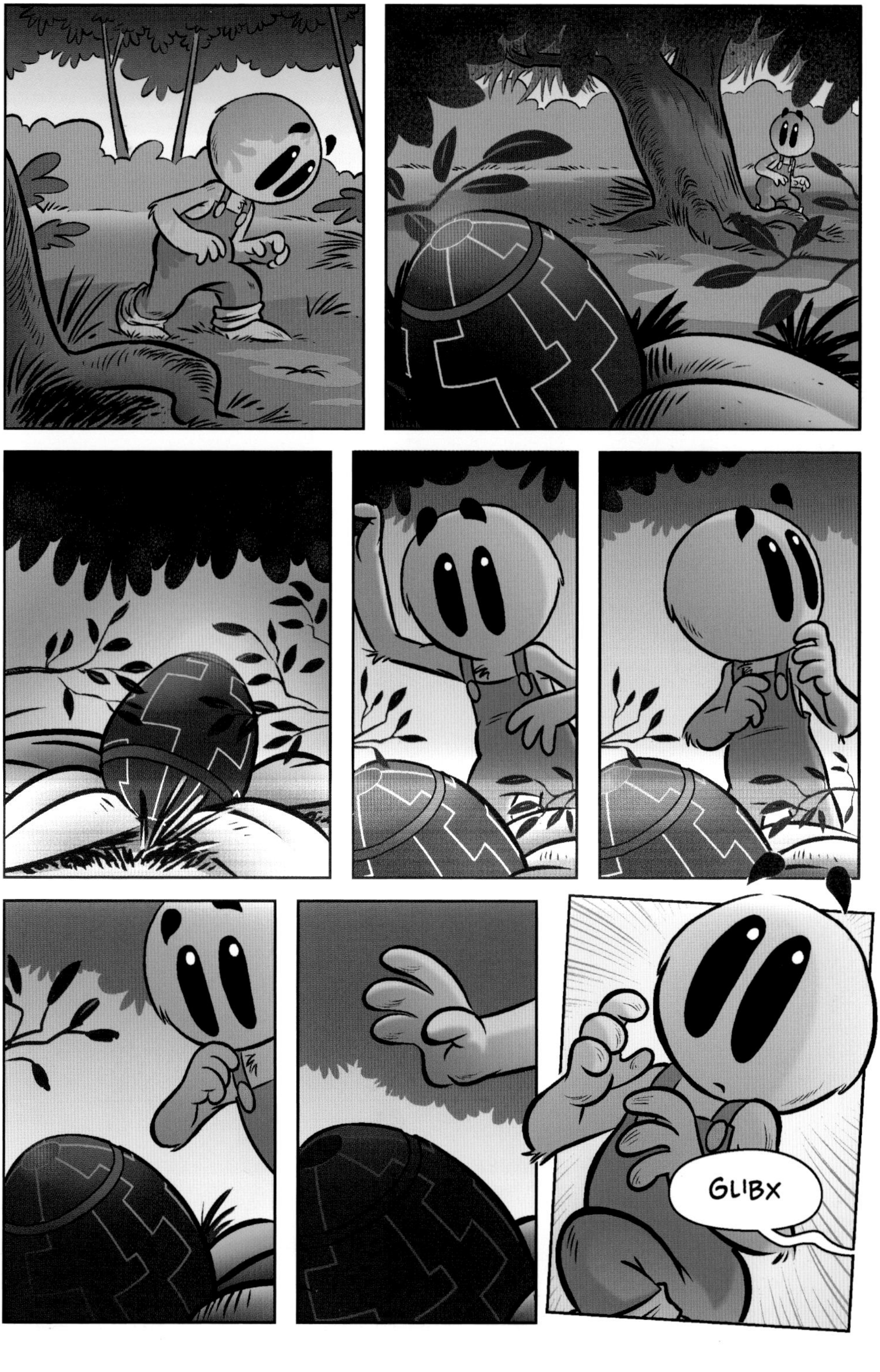
GLIBX

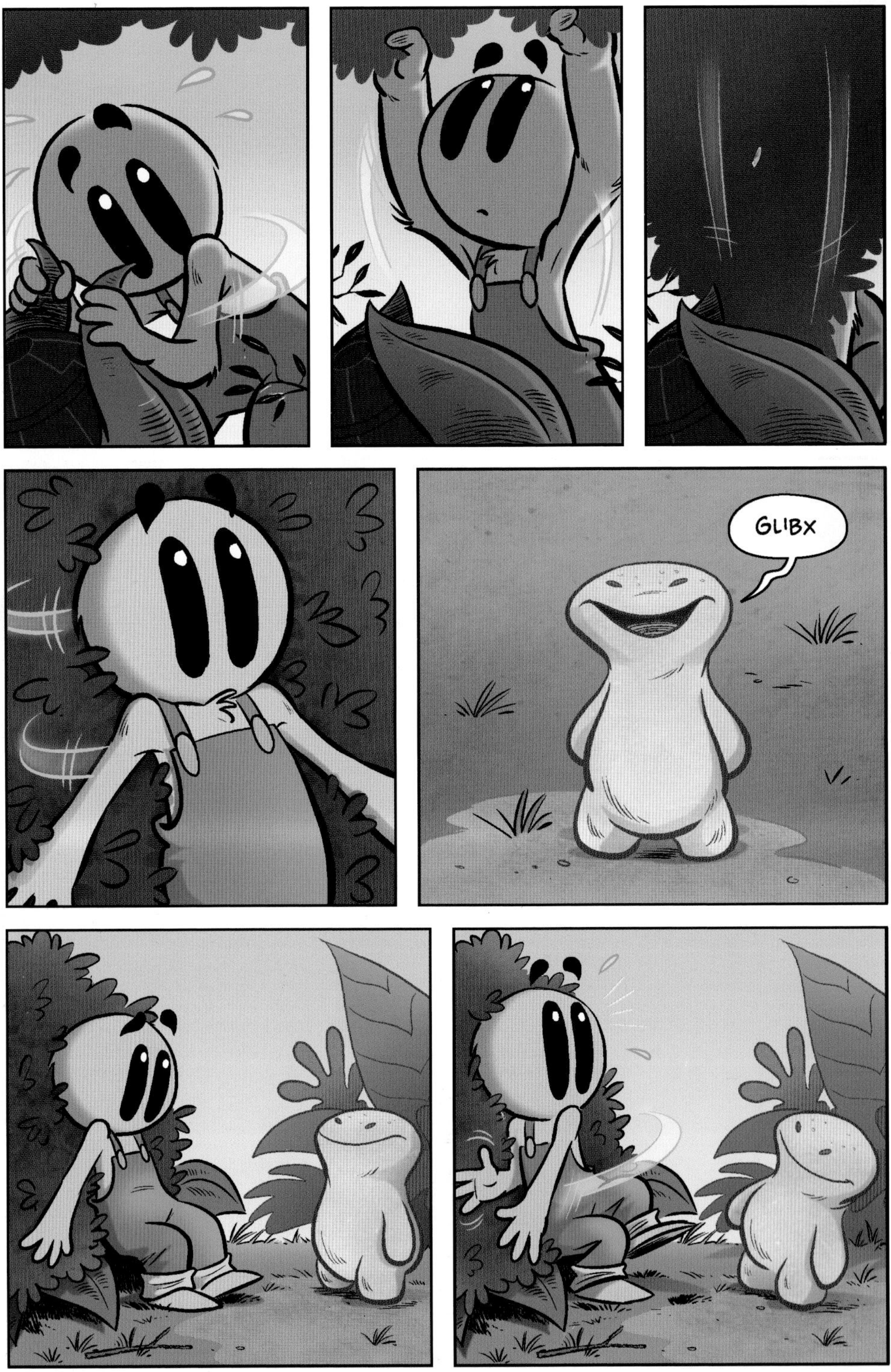
GLIBX

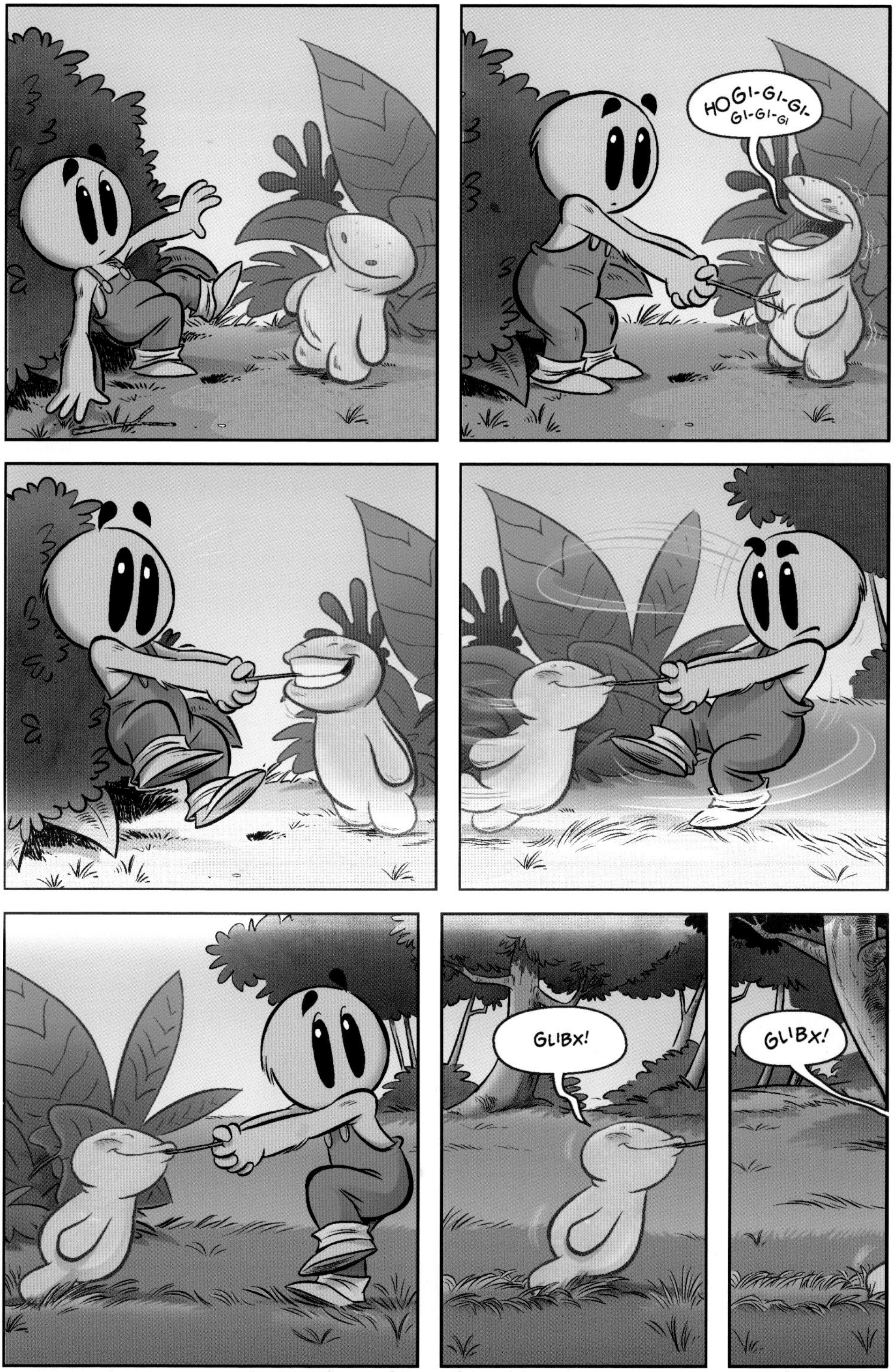
HOGI-GI-GI-GI-GI-GI
GLIBX!
GLIBX!

YOU *STILL* HERE?

I THOUGHT YOU'D BE *LONG GONE* BY NOW!

WELL, I'M GLAD YOU'RE AWAKE, BECAUSE I *DIDN'T* GET A CHANCE TO TELL YOU SOMETHING LAST NIGHT...

GO AWAY!

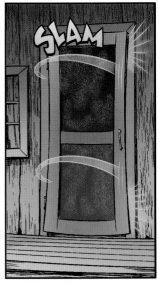

SLAM

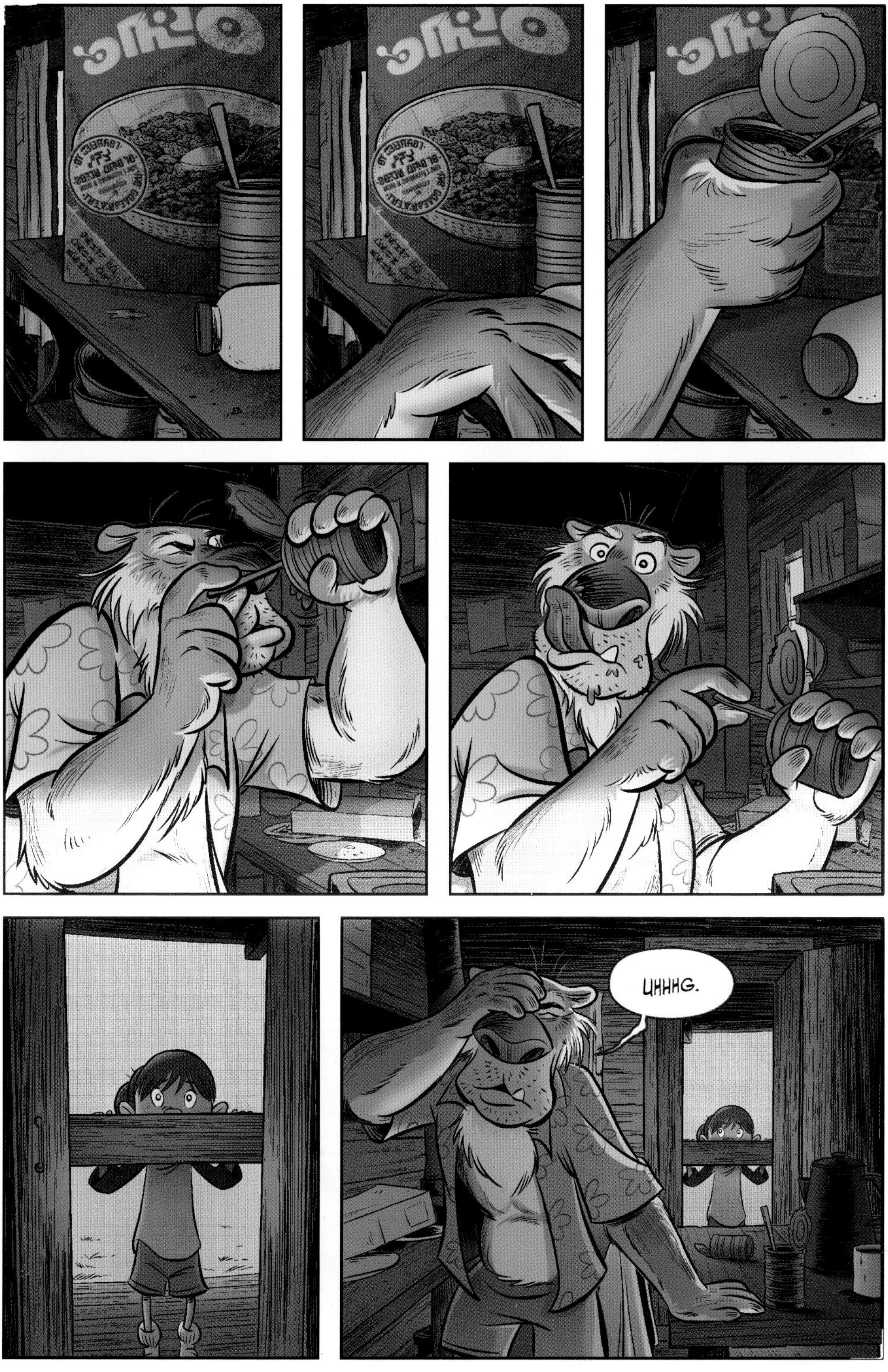
UHHHG.

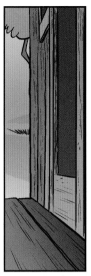

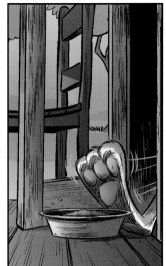

SLAM

YA KNOW, I'VE BEEN LOOKING THROUGH **BOOKS** 'N' **CHARTS** ALL MORNING AND CAN'T SEEM TO FIND A SPECIES LIKE YOU ANYWHERE **ON** THIS PLANET.

NOW **WHY** DO YOU SUPPOSE THAT IS?

WELL...

MAYBE IT'S BECAUSE...

...AHM NOT FWOM AWOUND HERW.

YA DON'T SAY?

WHU-HUH!

146

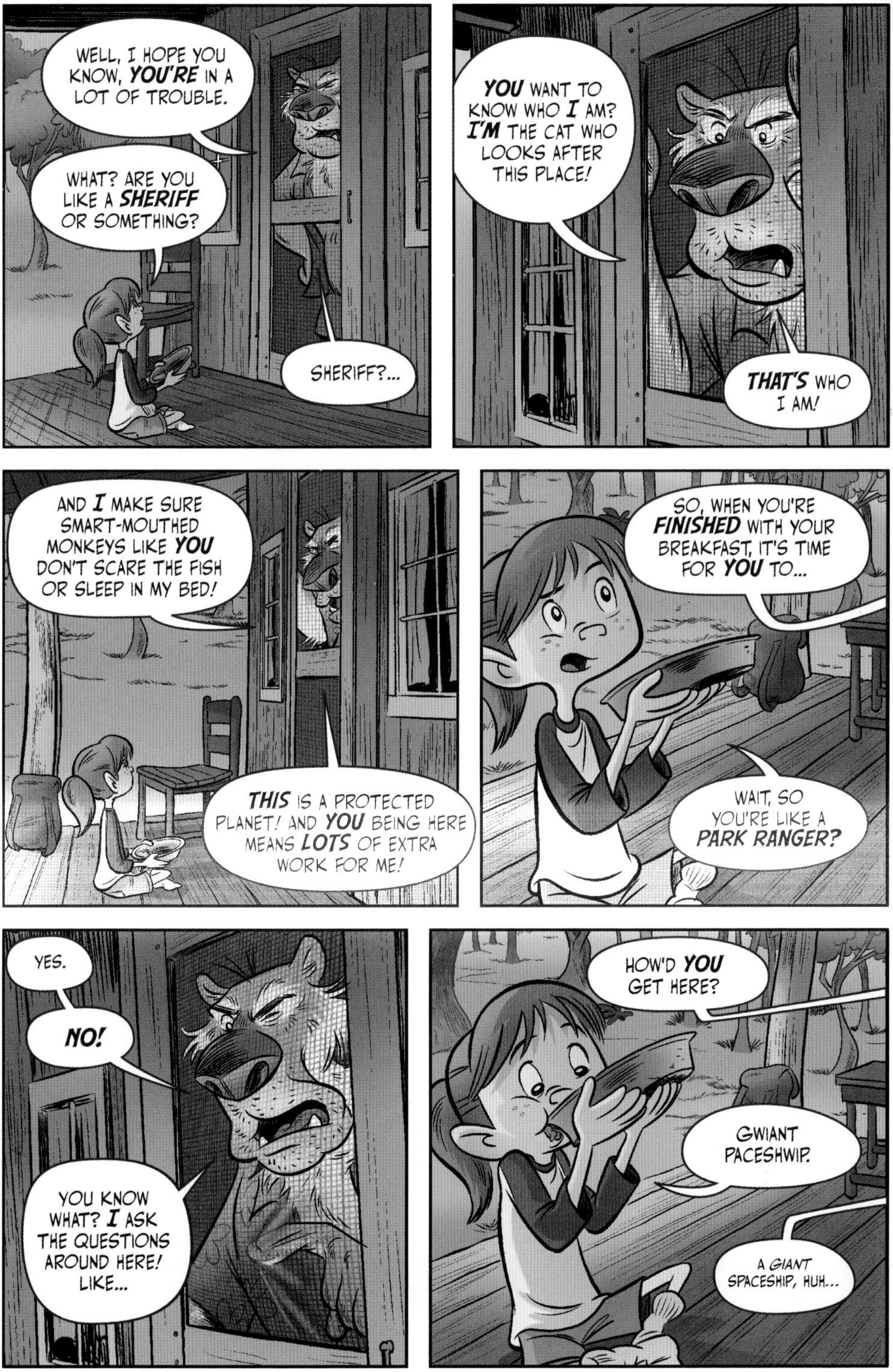
WELL, I HOPE YOU KNOW, YOU'RE IN A LOT OF TROUBLE.
WHAT? ARE YOU LIKE A SHERIFF OR SOMETHING?
SHERIFF?...
YOU WANT TO KNOW WHO I AM? I'M THE CAT WHO LOOKS AFTER THIS PLACE!
THAT'S WHO I AM!
AND I MAKE SURE SMART-MOUTHED MONKEYS LIKE YOU DON'T SCARE THE FISH OR SLEEP IN MY BED!
THIS IS A PROTECTED PLANET! AND YOU BEING HERE MEANS LOTS OF EXTRA WORK FOR ME!
SO, WHEN YOU'RE FINISHED WITH YOUR BREAKFAST, IT'S TIME FOR YOU TO...
WAIT, SO YOU'RE LIKE A PARK RANGER?
YES.
NO!
YOU KNOW WHAT? I ASK THE QUESTIONS AROUND HERE! LIKE...
HOW'D YOU GET HERE?
GWIANT PACESHWIP.
A GIANT SPACESHIP, HUH...

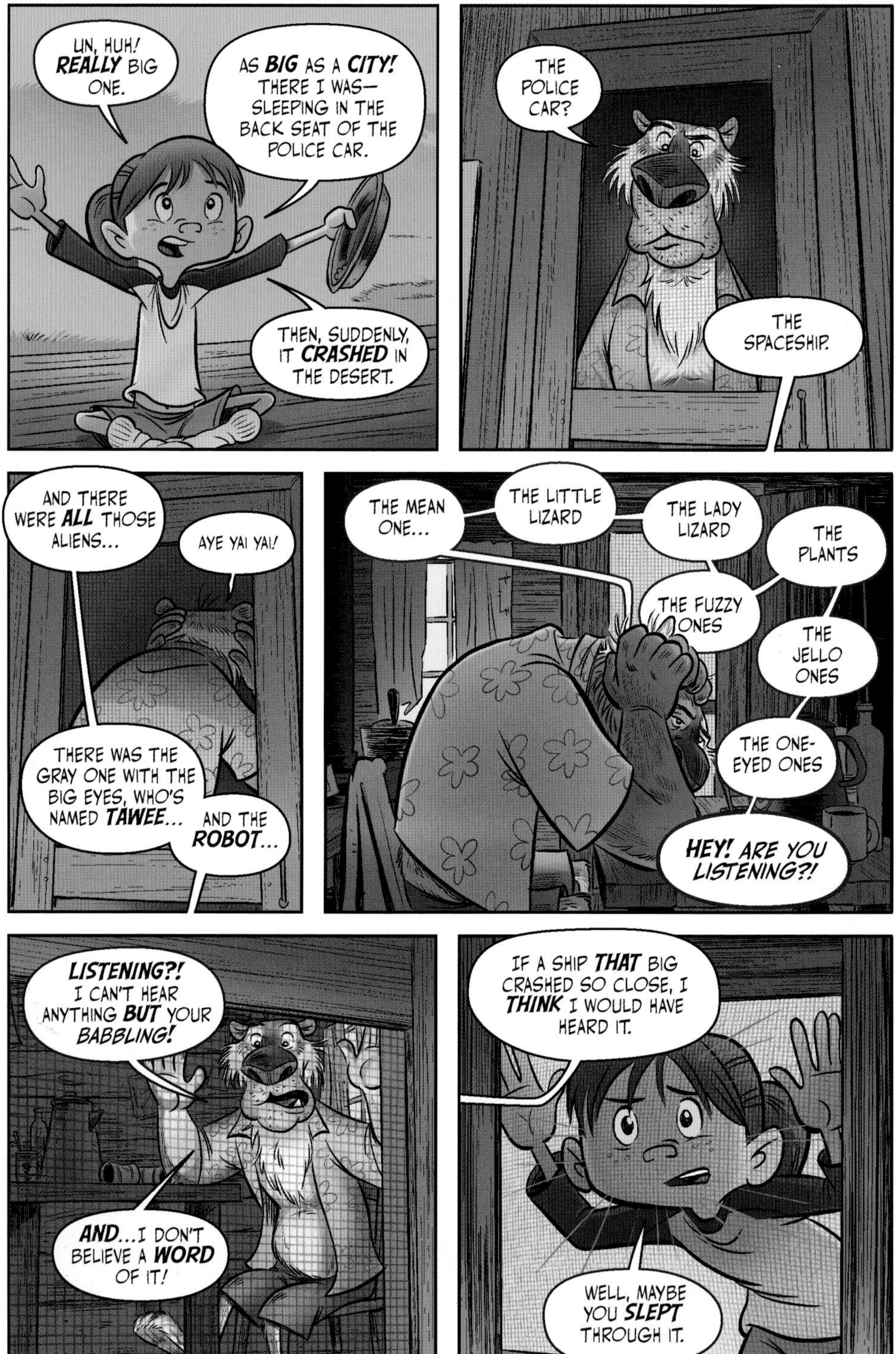
UN, HUH! REALLY BIG ONE.
AS BIG AS A CITY! THERE I WAS— SLEEPING IN THE BACK SEAT OF THE POLICE CAR.
THEN, SUDDENLY, IT CRASHED IN THE DESERT.
THE POLICE CAR?
THE SPACESHIP.
AND THERE WERE ALL THOSE ALIENS...
AYE YAI YAI!
THERE WAS THE GRAY ONE WITH THE BIG EYES, WHO'S NAMED TAWEE...
AND THE ROBOT...
THE MEAN ONE...
THE LITTLE LIZARD
THE LADY LIZARD
THE PLANTS
THE FUZZY ONES
THE JELLO ONES
THE ONE-EYED ONES
HEY! ARE YOU LISTENING?!
LISTENING?! I CAN'T HEAR ANYTHING BUT YOUR BABBLING!
AND...I DON'T BELIEVE A WORD OF IT!
IF A SHIP THAT BIG CRASHED SO CLOSE, I THINK I WOULD HAVE HEARD IT.
WELL, MAYBE YOU SLEPT THROUGH IT.

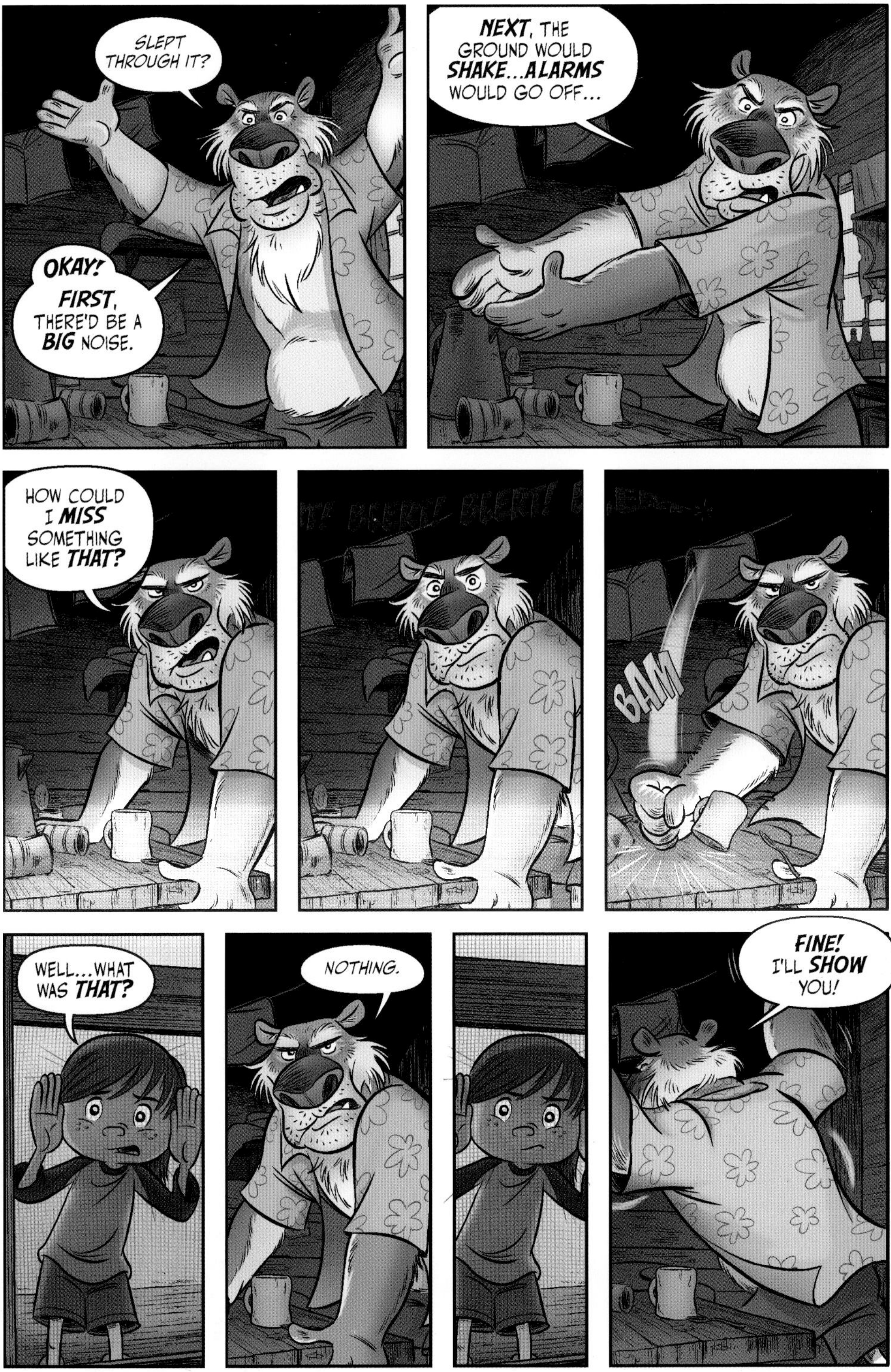
SLEPT THROUGH IT?
OKAY! FIRST, THERE'D BE A BIG NOISE.
NEXT, THE GROUND WOULD SHAKE...ALARMS WOULD GO OFF...
HOW COULD I MISS SOMETHING LIKE THAT?
BAM
WELL...WHAT WAS THAT?
NOTHING.
FINE! I'LL SHOW YOU!

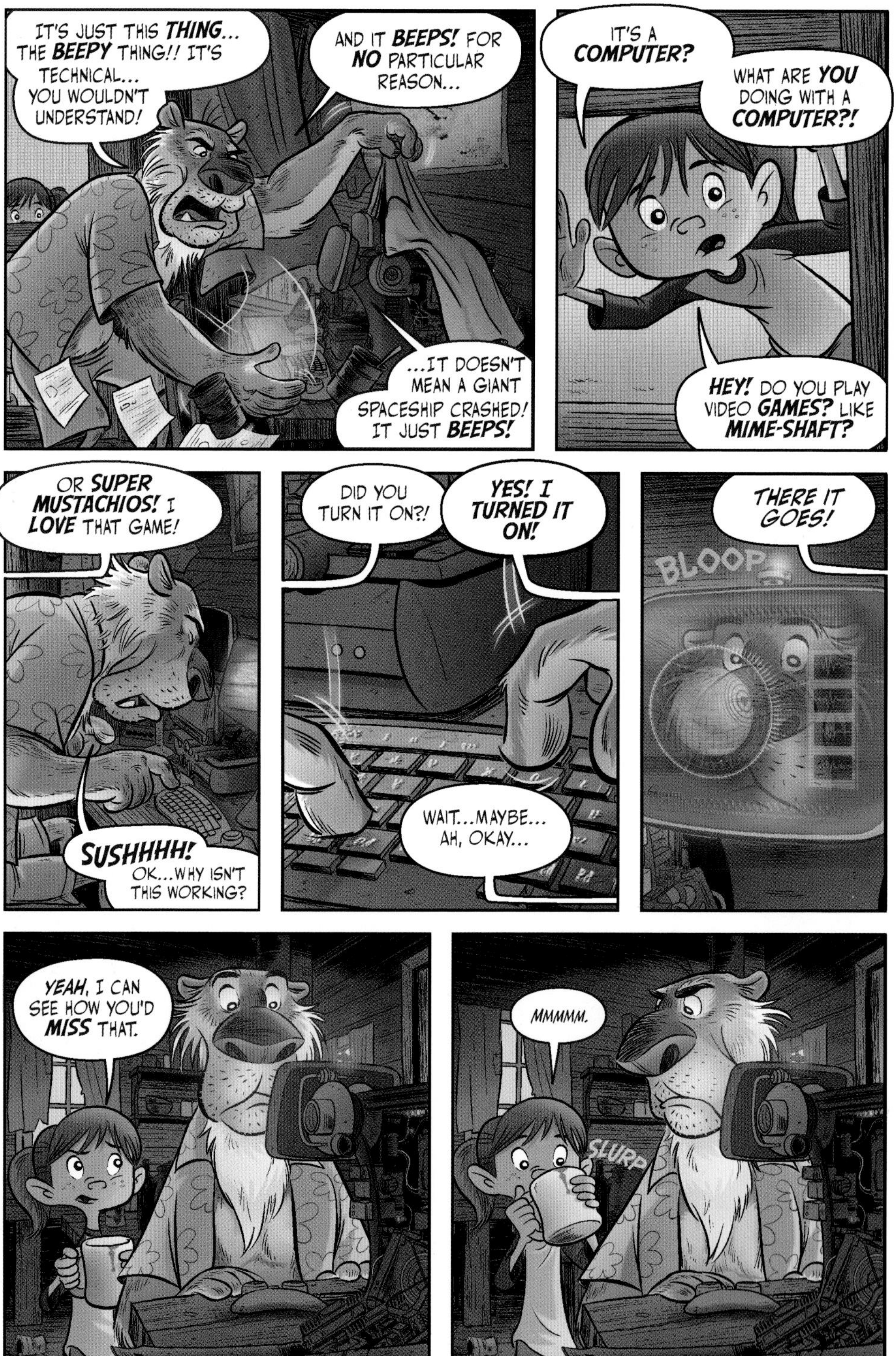
IT'S JUST THIS THING... THE BEEPY THING!! IT'S TECHNICAL... YOU WOULDN'T UNDERSTAND!
AND IT BEEPS! FOR NO PARTICULAR REASON...
...IT DOESN'T MEAN A GIANT SPACESHIP CRASHED! IT JUST BEEPS!
IT'S A COMPUTER?
WHAT ARE YOU DOING WITH A COMPUTER?!
HEY! DO YOU PLAY VIDEO GAMES? LIKE MIME-SHAFT?
OR SUPER MUSTACHIOS! I LOVE THAT GAME!
SUSHHHH!
OK...WHY ISN'T THIS WORKING?
DID YOU TURN IT ON?!
YES! I TURNED IT ON!
WAIT...MAYBE... AH, OKAY...
THERE IT GOES!
BLOOP
YEAH, I CAN SEE HOW YOU'D MISS THAT.
MMMMM.
SLURP

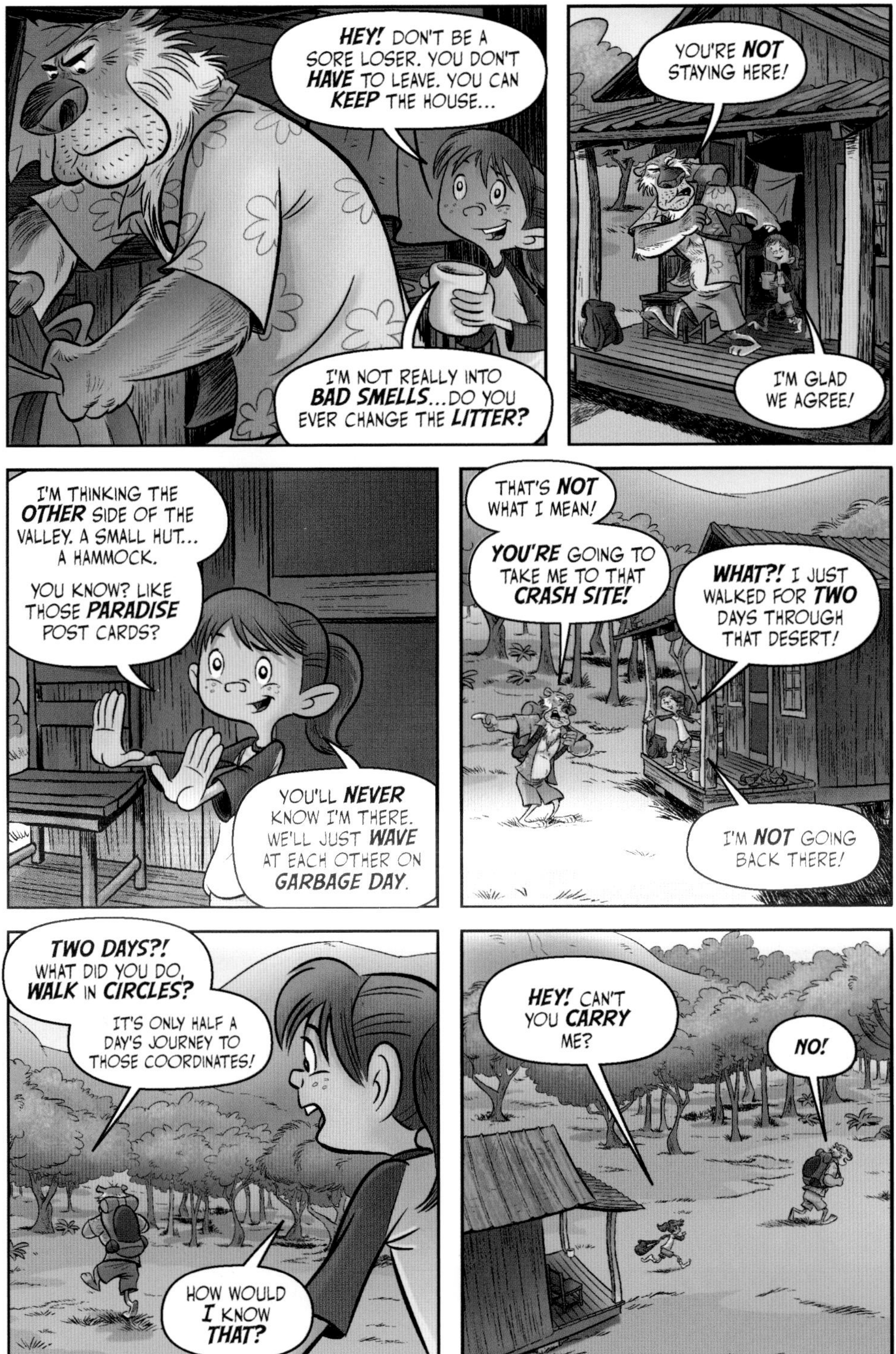
HEY! DON'T BE A SORE LOSER. YOU DON'T HAVE TO LEAVE. YOU CAN KEEP THE HOUSE...
I'M NOT REALLY INTO BAD SMELLS...DO YOU EVER CHANGE THE LITTER?
YOU'RE NOT STAYING HERE!
I'M GLAD WE AGREE!
I'M THINKING THE OTHER SIDE OF THE VALLEY. A SMALL HUT... A HAMMOCK.
YOU KNOW? LIKE THOSE PARADISE POST CARDS?
YOU'LL NEVER KNOW I'M THERE. WE'LL JUST WAVE AT EACH OTHER ON GARBAGE DAY.
THAT'S NOT WHAT I MEAN!
YOU'RE GOING TO TAKE ME TO THAT CRASH SITE!
WHAT?! I JUST WALKED FOR TWO DAYS THROUGH THAT DESERT!
I'M NOT GOING BACK THERE!
TWO DAYS?! WHAT DID YOU DO, WALK IN CIRCLES?
IT'S ONLY HALF A DAY'S JOURNEY TO THOSE COORDINATES!
HOW WOULD I KNOW THAT?
HEY! CAN'T YOU CARRY ME?
NO!

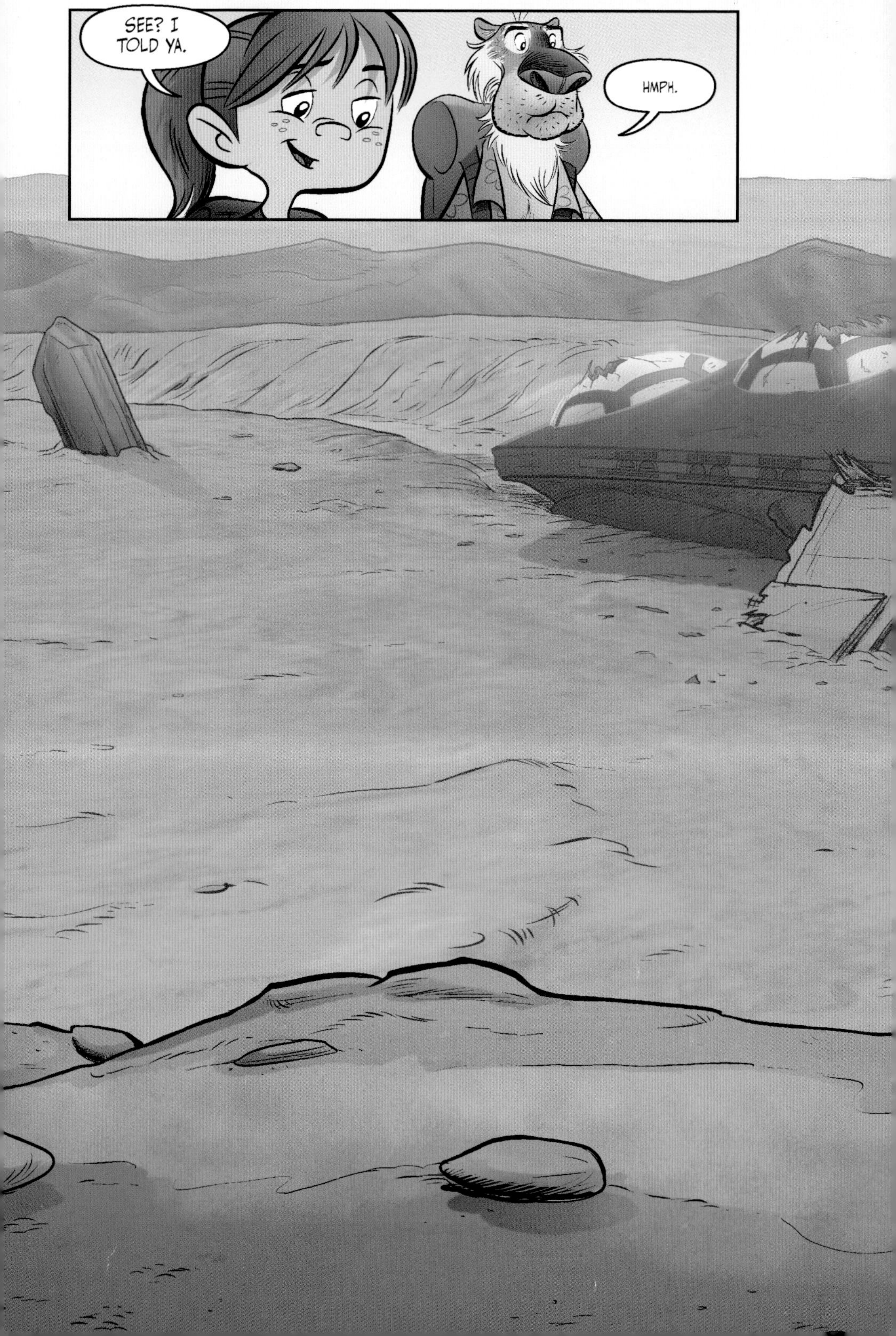
SEE? I TOLD YA.
HMPH.

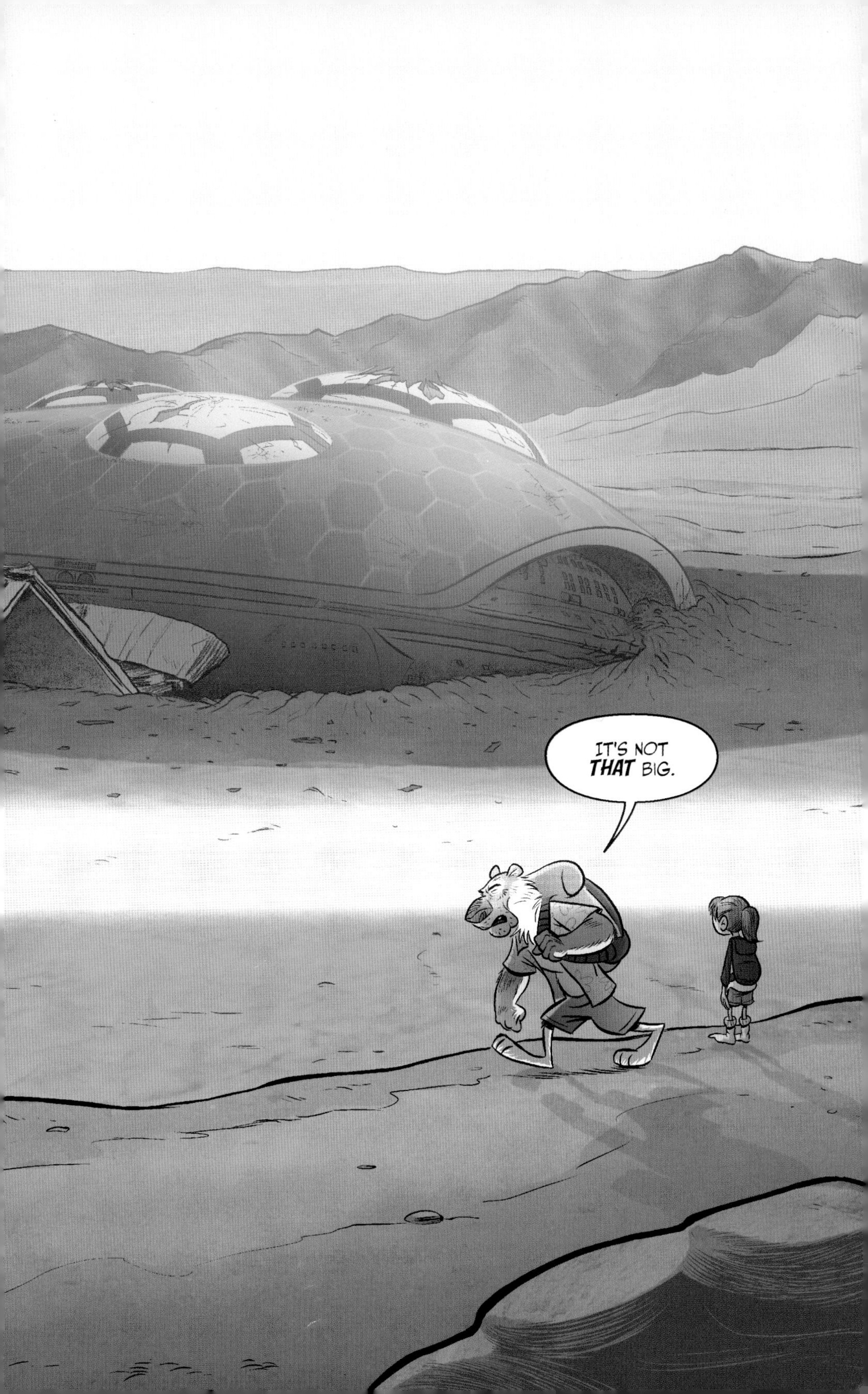
IT'S NOT **THAT** BIG.

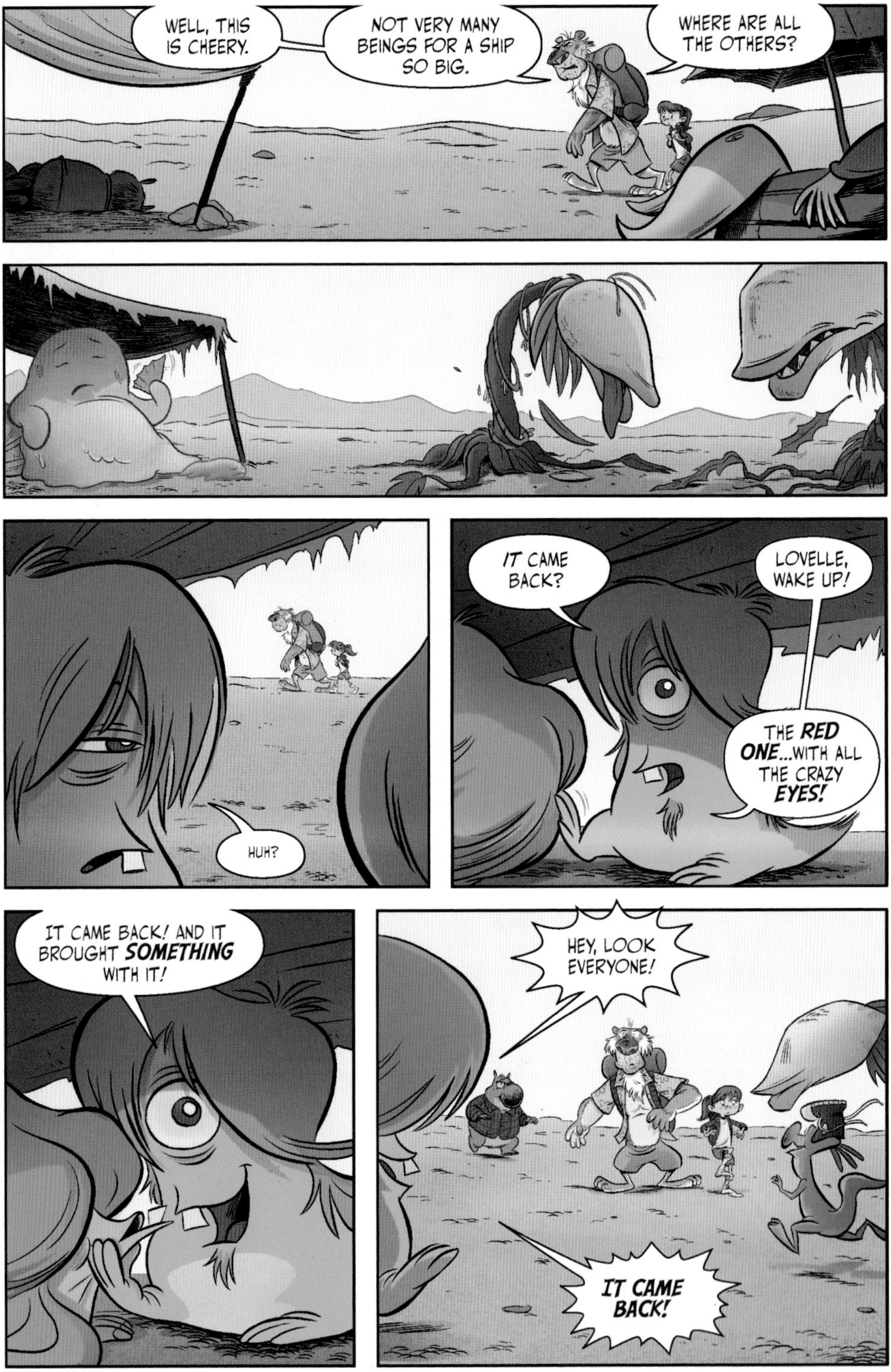
WELL, THIS IS CHEERY.
NOT VERY MANY BEINGS FOR A SHIP SO BIG.
WHERE ARE ALL THE OTHERS?
HUH?
IT CAME BACK?
LOVELLE, WAKE UP!
THE RED ONE...WITH ALL THE CRAZY EYES!
IT CAME BACK! AND IT BROUGHT SOMETHING WITH IT!
HEY, LOOK EVERYONE!
IT CAME BACK!

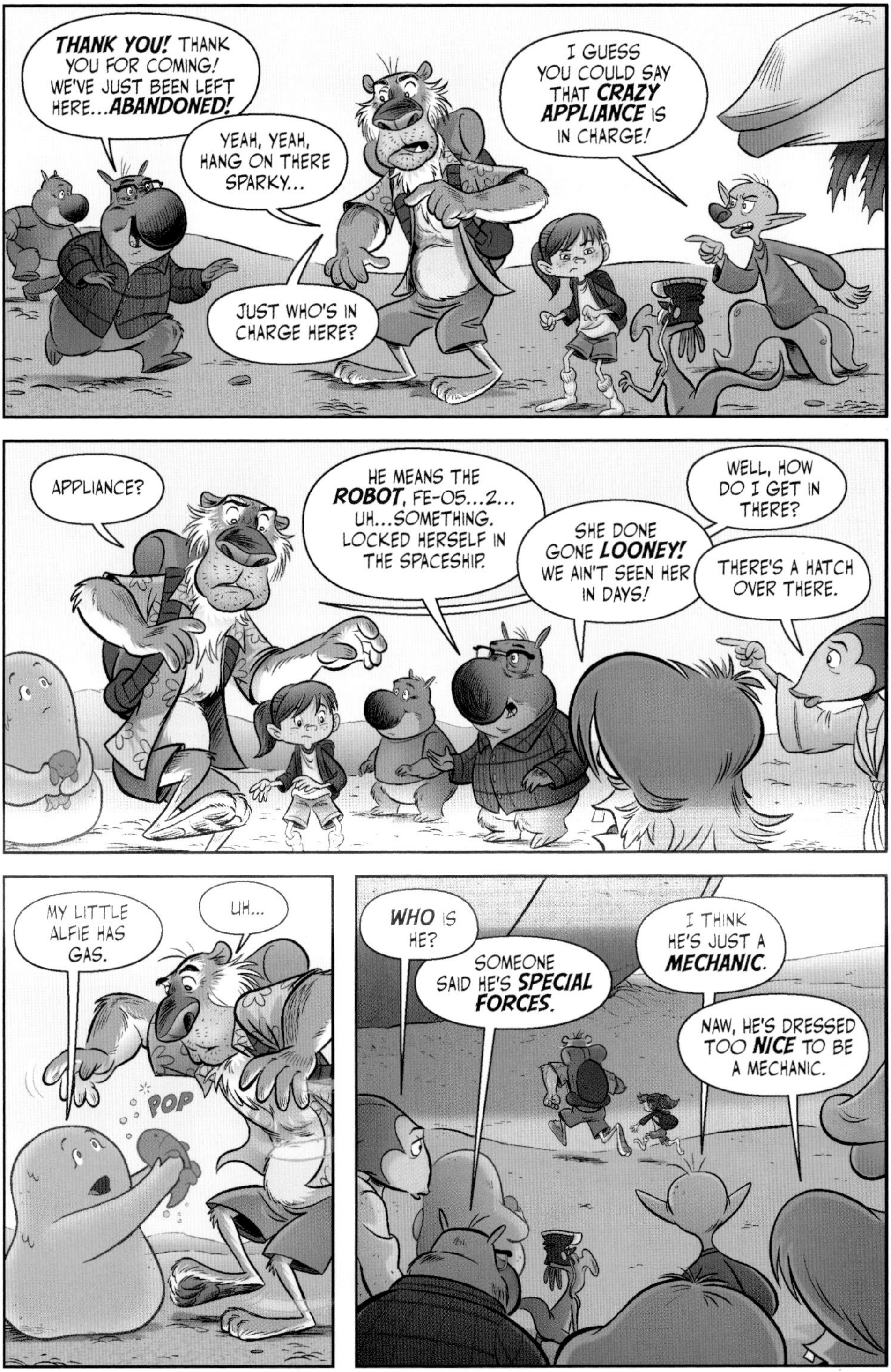
THANK YOU! THANK YOU FOR COMING! WE'VE JUST BEEN LEFT HERE...ABANDONED!
YEAH, YEAH, HANG ON THERE SPARKY...
JUST WHO'S IN CHARGE HERE?
I GUESS YOU COULD SAY THAT CRAZY APPLIANCE IS IN CHARGE!
APPLIANCE?
HE MEANS THE ROBOT, FE-05...2... UH...SOMETHING. LOCKED HERSELF IN THE SPACESHIP.
SHE DONE GONE LOONEY! WE AIN'T SEEN HER IN DAYS!
WELL, HOW DO I GET IN THERE?
THERE'S A HATCH OVER THERE.
MY LITTLE ALFIE HAS GAS.
UH...
POP
WHO IS HE?
SOMEONE SAID HE'S SPECIAL FORCES.
I THINK HE'S JUST A MECHANIC.
NAW, HE'S DRESSED TOO NICE TO BE A MECHANIC.

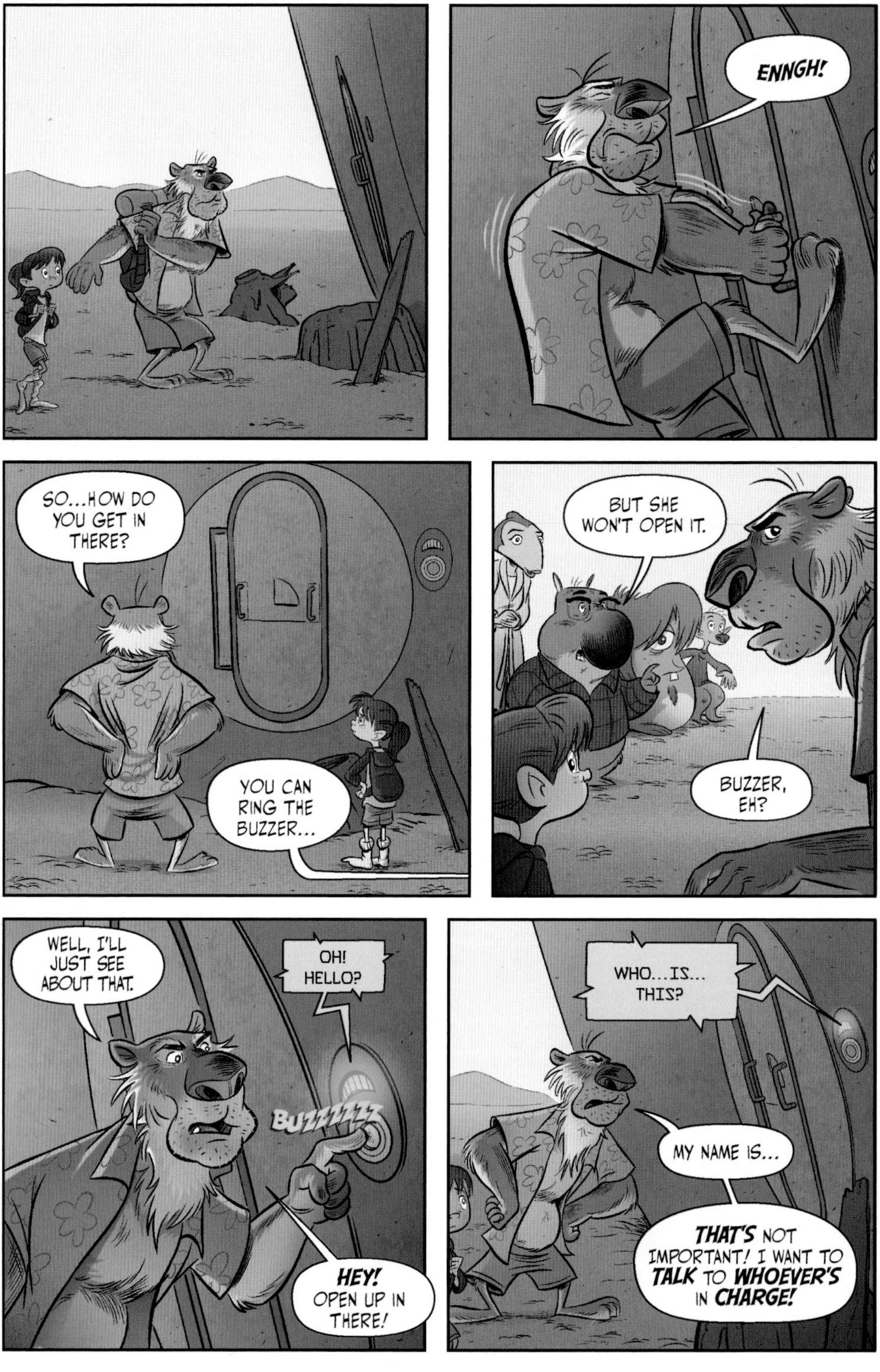
ENNGH!
SO...HOW DO YOU GET IN THERE?
YOU CAN RING THE BUZZER...
BUT SHE WON'T OPEN IT.
BUZZER, EH?
WELL, I'LL JUST SEE ABOUT THAT.
OH! HELLO?
BUZZZZZZ
HEY! OPEN UP IN THERE!
WHO...IS... THIS?
MY NAME IS...
THAT'S NOT IMPORTANT! I WANT TO TALK TO WHOEVER'S IN CHARGE!

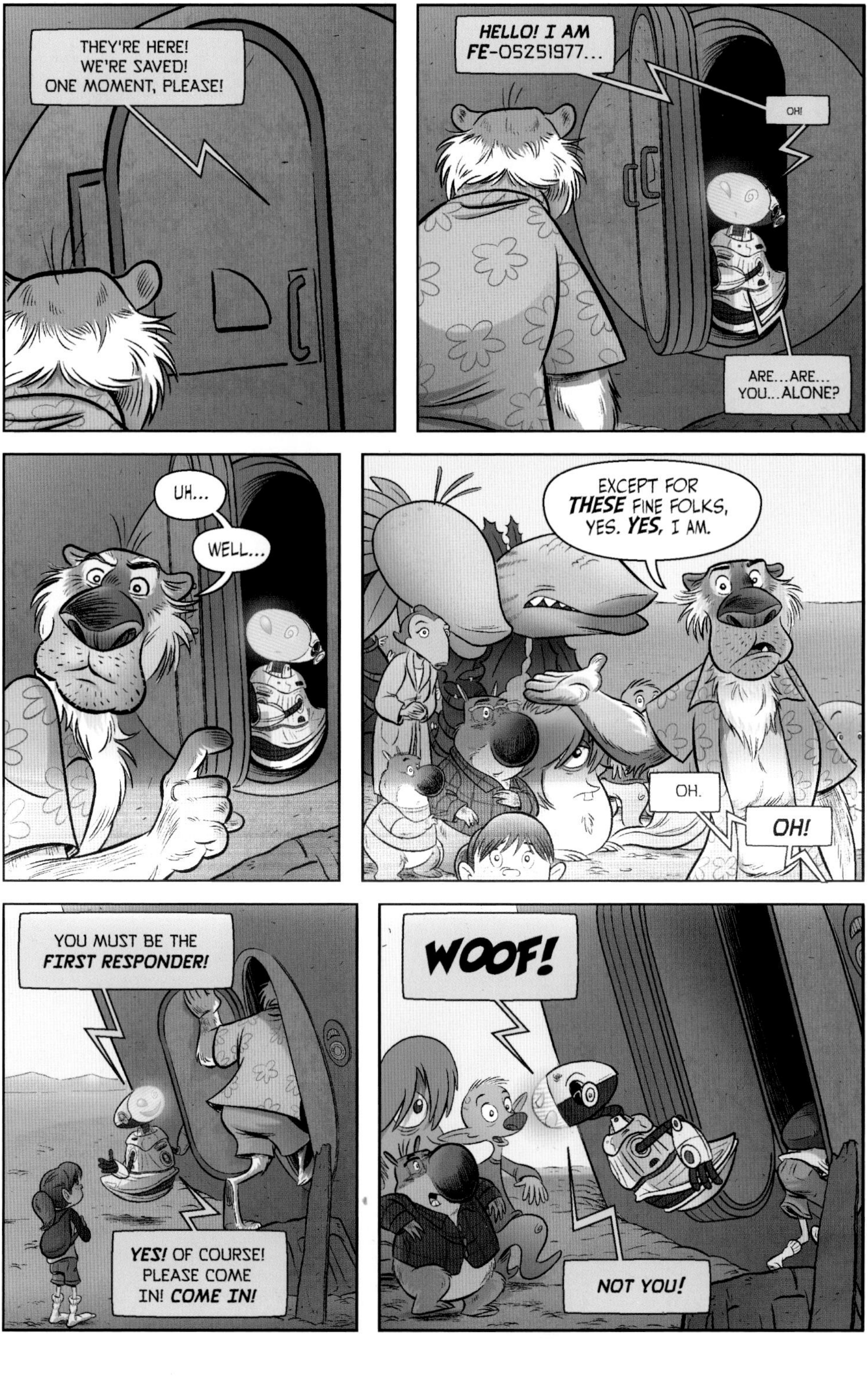
THEY'RE HERE! WE'RE SAVED! ONE MOMENT, PLEASE!
HELLO! I AM FE-05251977...
OH!
ARE...ARE... YOU...ALONE?
UH...
WELL...
EXCEPT FOR THESE FINE FOLKS, YES. YES, I AM.
OH.
OH!
YOU MUST BE THE FIRST RESPONDER!
YES! OF COURSE! PLEASE COME IN! COME IN!
WOOF!
NOT YOU!

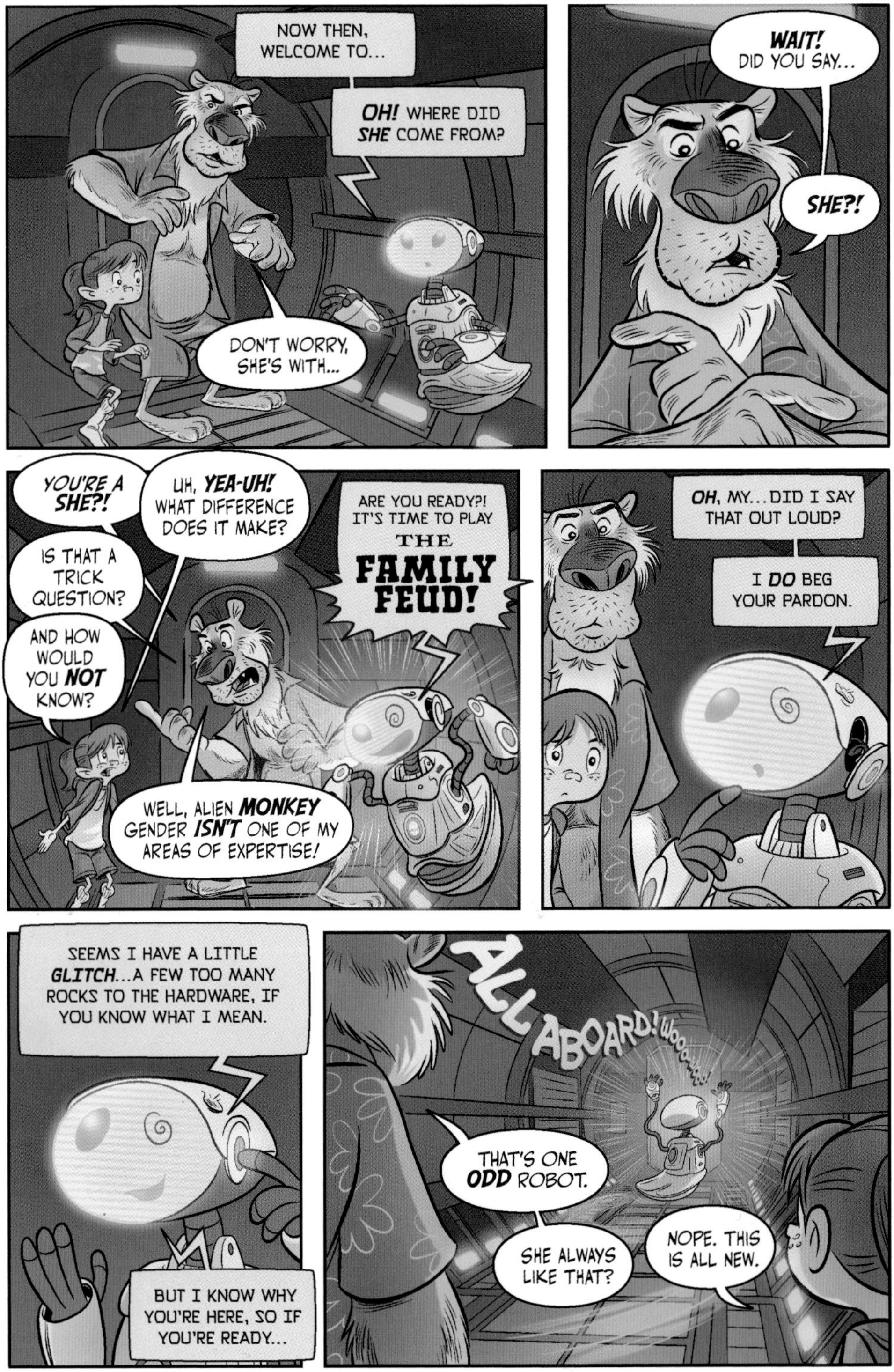
NOW THEN, WELCOME TO...
OH! WHERE DID SHE COME FROM?
DON'T WORRY, SHE'S WITH...
WAIT! DID YOU SAY...
SHE?!
YOU'RE A SHE?!
UH, YEA-UH! WHAT DIFFERENCE DOES IT MAKE?
IS THAT A TRICK QUESTION?
AND HOW WOULD YOU NOT KNOW?
ARE YOU READY?! IT'S TIME TO PLAY THE FAMILY FEUD!
WELL, ALIEN MONKEY GENDER ISN'T ONE OF MY AREAS OF EXPERTISE!
OH, MY... DID I SAY THAT OUT LOUD?
I DO BEG YOUR PARDON.
SEEMS I HAVE A LITTLE GLITCH... A FEW TOO MANY ROCKS TO THE HARDWARE, IF YOU KNOW WHAT I MEAN.
BUT I KNOW WHY YOU'RE HERE, SO IF YOU'RE READY...
ALL ABOARD! WOOO-HOO!
THAT'S ONE ODD ROBOT.
SHE ALWAYS LIKE THAT?
NOPE. THIS IS ALL NEW.

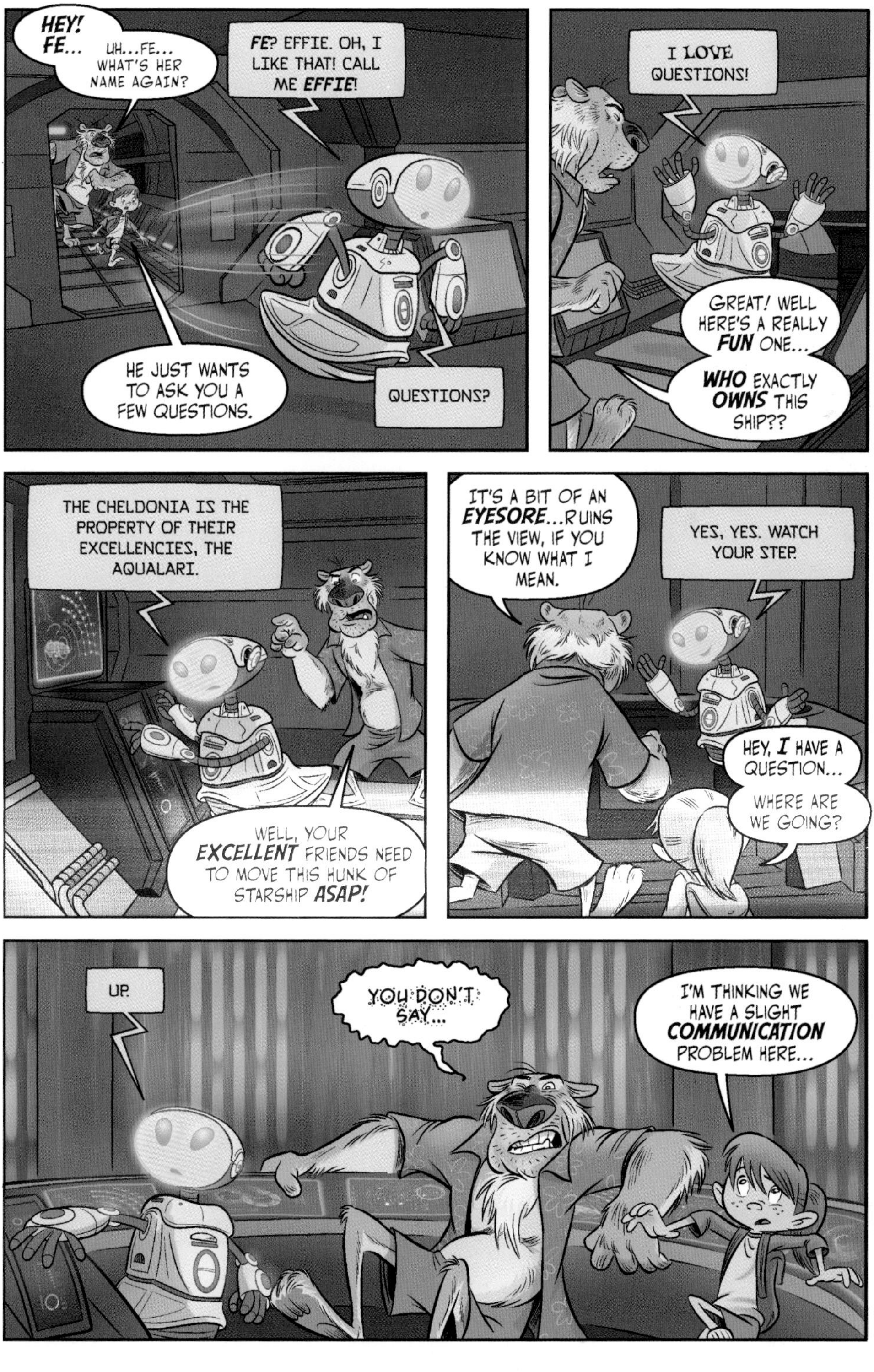
HEY! FE...
UH...FE... WHAT'S HER NAME AGAIN?
FE? EFFIE. OH, I LIKE THAT! CALL ME EFFIE!
HE JUST WANTS TO ASK YOU A FEW QUESTIONS.
QUESTIONS?
I LOVE QUESTIONS!
GREAT! WELL HERE'S A REALLY FUN ONE...
WHO EXACTLY OWNS THIS SHIP??
THE CHELDONIA IS THE PROPERTY OF THEIR EXCELLENCIES, THE AQUALARI.
WELL, YOUR EXCELLENT FRIENDS NEED TO MOVE THIS HUNK OF STARSHIP ASAP!
IT'S A BIT OF AN EYESORE...RUINS THE VIEW, IF YOU KNOW WHAT I MEAN.
YES, YES. WATCH YOUR STEP.
HEY, I HAVE A QUESTION...
WHERE ARE WE GOING?
UP.
YOU DON'T SAY...
I'M THINKING WE HAVE A SLIGHT COMMUNICATION PROBLEM HERE...

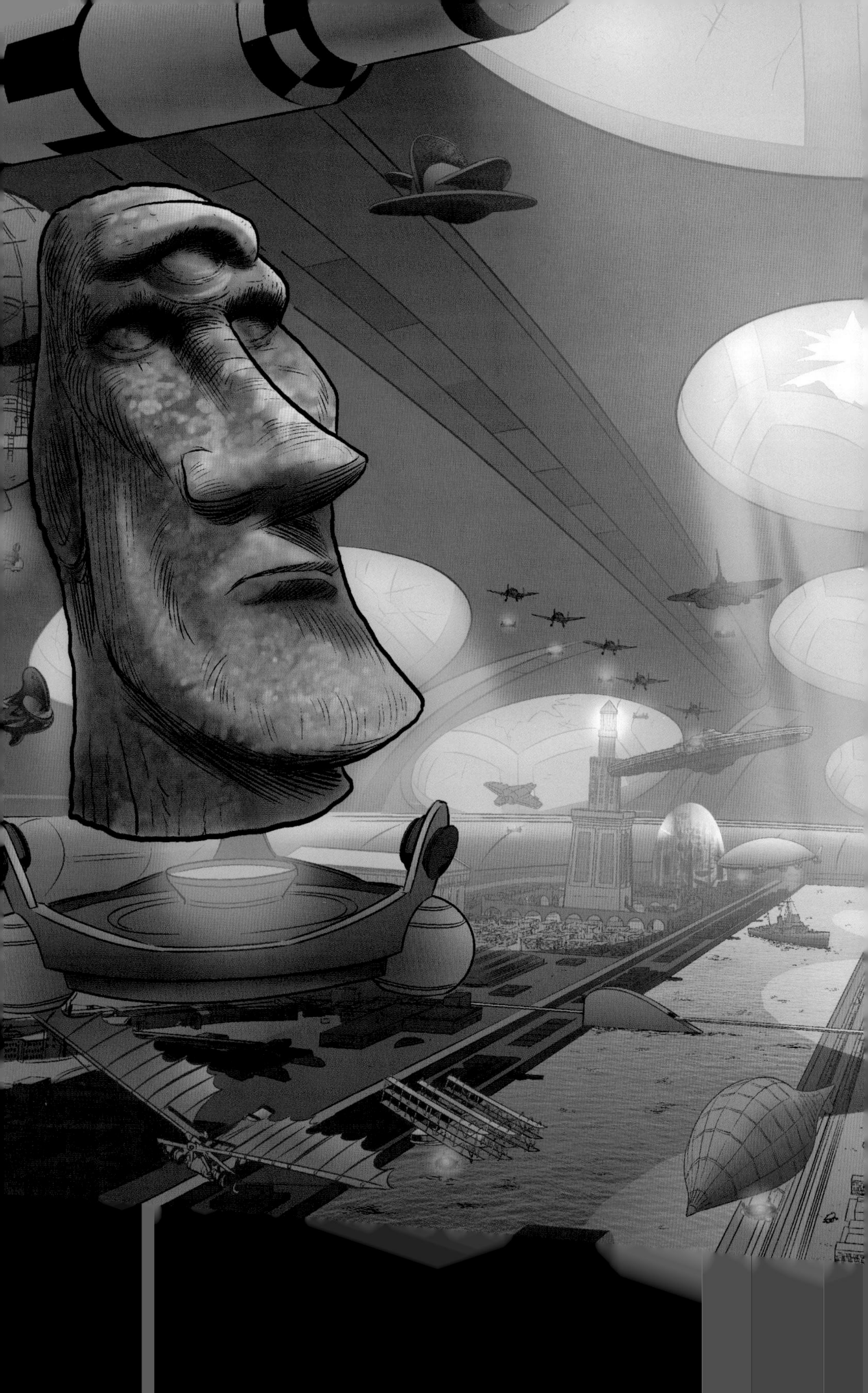

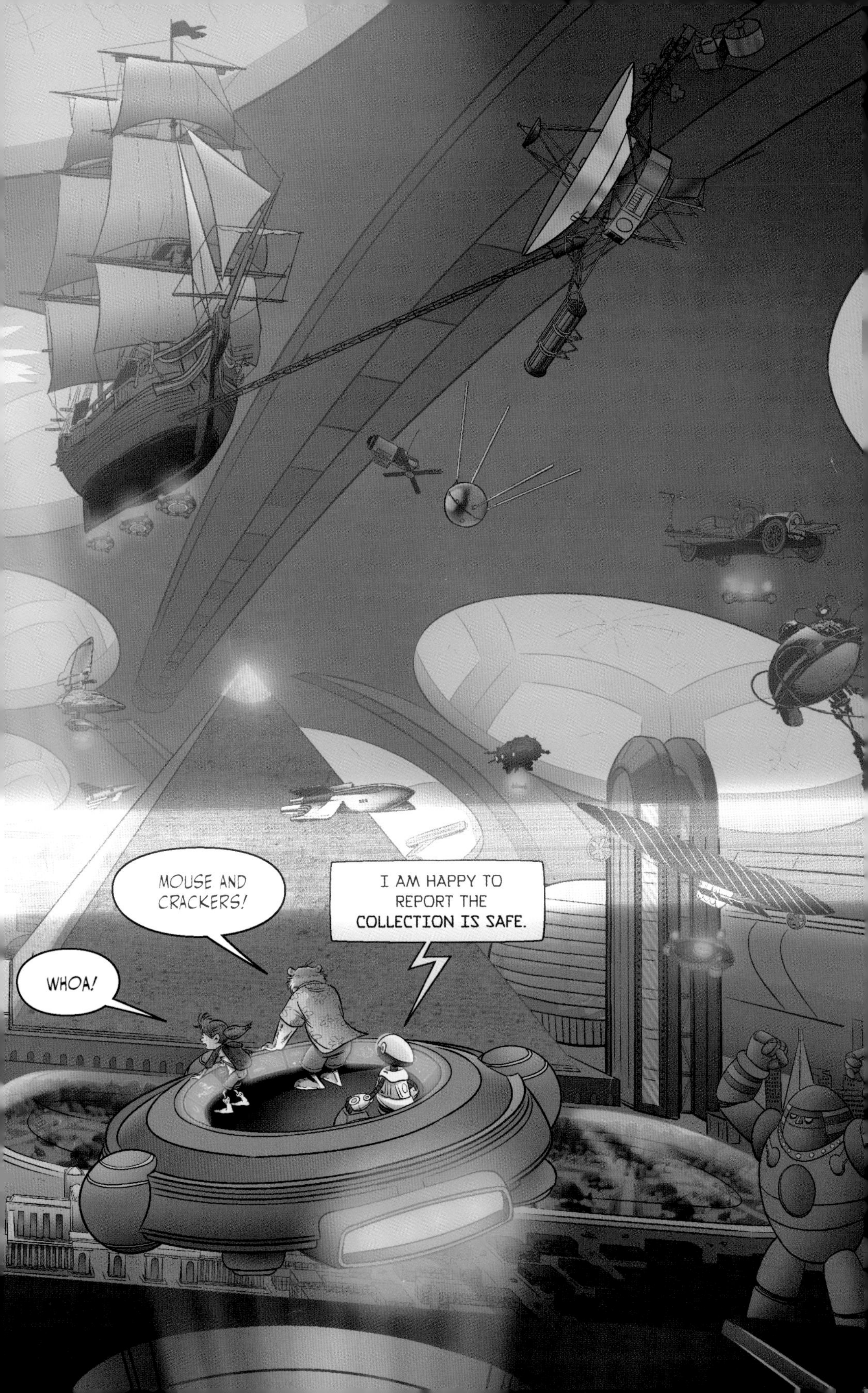
WHOA!
MOUSE AND CRACKERS!
I AM HAPPY TO REPORT THE COLLECTION IS SAFE.

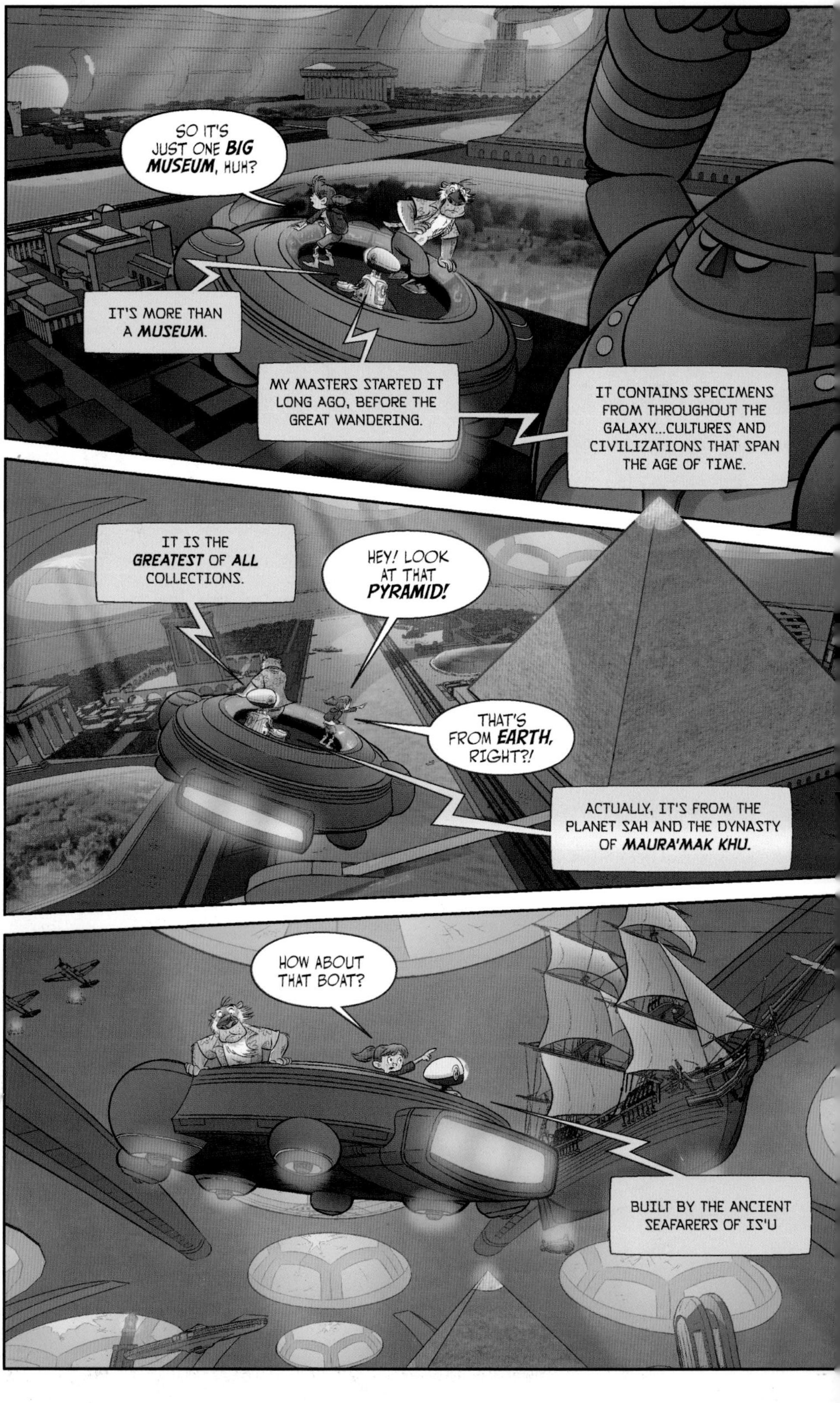
SO IT'S JUST ONE BIG MUSEUM, HUH?
IT'S MORE THAN A MUSEUM.
MY MASTERS STARTED IT LONG AGO, BEFORE THE GREAT WANDERING.
IT CONTAINS SPECIMENS FROM THROUGHOUT THE GALAXY...CULTURES AND CIVILIZATIONS THAT SPAN THE AGE OF TIME.
IT IS THE GREATEST OF ALL COLLECTIONS.
HEY! LOOK AT THAT PYRAMID!
THAT'S FROM EARTH, RIGHT?!
ACTUALLY, IT'S FROM THE PLANET SAH AND THE DYNASTY OF MAURA'MAK KHU.
HOW ABOUT THAT BOAT?
BUILT BY THE ANCIENT SEAFARERS OF IS'U

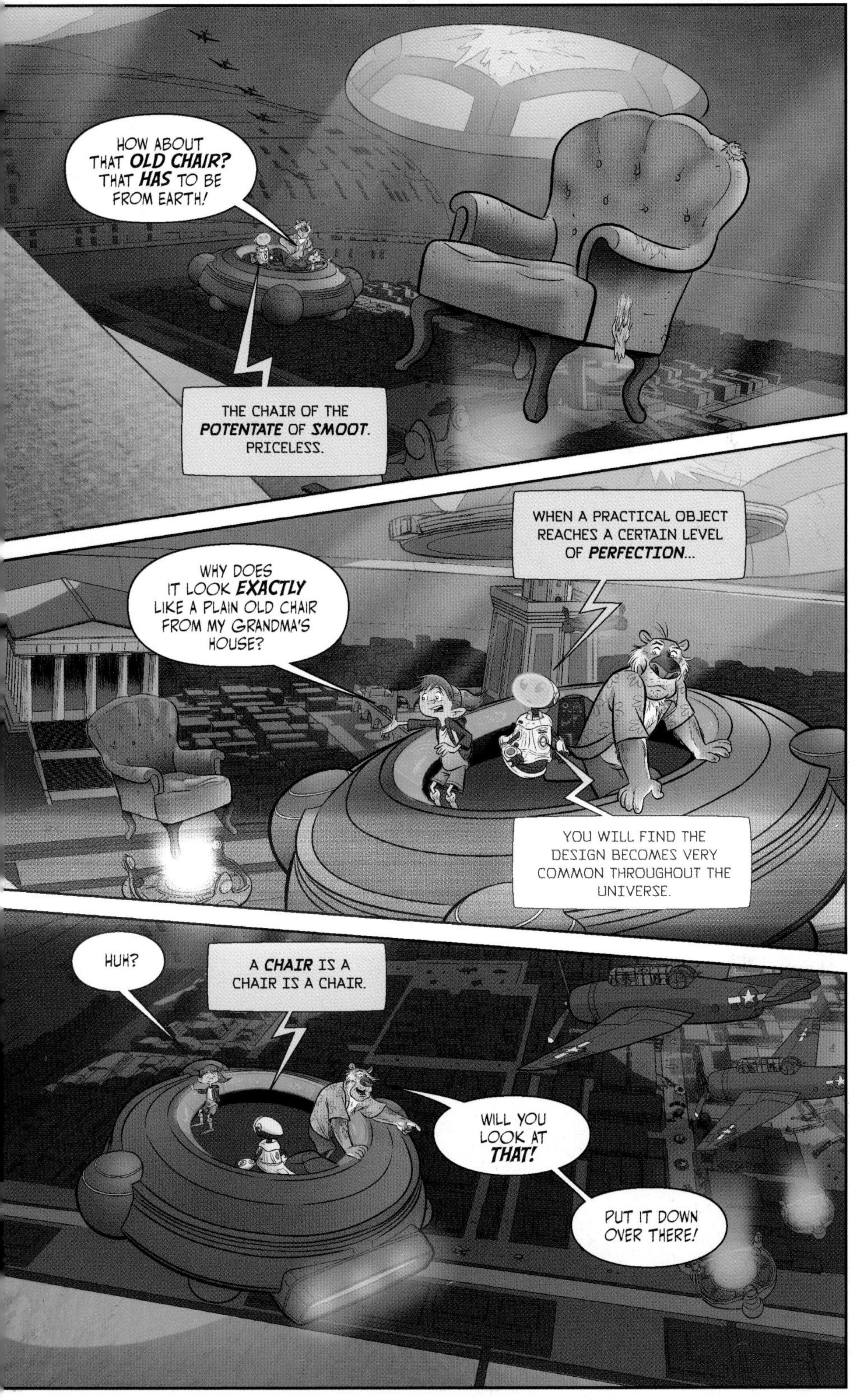
HOW ABOUT THAT OLD CHAIR? THAT HAS TO BE FROM EARTH!
THE CHAIR OF THE POTENTATE OF SMOOT. PRICELESS.
WHY DOES IT LOOK EXACTLY LIKE A PLAIN OLD CHAIR FROM MY GRANDMA'S HOUSE?
WHEN A PRACTICAL OBJECT REACHES A CERTAIN LEVEL OF PERFECTION...
YOU WILL FIND THE DESIGN BECOMES VERY COMMON THROUGHOUT THE UNIVERSE.
HUH?
A CHAIR IS A CHAIR IS A CHAIR.
WILL YOU LOOK AT THAT!
PUT IT DOWN OVER THERE!

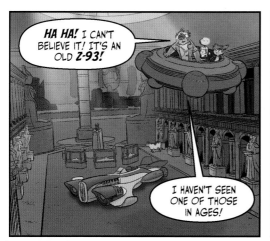

HA HA! I CAN'T BELIEVE IT! IT'S AN OLD *Z-93!*

I HAVEN'T SEEN ONE OF THOSE IN AGES!

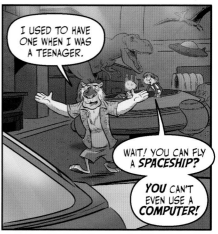

I USED TO HAVE ONE WHEN I WAS A TEENAGER.

WAIT! YOU CAN FLY A *SPACESHIP?*

YOU CAN'T EVEN USE A *COMPUTER!*

SPACESHIP?! IT *ISN'T* A SPACESHIP!

THIS IS A FINELY TUNED *PRECISION* MACHINE! THE FINEST *HOV-ROD* EVER MADE.

WHAT IS UP WITH EVERYONE AND THEIR *STUPID* CAR LOVE?!

WHERE DID ALL THIS STUFF COME FROM?

DIFFERENT MEANS OF ACQUISITION.

DEALERS, ESTATE SALES, GIFTS, INTERNET AUCTIONS.

IT MUST BE WORTH...

I CAN'T GET MY HEAD AROUND IT.

THE COLLECTION IS PRICELESS.

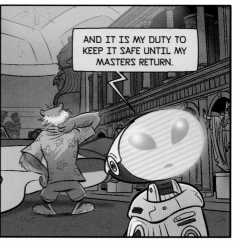

AND IT IS MY DUTY TO KEEP IT SAFE UNTIL MY MASTERS RETURN.

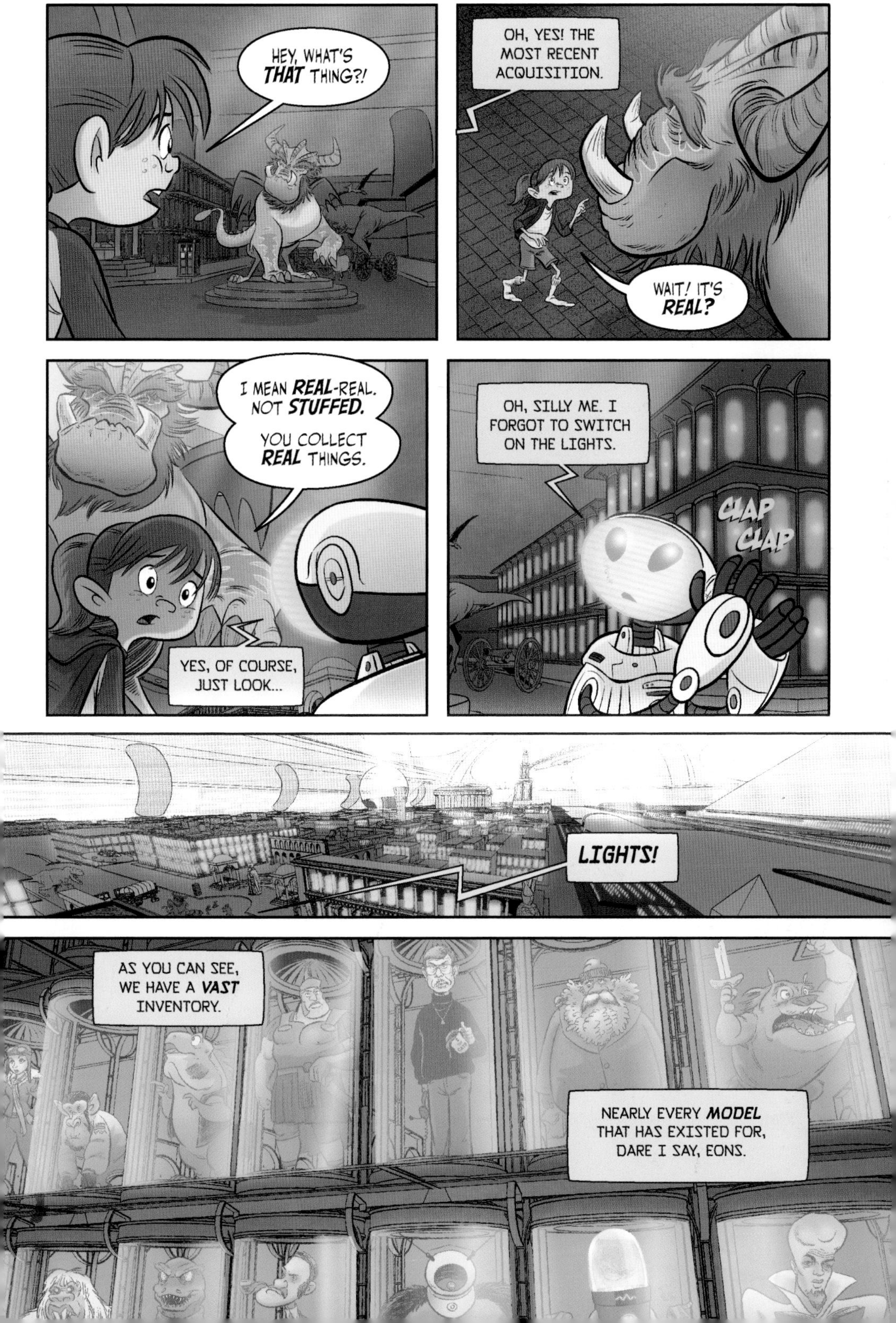
HEY, WHAT'S **THAT** THING?!
OH, YES! THE MOST RECENT ACQUISITION.
WAIT! IT'S **REAL?**
I MEAN **REAL**-REAL. NOT **STUFFED.**
YOU COLLECT **REAL** THINGS.
YES, OF COURSE, JUST LOOK...
OH, SILLY ME. I FORGOT TO SWITCH ON THE LIGHTS.
CLAP CLAP
LIGHTS!
AS YOU CAN SEE, WE HAVE A **VAST** INVENTORY.
NEARLY EVERY **MODEL** THAT HAS EXISTED FOR, DARE I SAY, EONS.

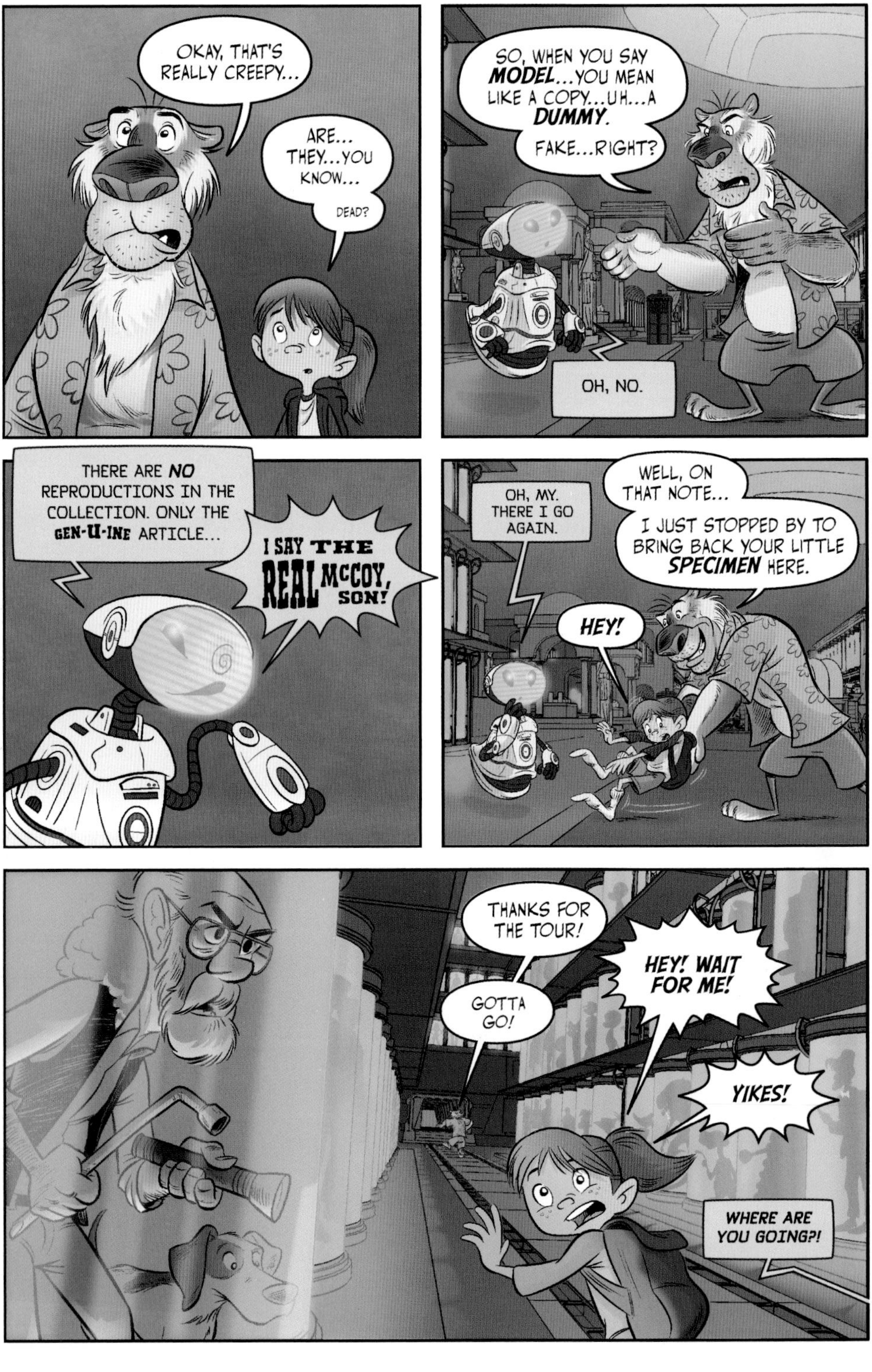
OKAY, THAT'S REALLY CREEPY...
ARE... THEY...YOU KNOW...
DEAD?
SO, WHEN YOU SAY MODEL...YOU MEAN LIKE A COPY...UH...A DUMMY.
FAKE...RIGHT?
OH, NO.
THERE ARE NO REPRODUCTIONS IN THE COLLECTION. ONLY THE GEN-U-INE ARTICLE...
I SAY THE REAL McCOY, SON!
OH, MY. THERE I GO AGAIN.
WELL, ON THAT NOTE...
I JUST STOPPED BY TO BRING BACK YOUR LITTLE SPECIMEN HERE.
HEY!
THANKS FOR THE TOUR!
GOTTA GO!
HEY! WAIT FOR ME!
YIKES!
WHERE ARE YOU GOING?!

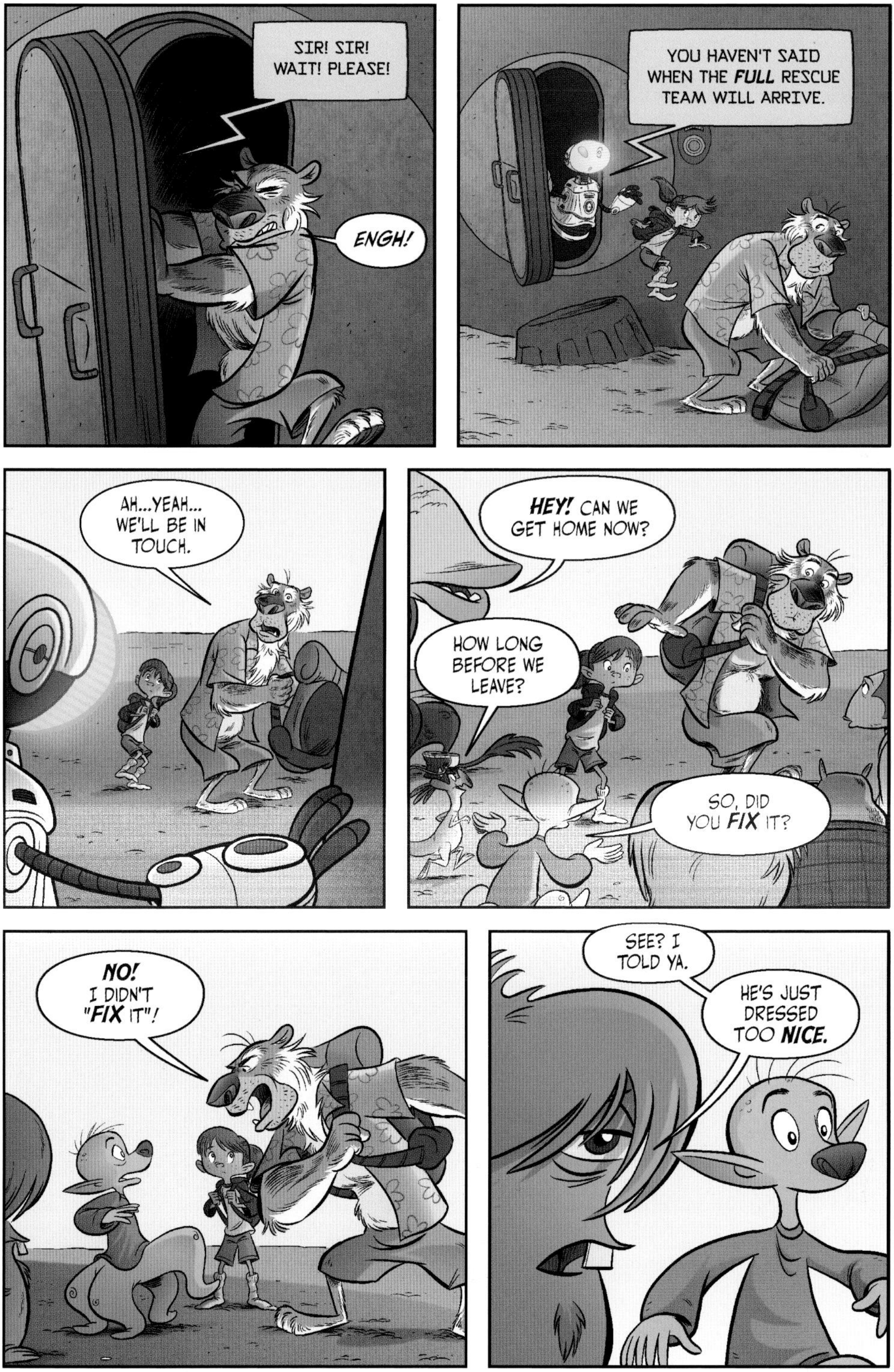
SIR! SIR! WAIT! PLEASE!
ENGH!
YOU HAVEN'T SAID WHEN THE **FULL** RESCUE TEAM WILL ARRIVE.
AH...YEAH... WE'LL BE IN TOUCH.
HEY! CAN WE GET HOME NOW?
HOW LONG BEFORE WE LEAVE?
SO, DID YOU **FIX** IT?
NO! I DIDN'T "**FIX** IT"!
SEE? I TOLD YA.
HE'S JUST DRESSED TOO **NICE.**

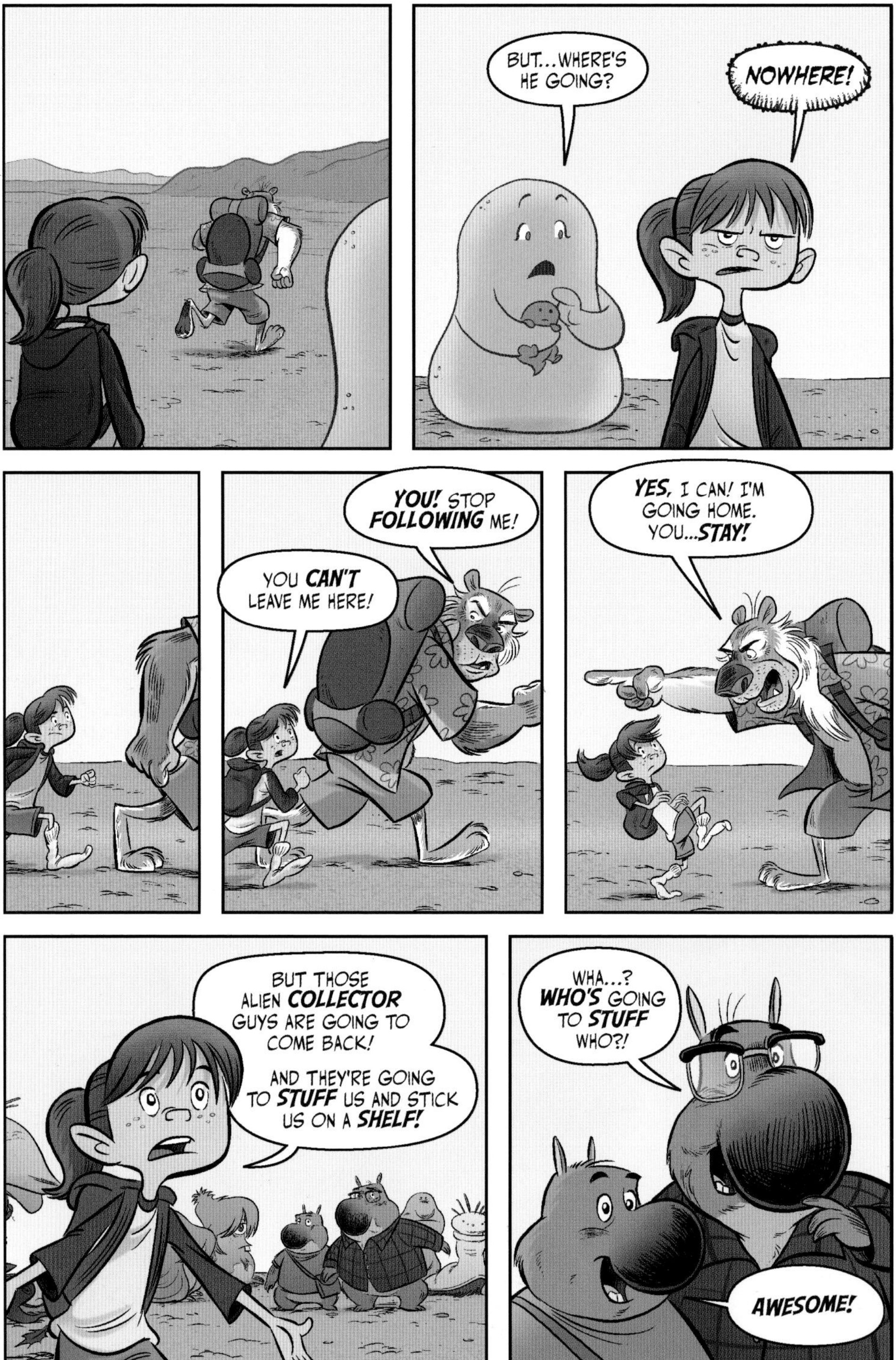
BUT...WHERE'S HE GOING?
NOWHERE!
YOU! STOP FOLLOWING ME!
YOU CAN'T LEAVE ME HERE!
YES, I CAN! I'M GOING HOME. YOU...STAY!
BUT THOSE ALIEN COLLECTOR GUYS ARE GOING TO COME BACK!
AND THEY'RE GOING TO STUFF US AND STICK US ON A SHELF!
WHA...? WHO'S GOING TO STUFF WHO?!
AWESOME!

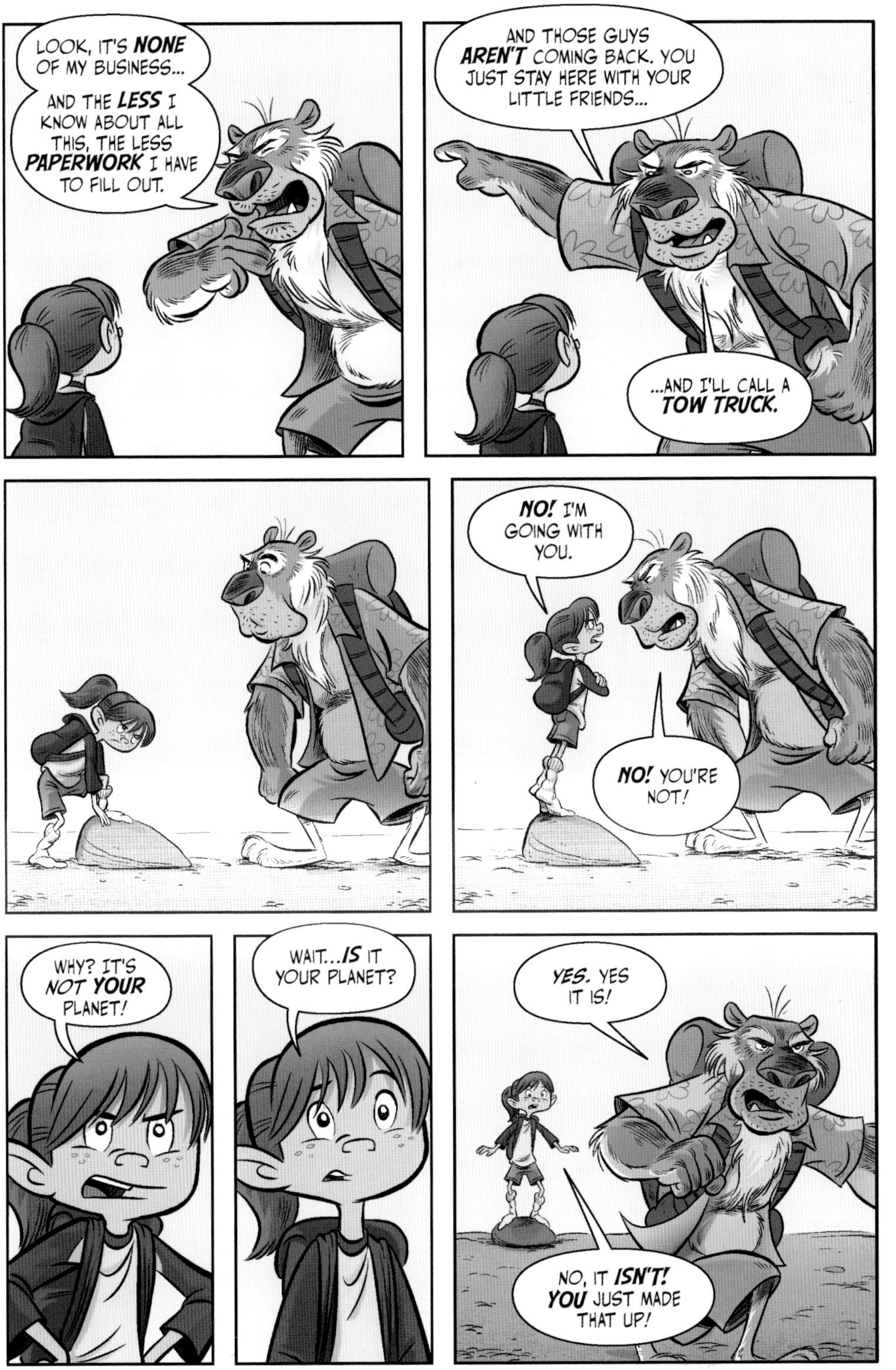
LOOK, IT'S NONE OF MY BUSINESS...
AND THE LESS I KNOW ABOUT ALL THIS, THE LESS PAPERWORK I HAVE TO FILL OUT.
AND THOSE GUYS AREN'T COMING BACK. YOU JUST STAY HERE WITH YOUR LITTLE FRIENDS...
...AND I'LL CALL A TOW TRUCK.
NO! I'M GOING WITH YOU.
NO! YOU'RE NOT!
WHY? IT'S NOT YOUR PLANET!
WAIT...IS IT YOUR PLANET?
YES. YES IT IS!
NO, IT ISN'T! YOU JUST MADE THAT UP!

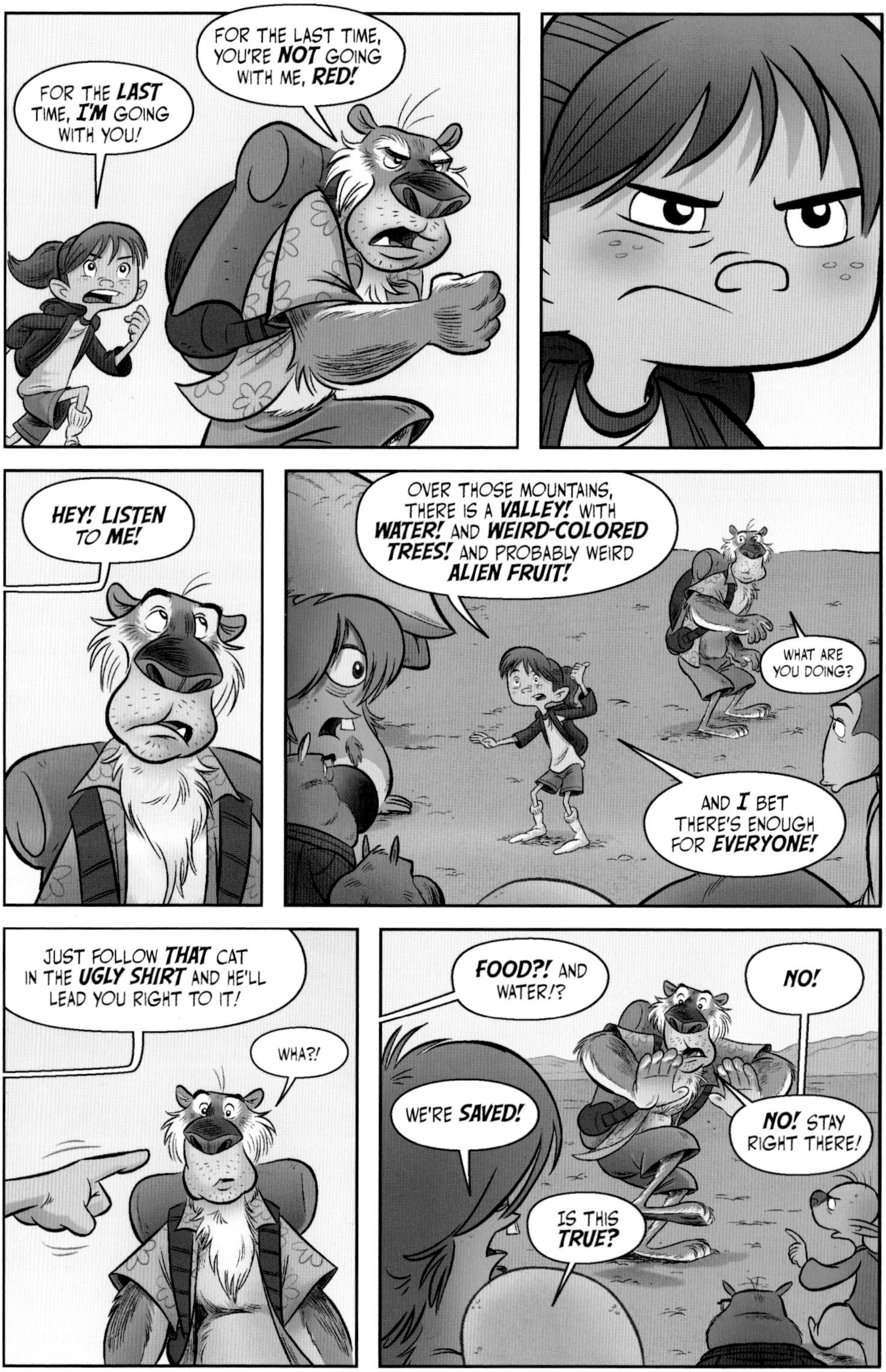

FOR THE LAST TIME, I'M GOING WITH YOU!
FOR THE LAST TIME, YOU'RE NOT GOING WITH ME, RED!
HEY! LISTEN TO ME!
OVER THOSE MOUNTAINS, THERE IS A VALLEY! WITH WATER! AND WEIRD-COLORED TREES! AND PROBABLY WEIRD ALIEN FRUIT!
WHAT ARE YOU DOING?
AND I BET THERE'S ENOUGH FOR EVERYONE!
JUST FOLLOW THAT CAT IN THE UGLY SHIRT AND HE'LL LEAD YOU RIGHT TO IT!
WHA?!
FOOD?! AND WATER!?
NO!
WE'RE SAVED!
NO! STAY RIGHT THERE!
IS THIS TRUE?

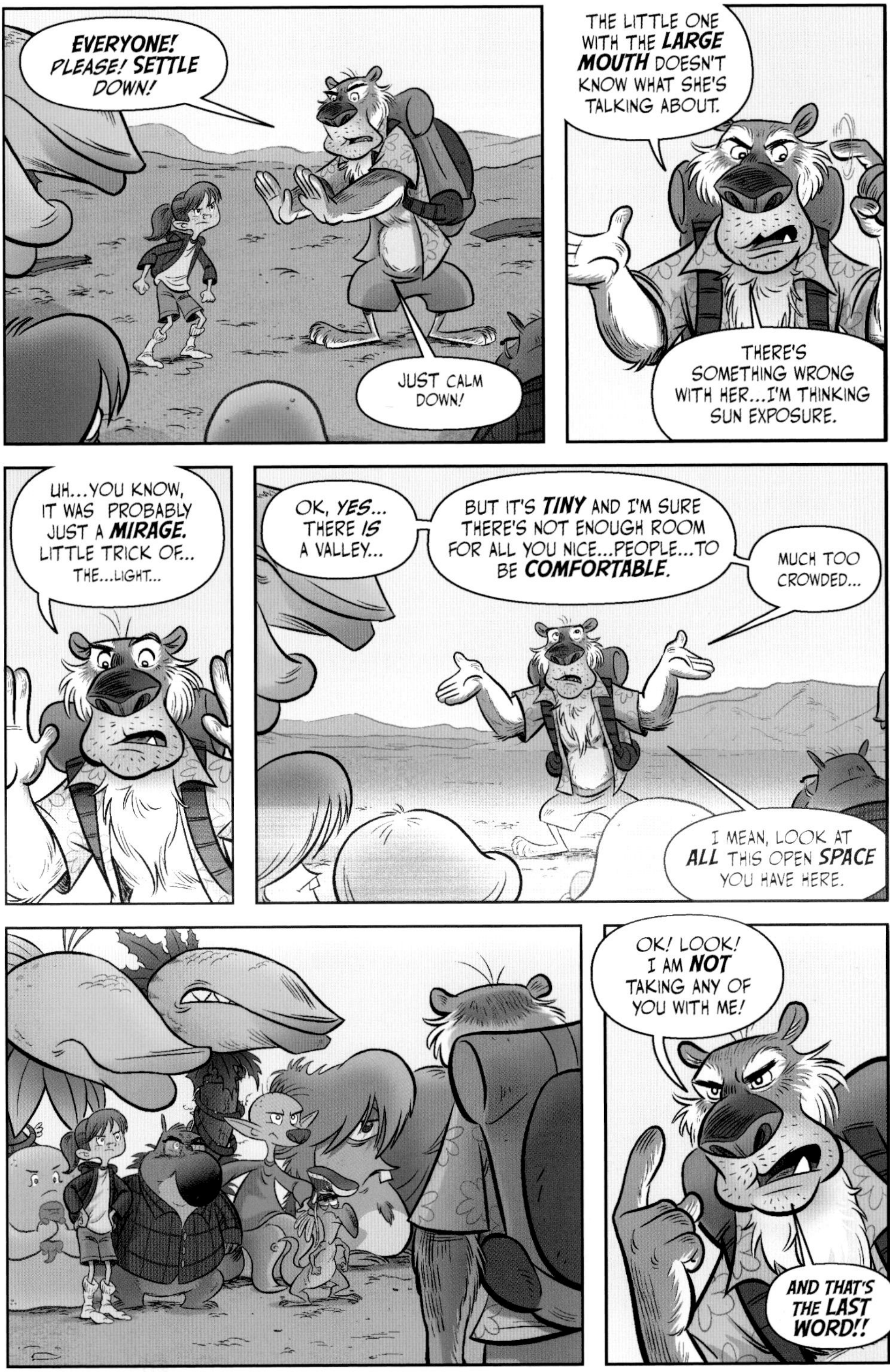
EVERYONE! PLEASE! SETTLE DOWN!
JUST CALM DOWN!
THE LITTLE ONE WITH THE LARGE MOUTH DOESN'T KNOW WHAT SHE'S TALKING ABOUT.
THERE'S SOMETHING WRONG WITH HER...I'M THINKING SUN EXPOSURE.
UH...YOU KNOW, IT WAS PROBABLY JUST A MIRAGE. LITTLE TRICK OF... THE...LIGHT...
OK, YES... THERE IS A VALLEY...
BUT IT'S TINY AND I'M SURE THERE'S NOT ENOUGH ROOM FOR ALL YOU NICE...PEOPLE...TO BE COMFORTABLE.
MUCH TOO CROWDED...
I MEAN, LOOK AT ALL THIS OPEN SPACE YOU HAVE HERE.
OK! LOOK! I AM NOT TAKING ANY OF YOU WITH ME!
AND THAT'S THE LAST WORD!!

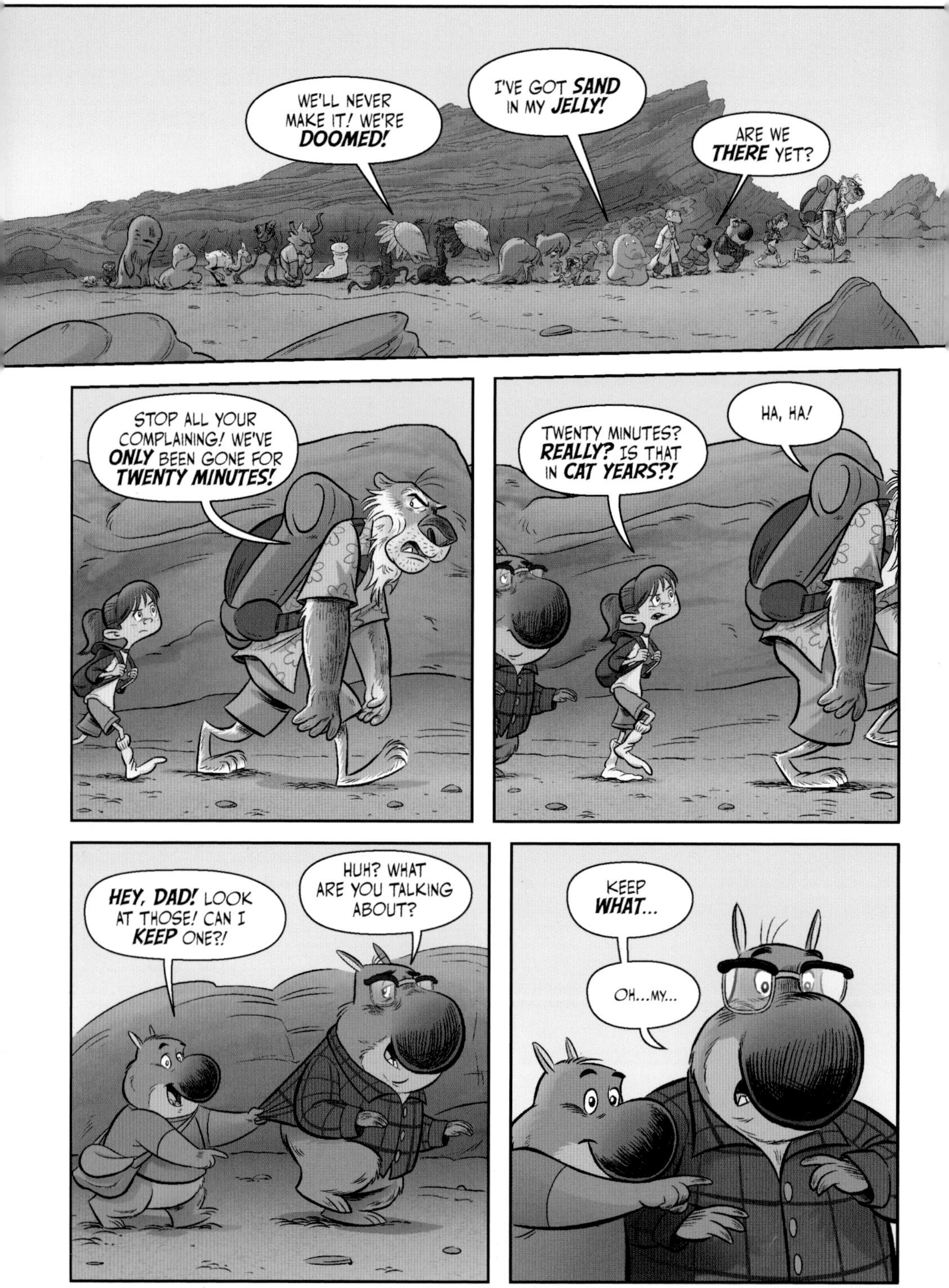
WE'LL NEVER MAKE IT! WE'RE DOOMED!
I'VE GOT SAND IN MY JELLY!
ARE WE THERE YET?
STOP ALL YOUR COMPLAINING! WE'VE ONLY BEEN GONE FOR TWENTY MINUTES!
TWENTY MINUTES? REALLY? IS THAT IN CAT YEARS?!
HA, HA!
HEY, DAD! LOOK AT THOSE! CAN I KEEP ONE?!
HUH? WHAT ARE YOU TALKING ABOUT?
KEEP WHAT...
OH...MY...

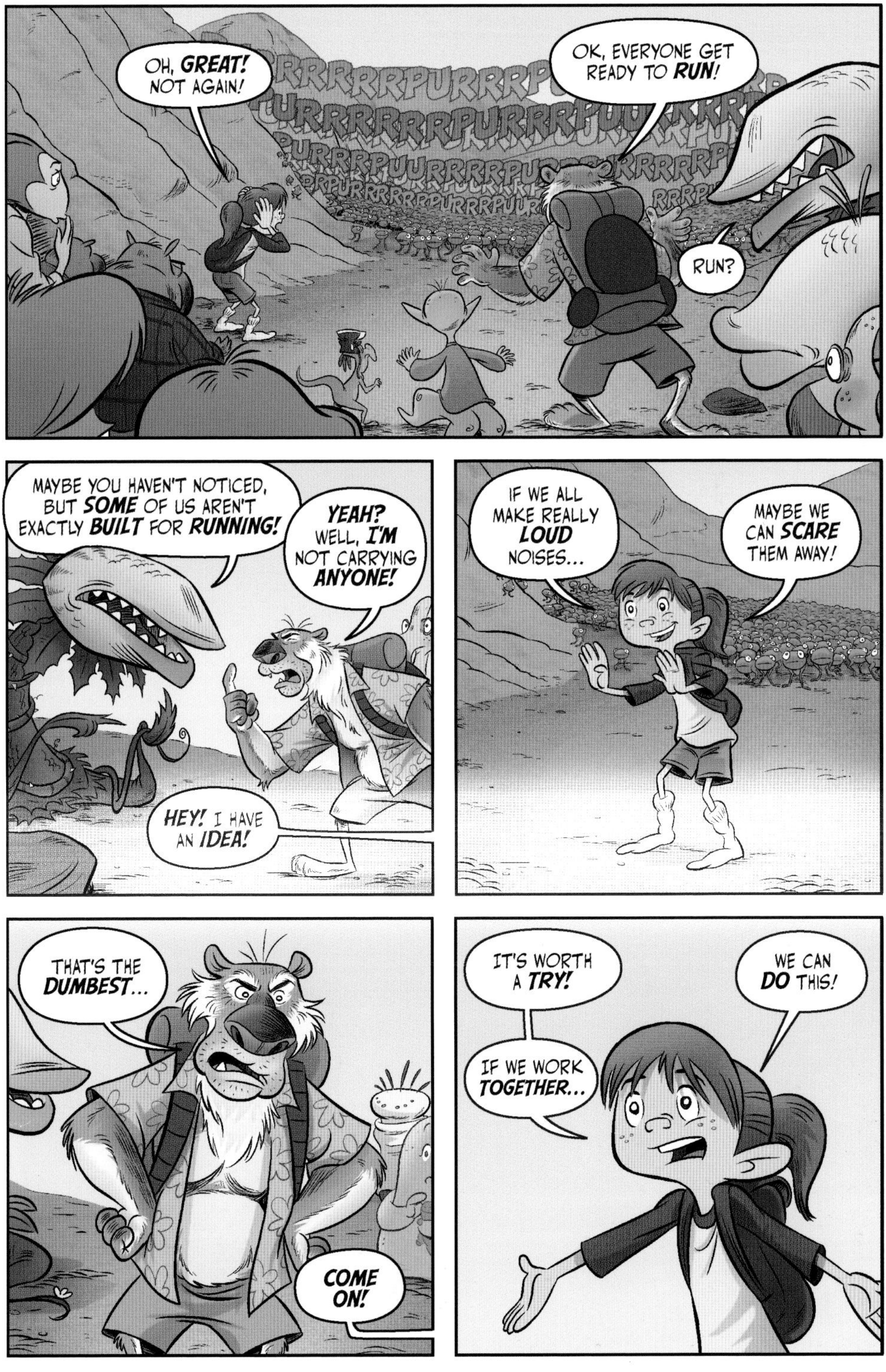

OH, GREAT! NOT AGAIN!
OK, EVERYONE GET READY TO RUN!
RUN?
MAYBE YOU HAVEN'T NOTICED, BUT SOME OF US AREN'T EXACTLY BUILT FOR RUNNING!
YEAH? WELL, I'M NOT CARRYING ANYONE!
HEY! I HAVE AN IDEA!
IF WE ALL MAKE REALLY LOUD NOISES...
MAYBE WE CAN SCARE THEM AWAY!
THAT'S THE DUMBEST...
COME ON!
IT'S WORTH A TRY!
IF WE WORK TOGETHER...
WE CAN DO THIS!

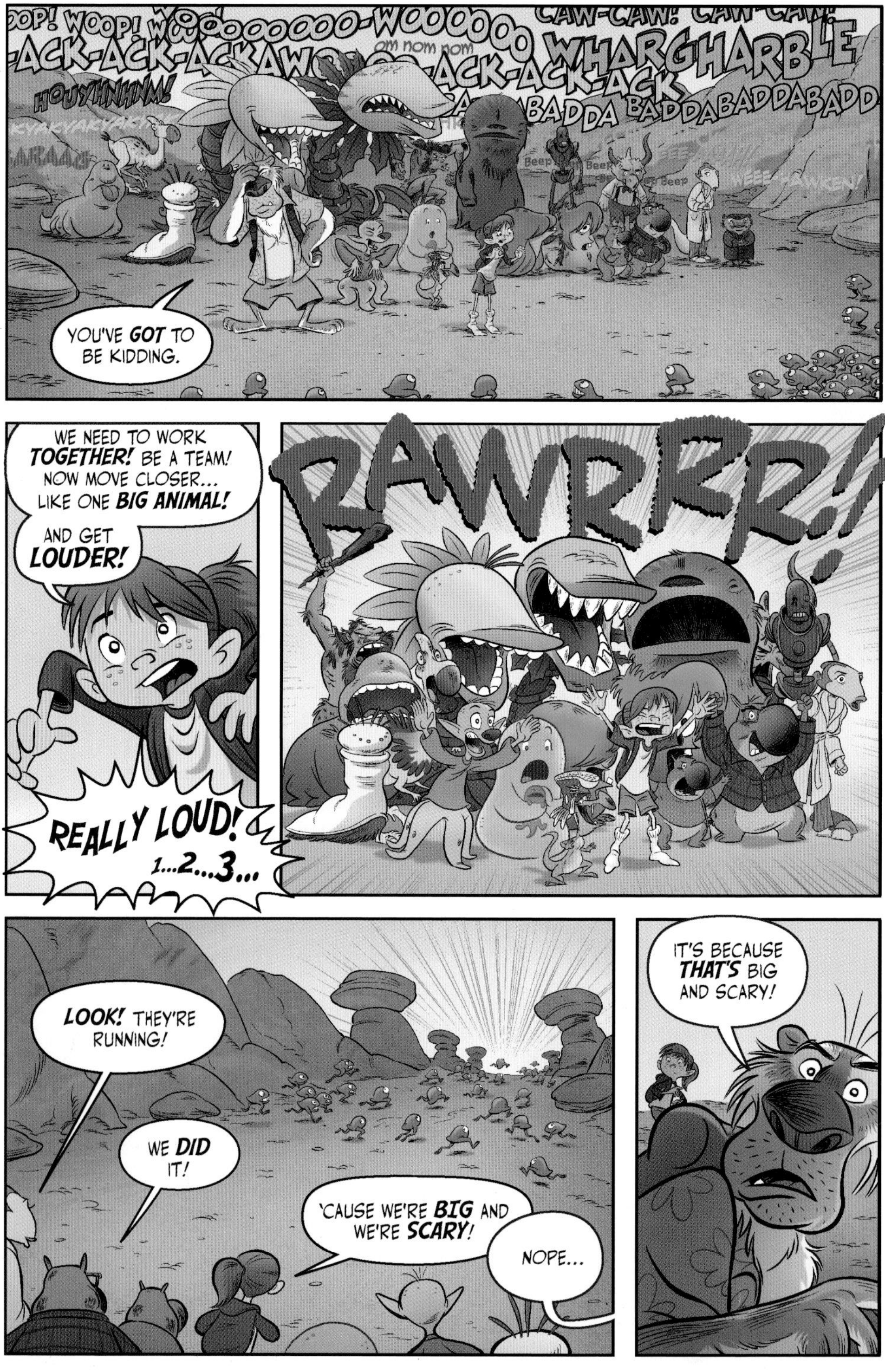
WOOP! WOOP!
WOOOOOOOOO-WOOOOOO
CAW-CAW! CAW-CAW!
om nom nom
-ACK-ACK-ACK
WHARGHARBLE
HOUYHNHNM!
BADDA BADDABADDABADD
Beep Beep Beep
WEEE-HAWKEN!
YOU'VE **GOT** TO BE KIDDING.
WE NEED TO WORK **TOGETHER!** BE A TEAM! NOW MOVE CLOSER... LIKE ONE **BIG ANIMAL!**
AND GET **LOUDER!**
REALLY LOUD! 1...2...3...
RAWRRR!!
LOOK! THEY'RE RUNNING!
WE **DID** IT!
'CAUSE WE'RE **BIG** AND WE'RE **SCARY**!
NOPE...
IT'S BECAUSE **THAT'S** BIG AND SCARY!

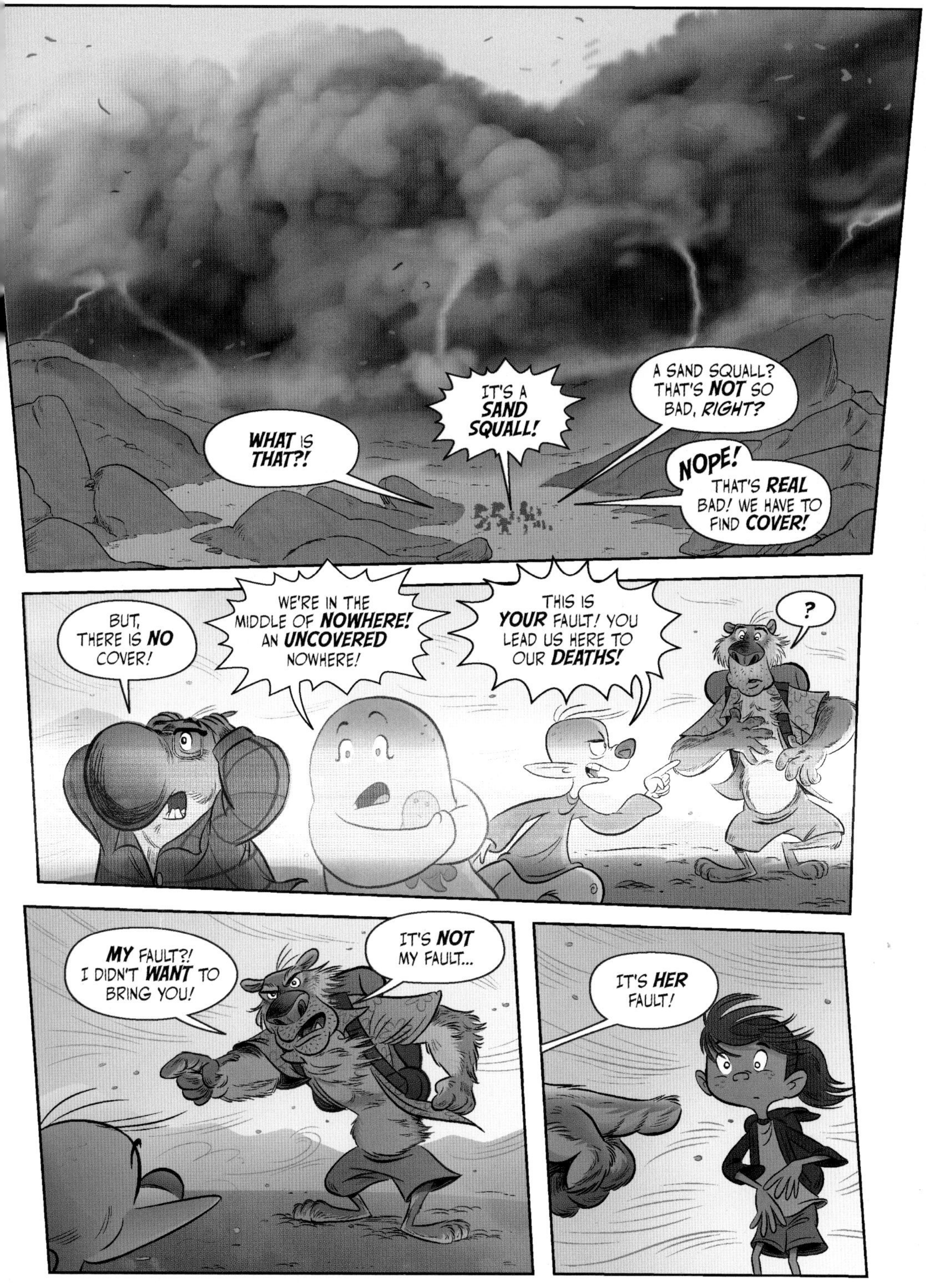
WHAT IS THAT?!
IT'S A SAND SQUALL!
A SAND SQUALL? THAT'S NOT SO BAD, RIGHT?
NOPE! THAT'S REAL BAD! WE HAVE TO FIND COVER!
BUT, THERE IS NO COVER!
WE'RE IN THE MIDDLE OF NOWHERE! AN UNCOVERED NOWHERE!
THIS IS YOUR FAULT! YOU LEAD US HERE TO OUR DEATHS!
?
MY FAULT?! I DIDN'T WANT TO BRING YOU!
IT'S NOT MY FAULT...
IT'S HER FAULT!

YEAH! IT'S RED'S FAULT! SHE TALKED US INTO THIS!

WE COULD HAVE FOUND SHELTER AT THE SHIP!

ARE YOU KIDDING?!

I WAS JUST TRYING TO HELP!

YOU WERE TRYING TO HELP YOURSELF!

YEAH, HE WASN'T GOING TO SAY "NO" TO EVERYONE!

I DON'T THINK THERE EVEN WAS A VALLEY!

NO!

AND NOW WE'RE ALL DOOMED!

GET HER!

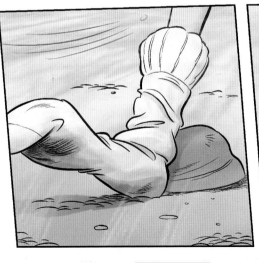

WHOA!

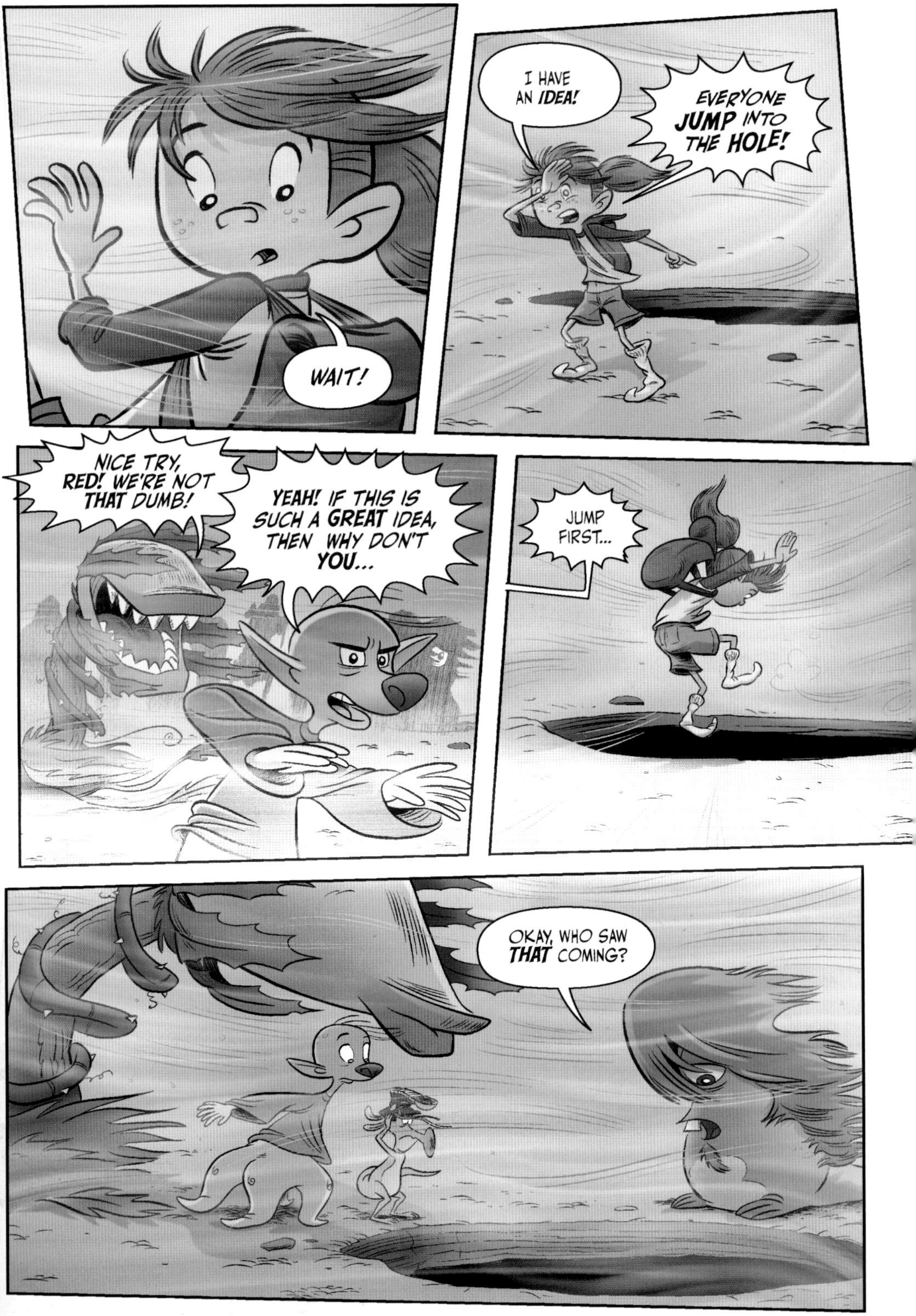
WAIT!
I HAVE AN IDEA!
EVERYONE JUMP INTO THE HOLE!
NICE TRY, RED! WE'RE NOT THAT DUMB!
YEAH! IF THIS IS SUCH A GREAT IDEA, THEN WHY DON'T YOU...
JUMP FIRST...
OKAY, WHO SAW THAT COMING?

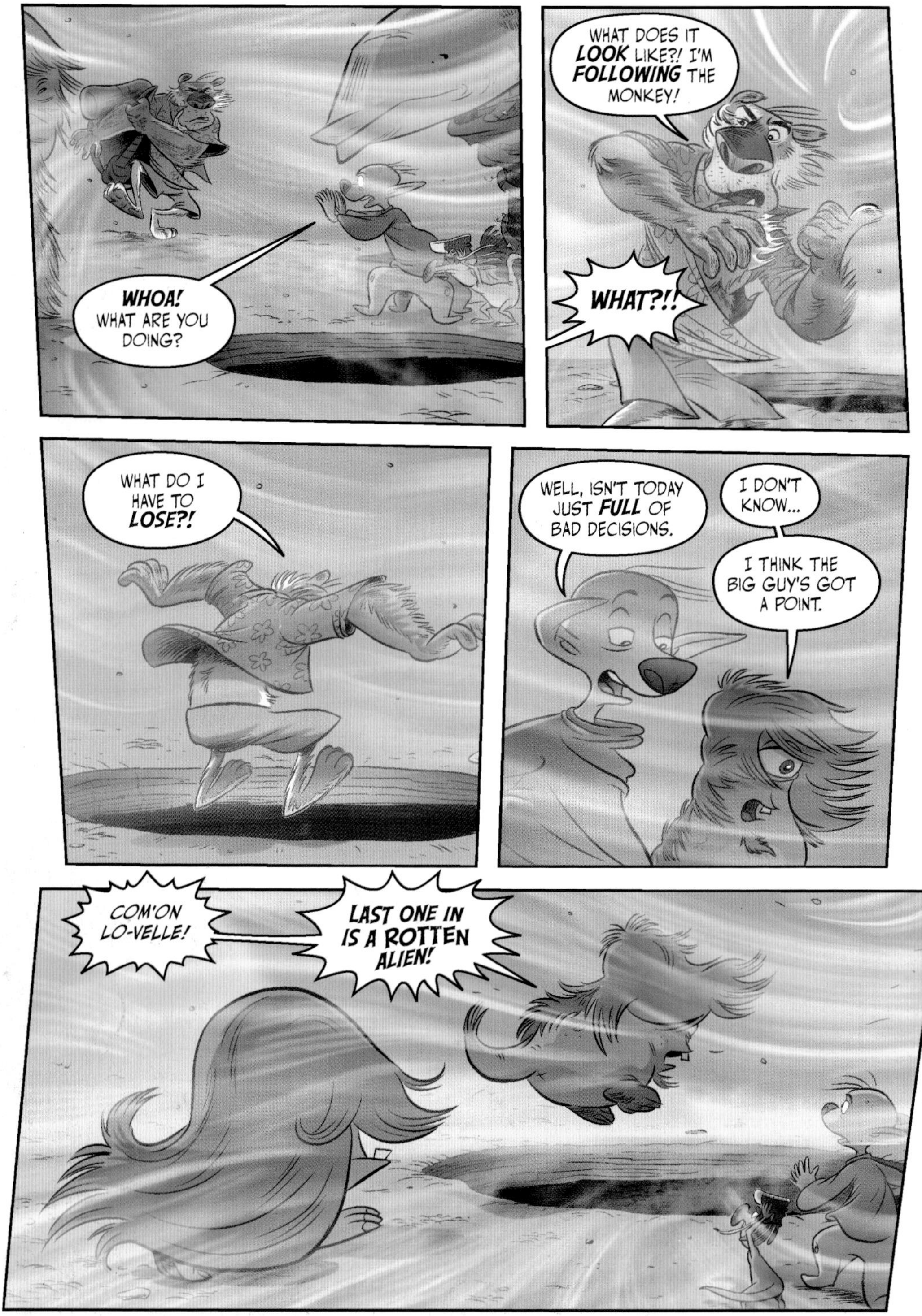
WHOA! WHAT ARE YOU DOING?
WHAT DOES IT LOOK LIKE?! I'M FOLLOWING THE MONKEY!
WHAT?!!
WHAT DO I HAVE TO LOSE?!
WELL, ISN'T TODAY JUST FULL OF BAD DECISIONS.
I DON'T KNOW...
I THINK THE BIG GUY'S GOT A POINT.
COM'ON LO-VELLE!
LAST ONE IN IS A ROTTEN ALIEN!

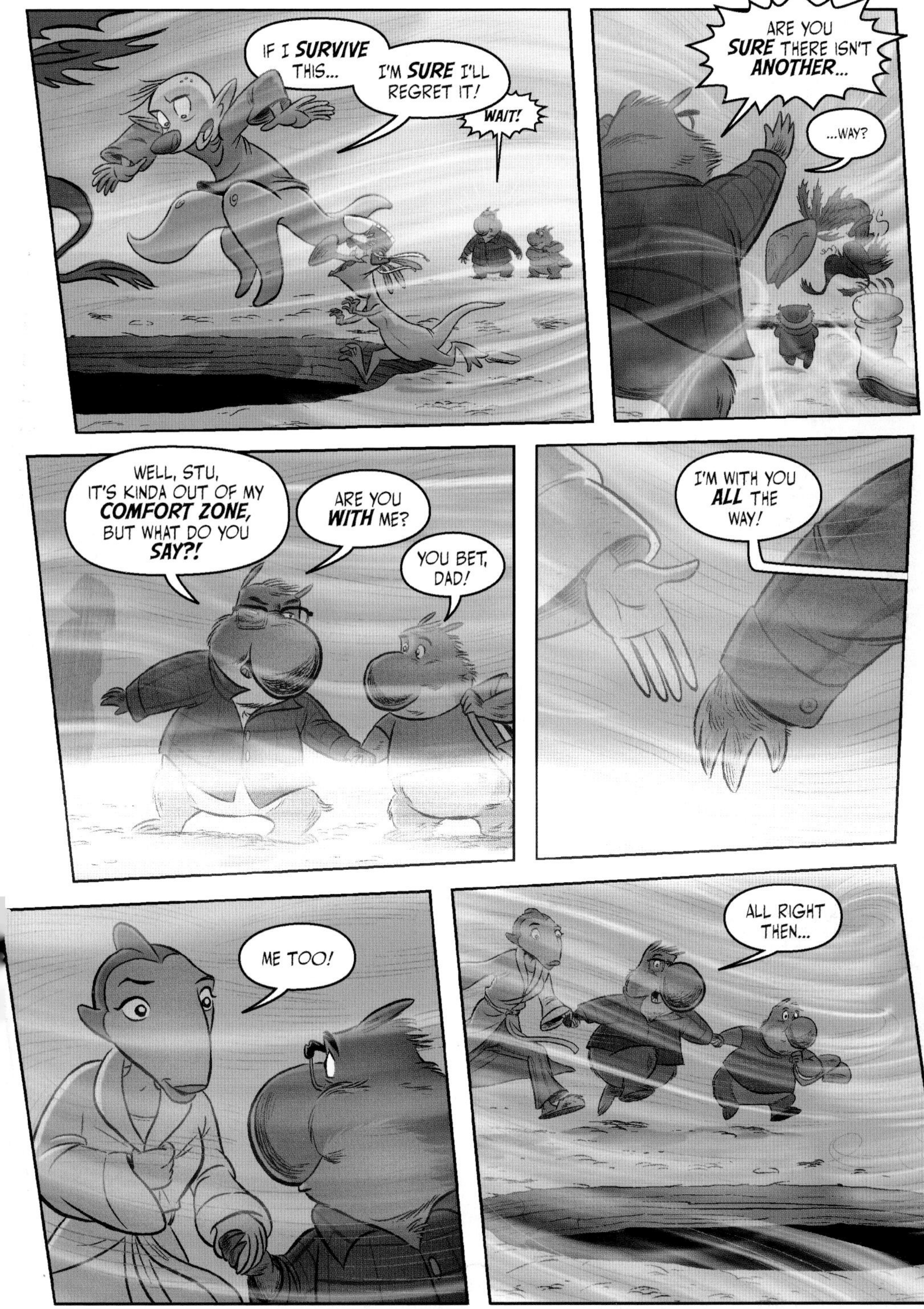
IF I SURVIVE THIS...
I'M SURE I'LL REGRET IT!
WAIT!
ARE YOU SURE THERE ISN'T ANOTHER...
...WAY?
WELL, STU, IT'S KINDA OUT OF MY COMFORT ZONE, BUT WHAT DO YOU SAY?!
ARE YOU WITH ME?
YOU BET, DAD!
I'M WITH YOU ALL THE WAY!
ME TOO!
ALL RIGHT THEN...

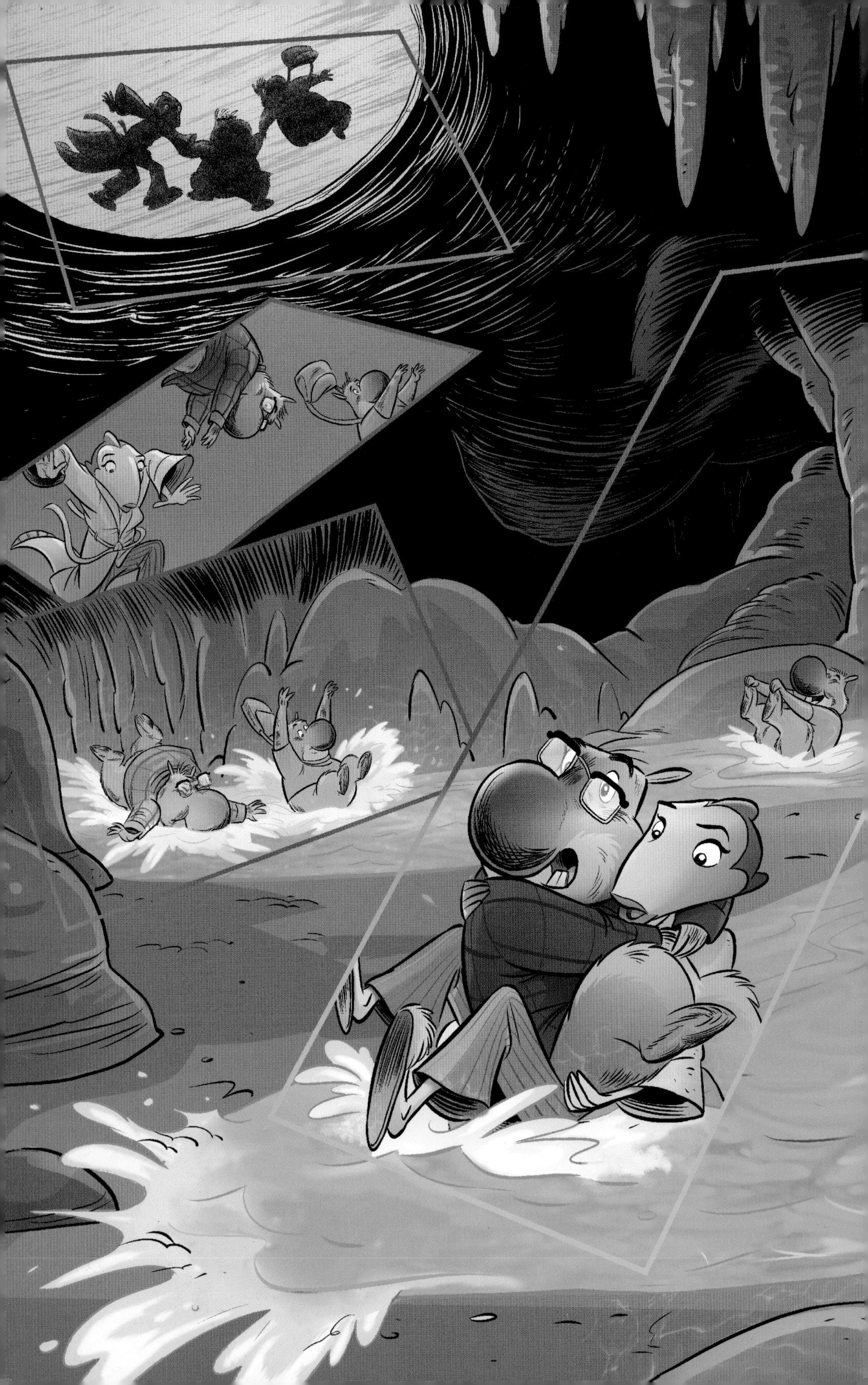

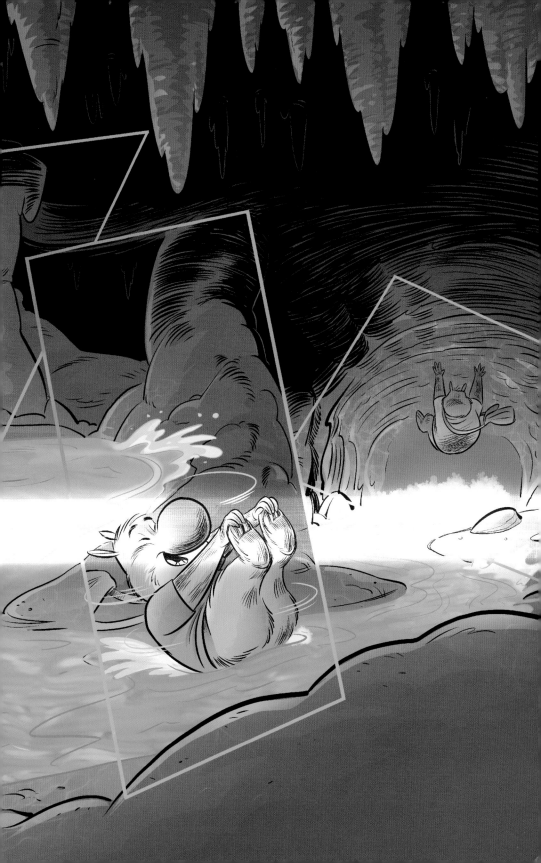

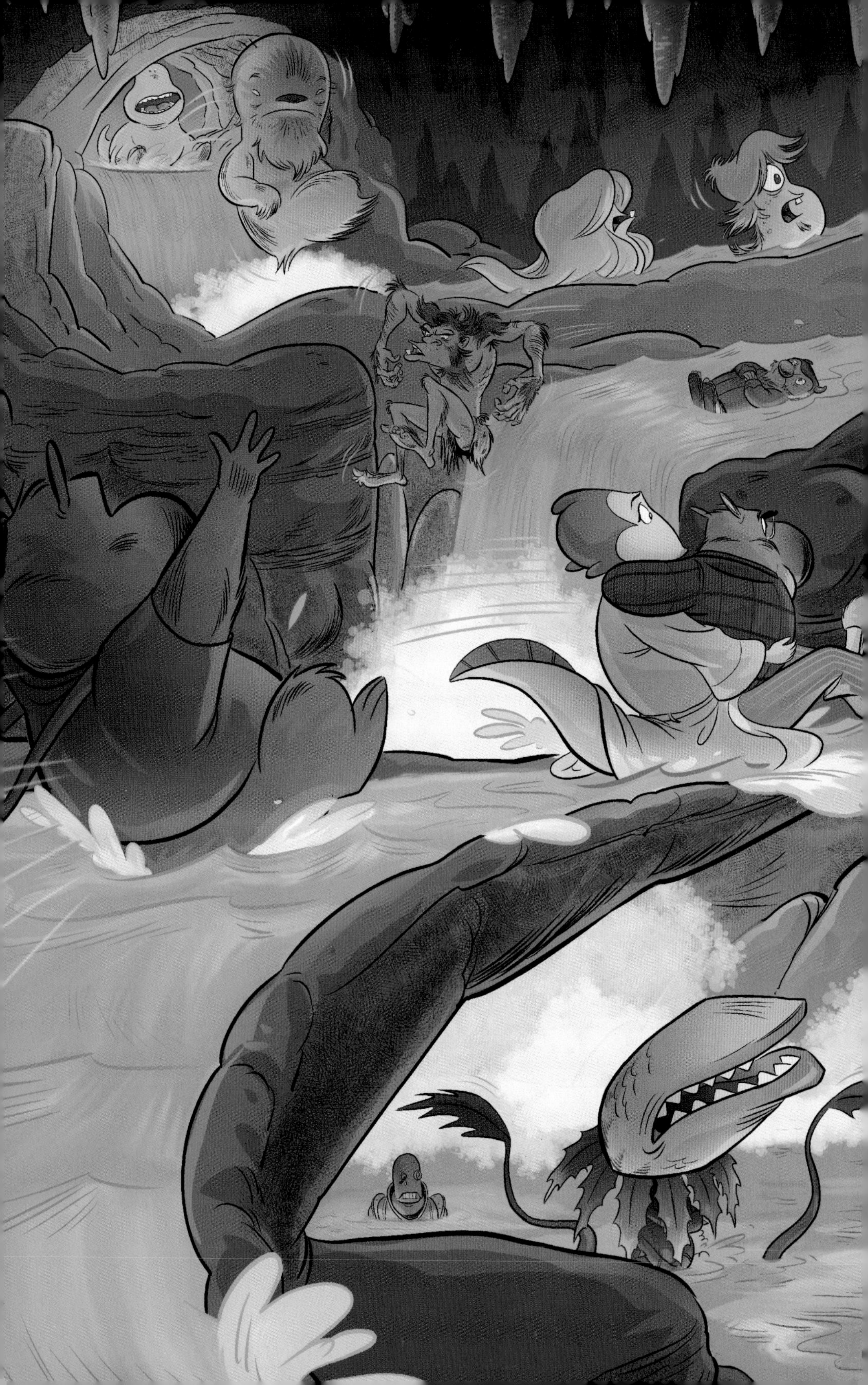

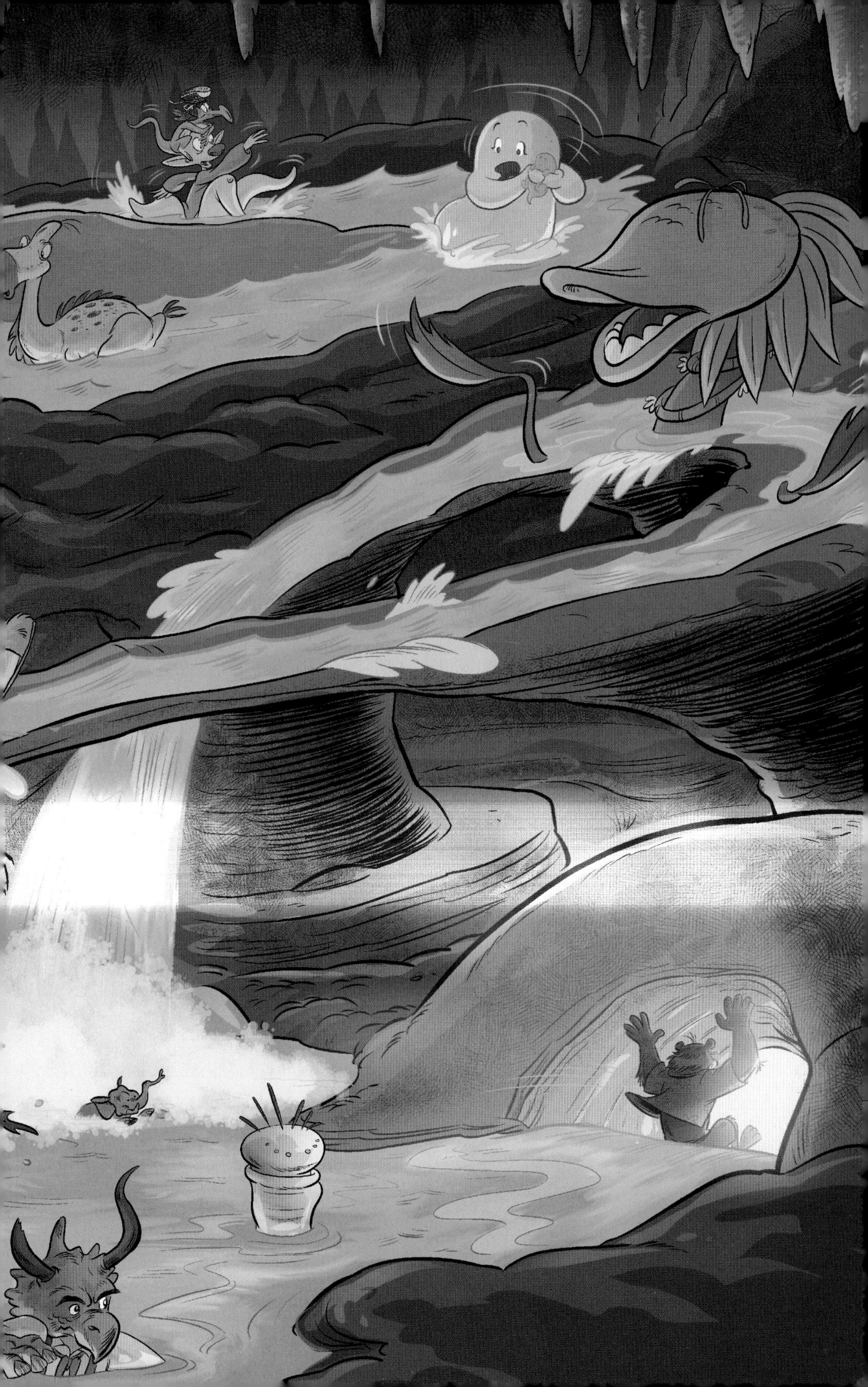

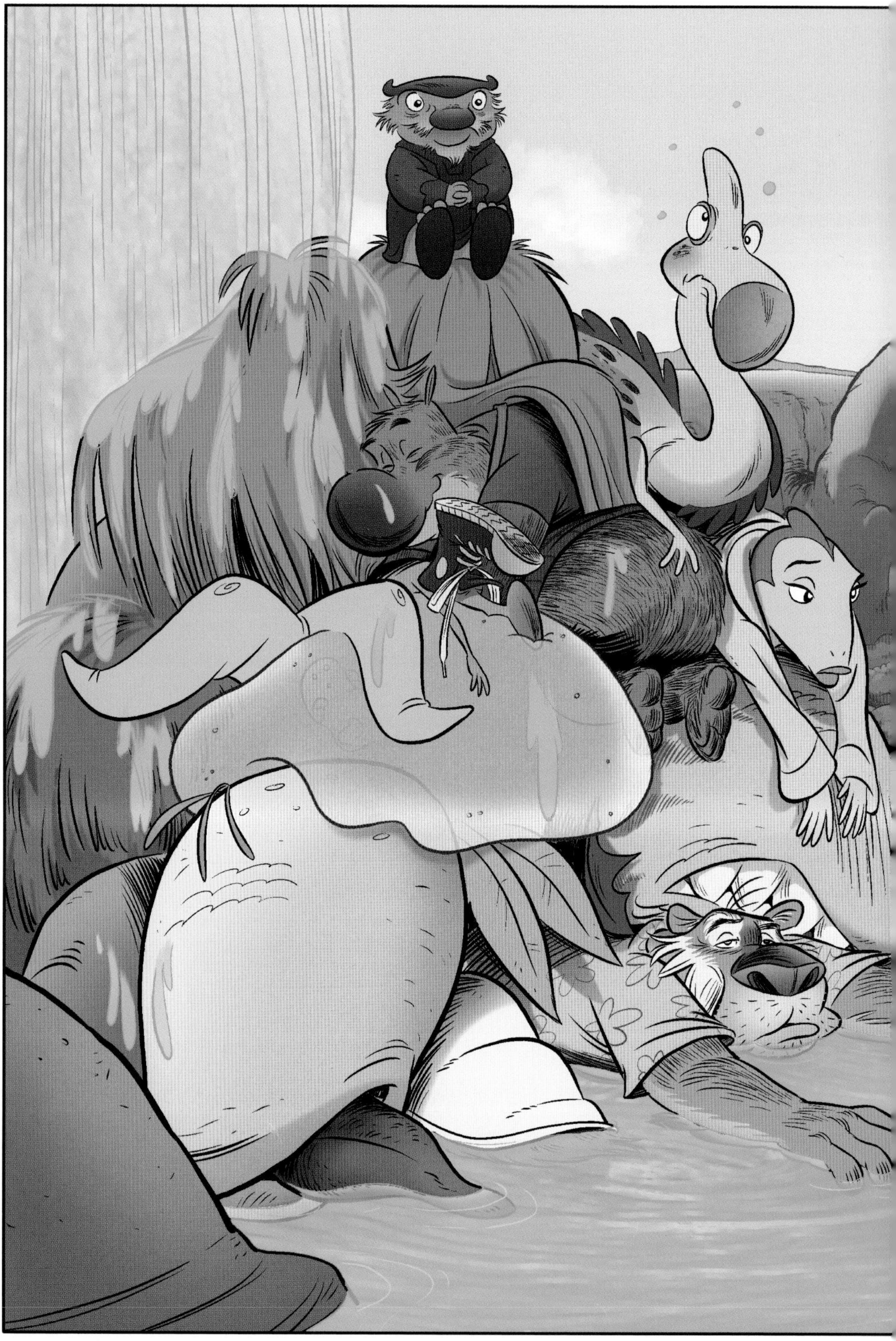

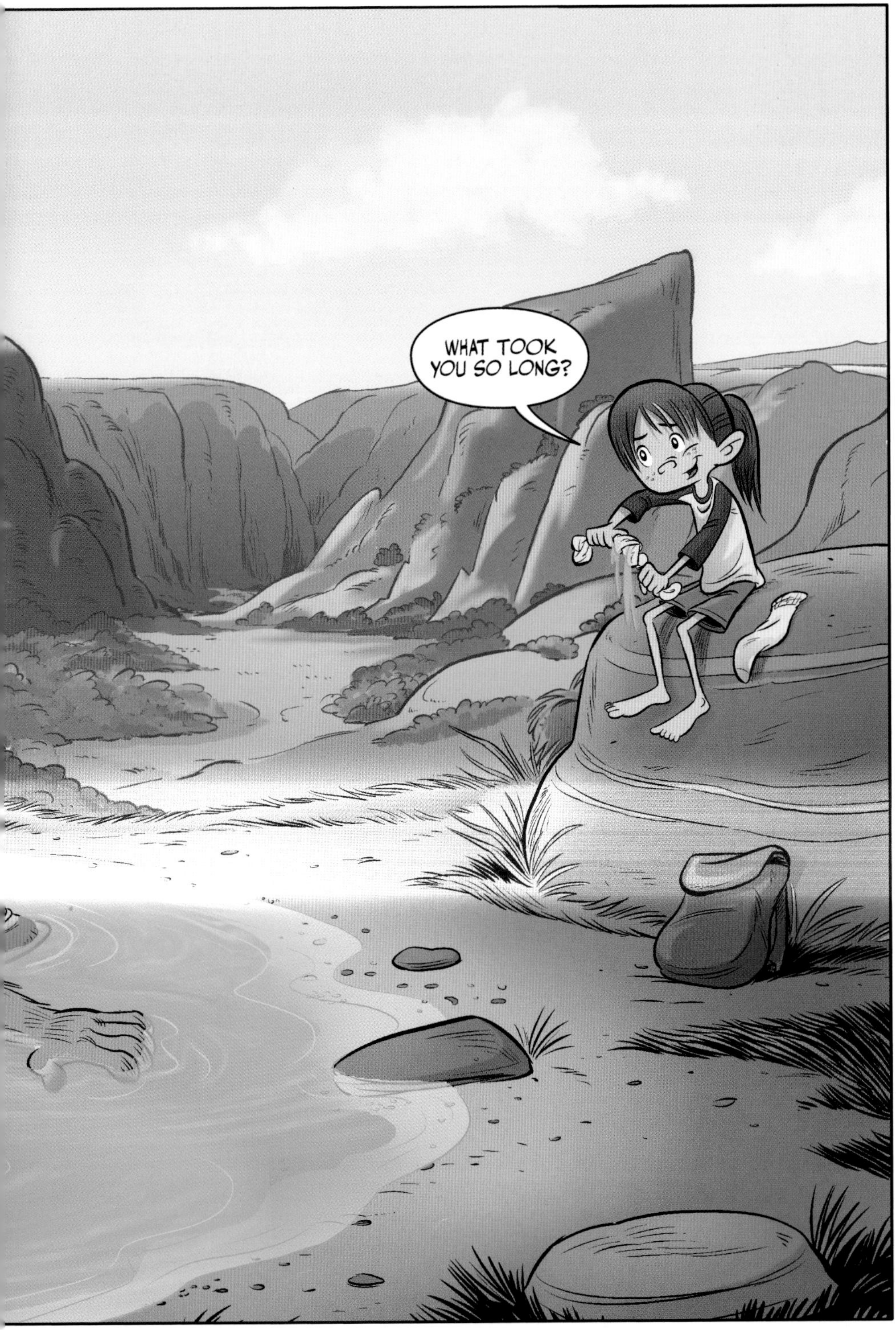
WHAT TOOK YOU SO LONG?

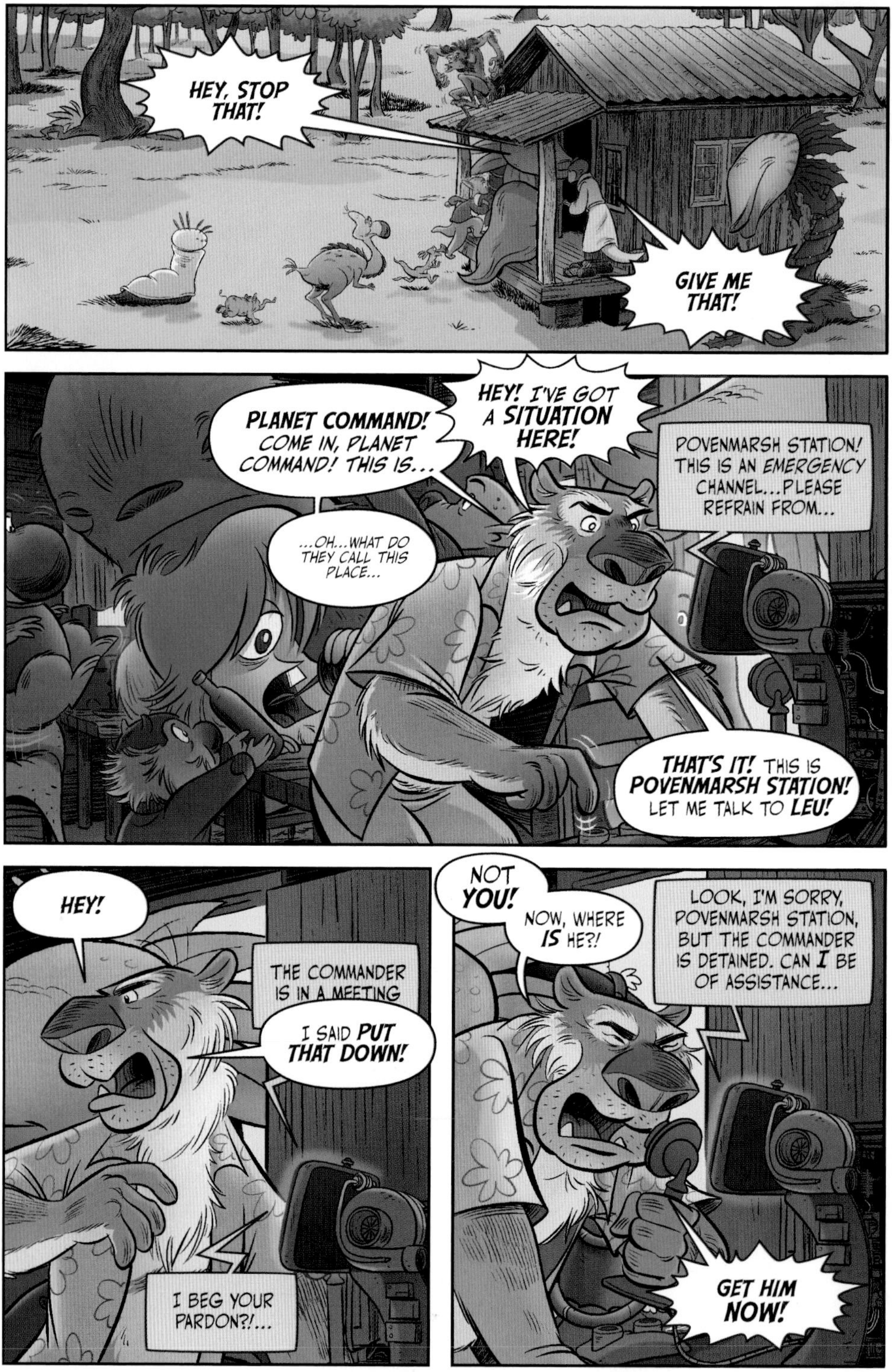
HEY, STOP THAT!
GIVE ME THAT!
PLANET COMMAND! COME IN, PLANET COMMAND! THIS IS...
HEY! I'VE GOT A SITUATION HERE!
POVENMARSH STATION! THIS IS AN EMERGENCY CHANNEL...PLEASE REFRAIN FROM...
...OH...WHAT DO THEY CALL THIS PLACE...
THAT'S IT! THIS IS POVENMARSH STATION! LET ME TALK TO LEU!
HEY!
THE COMMANDER IS IN A MEETING
I SAID PUT THAT DOWN!
I BEG YOUR PARDON?!...
NOT YOU!
NOW, WHERE IS HE?!
LOOK, I'M SORRY, POVENMARSH STATION, BUT THE COMMANDER IS DETAINED. CAN I BE OF ASSISTANCE...
GET HIM NOW!

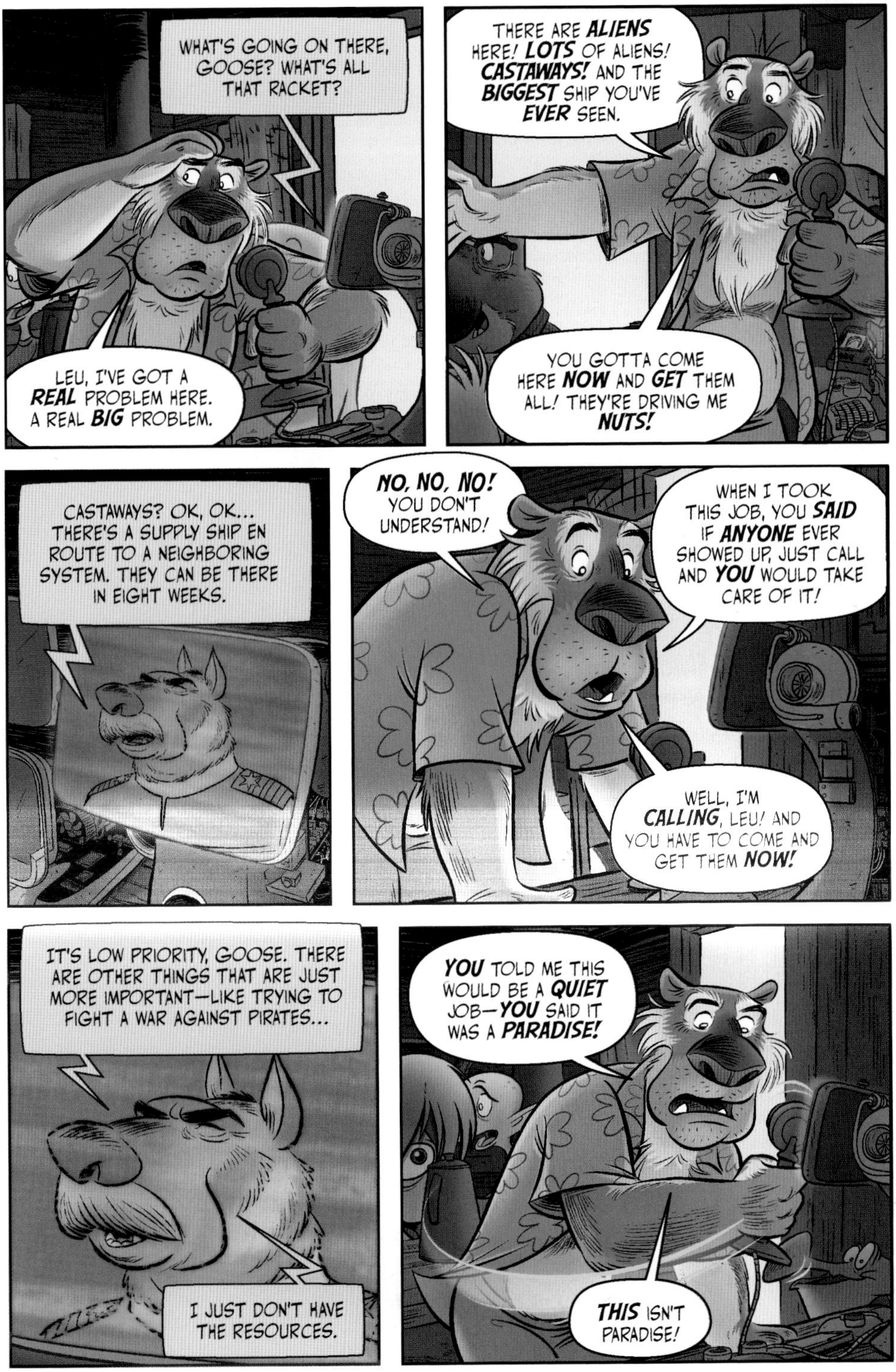
WHAT'S GOING ON THERE, GOOSE? WHAT'S ALL THAT RACKET?
LEU, I'VE GOT A REAL PROBLEM HERE. A REAL BIG PROBLEM.
THERE ARE ALIENS HERE! LOTS OF ALIENS! CASTAWAYS! AND THE BIGGEST SHIP YOU'VE EVER SEEN.
YOU GOTTA COME HERE NOW AND GET THEM ALL! THEY'RE DRIVING ME NUTS!
CASTAWAYS? OK, OK... THERE'S A SUPPLY SHIP EN ROUTE TO A NEIGHBORING SYSTEM. THEY CAN BE THERE IN EIGHT WEEKS.
NO, NO, NO! YOU DON'T UNDERSTAND!
WHEN I TOOK THIS JOB, YOU SAID IF ANYONE EVER SHOWED UP, JUST CALL AND YOU WOULD TAKE CARE OF IT!
WELL, I'M CALLING, LEU! AND YOU HAVE TO COME AND GET THEM NOW!
IT'S LOW PRIORITY, GOOSE. THERE ARE OTHER THINGS THAT ARE JUST MORE IMPORTANT—LIKE TRYING TO FIGHT A WAR AGAINST PIRATES...
I JUST DON'T HAVE THE RESOURCES.
YOU TOLD ME THIS WOULD BE A QUIET JOB—YOU SAID IT WAS A PARADISE!
THIS ISN'T PARADISE!

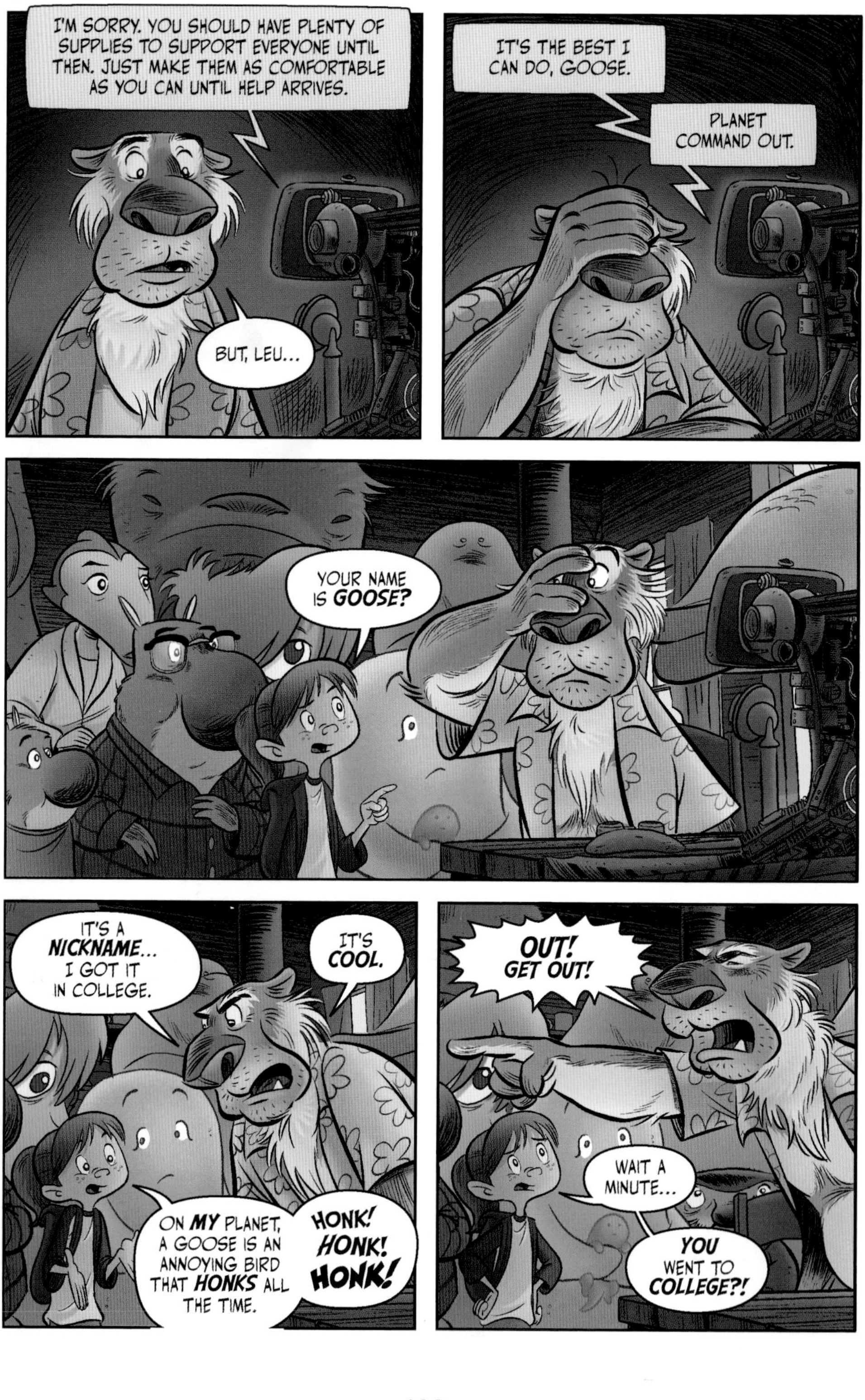
I'M SORRY. YOU SHOULD HAVE PLENTY OF SUPPLIES TO SUPPORT EVERYONE UNTIL THEN. JUST MAKE THEM AS COMFORTABLE AS YOU CAN UNTIL HELP ARRIVES.
BUT, LEU...
IT'S THE BEST I CAN DO, GOOSE.
PLANET COMMAND OUT.
YOUR NAME IS GOOSE?
IT'S A NICKNAME... I GOT IT IN COLLEGE.
IT'S COOL.
ON MY PLANET, A GOOSE IS AN ANNOYING BIRD THAT HONKS ALL THE TIME.
HONK! HONK! HONK!
OUT! GET OUT!
WAIT A MINUTE...
YOU WENT TO COLLEGE?!

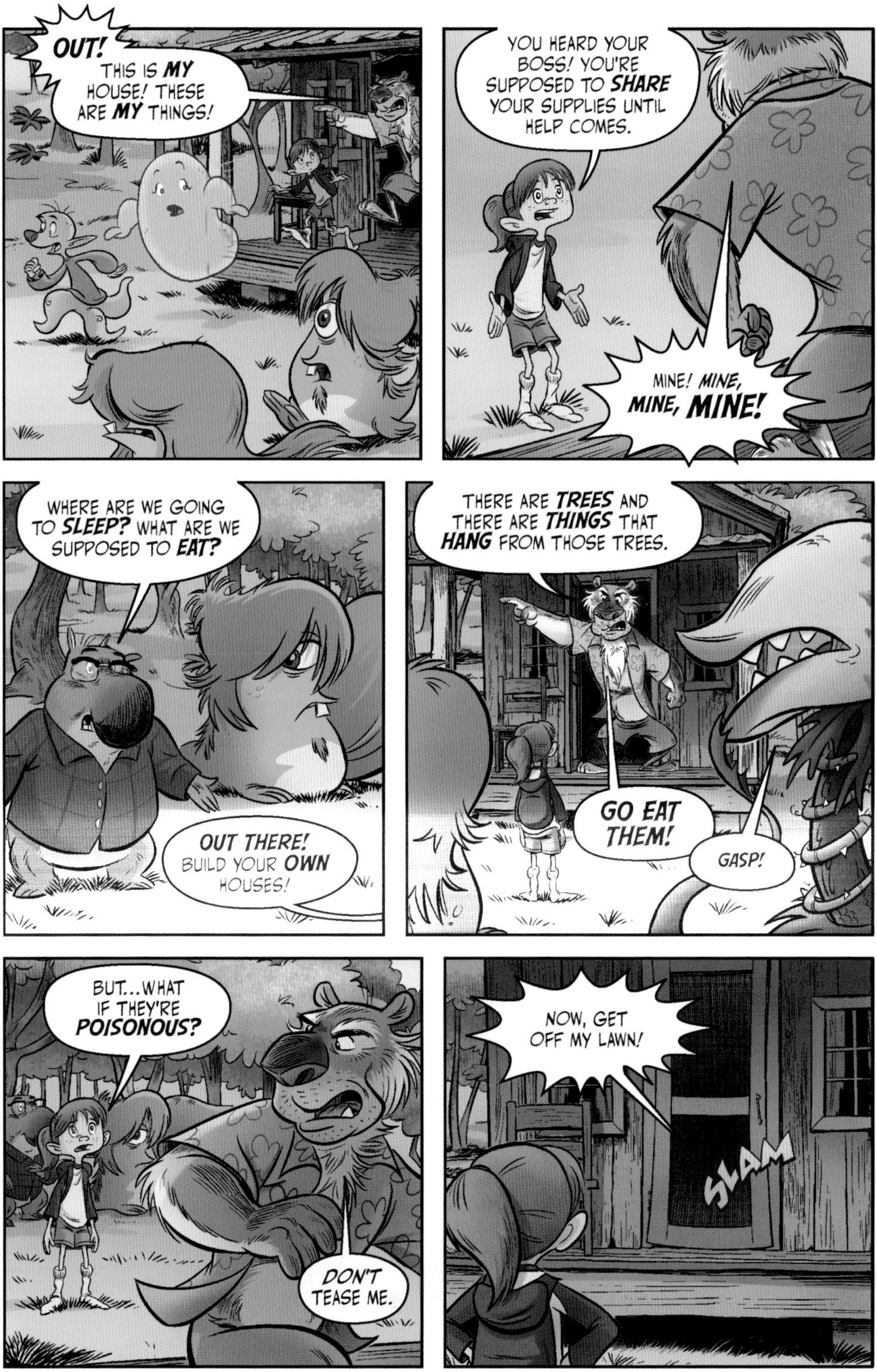
OUT! THIS IS MY HOUSE! THESE ARE MY THINGS!
YOU HEARD YOUR BOSS! YOU'RE SUPPOSED TO SHARE YOUR SUPPLIES UNTIL HELP COMES.
MINE! MINE, MINE, MINE!
WHERE ARE WE GOING TO SLEEP? WHAT ARE WE SUPPOSED TO EAT?
OUT THERE! BUILD YOUR OWN HOUSES!
THERE ARE TREES AND THERE ARE THINGS THAT HANG FROM THOSE TREES.
GO EAT THEM!
GASP!
BUT...WHAT IF THEY'RE POISONOUS?
DON'T TEASE ME.
NOW, GET OFF MY LAWN!
SLAM

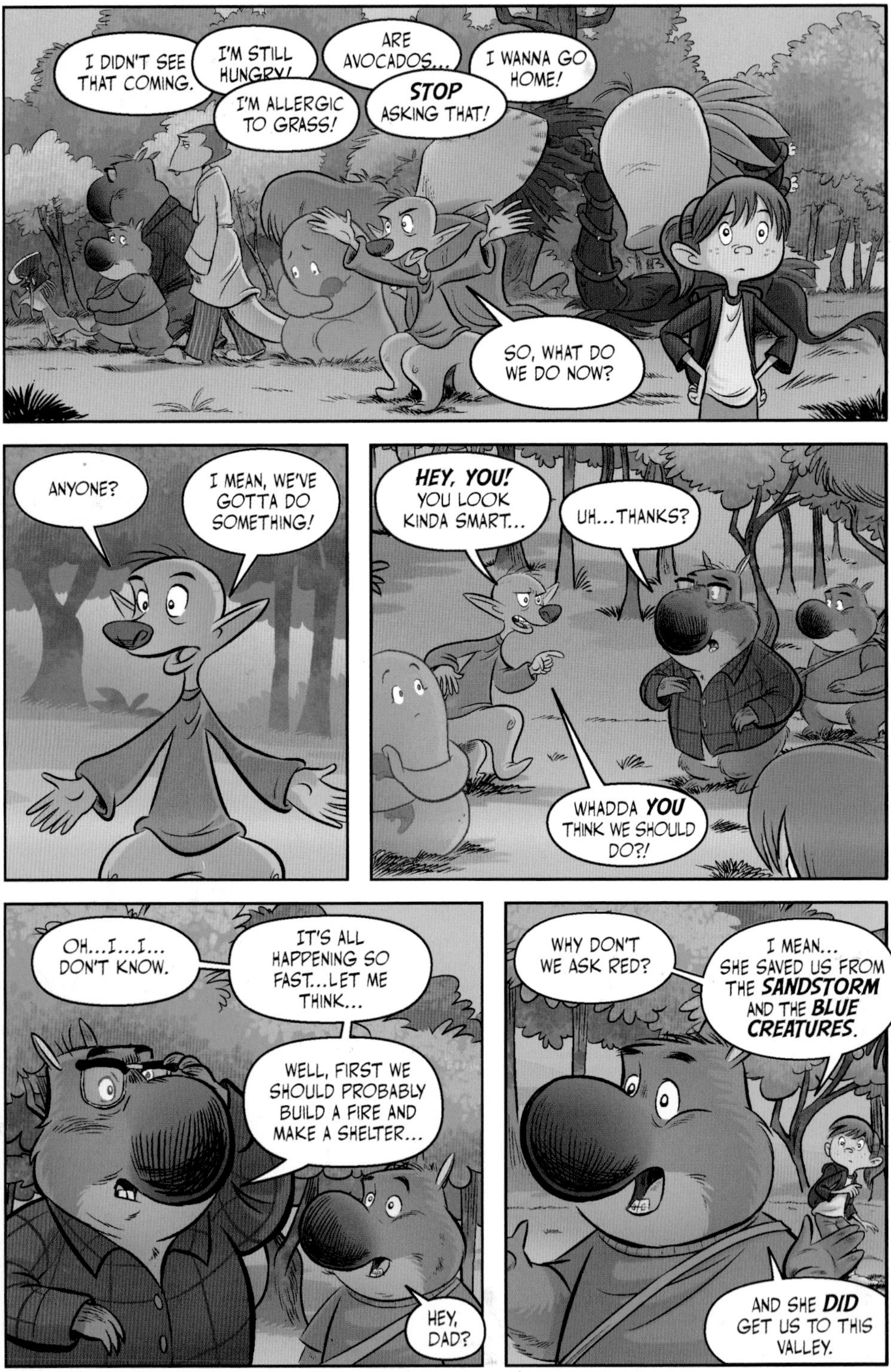
I DIDN'T SEE THAT COMING.
I'M STILL HUNGRY!
I'M ALLERGIC TO GRASS!
ARE AVOCADOS...
STOP ASKING THAT!
I WANNA GO HOME!
SO, WHAT DO WE DO NOW?
ANYONE?
I MEAN, WE'VE GOTTA DO SOMETHING!
HEY, YOU! YOU LOOK KINDA SMART...
UH...THANKS?
WHADDA YOU THINK WE SHOULD DO?!
OH...I...I... DON'T KNOW.
IT'S ALL HAPPENING SO FAST...LET ME THINK...
WELL, FIRST WE SHOULD PROBABLY BUILD A FIRE AND MAKE A SHELTER...
HEY, DAD?
WHY DON'T WE ASK RED?
I MEAN... SHE SAVED US FROM THE SANDSTORM AND THE BLUE CREATURES.
AND SHE DID GET US TO THIS VALLEY.

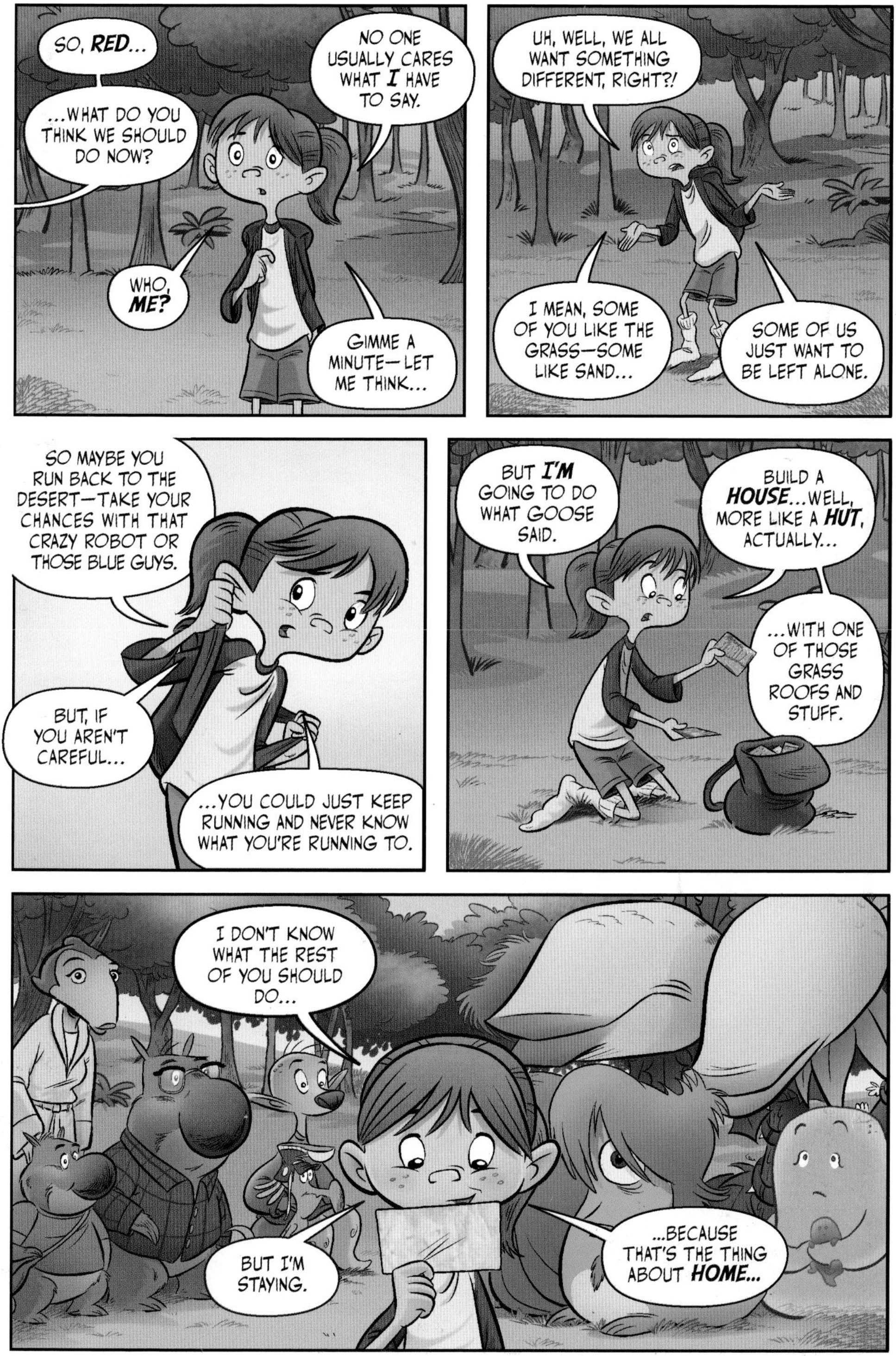
SO, RED...
...WHAT DO YOU THINK WE SHOULD DO NOW?
WHO, ME?
NO ONE USUALLY CARES WHAT I HAVE TO SAY.
GIMME A MINUTE—LET ME THINK...
UH, WELL, WE ALL WANT SOMETHING DIFFERENT, RIGHT?!
I MEAN, SOME OF YOU LIKE THE GRASS—SOME LIKE SAND...
SOME OF US JUST WANT TO BE LEFT ALONE.
SO MAYBE YOU RUN BACK TO THE DESERT—TAKE YOUR CHANCES WITH THAT CRAZY ROBOT OR THOSE BLUE GUYS.
BUT, IF YOU AREN'T CAREFUL...
...YOU COULD JUST KEEP RUNNING AND NEVER KNOW WHAT YOU'RE RUNNING TO.
BUT I'M GOING TO DO WHAT GOOSE SAID.
BUILD A HOUSE...WELL, MORE LIKE A HUT, ACTUALLY...
...WITH ONE OF THOSE GRASS ROOFS AND STUFF.
I DON'T KNOW WHAT THE REST OF YOU SHOULD DO...
BUT I'M STAYING.
...BECAUSE THAT'S THE THING ABOUT HOME...

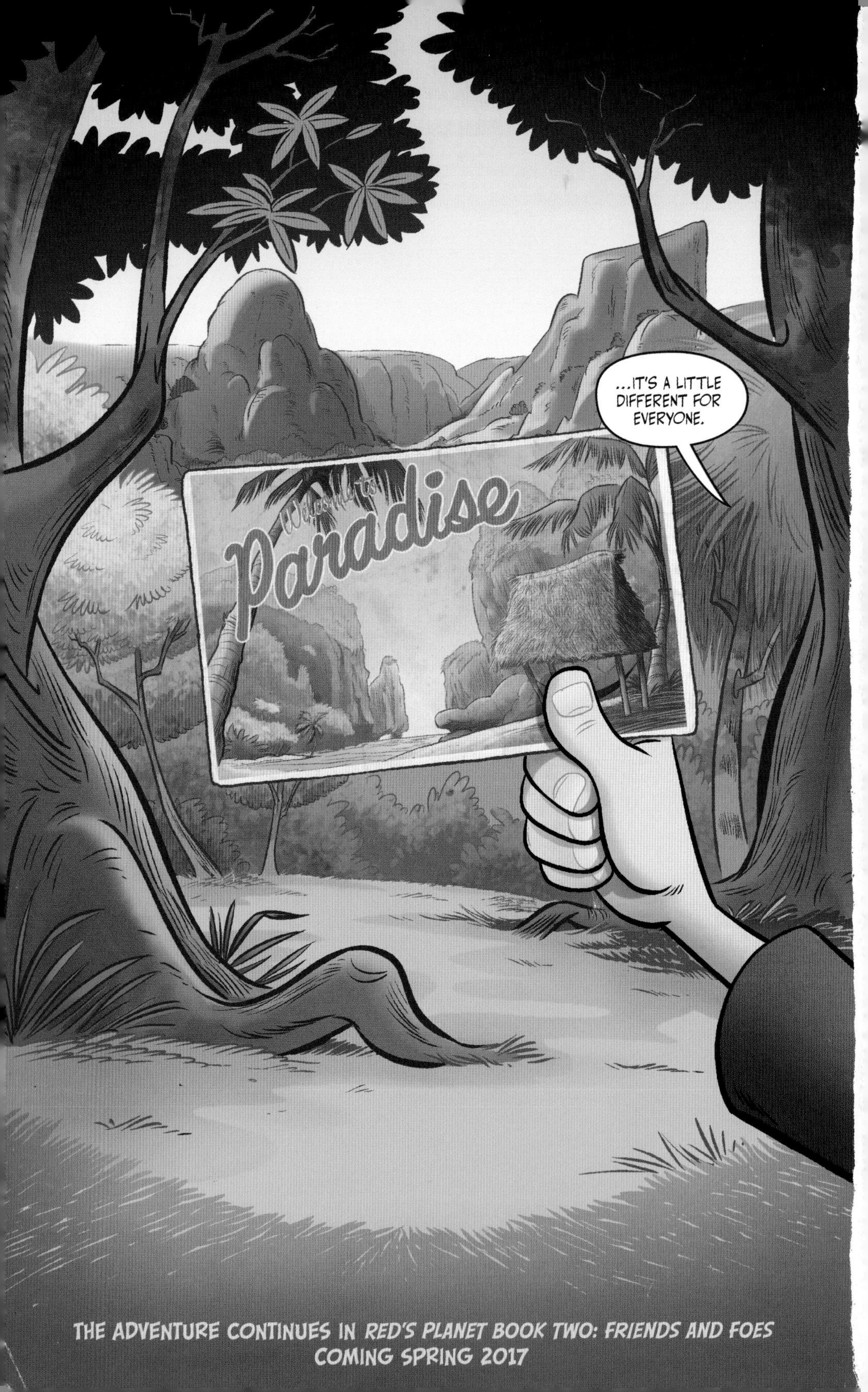
Paradise
...IT'S A LITTLE DIFFERENT FOR EVERYONE.

THE ADVENTURE CONTINUES IN *RED'S PLANET BOOK TWO: FRIENDS AND FOES*
COMING SPRING 2017

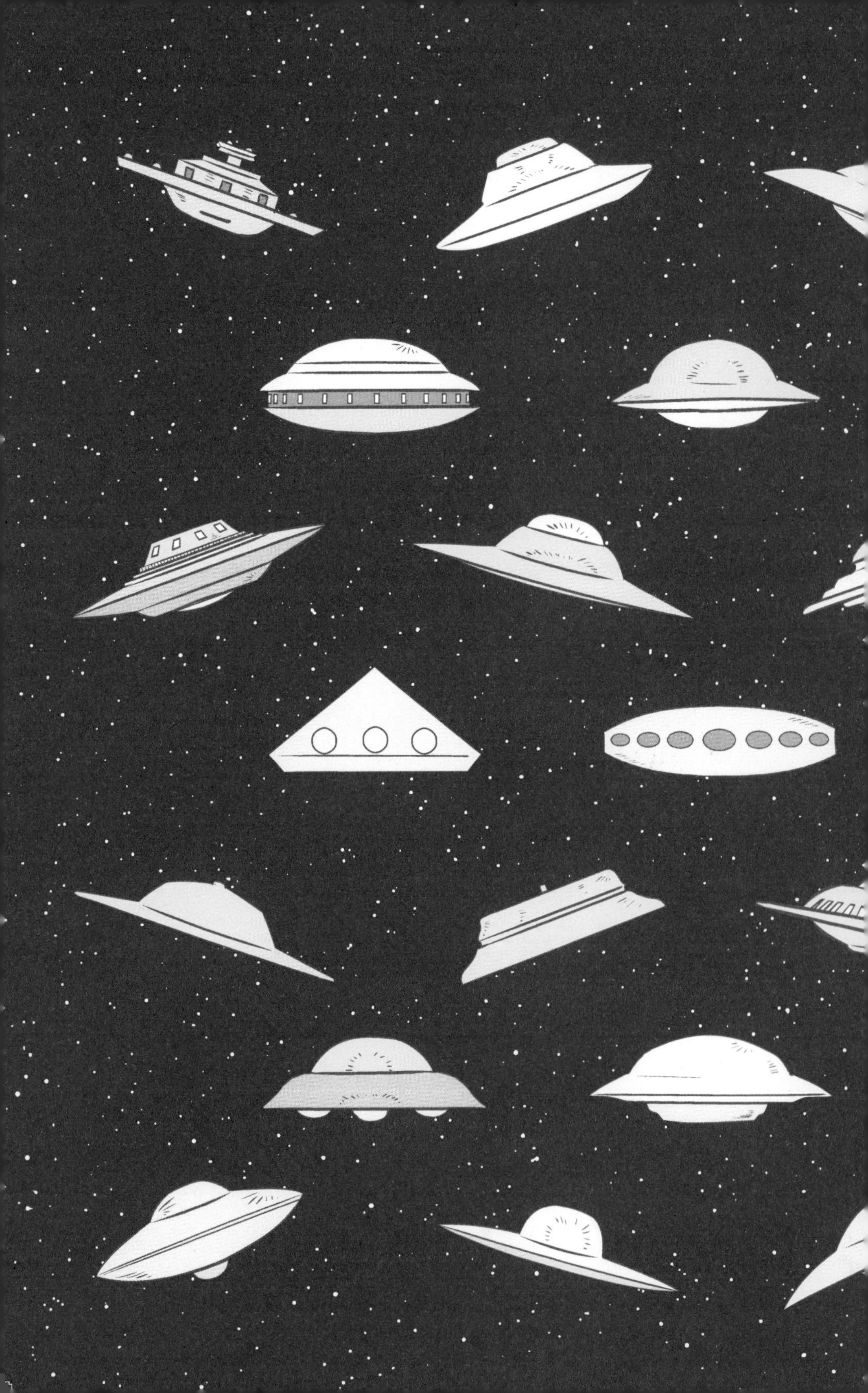